Seven Years Between

୬୬୬

Pamela McDavid

Published by Pamela McDavid
Oregon
Author contact: pjmcdavid@gmail.com

Author's note: This is a work of fiction. Many of the names are real people,
but are used fictitiously. This book is loosely based on the childhood of
Carol Suzanne Carlson-Moran, my mother.

ISBN: 978-0-9852514-0-6

This book is dedicated
to my sisters,
Paula Sue
and
Kathleen Sarah

With special
heart-felt thanks to my
cover creator, editor, and the
Love of my life~
Andy

And to the Kyllo family…
Thank you for the inspiration!

Part One

December, 1937

1

The first time I got the death pains I was six. I was jolted awake by the sound of shattering glass coming from the kitchen. It was still dark outside but felt like morning. I smelled coffee and heard voices. Angry voices. Mama was hollering and Father was mumbling, and every time her hollering got louder, his mumbling got smaller and farther away. I'd never heard words like that come from my mother before. I questioned if it really was her, the voice didn't have the right cadence. She wasn't usually given to much carrying on. Her voice was gentle and deliberate, but this voice was angry and sporadic. Her tirade had a paralyzing effect on me and a heaviness fell on my chest. I brought my hand up to find the source of the pressure, but there was nothing there. Fear alone was pressing me down. In spite of this cruel force, it felt like my heart might catapult right out of my body.

The rusty screech of the storm door signaled someone either coming or going. I listened carefully to know which it was. The door answered with an angry slam. Everything was quiet for a few seconds, then a shattering crash sent me cowering further under my covers. My throat closed and my face got hot, and everything sounded fuzzy. I concentrated on breathing, because if you don't breathe you'll die. Mama said that. After a minute, I thought I could hear mama crying and blowing her nose. So I peeked out from under my blanket, fumbled for my glasses, and watched the long hand go past the twelve two times.

A curly moan echoed from the kitchen. It was the sound Mama made when she heard a sad story, or saw a dead animal on the side of the road. She blew her nose again, sniffed, and took a deep breath. Then everything got quiet.

"Mama?" My voice got caught like a scream in a nightmare. "Mama?" I tried again, but I couldn't make my voice go very far, and got no answer.

When my curiosity outweighed my fear, I slipped from my bed with my faded-pink blanket wrapped around my neck. The pressure on my chest didn't fall off when I got up. I tip-toed across the cold, wood floor and peeked around the door jam, into the kitchen. It was dark except for a dim light over the stove. I didn't see my mother, so I called again, "Mama?"

"Hmmm?" a muffled voice answered.

I still couldn't see her, so I tip-toed into the kitchen. The floor was cold and a little bit wet. I stepped on something sharp.

"Mama, where are you?" I limped over to wipe my foot on a towel that was sticking out of a pile of dirty laundry waiting to be washed. It moved and I screamed.

That pile of laundry turned out to be my mother. She had a towel turbaned around her head that covered her face, and her blue quilted bathrobe was wrapped around her body. The kitchen table cloth, still clutched in her right hand, trailed across her legs. She was curled up like a baby, crying the cry of someone who doesn't want you to hear. I got right down next to her, found her face, and dried her tears with the silky part of my blanket. This made her cry harder. She wiped her nose with the table cloth, and then motioned for me to lie down next to her. She spooned me into her belly and put her hand on the heavy place in my chest. We stayed like this for a good long time and when she could speak she said, "It's okay, Carol. Mama's here." Eventually her breath slowed, and her arm relaxed over me until it felt too heavy and I started to squirm. She gave me a squeeze, kissed my hair and whispered, "I miss my Mama." I rolled over and kissed her wet, salty cheek, then licked it. She tried to smile and scrunched her nose.

"Don't be sad, Mama. It's Christmas."

"So it is, and you are my own Christmas Carol."

2

The kitchen floor was dangerous territory that morning. Most of the glass from the first whiskey bottle landed on the steps outside the kitchen door. But, as Mama confessed to Uncle Virg later, the feeling of reeling that bottle at someone so thoroughly marinated in what had been its own contents satisfied something deep inside her, so she threw another one, half full this time. The second projectile shattered into the wall, sending whiskey and glass shrapnel into every corner of the tiny kitchen.

Mama got up off the floor and sat me on the kitchen counter. She checked my feet and plucked out a tiny piece of glass. Then she lit a cigarette and turned on the hot water, letting it run for a minute as she looked out the window and I looked at her. She tested the warm washcloth to her cheek and wiped my feet with it. Then she kissed my foot where the glass had been.

"All better," she said. "Stay there Peach, I need some better shoes." A thin stream of smoke trailed behind her as she scuffed across the kitchen.

I perused the view from my perch. There was an arched opening in the wall between the living room and the kitchen. A chair, a small sofa, and Mama's sewing machine competed for what little space there was. Our Christmas tree sat on a table by Father's chair, for lack of space to put it anywhere else. Father said a smaller tree was easier to cut down, cheaper to decorate, and faster to dispose of when the "bless-ed holidays" were over. He made the word "bless-ed" sound like a cuss word. I craned my neck to see something sticking out from in back of Father's chair and the anxiety of the morning now had a new target. I wasn't sure, but thought it could be. I leaned out a little farther and saw the wooden dowel of what might be a handle. It was attached to a length of black, curvy metal. I leaned way down and saw what was surely the shape of a wheel. He brought it! My heart bubbled in my chest again, but this time for an entirely different reason—my baby buggy. The reality of Santa actually coming through with it consumed me. I'd almost traded the dreaded death pains for happy anticipation, when Mama tapped back into the room. She was still wearing her bathrobe but had wound her hair up into a sloppy French twist and was sporting her navy blue platform high heels.

"These should keep me out of the danger zone while I clean up this mess," she said. She planted her cigarette in the corner of her lips and started sweeping. I stole glances into the living room when she wasn't watching.

A few days earlier, mostly looking at Father even though she was talking to me, Mama had argued that dolls don't need carriages, only real babies do, and if I wanted a buggy to schlep my doll around, I'd better be hoping Santa didn't realize how particularly foolish and unnecessary it was. She said that even a stamp was beyond our means this year, and if I wanted to send Santa Clause a letter, I could just fold it up into a paper airplane, throw it out the window of the Empire State Building, and hope it got to the North Pole. I thought how silly that was because it would cost way more to get to the Empire State Building than to use one stamp. So I took it to Mr. Bateman down at the corner store. He said if anyone passing through was going to the Empire State Building, he would be sure to give it to them for safe delivery. I suggested anyone going to the North Pole could also deliver it straight away.

I watched as Mama swept the last bit of glass into the dustpan.

"When can we open presents?" I said, as I wiggled back and forth on the counter with my ankles crossed.

"Soon as you go pee, and I get dressed," she said, lifting me from the counter.

I wrapped my legs around her waist and my arms around her neck like a baby Koala bear.

"Where's Father?" I whispered in her ear.

She backed up, sat down in a kitchen chair and lowered me to her lap. Then she wrapped both my hands in hers, brought them to her chest and looked me right in the eyes. I could see that hers were holding back a spill.

"Your father is gone, Peach. I'm not sure when we'll see him again. Your father is a liar, and I cannot tolerate liars."

A worry welled up in me that I can't explain. My chest got tight and fell into my stomach, then pressed on my bladder and I peed all over my mother's legs and navy blue high heels. She didn't say anything, just lifted me like a wet cat and carried me to the bathroom.

Mama washed my hair and I cried. The bathtub is a good place to cry because you can't count your tears and you can let your nose just drip all it wants. I bet by the time I got out of that tub it was as salty as the Dead Sea. I felt like I needed another bath just to get the sad off. Mama wrapped me in a towel, sat on the toilet seat and rocked me while she hummed the tune to Silent Night.

"I miss my Daddy," I said, before I drifted off to sleep in her arms.

3

The second time I woke up on Christmas morning, it was daylight and I was in my parent's bed. At first I wondered why I was wrapped in a towel, but then I remembered about Father, and the kitchen floor, and the bath.

"You feeling better Peach?" Mama was laying my clothes out on a chair.

"I think so."

"How's your foot?"

I wiggled it around to check. "Fine."

"Good." She kissed me, then turned in response to the kitchen timer. "My pies are ready, why don't you get dressed. Uncle Virg will be here in about an hour."

I lay there for a while, looking at the familiar pattern on the ceiling and the dirty smudges on the wall. As far back as I can remember I liked to lay sideways on my bed and tap dance on the wall with my bare feet. It's a good way to wake up, but that day I wasn't in the mood for dancing.

Mama, Father and I had lived in that one bedroom basement apartment since I was born. They probably lived there before that, but I don't know for how long. I can only remember back to when I was three. In our room there was a chair, a dresser as tall as me, my little white painted iron bed and Mama and Father's big bed. Between the beds was a wooden watermelon box for our lamp, and the wind-up alarm clock that Aunt Marion and Uncle Virg gave me for my birthday on December 16th. Aunt Marion said that six was a good age to start taking responsibility for ones' self, so I put myself in charge of waking up with my alarm clock. Sometimes I used it to time myself. I made up rewards for beating the clock. If I got my teeth brushed, clothes on, and bed made in less than ten minutes, then I would have a good day and no one would ask me to do any more chores. Mama said I was an excellent self-manager and good for me because I didn't need anyone else to boss me around anyway.

From the kitchen I could hear a man on the radio telling the whole world how unusually warm it was for Christmas in Western New York. Mama had put way too many clothes on that chair for an unusually warm Christmas day, so I decided to forfeit the wool leggings and wear my white tights instead. I'd wear no tights at all, just socks, except I saw that Mama had laid out the wool skirt that Aunt Marion and Uncle Virg had gotten me for Christmas the previous year. It was so scratchy that I couldn't stand it next to my legs. Up until now I hadn't been able to wear it at all because it slipped right down over my bottom. I don't know why she bought a size 6 when I was only a size 5. I think people do that so a thing will last longer, but what good is anything if it doesn't fit when you get it. Aunt Marion repeatedly complained of how painfully thin I was, and tried to feed me all kinds of high-calorie concoctions. Mama said I was perfect and that I should only eat when I am hungry. These are the things I liked to eat: pot roast sandwiches with mayonnaise, pork chops—especially the fat around the edges, pistachios, mashed potatoes, celery with peanut butter, crumpets with coddled cream—which I only got at my grandmother's house—egg salad sandwiches, and chocolate cake. Those were my favorites. I despised sweet potatoes, okra, lemon bars, chicken legs, and biscuits and gravy.

I tried on the skirt and it fit. Mama had moved the button over. She said I looked like a school girl and helped me tuck in the white blouse, which helped with the itchiness. I felt cute, but stiff, even without putting on the sweater and my bulky, wool coat that still hung on the back of the chair.

The next thing on my list was to get my hands on that baby buggy. Mama said I needed to eat before presents and that there was oatmeal on the stove, so I headed into the kitchen and made myself a bowl and sat down at the kitchen table to eat it. Oatmeal was not my favorite, nor was it something I hated. I just ate it because if she made it and I didn't eat it, I'd get nothing. That's just how we did it. If I went to Aunt Marion and Uncle Virg's house, all I'd have to do is look at the oatmeal with a sad face and Uncle Virg would make me cinnamon toast and chocolate milk to dip it in. Uncle Virg is the nicest man I've ever known. The oatmeal that day had raisins in it which made it more interesting, but I had to be careful not to over-raisin any one bite so that they would last until the end. It worked out perfectly.

I heard Mama walking around in her navy blue high heels and I was mortified to think that she was still wearing those piss shoes. She came into the kitchen, stopped in the doorway and put both hands on her hips, waiting for me to say, "Who's the most beautiful woman in the entire nation?" like Father always did.

"Why, thank you so much, Peach, and I do not deny it," she said. "If you can't look in the mirror and say you're beautiful, nobody else will."

My mother had a confidence that was comforting. Her beauty came more from the inside, than outward adornment. When she looked in the mirror and told herself she was beautiful, it was almost like she was trying to talk herself into it. She always wore a hat when we went out, even to the market. She owned two and that day she wore her church one, with three feathers on the side. I scooted my chair away from the table and looked under it to assess the condition of her shoes. She knew as much and said, "There is no harm done from a little bit of pure, sterile urine, and don't you say one more thing about it, Carol. It wiped right off and these shoes are perfect with this skirt."

Then she walked directly into the living room, crawled behind the sofa, and plugged in the Christmas tree lights. I climbed into the chair, knowing full well that my present was right behind me. I waited for her to bring it out, practicing in my mind how I would act surprised.

"All right then," she announced. She sat on the floor, reached for the ash tray, and lit the half-smoked cigarette that was sitting in it. "Let's play *Hot and Cold* to find your present."

We played this game a lot, so I knew to stand in the middle of the living room, close my eyes, and turn around a few times before I started forward with my hands out in front of me, like blind man's bluff.

"Cold, cold, cold."

I turned around.

"Warmer..."

I turned left.

"Cold, colder, freezing!"

I giggled and turned around again, covering my eyes with my hands. The temptation to open them was almost more than I could bear. I walked forward and bumped my knees into Father's chair.

"Hot!" she said.

I climbed into the chair and felt all over the seat and up the back, pretending to be curiously stumped.

"Almost boiling!"

I stood up on the seat cushion and reached over the back of the chair.

"Boiling hot, steaming, burning, hot-hot-hot!" Mama yelled.

I felt the wicker hood of the carriage and opened my eyes, "Oh Mama!" I scrambled over the arm of the chair and maneuvered the treasure out of its snug hiding place. "This is just like a real buggy, with rubber wheels!"

There was a card on the soft white pillow in the buggy. I opened it. "For Carol, with love from Father," I read slowly. I looked at Mama, "Santa didn't bring it?

"Why no, Carol, Santa doesn't bring presents, parents do," she said absentmindedly, then rose gracefully from the floor and proceeded into the kitchen to find her coffee cup.

"You might as well know the truth now, Peach. Nothing comes for free, and most costs more than it's worth. Uncle Virg will be here in a few minutes, did you brush your teeth?"

"Yes, Mama." I felt heartsick. I even considered she might be lying about Santa.

I went to my bed and found Jesse, my doll. I swaddled her in a piece of flannel fabric and tucked her in the fancy new buggy. They were a perfect fit for each other.

"Can I take Jessie and my buggy to Uncle Virg and Aunt Marion's?"

"If Virgil has room in the car and it fits, sure. If not, Jessie can come but the buggy will have to stay. Your suitcase is by the door. We're staying a few days, so put your toothbrush in there — and a book if you want."

I had a toothbrush at Uncle Virg's already, but I packed three books.

4

Uncle Virg had a 1931 Ford Model A, Tudor Sedan. He bought it brand new and paid four hundred ninety-five dollars for it, but treated it like it was worth a million bucks. It was two-tone green and spotlessly clean, inside and out. He dusted the exterior of that car with a real sheep fleece, as if it was a piece of fine furniture. The rubber mats on the floor were as clean as Aunt Marion's kitchen floor, and that was clean. Uncle Virg kept a whiskbroom under the driver's seat and rarely put the car away for the night without giving it a good sweeping out.

The minute Uncle Virg arrived I let him know about the matter of the buggy. He made sure that the buggy, Jessie, and I fit in the back seat with no problem. The handle of the carriage came up over my legs, and of course I held Jesse while we sat up on the back seat all by ourselves.

"You know Carol, your first car ride was in this fine automobile, coming home from the hospital. She was only eleven days old, and so were you," Virgil remembered out loud.

"Where's Gust?" Uncle Virg asked Mama, as he opened her door.

"Not coming," she said.

"All right then," said Uncle Virg, "All aboard!"

Mama got in the front seat and we were off. We turned right out of our driveway and headed down Tower Street, passing the market at the end of the block. Mama was applying the finishing touches on her lipstick in her compact mirror and I was looking out the window at Mr. Bateman's store, dark and shut up tight for Christmas day. I muffled a gasp as we drove past. My father was sitting on a crate under an awning on the side of the market. He had a brown paper bag between his legs and his hat hung off one knee. My chest fell into my stomach as our eyes met. I wanted to holler out, but something stopped me. He winked and held up his curved pinky-finger. That was our secret hand shake—pinky swear. I watched him for as long as I could see him, then slowly turned my head to the front. Uncle Virg directed the rear view mirror so I could see his eyes. They spoke volumes, but he didn't say a word. His expression said something like, "It's all right Peach. Let him go. And whatever you do, don't tell your mother that you saw your dad sitting next to the market with a bottle of whiskey in his lap and nowhere to go on Christmas day."

In a robust voice, Uncle Virg began singing, "God rest ye merry gentlemen..."

Mama interrupted, "Virgil?"

"Yes Virginia."

"Do you remember what the Christmas Truce of 1914 was?"

"I do," said Virgil.

Mama closed her compact and slipped it into her purse. "Well I believe it was the last documented moment in which people were truly nice. It seems like people are not nice anymore. They don't do what they say they are going to do. They lie and do what's easy or what will cover up for their selfishness." She blotted her lips on a kleenex. "I need to try to make a truce, just for today to be nice."

"What nature of a truce are you about, Virginia?" said Uncle Virg, in his school superintendent voice. I felt the Model-A slow ever so slightly.

"The Christmas truce of 1937. Please turn the car around Virg, I can't do this today," said Mama.

Uncle Virg pulled the car over to the side of the road. He kept his hands on the steering wheel, kept his eyes forward, and said nothing. Mama said nothing. I wrapped Jessie's blanket around her a little bit tighter.

"I saw him back there by the market Virgil. I pretended not to see him. I wanted not to see him, but I did, and I can't go on my merry way with him sitting there on Christmas day with a bottle of whiskey as his only friend. Two wrongs don't make a right."

"You will never be able to match the wrongs that have been done to you, Virginia."

"So let's not try."

Uncle Virg turned toward her with a look of total obedience, trying to understand a heart more forgiving than his. "You're too good."

"I'm not good—I'm confused. Just go back before I change my mind," Mama said, with a fluttery wave of her hand.

We drove back in silence. Father was sitting there just as before. He didn't look up as Uncle Virg brought the car to a gradual stop across the street. Mama got out, left the car door open, and walked up to him. I couldn't hear what she was saying, but she had her arms folded and her body was completely still except for a barely noticeable, but constant and steady tap of her right heel. She did that with her foot to release just enough tension so she wouldn't cry, yell, or faint. I know because I do the same thing. He slowly lifted his eyes to her face. She placed her hands on her hips and her heel tapped faster. Finally, he stood up. Picking up the brown bag, he paused for a moment, then dropped it in the trash can beside the crate. He put on his hat and followed my mother to the car. Mama got in next to me and curled her legs up onto the seat to avoid the buggy. Father got in the front.

"Thanks Virgil, Merry Christmas," mumbled Father.

"No thanks to me Gust—not my idea," said Uncle Virg. He offered Father a cigarette. Father took two, lit both, and handed one back to Mama.

The second time Uncle Virg turned the car around on Tower Street that Christmas day, we were a family again. No one spoke for a while, but when the thought came into my head I asked, "Uncle Virg, what *was* the Christmas truce of 1914?"

He took a long deep breath and thought a moment before answering. "Well, it was during World War One, when some clever boy sent a message over—probably threw it wrapped around a grenade without the pin pulled or just hollered across no man's land. They might have said something like, 'Let's have a party. Let's meet in the middle. No shooting between the lines.' So, the British in their khaki, and the Germans in their grey, both got up out of their trenches, left their rifles behind and met at enemy lines. They swapped cigarettes and addresses, asked about friends or relatives they knew from each other's hometowns. A few of the Germans had actually worked in London before the war and had to leave their jobs and loved ones in London to join the ranks that would bomb the same city and friends they left behind. But that Christmas eve, they left the fighting in the trenches and treated each other like brothers. There was an unspoken understanding that after Christmas they'd go back to fighting, but for that one day they would trust each other to act cautiously civil and attempt to put away their differences."

"Oh," I said. "Too bad they had to go back to fighting."

Father leaned his head against the window and closed his eyes. Mama looked out her window and commented on the things she observed, like the pretty street decorations uptown and the ornate window displays in Bigelow's Department store. It was a three hour drive each way to Greenwood, where Uncle Virg lived. I hoped Mama wouldn't act this odd way for the entire drive.

Once we got out onto the big highway, little rivers of accumulated rain streamed down the hills along the highway. Every once in a while the tires sent fans of water off to each side. The damp made it feel close and steamy inside the car. I wrote my name on the fogged-up glass of the window. On the outside, the window held little drops of moisture that worked like a kaleidoscope when I put my eye up-close. Looking through them brought the saturated greens, blues and browns of the passing countryside to life. The skeletons of the leafless trees sent droplets from branch to twig to twig, like trapeze artists swinging from limb to limb, and occasionally a giant raindrop would fall from the canopy of trees along the road. There would be no walks with the buggy on the sidewalk in front of Uncle Virg's house that day. But their house had a covered porch that wrapped all the way around and I already knew it would be the perfect place for Jessie and me to take our maiden voyage with the buggy.

I was anxious to get out of the car as soon as we pulled up to the house but Mama told me to stay put. We were going to church, and we needed to make room for Aunt Marion in the car. Mama opened her door and guided the baby buggy out to Uncle Virg. He carried it up onto the porch, opened the front door and rolled it over the threshold. Aunt Marion's Boston bull terrier, Butch, sneaked out the door to greet us, but as soon as his paws felt the rain, he high-tailed it right back into the house. Butch was just about as spoiled rotten as a dog could be. He had his own bed in the corner of the kitchen by the wood stove and several hand knit sweaters made by Aunt Marion herself. Aunt Marion was still talking baby-talk to Butch when she shut the door. Uncle Virg helped her down the steps. One of her legs was a little shorter and skinnier than the other because of Polio when she was a little girl. She always said she was lucky to have a leg at all. Mama scooted over next to Jessie and me so Aunt Marion could get in the back with us.

"Merry Christmas Carol...Gust. Merry Christmas Virginia," said Aunt Marion. She laid her hand on top of my mom's and gave it a "Good to see you" squeeze.

"You're longer than I expected, did the rain slow you down?"

"No Marion, we had to go back and get something we forgot," said Mama. "Oh no, I forgot the pumpkin pies!" Mama tapped her hand to her forehead and sank down in frustration.

"Oh Virginia, don't think about it for even one minute. I made my minced meat pie and chocolate cake and we had the pleasure of your pies at Thanksgiving. Take them to the hospital. They won't last five minutes in the hospital dining room."

Mama was obviously disheartened, but smiled with a nod.

"Of course you could always feed them to Carol for breakfast, lunch and dinner. The child is so painfully thin." She leaned over and looked across the seat to me. "I see you finally fit into your skirt."

"And she looks very smart in it, I might add," said Uncle Virg.

I lifted Jessie to better show off my skirt and started to say how much I liked it but she interrupted, carrying on about how Pendleton Wool came from Oregon and was some of the finest wool made in the whole United States.

"When you grow out of it, you should preserve it in moth balls and save it for your own children because it will last forever," said Aunt Marion. This was probably only the seventeenth time I'd heard this lecture. I vowed never to make my children wear Aunt Marion's skirt.

It was a short drive to the church. I loved going to church with Aunt Marion and Uncle Virg. Whenever we stayed over a Sunday in Greenwood—which included the past three Christmases—we'd go to whatever service or gathering the church was having and were always greeted like celebrities. On Sunday mornings, whenever it was one of the children's birthday week, they got to go up in front of the congregation during the offering and put a penny in the little ceramic, church-shaped bank. I always asked Mama for two pennies, one for me and one for the Christ Child, as our birthdays are only nine days apart. For my birthday that year Mama had gotten me a book called *The Birds' Christmas Carol*, by Kate Douglas Wiggin. It is about a little girl named Carol Bird who is bedridden and sickly but was most certainly the nicest girl I would ever hope to meet. She was born on Christmas day so her parents called her their own Christmas Carol, just like Mama called me. I actually think Mama got the idea from the book, but that's okay. I wished I *was* Carol Bird, except for the part when she dies. Mama and I bawled our eyes out when we read that part. That was the first book that made me love to read. It seemed so real. So, in honor of my new imaginary friend, Carol Bird, that year I asked Mama for three pennies: one for me, one for Jesus, and one for Carol Bird.

Another thing I liked about the Greenwood Church was the shoes. I always made sure to sit on the end of the pew, near the aisle, so when everyone went up to get the bread and juice, I could watch the different styles of shoes pass by. I had two pairs of shoes, one for church and one for school. I usually went barefoot when it got warm in the summer. As I got older, what shoes I got for the next school year greatly depended on what I saw walking the isle at Greenwood Baptist.

Our church in Jamestown had a piano, and Pastor Friedland's wife played it in such a manner as made me want to march. At Greenwood, there was a pipe organ with a giant row of pipes all along the wall above the altar. The organ was stately and serious. It filled every corner of the sanctuary with thrones for the Holy Spirit. I could sing as loud as I wanted and never go off key. They also had a harp that made me think of magical wonders in heavenly places. Listening to it, if I closed my eyes, I could picture myself dressed in a white frock with wings lifting me up to sit right on Jesus' lap, like the pictures in the Sunday school room. On this particular Christmas day, after I had deposited my pennies, we were singing "Oh little town of Bethlehem" with the harp as the accompaniment. I looked up at Father sitting next to me. He wasn't singing, but he had his eyes closed and wore a thin, wide smile. He looked joyful and different.

I tapped him on the shoulder and motioned with my index finger for him to bend down. I whispered in his ear, "Thanks for my baby buggy."

He kissed my forehead. The smell of tobacco and whiskey clung to his breath, and his coat, and my memory. I threaded my arm through the crook of his elbow, rested my head on him and listened. I held on tight to my father's arm, thinking I might lift right off the pew with all the joy I was feeling. The drone of Pastor Clarence's voice usually made me sleepy, but today was different. I couldn't think of anywhere I'd rather be. I didn't know it then, but that was the last time I would ever sit in church with my dad.

5

After church Mama announced that she and Father would walk back to the house, and asked if Marion and Virgil would take me home with them. Aunt Marion tried to talk Mama into going downstairs to the fellowship hall for pastries and coffee, but Uncle Virg intervened and off they went. I ended up being the only celebrity and got all the attention and two pastries. On our way home in the car we passed Mama and Father but they didn't see me waving to them out the window. Father was talking with a serious face, waving his hands around like Mrs. Indellicati, the sausage lady.

Since we got home before them, I settled Jesse in her carriage and made several trips around the porch. Butch trotted along beside me as I promenaded. After the fourth time around, Butch retired to a temporary patch of sunlight on the front door mat. His little legs were plumb worn out. So on my next trip around I made room in the buggy and told him to lay down, but he had no intention of being my other baby. He propped himself up with his paws on the side of the buggy and enjoyed the view from his new perspective. The slatted boards of the porch made a bumpity noise and the vibration seemed to help Jesse fall asleep. I was feeling a little tired too, so we stopped. I sat in the wicker chair on the side of the house and as soon as I was settled in, Butch jumped onto my lap and curled up for a little nap.

This house was grand, compared to our basement apartment. Aunt Marion called it her "Victorian Beauty" and said she never would move, as long as she could climb the stairs. She spent most of her free time in spring and summer in the yard and vegetable garden. After she went back to teaching at the University in the fall, she spent weekends in September and half of October, canning the bountiful harvest of fruits and vegetables that she and Uncle Virg grew. When the canning was done she took to crocheting. She used a tiny hook and very fine cotton thread to make doilies, collars, lace and sundry other useful, if frivolous, creations. From each of the upstairs windows, there hung intricately crocheted curtains. When the windows were open, the fringe waved in the wind and made pretty shadows on the walls. Their house was fancy and breakable. I liked being outside more than in and my favorite part about the house, other than the porch, was the roof. It had five tall peaks and a turret over their bedroom that looked like a hat, topped with an angel blowing a trumpet in the direction of the wind. It was an easy climb up to the roof from the balcony off of the guest room, but I only went up there when Aunt Marion wasn't home. I liked being at Aunt Marion and Uncle Virg's house, I never felt like company.

Mama arrived back before Father did. She looked tired and her cheeks were pink from the walk. She took off her rain bonnet and pulled the collar of her coat up around her neck, then she sat in the wicker love seat across from me.

"When you were a baby, I'd wrap you up in a bunting and put you outside on the covered porch in your bassinet to get some fresh air, even in the winter," Mama said.

"Didn't I get cold? Weren't you afraid I'd get sick?" I said.

"Nope, you had lots of blankets and kept nice and warm. I'd let you lay out there and cry and get mad so you would be good and tired by the time your father came home. You'd wail for five or ten minutes while you flailed your arms and legs around. It was good for your lungs. Then I'd bring you in with your face all red and wet and cuddle you up for a snack, and you'd sleep for a few hours, snug as a bug." Mama got up from her seat and started toward the kitchen door around back of the house. "It's probably getting time for dinner Carol. Let's see if Aunt Marion needs some help."

I got up and followed her with Jesse in the buggy, and Butch under my arm, bumping over the kitchen threshold and into the steam of boiling potatoes.

"Need help?" Mama asked.

Aunt Marion was giving Butch a taste of the gravy straight from her stirring spoon. She took a taste herself and started right in giving orders and delegating responsibilities. As usual I was in charge of the silverware.

***

Dinner was uncomfortable. Usually Uncle Virg told stories and shared remembrances of when he and Mama were growing up. Aunt Marion liked to re-cap the news headlines and offer her opinions and conclusions. That day it felt like they were quizzing Father on a chapter of a book he hadn't read.

"How's the job search, Gust?"

"Not so good, Virgil."

"What nature of work are you looking for?" Aunt Marion probed.

"Can't say. Carpentry maybe."

"There's a service station, Texaco I think, going in at the North part of Jamestown. You could see if they need any help," Uncle Virg suggested as he passed the peas.

"Could." Father took a small spoonful, like he didn't deserve more.

"Well times certainly are tough," offered Aunt Marion. "I've lost my assistant and they've given me a student volunteer. The girl doesn't know diddly about being a secretarial assistant. Can't type, or file, or answer the phone with any civility. She's more interested in the health of her cuticles than the growing pile of papers on her desk. How's your typing, Gust?"

"Don't type." His jaws pulsed, not from chewing but from clenching. He did this when he didn't want to talk about it.

I dove in to save him, "Wanna play checkers after dinner, Father?

"We'll see, Peach" He didn't smile.

***

When Father went out for his after-dinner cigarette, he didn't come back. Aunt Marion walked around with a questioning furrow on her brow. Mama seemed relieved. Uncle Virg and I played checkers in the corner of the kitchen by the wood stove while Aunt Marion and Mama washed dishes.

The kitchen sink was under a set of double-hung windows that looked out onto the back yard and the creek beyond. Naked weeping willows hung over the muddy water, which ran swiftly on this dark, drippy day. Mama was taking special care to clean off the dried gravy under the pour spout of the gravy boat. Aunt Marion dried the glasses with a special towel that had the word "glass" woven right into it. She held each glass up to the light of the window before she returned it to the paper-lined shelf.

"Virgil," said Aunt Marion, still drying and checking, and double checking, "why don't you and Carol go out to the parlor for a while. Make a fire if you want to, I think *Jack Armstrong, The All American Boy,* is on the radio."

"What is it you had in mind, Marion?" said Uncle Virg.

"Nothing a young girl and her Uncle would be interested in. Go on then. I'll be out shortly with dessert. Do you care for coffee Virgil?"

"Bet yer life!" Uncle Virg said, and then looked at me with his Cheshire cat smile and bouncing eyebrows. "A little minty cocoa might be a nice libation for my opponent. We have a championship to play, and the winner gets a double portion of chocolate cake." He winked at me and carefully raised the checkerboard from the table. We left through the kitchen door. It swung three times before resting in its place.

"I'll be right back Uncle Virg," I said and detoured to the bathroom.

"Don't hurry, I'll be planning my strategy," he chided.

Thanks to a large vent that allowed the wood stove heat to flow into the bathroom, I could hear everything Aunt Marion and Mama said from the kitchen. Consequently my trip to the bathroom lasted a little longer than I had intended.

"Virginia, what in the world is going on with you and Gust? There couldn't have been five words shared between the two of you during that entire meal, and he never did look me in the eye, not a single time."

Mama didn't speak right away. I imagined her staring silently out the window, past the creek and the trees, past the sky and rain clouds, and all the way back around to her heart. I was worried she would cry again. I couldn't do what I went into the bathroom to do. My stomach ached.

Finally the words churned through her lips. "He doesn't...love me. I still love him, but he doesn't love me," she wept.

Aunt Marion growled. I heard the clink of coffee cups, the snap of the canister lid, and water running. Then the kitchen was quiet for a time.

I heard Uncle Virg's voice, "How's the coffee coming, sweetheart?"

"Bad timing," Marion barked.

The kitchen door swung three more times as Uncle Virg retreated. I stayed seated, rocking back and forth, trying to calm the gurgling in my stomach. I looked out the window and traced the terminal branches of the oak tree with my eyes. A blue jay landed and enjoyed the bobbing of the branch a few seconds before it pulled a piece of moss from a gnarly twig and flew away.

When Mama's sobbing stopped, Aunt Marion asked, "Why do you think he doesn't love you?"

Mama's words came slowly, with a chesty tension that made it difficult for me to listen to, but I couldn't help myself. "Love is patient, love is kind. It does not envy, it does not boast, it is not proud, rude or selfish. It is not easily angered and keeps no records of wrongs. Love does not delight in evil but rejoices in the truth. Love always protects, trusts, always hopes... and always perseveres." She blew her nose. "Love doesn't come home on payday with liquor on his breath and no check. Love is there when your daughter is born and when your mother dies. Love knows the difference between working late, and carousing around with the boss's daughter."

"Oh dear God, Virginia," Aunt Marion said.

Both women wept.

"It'll be all right Marion, I'll be okay," Mama said. "He's moving out and I'm moving on."

"I'm so sorry. I had no idea. Virginia, you don't deserve this. What will you do? How will you get by? I need a secretary, how's your typing?"

"I'm an excellent typist, but that's not what I'll do. Carol and I will be fine, it's Gust I'm worried about. Seems the booze has sucked the life out of him, just doesn't act rational anymore. He's sad and puny most of the time and when he's happy it's because he has some grandiose pipe dream that's gonna bring our ship into harbor and set us up for life."

So I knew a secret. We all knew a secret, for when I came out of the bathroom Uncle Virg still had his ear up to the kitchen door. My father was more than a liar. My father had secrets too. I may have been only six, but I understood the story my mother told through her tears.

We swept our four-way secret under the nearest rug, each for the sake of the others, and continued to let it be Christmas.

6

The day after Christmas was Boxing Day. For Aunt Marion this didn't mean giving gifts to the less fortunate, or a Bank holiday for Canadians. Boxing day at Aunt Marion and Uncle Virg's meant boxing up all the decorations from the holidays to be stored away for next year. To me it seemed sad to whisk it all away after such a short time, but things were done with order and design at Aunt Marion's house, and a proper putting-away was just as important as an efficient getting-out.

Every year, right after Thanksgiving, Mama and Aunt Marion were always single minded about one thing, getting Christmas out. Getting Christmas out for Mama meant putting the pinecone candleholders, with new green candles, on the coffee table. She hung five silver bells in the kitchen above the sink, changed the salt and pepper grinders to the ceramic Christmas tree shakers, and traded her Amish quilted apron for the red and green one with an appliqued snowman on the front. But for Aunt Marion the transformation took days. I loved being there for the getting-out. It was a day of memories and responsibilities. As soon as breakfast was over, Uncle Virg would start bringing boxes down from the attic. The boxes were labeled in numerical order: 1 of 12, 2 of 12, 3 of 12, and so on. The Nativity set was always 1 of 12 and from the time I was four, setting up the Nativity was my responsibility. I always hid Jesus up on the mantle until Christmas day because he wasn't born yet. Anyway, the cows and sheep needed to eat out of the manger until The Baby was born.

But, on Boxing Day it all went back. Everything was categorized, labeled, wrapped, and hauled back up to the attic for next November. This was always a gloomy day for me. Maybe it was the actual work involved, or maybe it was the feeling that it was all over, and it didn't turn out quite the way I thought it would.

That year, on Boxing Day, I woke up knowing that I would be expected to wrap Baby Jesus back up in the blue tissue paper, the wise men in the white tissue paper, and Joseph and Mary, the sheep, and the Angel of the Lord, back in the pink silky fabric that used to be Aunt Marion's honeymoon nighty. I knew we would have waffles. I knew we would take a nap in the afternoon. I knew we would eat cold turkey sandwiches for lunch and hot turkey gravy over mashed potatoes for dinner. But I didn't know where my father was.

***

That evening, Uncle Virg drove us home. When we pulled up to the house, it looked abandoned. There were no lights making the windows glow a pretty yellow to welcome us home. Mama rummaged around in the bottom of her purse for her key and searched for the right way to unlock the door. I think this may have been the first time Mama had ever had to unlock the door for us at night. Father usually took the lead, opened the door, flipped on the light and said, "Home again, home again jiggidy- jig!" Mama flipped the light on this time and as she did, a bright flash and popping noise startled us. Uncle Virg stopped short when he met us at the dark doorway.

"Kitchen light must have burned out. Stay right here." He squeezed past us, found his way through the kitchen, and flipped on the switch in the hallway. The light was sufficient for us to make our way through the kitchen and the hall, where the rest of the lights seemed to be just fine. We dropped our bags and packages on Mama's bed, I laid Jesse on my bed, and Uncle Virg set the boxed-up leftovers on the kitchen table.

"Got another light bulb Virginia?"

"Under the kitchen sink. Thanks, Virg!" she answered from the bedroom.

I raced to the kitchen and found the light bulb before Uncle Virg had a chance. He pulled the kitchen chair over to the middle of the room, hoisted himself up, removed the globe from the fixture and handed it to me.

"Here, Peach, rinse the bugs out and wipe it with a towel, would ya?" he said on his way out to the car to get some more stuff.

I pushed my stool up to the kitchen sink and filled the globe up like a swimming pool full of bugs. Some of the bugs were cooked to the inside of the globe and I had to scratch them off with my finger nail. A big moth, with eyes on her wings, floated out with the water and got lost down the drain. I was carefully drying the globe, when Mama came into the kitchen, already wearing her bathrobe and slippers. She lifted the globe out of my hands, warning me that it was breakable and for me to let her help. Uncle Virg wheeled my buggy into the kitchen as she was taking the globe from my hands.

"Good job, Peach. Wanna help?" he said.

"Bet yer-life," I said and saw Uncle Virg wink at Mama and smile.

He parked the buggy, lifted me onto his shoulders and positioned me under the ceiling fixture. He held one hand under mine to catch the bulb if I dropped it, which I didn't, and we were in business again. Then he walked over to the light switch with me still on his shoulders, bent down so I could reach it from my perch on his tall frame, and I flipped on the light.

He spun around with me on his shoulders. "Whoo-Hoo! You did it!"

Mama was on the chair now, replacing the globe. She held it with her left hand and was twisting the little screw in with the other.

"You need help?" Virgil asked.

"Nope, got it. Time to learn to do some things on my own."

As soon as she got down off the chair and moved back to assess our handiwork, the globe fell from the ceiling, and crashed to the floor.

I instinctively brought my hands up to my eyes, blindly anticipating what would happen next. When I peeled my palms from my face, I saw that Mama also had her hands over her face. She didn't move. I felt nervous. Maybe I would have done a better job putting the globe up. Maybe Uncle Virg should have done it. But Mama, who usually did most things well, did it, and now it was broken and she was sad again. I hated this kitchen with the broken glass all over the floor all the time.

"I need a minute," Mama said from inside her hands.

Uncle Virg lifted me down from his shoulders into his big arms and walked across the crunchy floor past Mama. He carried me to my bed, turned on the bedside lamp, and pulled the chair between the beds. I got out of my bed and crawled up into Mama's.

"Would you like a story?" He asked.

"Shouldn't we help Mama?"

"No, she'll be fine."

I picked out *The Birds' Christmas Carol* of course. We had just started the second chapter when Mama came in and lay down with me. I fell asleep even before Carol Bird had the idea of inviting all the Ruggles' over for Christmas dinner.

That night I dreamed I was swimming deep down in the ocean in a great blue hole that was thickly populated with every color and size of fish. Their slippery scales touched me as they swam. There was a prickly seahorse floating around that looked like a plastic toy. He looked mean, so I didn't touch him, and he kept a safe distance away from me too it seemed. An eel slithered on the sandy floor making dust with its tail. A school of tiny pink and orange fish danced around like a troop of ballerinas, following each other's every move. The water was warm, and unlike real life, I was a good swimmer. I could propel myself by pointing my toes, and little bubbles came out of my feet. I was alone, except for the fish, but I was not afraid until I ran out of breath and tried to make my way to the surface and realized it was very far away. When I paddled my feet and moved my arms, I slowed down, but if I just pointed my toes I went faster. I was completely unable to do anything else to hurry myself along. I panicked. I was running out of air and still very deep in the sea with the surface nowhere in sight. Finally, when I could hold my breath no longer, I gave up. I pointed my toes as straight as I could, lowered my arms to my sides, and took a full breath of water into my lungs. I expected to drown, but I didn't. Nor did I cough, or choke, or faint. I was breathing underwater.

**

In the morning when I woke up, Mama was lying next to me on her back, purring. I wondered if we had eggs, because I did not want oatmeal. I carefully climbed over Mama so I wouldn't wake her. I had a plan, and her waking up would ruin it. I successfully crawled out of the bed and got a pair of socks out of the top dresser drawer. This took some time because the drawer was not easy to pull out and sometimes made a squeaking noise. If I pulled the drawer out in tiny tugs, it didn't make a noise

My plan was to make breakfast for Mama and serve it to her in bed. I knew she would want coffee first, so I went about making it. I put two spoons of sugar into her favorite mug, and filled it up halfway with milk. I pulled the percolator to the front of the counter and filled it to the six line, and put four tablespoons of coffee in the metal basket. I had watched Mama do this seven thousand times, and had helped her probably twenty-five times, so I knew this was right, and it would be just how she liked it. Then I went to the refrigerator to get the eggs but stopped to feel the letters on the front of the freezer door. They were raised metal letters that read: P-H-I-L-C-O. Ever since I was a baby, I remember Mama holding me up on her hip to see and recite the letters. It was my first spelling word. Philco. I knew all of these letters, plus the letters to my own name, long before I went to school. I am sure my teacher was impressed that my mother was such a good teacher, but the truth is we just did it for fun. Most everything we did seemed to be just for fun, and if it ended up teaching me how to spell, or make coffee, or fold a perfect hospital corner with a sheet, that was just gravy.

I went about the preparations for breakfast. I broke three of Aunt Marion's brown chicken eggs into a bowl, one for each person plus one, then scrambled them up, and put them in a pan with butter and a splash of water. Mama kept long matches by the stove for lighting the flame. I turned the dial to where the 3 would be if it wasn't worn off the porcelain knob, and scraped the match on the side of the box. Carefully, I lit the flame with an outstretched arm. The tiny blue tongues of fire whooshed around the burner. After I put the egg pan on the flame, I turned the knob to 5 and put two pieces of bread in the toaster. We always kept soft butter in the cupboard above the toaster, so I got that down, using my stool, and was all ready for when the bread popped up. The eggs were getting bubbly, which made me wonder why the percolator wasn't bubbling. I pushed my stool over to check the coffee. The water was cold. I'd forgotten to plug it in, so I did. I buttered the toast, turned the eggs down to 1 to keep them warm and poured two glasses of orange juice. Then I put everything on a big tray and took inventory like I had heard Mama do whenever she was setting the table: "Bread n' butter, salt n' pepper, cream n' sugar, linen-cutlery-candles." I put two cloth napkins on the tray, decided against candles, drank half of my juice, and re-filled it. Breakfast was ready but the coffee wasn't, so Mama would have to have coffee after breakfast today. I made it all the way to the bedroom without spilling, put the tray on the watermelon crate, climbed up on the bed and woke Mama with a butterfly kiss. She didn't open her eyes, but she smiled and said, "I smell something yummy, did you make breakfast?"

"I made eggs and toast all by myself," I said and climbed over her onto the other side of the bed.

She opened her eyes and looked at me, still smiling, but looking away quickly. She was probably picturing me in the kitchen, using the stove all by myself, and feeling panicked and trying not to show it. She sat up, looked around, and found the breakfast to her left.

"Wowee! Look at you. You did this all by yourself?" she beamed.

"Yep!"

"What a treat."

"Wait right there," I said, and scrambled down to go and check the coffee.

"Check the burners and unplug the toaster!" she hollered down the hall.

"Don't tell me how to cook in my own kitchen!" I hollered back, quoting my Aunt.

"Oh, Okay Marion!" there was a smile in her voice.

When I got back with the coffee Mama was sitting up with the pillows stacked in back of her. She'd made a similar nest next to her for me. She reached down and took the coffee, smelled it as she cradled it in her palms, and gave an appreciative moan of pleasure. Steam billowed off the surface as she took a sip, "Perfect," she said. I made a permanent place in my mind for this memory. Perfect.

Mama drank her coffee, and I ate most of the breakfast while I told her about my dream.

"Huh," she said, "that sounds like fun."

"It was, and it felt really real," I said.

"Maybe it means something," she said.

"Like what?"

"Maybe you're gonna grow up to be a deep sea diver."

"That would be scary," I said.

"Not if you can breathe under water," she said. "You can be anything you want to be. Always believe that."

Mama put the empty plates on the watermelon crate and I laid my head on her lap. She combed her fingers through my hair and finished her coffee.

"Mama?"

"Well."

"How many days till I go back to school?" I asked.

"Four," she answered, "why?"

"How about we just lay here for four days and we can read books, and eat eggs, and listen to the radio, and paint our toe nails."

"Sounds good to me," she said.

But as soon as she said it, there was a frantic pounding on the door.

7

The house we lived in was divided into three apartments. We lived in the basement, Lena and Leonard Harrison lived in the apartment above us, and Mrs. Nigren lived in the top with her two teenaged sons, Mitchell and Michael.

We knew before we got to the door that it was Lena out there because she was hollering and pounding and wriggling the doorknob to get in. Mama undid the latch and Lena came barreling through the door, followed by Mrs. Nigren, panting and red-faced.

"Mitchell has a piece of apple lodged in his throat and he can't breathe!" hollered Lena. She pulled Mama out the door and up the two flights of stairs to the Nigren's apartment.

Mrs. Nigren followed them in her mint-green bathrobe, so I didn't hesitate to follow suit in my flannel nightgown. As we passed the Harrison's landing, Leonard was standing in the open doorway, poking his head through a white t-shirt. He followed behind me. All three women bolted through the Nigren's door and headed straight for the kitchen where it appeared Michael was trying to beat the apple out of his brother. Mitchell lay prostrate on the floor and Michael was trying to dislodge the apple by pounding his brother on the back. Mama hollered at Michael to get off, and then she rolled Mitchell over onto his back. She lifted her nightgown, stepped right over him and squatted down. Then she placed her hands just under his ribs, and thrust so hard that her feet came off the floor. Her head was right above his when the apple, and everything else he had eaten for breakfast, came hurling out of his blue face and covered Mama with a chunky gray mess. I was sure it was oatmeal. She rolled him onto his side and he coughed and puked and coughed some more until he could take a breath. Everyone was clapping and hooting and praising God, slipping through the slime just to come over and welcome him back to the living. Mrs. Nigren went to the sink to get Mama a towel to wipe off, but she had already wiped her face with her sleeve and was using a quiet voice to speak encouraging direction to Mitchell, while her left hand was on his wrist, feeling for his pulse.

"He's pinking right up," she assured us over her shoulder. "Think you can get up?" she asked Mitchell.

He nodded his head, took several shallow breaths, and slowly sat up.

"Thanks Mrs. Carlson." His voice was raspy and shallow.

"You'll be fine," said Mama.

"Yeah," Mitchell nodded, then smiled a thin smile of embarrassed gratefulness.

Mama got up and looked down at her front. Her nighty was plastered with Mitchell's breakfast. She gagged a little and pulled the slimy mess away from her torso, then made a beeline for the door. She didn't stop until she reached our bathtub and turned on the shower. She got right in, not even bothering to take off her nightgown.

I was right on her heels, "Are you all right, Mama?"

"Yes honey, are you?"

"Yeah, I think." I thought about it for a minute.

"Shut the door, it's cold," she said.

"Can I get in with you?" I asked.

"Wait till I rinse off this mess," she threw her twisted nightgown over the shower curtain and gave a big sigh. "Okay, I think it's safe now, come on in."

I shed my nightgown and found the opening of the shower curtain and climbed into the big claw-foot tub. I sat down and let the water rain on me with my face down so it wouldn't go up my nose.

"Mrs. Nigren said you're her hero, Mama," I said.

"Hero huh?" She smiled down at me. "You're my hero."

"Why am I your hero, Mama?"

"Cuz I love you so much I couldn't live without you."

I smiled. "I love you more."

"I love you the mostest," she said.

She rinsed her hair and got out of the tub. I shut the water off and rubbed soap up the slanted part of the tub so I could slide down. I did this until I was too cold, then rinsed off and got out and grabbed the towel that Mama had hung to warm near the radiator.

When I came out, Mama was already dressed looking as if she was ready for an outing. She was in the living room, sorting through a stack of Christmas cards. The Christmas tree was still there, but the ornaments were off and the boxes were stacked up, waiting to be stored away. Newspaper shreds and packing materials littered the floor.

"So much for lying in bed all day and painting our toe nails. Shall we go check on Mitchell?" she said.

I got dressed. No scratchy skirt this time. We played stair-school on the way up the stairs to the Nigren's.

"Spell cat," Mama said.

"Cat, c-a-t, cat," I said. And we went up two steps.

"What do you get when you mix red and blue?" Mama said.

"Purple," I said. And we went up two more.

"Okay, say the days of the week, one step for each day you get right."

I said them all and climbed seven more steps. When we were one step away from the top she thought hard and smiled, "Who's the smartest first grader at Willard School?"

"Me?" I said, looking up at her.

"You!" she said, while we took the last step with pride and victory.

The Nigren's kitchen smelled of disinfectant. Mrs. Nigren was putting a chicken in a big kettle of steaming water on the stove, and started right in explaining that the whole apple episode never would have happened if Mitchell wasn't always in such a hurry. He was too eager to get back out to the garage and work on that deathtrap of his. As far as Mrs. Nigren was concerned, if the apple didn't kill him, the motorcycle would. She started in about how she had a dead husband and didn't need a dead son to top off her grief.

"The people around me don't take into account how their actions are going to affect anyone else," she fretted as she cut a carrot into thin medallions. "I just can't bear another tragedy in my life and..."

"Mom! Knock it off. I'm fine. I choked. Stop pounding nails into my coffin!" erupted Mitch, as he walked through the kitchen with his tool box in his grip. He passed Mama and me in the doorway. "Skuze me Mrs. Carlson."

Mrs. Nigren stood speechless, her chin pulled back into her neck and her hurt feelings puddling up in her eyes.

"Christine, sit down and gather yourself. Goodness sakes you've had a morning," said Mama.

Mama knew that there were specific times to make coffee and others to boil water for tea. She filled the teakettle and lit the stove, found the tea and cups, then put her hand on the handle of the teakettle as if pressing it down on the stove would make it boil faster. She suggested that I go in and play the piano, if that was all right with Mrs. Nigren. Mrs. Nigren said that would be fine, then repeated what she always said when I played her piano.

"Carol is gifted, Virginia. That child can play by ear. When a child starts to read, is the pivotal time to introduce formal music training. You may miss her window of opportunity." Mrs. Nigren's head bobbled when she said "window of opportunity."

Mrs. Nigren was a piano teacher. That is how she'd made a living since her husband died three years before. I hadn't taken lessons from her because it was too expensive for us, but every once in a while she let me play, and I always liked finding familiar tunes in my head, and plunking them out. So I went in and started fiddling around on the black keys, because that sounded like the mood that was fogging us in.

A few minutes later, Lena came upstairs and joined Mama and Mrs. Nigren. All three women chatted, smoked their Chesterfields, and drank tea. In between my made-up piano songs, I listened to them talk.

"Thanks for saving my son's life Virginia. Don't see any signs of brain damage as of yet, he's still sassy as ever," Mrs. Nigren lamented. "Do you know what he did as soon as you left? Well, first he took a shower, but then he marched right out here to the kitchen and ate an apple—the very fruit that almost killed him. He just bit right into another one like nothing ever happened."

"Guess it's good to get right back on the bike and try again. No sense avoiding apples if the Lord has planned for a streetcar to kill you," Mama said.

"Just as easy to drown in a teacup of water as it is in a lake,' Stu used to say. He let those boys run wild as foxes. He's the one taught them not to take any mind for the danger of a thing. 'Just have fun, be young while you're young,' he'd say. Well, I say be careful while you're young or you'll likely never see thirty."

"Why's that bad?" said Lena. "I'd rather have fun and live a short life than sit and be bored to death till I'm ninety."

"Oh you just don't understand. You two live a charmed life with husbands and money and hope on the horizon. These two boys is all I have," said Mrs. Nigren, noticeably rattled.

"I don't have money!" said Lena. "Leonard's been laid off for two weeks, and if they need him back for next month it will only be thirty hours a week. We're broke."

"And I'm shy one husband and left without a pot to piss in," Mama said.

"Lands," said Mrs. Nigren. "We do have trouble. Seems like the devil himself has got his eye on our little piece of pie."

"I'm no visionary, but it seems like trouble comes in threes." Mama re-filled her tea cup and lit another cigarette. Then she went on, "Maybe with all of us having such a tough time of it, we can roll all these circumstances together and be done. You know, the devil only wants to meddle with the ones that make him mad. Maybe God's letting him have his way with us for a while and we're all in for a huge blessing if we persevere. Hmm. Remember Job?"

Mrs. Nigren got up to check her chicken. "Well, I've had my share and I'm counting on a better new year. The boys have jobs at the new Texaco service station. Money shouldn't be such an issue anymore. Lands, I need a new bra."

"Speaking of streetcars," Lena said, "I saw Virgil stop and pick you up on Christmas morning, then you all came back around and picked up Gust from Mr. Bateman's Market. Sounds like I'm spying on you, but I was just sitting by the window and happened to see. What's going on with Gust?"

"Speaking of streetcars?" Mama started laughing. Mrs. Nigren had just taken a substantial sip of tea and most of it came out her nose. Lena had followed her own train of thought perfectly, and found nothing funny about it.

"How do streetcars have anything to do with it?" Mama was laughing so hard she was hardly coming up for air.

"I don't know, someone was talking about streetcars just a second ago," Lena said, giggling along with Mama. I don't know why any of them found this funny, but they were all three laughing now and Mama was blowing her nose 'cuz it always ran when she laughed or cried.

I left my piano and went to investigate the goings on.

Lena good-naturedly punched Mama in the arm and in the process, spilled her tea. It splashed all over Mama, and a little on Lena. Lena gave a surprised snort and that instigated another full minute of hilarity. Mrs. Nigren went to the cupboard to get more tea, and came back with an empty tin.

She turned it upside down and a few tiny crumbs wafted to the floor.

"Speaking of hitting bottom," Mrs. Nigren said.

Well, that sent both Mama and Lena over the top. Lena was doubled over emitting a quiet raspy sound and Mama had to get up and hug Mrs. Nigren for being so witty. All three women were wiping tears from their faces and trying to catch their breath. It was good to see Mama laughing instead of crying.

When the hilarity died down Mama said, "Oh, I needed that," wiping her eyes and blowing her nose. "You know, they say laughing and crying give similar relief. I was ready to bawl my head off, but that was way more fun."

Lena gathered herself and re-visited her original question, "Streetcars or no, what *about* Gust?"

"Yeah, I guess we have to talk about Gust," Mama said, still recovering. She looked back at me, sensing I had stopped playing, and said, "Carol, how about playing something more lively, like—Round and round the mulberry bush?"

I went back to the piano and tried to play quiet enough to hear and be heard at the same time.

Mama went on. "Well...the successful businessman that I married turned out to be a bootlegger. He didn't even drink at that point, just ran rum as fast as he could get it. I thought he was delivering automobile parts, but I figured it out as soon as prohibition was over and the money ran out, and well... Then he got a job as a carpenter, he's actually a very good carpenter, but for some reason he took to drinking on the job, and that got him fired lickety-split. So he started working at a bank. I don't know how on earth he landed that job, but when you pay more attention to the bank manager's daughter than to the length of your lunch hour... It's all turned out to be a terrible mess. The bank manager called me and wanted to know why Gust was needed at home so often. I wasn't about to lie for him so I told him the truth; Gust never came home for lunch, I packed him one. So, his manager followed him one afternoon, straight to his own home, and well, Bob's your uncle."

"Good Lord!" Mrs. Nigren looked dumbfounded. "Why, you don't mean to say..."

"What I mean to say, and do say, is that I am suing Gust for divorce. He's gone already, though I'm not sure where, and can't say as I care really. I'm rid of him and his lies. Frankly, I'm relieved."

"You're relieved?" said Lena, "You don't look relieved. Sorry, but you look tired, and like you've lost about ten pounds that you didn't need to lose."

"I guess I'm just relieved to stop living in limbo. I've avoided the truth for so long, that when I heard him say it, I felt relieved. The truth is hard to hear, but it's easier to live with. I finally asked him if he wanted her or me. He said her. I would have tried anything if he was game, but he wasn't. So I'm on to plan B."

"I'm so sorry, Virginia," Lena said.

"Alcohol," said Mrs. Nigren, "it will rip a family apart faster than quick. An affinity for liquor will take an otherwise perfectly adequate man and pickle him into a cheating, stinky, lazy ol' sloth!"

"Well Christine, I'm sure he *was* drunk when he was sneaking around with the boss' daughter. One needs some sort of pickling to live inside a jar full of lies."

"Oh," Lena brought her hand to her chest. "This is terrible."

"Well, maybe not. One man's folly might be another man's gain," said Mama.

"What in the green world does that mean?" Mrs. Nigren rolled her eyes.

"Just that my misfortune might be just the thing to get at least some of us back on our feet," Mama said.

"What are you getting at?" said Lena. Her voice had taken on a sweet quality of mourning, with all the loss and tragedy that had caught up to her.

"How much do you need to make?" Mama asked Lena.

"I don't understand what you mean?" said Lena.

"Well, how much do you need, to make up for Leonard's lost wages?"

Lena's teaspoon tinkled on the sides of her cup while she made some mental calculations. "I don't know, at least twenty dollars a month."

"What if I paid you to look after Carol?" suggested Mama. "I need to go back to work."

At this point I stopped playing. There were no keys black enough to tell how I felt.

"I'm not sure. I was an only child myself and, well, Leonard and I, you know, Leonard wants children, and I'm sure I do too, eventually, but it just hasn't worked out that way and..."

"Think about it Lena, you'd be perfect with Carol— both only children and all." Then her countenance softened, for just a moment, "It would mean the world to me Lena, I don't know what else I'd do."

"I'll talk to Leonard, but really, Virginia, I know next to nothing about raising kids."

Mama called to me that it was time to go.

"Thanks for the tea Christine. When I get a job I'll buy you a new tin. Glad Mitchell's feeling better." She took my hand and we started out the door. But before she closed it, she leaned her head back in and whispered so I wouldn't hear, but I did. "She's six years old Lena, half raised already."

8

That night I couldn't sleep. The death pains were back. I called them the death pains because it felt like something terrible was going to happen, like someone might die. My stomach felt tight, and my chest was heavy with a deep sense of impending doom. Things were changing faster than I could keep track of, and it didn't seem I had much to say about it. My mother had just given me away to be "watched," whatever that meant, and I was learning things about my father that I didn't want to know. Lena couldn't raise me, nothing against Lena, she just wasn't my mom. She said herself that she didn't know anything about raising children. I wasn't sure what she knew much about. A certain naiveté went along with her sweet disposition.

"Mama?" I called from my bed.

The creaking of the floorboards announced her approach, "Well?" Her silhouette filled the doorway.

"Can I have a drink?"

"Ye-es," she said in a sing song voice. She was tired, I could tell, and wasn't really in the mood for this ritual. I only liked kitchen water, not bathroom water, and I liked it poured under my tongue out of a glass measuring cup while I was still lying down. Mama went to the kitchen and came back with the water.

"Open your mouth and lift your tongue," she said as she had a hundred times before, surrendering a smile. She poured a thin stream of water very slowly under my tongue so I wouldn't choke. She paused to let me swallow and repeated the process until all the water was gone. "Better?"

I nodded. "I have the death pains."

"Oh Peach. I'm sorry." She knew what I meant. "Turn over and I'll rub your back."

"It feels like something bad's gonna happen, like someone is gonna die."

"Nothing bad is going to happen, Carol. Whatever happens is because it is supposed to. Besides, how can you ever tell if what happens is really bad?"

"Father leaving is bad."

"How do you know that?" she took a deep breath.

I didn't answer. I didn't know how I knew it, it just felt bad.

"And the death pains, maybe they aren't death pains at all. Maybe they are the pains of life," she said.

"It feels like my heart is stretching," I said.

"It is, honey."

"I don't want Lena to *watch* me. I want to be with you," I cried.

"I know, Carol. This is going to be hard for both of us, but we have to figure something out to make this work. If I work nights, which is probably where I'll have to start, you can't stay by yourself. You're too little. And I don't want to ship you off with Uncle Virg or Grandpa because they're too far away. I want to be able to see you every day."

Mama rubbed my ear lobe and kissed my cheek. I rolled over as she was leaving the room, "Does Lena know how to make French toast?

"Yes, I'm sure Lena knows how to make French toast."

"What if it's soggy in the middle?" I said.

"Then you'll have to show her how it's done, "she sniffed, "Night-night, I love you."

"I love you Mama."

9

Monday morning came too fast, and as much as I wished it wasn't, Christmas vacation was over. I knew Mama was going to the hospital to see about a job today, but we didn't talk about it. I met Paul, Beanie, and Lydia on the sidewalk. They lived around the corner from me and we walked to school together. Beanie, who was in my class and also six, asked me what I got for Christmas.

"A doll buggy," I mumbled from under my hood.

"A doggy?" said Beanie.

"NO. A DOLL BUGGY!" I yelled as loud as I could, leaning toward her. I didn't feel like talking about Christmas.

"YOU DON'T HAVE TO YELL. Gosh!" Beanie dropped back to walk with her older sister, Lydia.

I was glad to be walking alone and in silence. A fresh dusting of snow had fallen in the night. It muffled the morning sounds and made things feel simple and clean. I was feeling very fortunate that I didn't have any sisters or brothers continually asking me stupid questions. I was also feeling very sorry for myself. I wondered where my dad was and when I would see him again. I couldn't imagine what it was going to be like not living with my mother or my father. Now I knew what Father meant when he said he had a lot on his mind.

Beanie caught back up to me when we arrived at Willard Elementary School. Neither of us said anything, but Beanie took my hand and we walked up the steps, down the hall, and turned into our classroom. There were first and second-graders together in the class. Our teacher's name was Mrs. Carlson, same as my last name. When she called roll on the first day, Mrs. Carlson remarked on our common surname. I felt a kindred attachment to her and immediately felt she was going to be my advocate. She had wavy brown hair that was swept up into a loose wispy knot on the back of her head. Her lips were pink, usually smiling, and sometimes got caught on a snaggle tooth that stuck out from her top lip. Her voice was calm and gentle, but if she raised it very much it rattled in her throat and sounded old and jittery. When this happened I always felt like I was in trouble, even though it was never me that caused her to raise her voice or clap her hands for our attention. I so badly wanted everyone to sit and listen, not giggle, not write on their desk, and keep their chairs on all four feet. It made me nervous when Mrs. Carlson had to be strict.

As soon as the bell rang I was seated at my desk in my wooden chair with both feet on the floor. I was ready to "be a good listener," Mrs. Carlson's most sought-after classroom skill. Alan, a second grader who spent most of his recess time cleaning erasers, sat in the seat next to mine. I stole a glance his way—mostly to make sure he was ready to be a good listener too. He had his hand over his mouth, holding back what was most certainly an outburst. I immediately got nervous. He took his hand down long enough to elbow Sven in the ribs. Sven got mad and looked like he was about to retaliate, but Alan quickly pointed to Mrs. Carlson at the blackboard. She had written three of our five spelling words on the dusty board and was just finishing the word m-a-t when I looked up and saw that the skirt of her dress was somehow tucked into her garter belt. Her entire left leg, and the hook holding up her stocking, was exposed for all the world to see. I gasped. The rest of the class caught on, and the result was a mixture of muffled cajoling from the boys, and embarrassed giggles from the girls. Mrs. Carlson looked over her shoulder to survey the class with a puzzled glance, then resumed her lesson. I froze. What happened next was humbling. I wish it had been me, but it wasn't. As Mrs.

Carlson was writing our last spelling word, Beanie walked right up to the front of the class, stood between us and Mrs. Carlson, and with one graceful tug, undid the problem of the exposed thigh. Mrs. Carlson understood immediately what had happened, as she felt the skirt of her dress float down. She smoothed the fabric self-consciously.

"Why, thank you Beanie," said Mrs. Carlson. "How kind of you."

Beanie said nothing, just nodded, and returned to her seat. Sven slipped way down in his chair with his arms folded across his chest. He was looking out the window, biting his top lip, red in the face. His eyes were watering and his shoulders bobbed from breathy laughter.

"Sven, please come to the board and write our last spelling word for the week," said Mrs. Carlson, not in her shaky mad voice, but in a gentle voice, carrying the weight of unwavering authority.

Sven rose from his best intentions of hiding, stood at the chalk board and waited for her to instruct him on what to write.

"The word is rude, r-u-d-e, rude." She delivered the word like a spelling bee champion. When he had finished writing, she asked, "Can you use this word in a sentence?"

More snickers and giggles arose from the children. Sven stood expressionless. He put the chalk on the metal chalk holder at the bottom of the board, and ran his finger along in the dust. He looked at Mrs. Carlson. She looked at him. She looked at the board. Up to this point, Alan had been able to keep his laughter suppressed, but now there were tears running down his face and he snorted, ruining all efforts to emit an air of innocence. He was pointing at the word that Sven had written. Sven looked at the board. It read; r-u-b-e. He rubbed the belly of the "b" off with his finger, picked up the chalk again, and added it back on the left side of the line. His face was red with anger. He seemed to be surveying the class for someone to blame and his eyes landed on Alan. Alan bit the skin from the side of his thumb and spit it off the tip of his tongue, onto the floor.

"Spitting is rude," recited Sven in a robotic voice.

"Thank you, Sven. You may take your seat."

Sven came back and sat down. As soon as Mrs. Carlson turned her back, Sven elbowed Alan in the ribs, hard. Alan's tears of laughter turned to a grimmace of pain, but he didn't let on.

Mrs. Carlson went on with the spelling lesson, but Sven was still making faces and gestures behind Mrs. Carlson's back. How come I cared? Why was I getting stomachaches from worrying if Sydney did his math page right, or if everyone would remember their permission slip for the field trip to the Fire Station? I felt embarrassed for Sven, and sad for Mrs. Carlson. I wasn't doing anything wrong and I still had the feeling I might get in trouble. I wished I could be more like Mrs. Carlson. She was so calm and self-assured.

I had watched Mrs. Carlson, and had taken particular notice of how she never got mad or nervous about what other people did. She didn't fuss over missed homework. She didn't seem to mentally follow a misbehaving student to the principal's office. She just went on with undivided attention to the lesson at hand, and assumed the rest of us were just as interested in silent e's as she was. Alan straightened desks during recess that day and Beanie was rewarded by being chosen to take the classroom bunny home the following weekend. I promised myself to be the one to go to her aid the next time her underwear caused a ruckus.

On the way home from school, winter got a second wind. Snow fell like powdered sugar and put a fresh frosting on all of Jamestown. Beanie and I took our time walking home. A light gust sent the billions of flakes aswirl, sticking to everything they touched. When we arrived home at my house the whole front yard was covered with a thick, snowy blanket. Lydia ran up behind us and walked right onto the grass, ruining the spotless white carpet. She dropped her book bag on the porch steps, lay down on her back, and slid her arms and legs out and in on the snowy grass. When she got up, she made a circle in the snow above the indentation of her head, making a halo. Beanie and I proceeded to cover the rest of the grass with snow angels, but the shapes disappeared quickly from the constant sifting of snowflakes from the sky. Lena called for us to come to the front door. She gave us little glass bowls and told us to pack them with snow, then she drizzled them with raspberry syrup. Maybe she did know something about raising kids.

Mama was still at the hospital, so we all traipsed into Lena's house, warm with a fire in the wood stove. We huddled around the radio and listened to Little Orphan Annie. We all felt disappointed when Annie and Joe still hadn't figured out who the lady in the black hat was, but we agreed to meet at my house the next day after school to hear the outcome of the story. I wanted to relive that day over and over, but it never happened quite that way again—so spontaneously. My days were soon to become much more regimented and less carefree.

10

Mama was a Registered Nurse. In 1925 she graduated from nurses' training at the Womens' Christian Association Hospital in Jamestown, New York, just a half mile from where we lived. She hadn't worked since I was born, and they were thrilled to have her back. She was hired for the night shift 11pm to 7am. She told them she could start working February 1st, three weeks from the day she interviewed.

Mama decided that I would move up to Lena and Leonard Harrison's apartment, and she would take a room in the nurses' housing. Mama said she would sleep while I was at school, then after school I could walk over to the hospital and visit. She'd eat dinner in the nurses' dining room, so I would need to be back to Lena and Leonard's house every evening by five-thirty for supper. Friday and Saturday were Mama's nights off, so we'd have weekends together.

Saturdays were our "special day." That meant that we did something that we didn't usually do like take the trolley uptown and sit at the counter in the back of Woolworth's to share a patty melt, or check the sale racks at Bigelow's. On Sundays we always went to church in the morning, then to either Grandpa Hussey's, or Aunt Honey's house in Levant for lunch.

Mama paid Lena twenty dollars a month to take care of me. The year was 1938. The United States was in the depression then, and Mama was thankful to have a career. There was never any question that I would go to college; it was assumed I would because "even if you are married, you never know what might happen to your husband." Mama said that.

***

A few days before Mama was to move out, and I was to move up, we started the tedious job of weeding through our belongings. Mama would need nothing as far as kitchen accoutrements, and decided that a jumble sale was in order. Lena came down to help and see if she wanted any of our treasures. There were three piles. The keeping pile, the Lena pile and the Saturday jumble pile.

"Carol, here's a good job for you." Mama put the entire silverware drawer on the floor and got a small red case out from underneath her bed. She unsnapped the straps on the sides of the case and it folded open revealing rows and rows of elastic bands.

"Each piece of silverware fits in one of these loops." She pointed to each area, "knives, forks, salad forks, tea spoons, soup spoons, and then this part is for serving pieces. You'll have to try and see what fits where. I haven't stored the silverware since I opened it."

This was a puzzle, if I ever saw one, and it was the perfect job for me. I dove into my task with great gusto.

"What is this?" Asked Lena, holding up a thin, three-inch-long cylinder made of light wood.

"That's Grandpa Perring's toothpick holder. I remember it always sitting on the windowsill in their house. I need to hold on to that," Mama said as she showed Lena how the top slid off and the two old toothpicks that were inside.

"Let me see! Who's Grandpa Perring?" I chimed in.

She showed me, let me hold it, open it, and check the toothpicks for bite marks. Then she carefully closed it and put it in her apron pocket, rather than on her pile.

"Grandpa Perring was my mother's father. He lived in Levant, right near the Wesleyan Church. They used to call him The Buttermilk Man. He had a dairy and sold milk and buttermilk from his horse-drawn cart, out of big metal milk cans." Mama said. "I think I have an article about him in my cedar chest." She went to her bedroom again and returned with a cigar box, set it down on the kitchen table and carefully filed through the newspaper clippings inside. "Here it is. From the Jamestown Messenger, September 30, 1882." She sat down and read aloud:

SHOT BY HIS FATHER

A DEPLORABEL ACCIDENT
WHICH HAS BROUGHT GRIEF
AND SORROW TO THE HOME OF
ROBERT PERRING AT LEVANT.

Again we are called upon to chronicle one of those sorrowful occurrences caused by the accidental discharge of a gun. Everybody knows the Buttermilk Man Mr. Robert Perring, who lives at Levant, and little Joe his ten year old son is almost as familiar to our citizens as he. This morning about seven o'clock as they were about to start out for their daily trip through our streets, the boy discovered a squirrel in a butternut tree near the house and asked his father to get out his gun and shoot it. While Mr. Perring was loading the gun, Joe stood and watched the little animal frisking about among the branches and as the father stood in the doorway, he also frequently glanced in that direction.

While thus looking up he placed a cap upon the table and must, in some way, have pressed the trigger, for the gun, which happened to be pointed in the direction of the child, was discharged. As the loud report rang out upon the still morning air, little Joe threw up his hands and with one shrill cry of pain, fell forward upon his face. The horror stricken father rushed to the spot and took the wounded boy in his arms. But as he lifted him from the ground, the sufferer glanced up to his face, then the boy closed his eyes for ever with one convulsive shiver of pain the child's spirit forsook the poor shattered body and Joe was dead. When the aggrieved parent realized that the little form he held in his arms was indeed lifeless, his grief and remorse overcame him. With a piercing shriek he dropped to the earth and for a time it was thought that the shock had killed him. Dr. H.P. Hall was at once telephoned for and after a time succeeded in bringing the unfortunate man back to consciousness, but he seems completely heart broken and prays in piteous tones that he might also die.

"Little Joe would have been your Great Uncle," said Mama.

I wiped my tears on Mama's apron and snuggled under her arm. "That's the saddest thing I've ever heard," I said.

"Tragic." Lena shook her head and stacked a box of canning jars on her pile.

We stayed lost in our own thoughts for a while. Mama lingered over some other newspaper clippings in the cigar box then flipped the top down and took a deep breath. The box went back in the cedar chest with some other things that she would take to her new apartment. I was curious about the cedar chest because it held Mama's personal things. I wasn't allowed to look in there unless she was with me. I do know that, other than the cigar box, there were diaries, Mama's wedding dress, and a bundle of letters. Also, at the very bottom of the chest was a small white box. Grandmother Carlson had given it to Mama and Father when they got married. Mama said that Grandmother Carlson wanted to make sure that nobody died without being baptized. So, the box had holy water, candles, and a little booklet that could lead someone in a prayer. I'm pretty sure it was for me if I ever got sick and needed a quick sprinkling to get me to heaven if it looked like I was going to die. Mama said that it wasn't the baptizing that got you to heaven; it was Jesus in your heart. She said that when I was ready, I could be baptized in the baptistery at church, or with the sprinkles from Grandma Carlson's bottle, or just as well in a puddle on the side of the road. She said it wasn't really the water that mattered, but the blood of Christ, so not to worry, we'd talk about it when I was older. So, I filed it away as something to ask her when I was seven.

"What about Little Joe, is he in heaven?" I asked.

"Yes, Peach. Little Joe is most certainly in heaven." Mama gave me a kiss on the forehead.

We kept up our sorting and packing and deliberating about what should go and what should stay. Lena was thrilled with the matching mixer and mixing bowls that Mama gave her. Father had given that to Mama last Christmas and it made me sad to see them go. Maybe I wanted it when I grew up. Mama didn't even ask me.

A knock on the door startled us all, but it was only Leonard asking if anyone was hungry.

"That means *he's* hungry," Lena said, rolling her eyes.

Just then Uncle Virg pulled up in his Model A. He was there to get the few things that Mama wanted to store at his house. These included things that were to be saved for me when I got older, and some special memorabilia that Mama couldn't get rid of, but didn't have room for in her room at the hospital. He walked in carrying a large pot, followed by Aunt Marion who had a basket lined with kitchen towels, containing several parcels wrapped in waxed paper.

"Who's hungry?" She announced, and crossed the kitchen to lay her offering on the table.

"Leonard is!" I said.

Mama and Lena smiled at each other. Leonard did his best at playing dumb.

"I was just asking. I didn't know that Carol was going to be my new good-luck charm and that my every wish would instantly come true," he chided as he walked over to the basket and took a deep breath, "But I do love corn bread!"

"Leonard, you are too presumptuous!" Lena scolded.

"There's plenty," said Aunt Marion "corn bread and chili, macaroni salad, and my own crazy chocolate cake."

"I cannot refuse such a lovely offer," announced Leonard, "It would be against all I stand for to decline when I have heard the words, "crazy chocolate cake."

Lena rolled her eyes again, "You are the most charming beggar I ever married!"

"Well that's perfect dear, because you are even prettier than my first wife. Oh, you *are* my first wife; you're getting prettier every year." He laughed at his own joke and hugged the love of his life.

Aunt Marion spread the food out on the table and put a low fire under the pot of chili. She attempted to open the missing silverware drawer, and then found it on the floor. I had not yet put the soupspoons in the storage case, so she snatched out six and laid them on the table, along with some cloth napkins she'd brought from home

"Help yourself!" she said, marveling at her generous creations.

"Thank You, Marion," Mama said, "How kind of you. I wasn't expecting this. I'm starving!"

"Well, we all have to eat, and I didn't expect you'd have time to prepare a decent meal with all of your comings and goings." She scooped a huge serving of macaroni salad into a bowl, and handed it to Uncle Virg. "There should be leftovers," she said with a glance at Leonard, who was lavishly enjoying his first spoonful of chili, "Unless, of course, we intend on feeding the rest of the neighborhood."

I looked at Mama to see what she would do with this comment. She winked at Leonard and said, "Marion, you are just about the most thoughtful person I know. Peach, be a dear and go up and ask Mrs. Nigren and the boys to join us. I'll bet they have never had *anything* as tasty as Aunt Marion's chili and cornbread."

Aunt Marion raised an eyebrow as she continued to cut the cornbread. I could tell she didn't approve of Mama's idea, because her arm movements got jerkier while the squares of bread got smaller. I grabbed a piece off the big end as I headed out the door to the Nigrens'.

After we all ate, including the Nigrens, and the leftovers were put away—yes leftovers—there were so many hands packing and cleaning and loading and folding, that we quickly finished all we needed to do for the jumble and for our exodus. Mama was going to sell the rest of Father's clothes, but the twins tried on a few things and found that either Michael or Mitchell could wear just about everything, so Mama said they could have them. Mitchell claimed the few shirts that were left. The pair of never-worn corduroy trousers, too long for Mitchell, was a perfect fit for Michael. There was one brown tweed blazer that could work for either brother, and they were fighting over it when Mrs. Nigren burst into the bedroom.

"Stop it this minute or I'll cut that thing right down the middle and you can each have half of it!" Her hands were flitting around and slapping anything they contacted, and the two grown boys cowered from their mother.

Mama was laughing so hard that she had to leave and take a walk up to the porch. I stayed and watched, but the scissors weren't necessary because the left sleeve ended up in Michael's hand, while the rest of the blazer hung from Mitchell's slight frame. They put both parts in the bag with the rest of the clothes and headed upstairs, angry at each other, but delighted with the prospect of having something new.

11

I moved in with Lena and Leonard on February 1st. They went to great lengths, trying to make me feel welcome. Leonard painted the walls of my new bedroom pale yellow, and Lena made blue gingham curtains that tied back to let the sun in. Out of the same fabric, she made throw pillows to go on the bed. Even the desk chair had a matching cover on the seat. Leonard painted the desk white and put cut glass drawer-pulls on the front. He hung a mirror above the desk and said it would suit me for schoolwork, a place to color, or a vanity. He said I needed a safe spot to keep my personal things and a place to brush my hair. I didn't have any "personal things" really, but I did keep my hair brush in the top left hand drawer of the desk. I stashed my pink blanket under the pillow when I made the bed because it didn't match the rest of the room. They tried so hard to help me make this transition. I felt embarrassed about the tear stains on my pillow but Lena never mentioned them.

It was all right living with Lena and Leonard but never really felt like home. I couldn't wait for my weekends with Mama, but I did like having my own room at Lena and Leonard's. Lena was kind and motherish. She helped me with my homework, and quizzed me on my spelling words while she made dinner.

Leonard was always jolly, always sober, always hungry, and could fix anything. He fixed the toaster when it broke, and good thing, because who could afford a new toaster? He fixed the broken kickstand on my scooter and Jessie's broken arm. Best of all, he could fix my bad mood or my hurt feelings. If he sensed I was gloomy or sad about something, he would get me going on a project or just make me laugh so hard I didn't have the energy to cry. Leonard liked to play games. Flinch, checkers or Mille Bornes were our favorites.

On the weekends, when Leonard wasn't working at the bakery, he liked to putter around in his workshop. I liked to watch him or help when he needed an extra hand to hold something together, or fetch a certain tool. Eventually, he hired me to paint the bird houses that he made and sold at the hardware store. He trusted me with even the small detail lines around the windows. He praised my work and paid me five cents for every birdhouse. I saved every nickel for Mama's birthday coming up on June 12th. I knew exactly what I was going to get her.

Mama and I liked to bomb around on Saturdays. Bombing around was sort of like window shopping, but it might include getting an ice cream cone, or returning library books, or checking the sale racks and testing the smelly-goods at Bigelows' department store. Mama tried one perfume each time we went to the smelly-good counter. Sometimes she liked what she tried, but more often she would make an unusually un-perfumy comparison. One fragrance smelled like wilted lettuce, another reminded her of her grandmother's top dresser drawer. Funny how smells dredge up memories. On this particular Saturday, Mama found what she would claim as her signature fragrance. It was a new perfume by Elizabeth Arden called Blue Grass. She smelled like a powder-puff garden all day long and kept lifting her wrist to her nose to smell the delightful aroma. Every so often she would jet her arm out to me and I knew to smell her wrist.

"No two people smell exactly the same when they wear the same perfume," she explained. "Your body chemistry mixes with the essential oils and it becomes your own aroma."

I had never seen her so goo-goo over anything before, so I set my heart on buying it for her as soon as I had two dollars and sixty cents. The week before her birthday, I was still twenty-five cents short, so I asked Leonard if I could paint five birdhouses all in one day. He didn't have any made, so he wrote up an I.O.U. in his elaborate curly penmanship. It read: I.O.U. Five birdhouse paintings. He had me sign it: Carol Carlson, professional birdhouse painter. He gave me thirty cents and told me I had gotten a raise. Then we rode bikes uptown. I felt very capable of going by myself, but Leonard said he needed the exercise, so he rode along. He rode a big, old, rusty, Elgin Oriole that he had nicknamed "The Limousine." I rode Lena's Road Master with the seat lowered. We took Chandler Street across the river, then bumped over the railroad tracks and followed 3rd street till we got to Bigelow's. Leonard locked our bikes to a tree trunk out front with a chain and padlock.

When we got to the perfume counter, my favorite clerk was there. She often wore the black dress that she was wearing that day. It was cinched around her waist with a white belt. Mama always said she looked like a sausage with her belt pulled so tight around her middle, but I thought she was the most glamorous woman I had ever seen in real life. She looked, quite nearly, like a movie star. Her eyebrows were dark and arched, penciled in where they might have been light. Her eyelashes were long, black, and perfectly spaced. She wore red lipstick and her cheeks were just slightly pink. Her blonde hair was pulled back in a high ponytail with a thick, black velvet, ribbon wrapped around the rubber band. However, the most intoxicating part of her whole self was her voice. It sounded like a grown-up little girl, who of course she was, but her voice had a high-pitched quality that you don't usually hear from adults, and her accent was from Tennessee, I think. She used phrases like "Oh, you sweet thing you," or "isn't that just the dreamiest little sweater." Sometimes she finished a sentence with a little catch in her throat like a hiccup, or half a giggle. I found myself staring at her, studying her, as if she were a piece of art. She was helping another woman buy a lipstick. When they were finished she came over to us.

"How may I help you?" she asked, looking at Leonard.

"Oh, I am only the chauffeur," Leonard said in his best French accent. "Mademoiselle is in need of your expertise." He sounded very convincing, but his scuffed shoes and dirty fingernails surely gave him away.

She directed her attention to me, "Oui, oui, Mademoiselle." Her face was serious and not condescending, "What can I show you?"

"I would like to see the Blue Grass line," I said in my mother's words.

"Oh, darlin'," she went back to her own signature voice, "you are not gonna believe your precious little nose when you smell this fragrance. It's scrumptious!" She snatched up the tester and reached for my arm.

"I already know what it smells like. I want the one that costs two dollars and sixty cents please," I said, just as I had practiced.

"Why of course, the half-ounce with the glass applicator—perfect choice. Is this for you, or is it a gift?" she continued as if I were twenty-seven, instead of six and a half.

"It's for my mother, for her birthday," I answered.

"Would you like that gift-wrapped?"

I looked up at Leonard for advice. My real concern was cost, and I was hoping he could advise me.

"What is the fee for professional wrapping?" my chauffeur asked.

"Wrapping is complimentary," she said, pleased with the generosity she was able to offer.

Leonard looked at me and nodded his head in a subservient manner, volleying the choice back to me.

"Yes please," I said.

While she wrapped the small blue and white box, I watched her every move. She didn't use tape but rather folded the pink paper around in a skillful way, creasing and tucking it into the folds so it stayed in place. Then she secured the parcel with a silky white ribbon. Her little red fingernails formed a perfect bow, and the result was classic simplicity, just like my mother.

My suede marble pouch hung inside my blouse and I suddenly became aware that I was going to have to fish it out very soon. I felt self-conscious and juvenile at not having a pocketbook, so I sauntered over to a rotating earring display where I would be out of direct sight of the sales lady, and quickly pulled the pouch out through the front of my blouse. It was heavily weighted with coins. I went back to the counter and carefully spread my savings on the glass case. I made four piles of ten nickels each, then a pile of six dimes, and presented them to the saleslady in that fashion. She counted each pile, and deposited the coins in her cash drawer.

"Two dollars and sixty cents exactly. My, my, your mother is a fortunate woman! And thank you so much. I needed nickels," she said as she handed me the bag containing the most important purchase I had ever made. "Ya'll have a nice day now."

"Thank you," Leonard and I chimed together.

I smiled the whole way home. My heart felt like it was going to burst right out of my chest with pride. I wasn't sure if I could wait three more days to give my mother her birthday present. I wanted to ride my bike straight over there and give it to her right then, but I promised myself I'd wait until Friday when Mama would come over to Lena and Leonard's for dinner and stay for a sleepover. I gave her my bed and I made an odd bed with the couch cushions on the floor, right next to her. The plan for Saturday was the most exciting of all. Uncle Virg and Aunt Marion would pick us up and the four of us would go to Lake Chautauqua for a birthday picnic.

***

I didn't say one thing about the perfume when I visited Mama after school each day, and that was not easy. I was good at keeping other peoples' secrets, but when it came to something I was excited about but had to wait for, I could hardly keep it under control.

When Friday finally arrived, I set the dinner table and put the present on her plate. We were having pork chops and applesauce with green beans and baked potatoes. The strawberries were ripe early that summer, so Lena made fresh strawberry pie for dessert.

At 4:45, Lena said I could walk down to King Street and meet Mama. She was pulling a little cart with all she would need for our sleep-over, and the picnic with Aunt Marion and Uncle Virg. She looked so fresh and pretty in her pink gingham sundress. It was my favorite of all her dresses. It had a twelve-inch gathered ruffle at the knee. Mama called these the shiffers, because she liked the way they shiffered around when she walked. Her lips were frosted with peachy-orange lipstick, and her wavy brown hair was peeking out from under a new creamy colored hat.

"You look smashing!" I said, and then giggled.

"Thank you Peach." She leaned down to give me a kiss and a hug.

We started our short walk back to the house, taking turns pulling the cart up the hill.

"You smell good," I said.

She smelled familiar.

"Thanks! Can you believe it? The girls on night shift all went in together and surprised me with that new perfume from Elizabeth Arden, the one I've been so crazy about."

My heart sank. A warm, gentle breeze encircled us and I was caught so off guard that I thought it might bowl me over.

"Blue Grass?" I said coyly.

"Yes, isn't it heavenly?" She waved her wrist under my nose.

I went through the motions of smelling her arm, but couldn't smell a thing. I was having a hard time breathing. I felt dizzy and the back of my hands were tingling. My next breath got caught in my throat. I struggled to hide my shock and disappointment, and fell two paces behind Mama as we walked up the brick pathway to the front porch. Mama reached the top step before I did. Leonard was waiting at the door.

"Hey girls! Happy Birthday Virginia." He opened the screen door and stood back, making room for us to pass. I looked up at him as I entered. His jovial smile bent downward when he read the distress on my face.

Leonard put his arm around Mama and led her through the dining room, into the kitchen. I went directly to the bathroom, locked the door and sat down on the floor. A beehive of emotions whirled around from my heart to my head. First I was mad at those stupid nurses for stealing my idea. Then I was impressed at their kindness. Next, I felt sorry for myself because now my gift was going to take a back seat. I considered not giving it to her, but then I'd have nothing at all to give. Besides, I wanted her to know the story of all my hard work and planning. I didn't know what to do, so I resolved myself to a good cry. Mama came to the bathroom door and knocked, asking if I was all right and letting me know that dinner was almost ready.

"Just a minute," I answered.

"All right, but hurry up. I'm starved and my mouth is ready for those pork chops!"

I was going to ruin Mama's birthday dinner with my hurt feelings if I didn't get my face washed and looking normal again. So I gave myself a good splashing, dried my face with the company towel and took a deep breath.

When I came out of my crying place, I was still feeling sorry for myself, and a good bit embarrassed. They were all having drinks in fancy glasses. A fourth fancy glass sat alone on the serving tray and I picked it up, knowing it was for me. I slunched down on the hearth of the fireplace and poked at the ice cubes in my punch. They all talked around me, not knowing what had happened in the last few minutes that would have sent me into such a funk.

Lena had been watching me, and excused herself from the circle. "Dinner should be ready in just a few minutes. Leonard will you help me open the pickle jar?" she said, and gave a gentle head tilt toward Leonard. They disappeared into the kitchen and we sat in silence until Mama spoke.

"What's wrong Peach?"

"Nothing," I lied.

"Why were you crying?"

"I can't say. It's a surprise, but I guess it's not really. Not anymore. Everything's ruined."

"Carol, what *are* you talking about?" she said. She was half smiling and half frowning. "Who ruined your surprise?"

"Not you."

"Well then, who?"

"I guess it's not really their fault, I'm just sad about it," I mumbled, still looking into my punch.

"About what?"

I put my glass down and she motioned for me to come to her. She sat back and I buried my face in her "pillows". My sobs were true and deep and mixed pathetically with my story as I blurted it out. I told Mama about the events of the past week; the birdhouses, the nickels, the trip to Bigelow's, my well-kept secret, and my nervous anticipation.

She listened quietly. Seriously. Her forehead and the purse of her lips revealed that she was just as upset as I was.

"I'm Sorry Mama."

"Sorry, nothing. You have good reason to be sad. You're right, it's no one's fault really, but what a disappointment." She rubbed my back and made the sad humming sound again. The one she makes when she is sad for someone else. "I know you think I won't appreciate your present as much because it isn't the only one, but that's just not true, Peach. I will cherish it all the more because I know how much hard work went into it. But I do know how you feel. It's hard to put so much effort toward one thing, and then have someone pull the rug out from under you. Believe me, I know how it feels. Don't let those nurses steal your joy, though. I'll love my perfume from you all the more, because it is from *you*." She rocked me on her lap while I tried to feel better. "You're the reason I get up each day. It's not because I have to go to work. It's because I know every day at three-fifteen you'll come running up the stairs to my apartment, and *that* is my best thing."

"I did want mine to be the only one," I said.

"I know, but it's always good to have a backup," she said.

"Yeah, but I wanted mine to be special."

"It is."

"Happy Birthday, Mama."

"Thank you, Peach. I love you so much."

Lena peeked around the kitchen wall, then retreated. Mama gave me one more, soft squeeze. I put on whatever suit of armor it took for me to make it through present-opening and pork chop-eating. The evening seemed to go just fine even though I wasn't the hero I wanted to be. I wanted Mama to be happy. What a huge relief it was to learn that Mama *was* happy, that I, not my gift, brought her joy.

12

The next morning, Mama opened my bottle of perfume and doused herself, yet again, with the glorious smell. She said my bottle smelled even better than the other one. I knew she was kidding, but I said, "that's because it has love in it."

Aunt Marion and Uncle Virg arrived to pick us up at ten o'clock. We were ready to go, beach bags packed and high spirits for the day ahead. But Uncle Virg wasn't in such a hurry. He took one look at the leftover strawberry pie and couldn't take his eyes off of it until Lena offered him a piece. He immediately sat himself down at the kitchen table and didn't pass up a cup of coffee either. The ladies took their coffee out to the porch. I was getting discouraged that this was going to turn into a chat-athon and slid down on my chair in a slump. Uncle Virg took his last bite of pie and heaved a satisfied sigh.

"Just what I needed," he said, rubbing his belly. Then he got up in a curious manner, like he was sneaking around, and went to check on the whereabouts of his sister, then came back with a knowing look on his face.

"Can you keep a secret, Peach?"

I nodded, curiously excited. "Cross my heart and hope to die!"

"I know you two think we're just going to the lake for the day, but I've made arrangements for us all to stay for the weekend and go to a play at the Theatre. There's another surprise too, so bring two dresses and your church shoes. Aunt Marion has arranged for clothes for your mother, but I need you to bring a grip with bedclothes, toothbrushes and the like. You'll need something to wear to the play and a change of clothes for the next day. Run up and do that; I'll occupy your mom. Here, use this," he handed me a brown paper grocery sack.

"Inconspicuous," he said.

"What play are we seeing?" I asked.

"*Funny Face*. It's a musical and your mother is dying to see it. She's crazy about the music. I think you may have heard one of the songs on the radio." He stood back and held his hand to his chest in a melodramatic way, tipped his head up in a crooning manner, and sang quietly so mama couldn't hear, "I love your funny face, your sunny funny face."

"Yeah, I know it! Mama sings it all the time! Are we really staying in a hotel?"

"Bet yer life! But ya can't tell," he whispered.

"I've never stayed in a hotel before," I said, wide eyed with anticipation.

"Neither has your mother."

13

Our plan worked famously, and we got out of the house with Mama being none the wiser. I was having a terrible time holding in my excitement, but felt energized by this new secret.

Mama and I were in the back seat. She must have felt me staring at her.

"What are you all smiles about?" she teased.

"Nothin'. Just excited to go swimming. Do you think we could take a ride on a steam boat?" I was trying to get my mind off the play.

"Seems like a good idea. Might as well live it up for our birthdays, huh Virginia?" Uncle Virg turned and smiled at Mama, then winked at me in the rear view mirror. "I think we can buy tickets for that at the Athenaeum Hotel, we'll have to stop there first and see if they have any seats left. It's a pretty hot day, probably be swamped with people."

Aunt Marion protested, "Boat ride? We won't have time for a boat ride. What about—"

Uncle Virg interrupted with an over-exaggerated throat clearing and looked at her over his glasses.

"Well, a boat ride might be just the thing," she succumbed.

We got to Lake Chautauqua in under an hour and drove down to the Athenaeum Hotel.

"They call this the Grand Dame of Chautauqua," Mama said. "Can you believe how beautiful it is? I would give my left leg to stay here."

I was just about ready to pee my pants. I could hardly stand it. Not much excited my mother enough for her to start giving away limbs.

"Virgil, can I go in with you? I want to take a walk around the porch while you check on the boat ride," Mama said.

"Why don't we all go in? We can have some iced tea on the porch," he said.

Mama didn't wait for Uncle Virg. She opened her own door and slid off the seat. I followed right behind her.

"I love this place. Have you ever seen anything so grand?" Mama stopped and was standing in the shade of a huge Sugar Maple tree. Uncle Virg walked up beside her. "Mother and Father had their honeymoon here," she said.

"Yep, quite a fancy-shmancy place for a farmer and his wife to stay," he said, smiling, "let's go see a man about a boat."

The Athenaeum hotel was perched like a palace sitting up on a hill, looking down on its village and moat. The massive structure was built in the Saratoga style with carved gingerbread and beaded posts all around. Up on the very top of the roof there was a domed turret, resembling a royal crown. The porch stretched along the wide expanse of the hotel and offered comfy couches and rocking chairs, just waiting for someone to come and laze the day away. We walked up the huge expanse of lawn past pic-nickers and croquet games. Ladies in fancy hats and pretty dresses sat in wicker chairs, sipping tea from fine china cups. Peach colored roses and lavender sprigs decorated the tables and scented the air. Light green fringe on the bottom of the tablecloths gave the impression that the tea tables had sprung up like mushrooms, right where they stood.

The lake was shimmering in the noon light and sailboats bobbed and glided along the swells of rolling blue and the occasional white tipped curl. Kids played in a roped-off area for swimming where two lifeguards sat in chairs, high up off the sand on stilted legs. Couples and families strolled along the boardwalk, and a line was assembling on the dock for the next cruise on the Steam Boat. We stood soaking in the lavish views and the inviting smells for a few minutes, then followed Uncle Virg into the Lobby.

Double doors opened up into a hallway that was as wide as a street. A colorful carpet led the way to the front desk. To each side of the carpet, the dark mahogany floors were calling me to remove my shoes and have a slide around on the shiny finish in my socks, but I suspected that would never happen. I had never been in a place as fancy as this and was determined to act as if I had. Halfway down the corridor I looked up. Even the ceiling was pretty. The whole thing was covered with white squares that had beautiful curly-Q engravings and chandeliers that hung from about a mile high. Mama leaned down and took my hand to encourage me to move along. We all bellied up to the smooth-as-glass wooden reception desk. I put my hands up on the round edge of the counter and when I took them off, the heat of my fingers left a silhouette of steam.

"May I help you, sir?" said a man in a navy blue double-breasted suit.

"Yes, please, I would like to inquire about booking a dinner cruise on the Steam Boat," said Uncle Virg.

"Dinner cruise?" Mama silently mouthed to Aunt Marion.

"Are you guests at the Hotel?" asked the man.

"Yes, we are," Uncle Virg said without skipping a beat.

"And your last name, sir?"

"Hussey. Virgil Hussey, party of four," he answered.

Mama elbowed him in the ribs and giggled under her breath, "Virgil. Stop it."

The man was fingering through a small wooden box of cards. Mama, sure he would not find Virgil's name and feeling a bit embarrassed by the charade, turned her back to the man and was fidgeting around in her purse for something.

"Yes, Mr. Hussey. We have you in the Edison suite, for two nights. This is one of our most desired apartments, as it is on the Northeast corner and has views of both the gardens and the lake," he congratulated us as he wrote some notes on the card. "And I see you are celebrating *two* birthdays. Has Virginia arrived?"

Slowly, Mama turned around, holding tight to the ledge of the desk for stability. Her eyes were as round as a come-upon doe.

"You must be Virginia," said the man, his somber, professional face taking on the curl of a smile. "Welcome to the Athenaeum. If there is anything we can do to make your stay with us more enjoyable, please ask." He handed her his personal card and their fingers touched in the exchange.

Mama held the card by the top and bottom edge with her thumb and first finger. She studied it, then looked at the man again.

"Thank you Mr. Danielson, I certainly will," she said, her nose tipped down and her eyes lifted.

Then she turned her attention to Uncle Virg and Aunt Marion. She dropped her purse that had been dangling from her left hand, and wrapped her arms around her brother and sister-in-law, half to keep standing, half to keep from floating away with bubbling gratitude. Uncle Virg had his eyes closed and brought his fist up to catch a tear or two. Aunt Marion was wide-eyed, looking all around to see who might be watching and finally pulled away leaving just Mama and Uncle Virg to finish the embrace. Mama stepped away from her brother and kissed him on the cheek, then she looked at Aunt Marion. "You married the sweetest man on the planet," she said.

Aunt Marion smiled in agreement as the bellhop approached us. "Will you need assistance with your luggage?" he offered.

"Yes, I'll bring the car around. Can you see the ladies to the porch for tea? I'll be back in five minutes," said Uncle Virg.

I was feeling very royal and fancy. We were shown to ladder-back rocking chairs on the mile long porch and served tea with lemon, sugar, mint and ice.

"Marion, I can't believe it! How did you ever come up with this?" gushed mama.

"Well, we've always wanted to stay here. I've heard rave reviews about the dining room, and knowing that it was your parents' honeymoon destination made it the perfect destination for your birthdays. For once we had the time *and* the money, so we just planned it and made it a surprise," she said.

"Where on earth does a person find money in this economy?" Mama said.

"You know the University textbooks Virgil and I have been working on for the past two years?" said Aunt Marion.

"The teaching textbooks?" Mama said.

"Yes. Well the publishers bought the books and have given us a handsome deal with money right up front that is supposed to encourage us to keep writing, but all it really did was encourage us to have a grand birthday party for you and Virgil with Carol and I gleaning all the benefits," she said, and winked at me.

"Marion! You're a published Author! Well la-di-da."

"Oops! I think Virgil wanted to announce it at dinner tonight," Marion said as she squeezed a lemon into her tea.

"I'll act surprised, but really I'm not," said Mama, "they are wonderful books. I'm thrilled for you!"

"The idea was all Virgil's, I can only take credit for the editing."

Aunt Marion was being awfully humble and gracious. Maybe I had her all wrong.

"And Carol, how long have *you* known about this?" Mama touched the tip of my nose when she said "*you*".

"I only found out this morning. We're staying over-night!" I said.

"Oh my," Mama sat up straight and looked down at herself, "All I have are the clothes on my back," she said.

"Don't worry, I think we've thought of everything," Aunt Marion assured her, "and if we don't have it, we'll buy it. Just relax and have a good time, Virginia. You deserve it. Happy birthday."

"I am sure that I've died and gone to heaven. I haven't even seen the room yet and I already know I'll want to live there for the rest of my life!" Mama marveled. She started to light a cigarette, but a voice from behind her interrupted.

"Allow me." Mr. Danielson, from the front desk, flipped open a silver lighter and offered her a light.

She put the cigarette between her lips, still holding it between her fingers, and waited for him to bring the flame to her.

"Thank you, Mr. Danielson," Mama said, then blew the smoke away from us.

"My pleasure." He flipped the lighter closed with his thumb.

I knew this sound. It was the sound of my father finishing something: a dinner, a project, a sentence. It was a comforting sound when associated with my father, I almost expected to see him now. I was lonely for him, and leery about this man. I didn't like the way he looked at my mother.

Uncle Virg walked up behind Mr. Danielson. "Have you ladies had sufficient refreshment? Would you like to take a turn around the hotel and visit your lodgings?" He said in a convincing British accent.

"Why of course, Mr. Darcy," Mama said, copying his tone.

Aunt Marion was smiling and rolling her eyes.

We rose and Mr. Danielson led the way. Our luggage went ahead in the elevator with a man in a flat cap, but we took one of the three sets of stairs. Uncle Virg and Aunt

Marion held hands, so did Mama and I. We went up two flights, then all the way down a long hallway with flowery carpet. Mr. Danielson opened our door with a skeleton key, and with a wave of his hand, bid us to enter. Aunt Marion entered first, then Mama, then me. Uncle Virg put a coin in Mr. Danielson's hand.

"At your service," said Mr. Danielson. He gave the key to Uncle Virg, offered a slight bow, and left.

We found ourselves in a sitting room that I can only describe as luxurious. The sofa and chairs were upholstered in silky, light yellow stripes. I attempted to sit daintily on the overstuffed down pillows of the sofa, but sank in so deep that I questioned my ability, or desire, to get up. Mama opened the drawers of a writing desk. She found paper and envelopes with "The Athenaeum" embossed at the top. A handsome pen set, also labeled with the hotel name, lay in indentations at the front of the drawer. Mama touched them with her fingertips but didn't pick them up.

Aunt Marion was looking out the window to the lake, but got sidetracked by tiny blue butterflies embroidered into the draperies. Uncle Virg stood in the middle of the room, smiling.

I interrupted the silent awe. "Where do we sleep?"

Uncle Virg pulled me out of my nest in the couch, and waltzed me over to a big white door. He turned the bronze knob, gave it a push, and backed away. It looked like a picture I might have seen in a magazine, or a place I conjured up from the pages of a fairy tale.

"Virginia, this is your and Carol's" room, he announced.

Mama hurried across the room and peeked in over me. "Will wonders never cease."

She walked around the perimeter of the room, floating her fingers over dustless wood, polished porcelain, and fine linens, before she rested on one of two full-sized beds. I took perch on the other. We both bobbed up and down, finding the perfect blend of springy and firm. Matching sinks in dark wood vanities guarded the closet door on each side. Another door led to the bathroom that revealed a huge bathtub and a toilet. A third door, at the far end of the bathroom, opened on its own and scared me and Mama both half to death, before we realized it was Uncle Virg.

"Hello ladies," he said and invited us in.

Aunt Marion was lying on the bed, feet still hanging off the side, with her arms spread wide and a smile on her face. The bed was enormous and had curtains all around it that were yet pulled back, but soon to be unfurled.

"I never ever..." said Mama," this is a palace!"

"Palace shmalace. I'm hot, let's go swimming," said Uncle Virg.

***

The afternoon was perfect. I swam in the roped off area, and met a girl named Eleanor. She was seven and was from Long Island. Her dad threw floating rings into the lake for us to retrieve and gave chocolate candies to the girl with the most rings. I've never been a great swimmer, so I lost every race, but Eleanor shared her chocolates with me anyway. She had an older sister who didn't swim, but sat in a wheelchair under a big umbrella with a light coverlet over her knees. She reminded me of the picture of Carol Bird on the cover of the *Birds' Christmas Carol*. We collected pretty rocks for her and poured buckets of lake water on her feet and hands. She smiled, but didn't speak. My heart felt sad for her, but she didn't seem sad. She always smiled and had the prettiest dark brown eyes.

Aunt Marion and Uncle Virg sat under an umbrella too, only coming out for frequent, short dips in the water. Mama was a good swimmer. She took a swim out past the ropes before organizing a game of Marco Polo with me, Eleanor, and another family of kids that had five boys and one girl, all between the ages of four and twelve.

After playing for over an hour we were all starving. Eleanor, her father, and sister had a catered lunch from the hotel. We were unpacking our pic-nic and noticed that the kids from the other family were not eating, but watching us. Their mother was not sitting under an umbrella, but on a blanket. She was knitting with yarn that she was unraveling from a large, tattered afghan. Aunt Marion had been watching her and mentioned that at one point she came to a hole in the afghan and had to tie the two ends of the yarn together. Aunt Marion marveled at her industry and resourcefulness. The kids kept peeking over at us, looking away when I looked at them.

"Carol," said Aunt Marion, "would you like to offer your friends a snack?" she handed me a big bundle of celery and a jar of peanut butter. I stuck the butter knife under my arm and ventured over.

"Have you ever had celery with peanut butter?" I was pretty sure Aunt Marion had invented the combination.

They mostly just looked at me until the oldest boy said, "Yep. It's my favorite!"

I didn't stop slathering peanut butter on celery until it was all gone. Cornelius, the four year old, licked the peanut butter clean off of his stalk, then took the celery to his mother who nibbled on it between rows of knitting. Everyone, including me, needed a dip in the lake to wash the remains off our faces and fingers. That started another game of Marco Polo which lasted until Mama had to bribe me out of the water with the promise that we could swim again tomorrow and a threat that I was going to turn into a prune. If I wanted a ride on the Steam Boat, it was now or never. Aunt Marion had gone on ahead of the rest of us. Said she needed time to put her face on.

"Are they going to let me on that fancy boat in my pedal-pushers?" she fretted.

"Virginia," said Uncle Virg, "would God send the birds out to fly without feathers?"

"No, Virgil," answered Mama in a sing-song voice.

"Would you send Carol to school barefoot?"

"No, Virgil," she sang again, turning her head and smiling at me.

"Would your sister-in-law allow you to accompany her on a dinner cruise without the appropriate attire?" He teased, all the while using a stern and authoritative voice.

"No Sir," said mama,

"Then stop your belly-achin' and trust me!" He put his arm around her and gave her a "sure-do-love-you" squeeze.

Upon reaching our rooms again, Uncle Virg stopped at the door and knocked three times. Aunt Marion greeted us, took the wet towels from Mama, and instructed me to put my bucket and shovel on the balcony. Mama stopped dead in her tracks when she saw the array of gifts on the coffee table. There were three shirt-size boxes, two small wrapped items, and one very small box, all piled on the table.

"Happy Birthday!" said Aunt Marion, more excited than I have ever seen her. "Go get cleaned up so you can open your presents!"

Mama took the longest bath in history. I was all ready and waiting when she came out, wearing a fluffy white robe embroidered with a silver "A."

I was feeling spoiled. I could only imagine how overwhelmed Mama felt. Aunt Marion and Uncle Virg sat in the "King and Queen" chairs and I sank down by Mama on the sofa.

All the gifts were wrapped in blue paper with yellow ribbon. Uncle Virg handed her the first box. She carefully unwrapped it, not tearing any paper and saving the bow. Inside, under a layer of white tissue paper, was a pretty yellow dress. It absolutely matched the room. Not bright, but not dull. Mama lifted it out of the box and held it up to her front. It had short sleeves and a double row of pearl buttons up the front. The skirt had half-inch pleats all the way around and fell just below her knees. At the waist was a thin belt with a small mother of pearl belt buckle.

"Size ten. It's perfect, said Mama. Exactly what I would have chosen!" She sashayed around the room for a minute, stopped to kiss Aunt Marion on the cheek, then laid the dress over the back of the desk chair. Aunt Marion went and got a hanger and hung it up.

Mama took hold of the next box and Aunt Marion handed the other biggish box to me.

"These are for you both to open at the same time," she instructed.

"Ready? Go!" said Mama, and we both ripped into the boxes, not caring a bit about saving the wrapping this time.

In unison, we each pulled out a crocheted shawl. Mama's was beige and mine was soft pink.

"Oh my!" We said together.

Aunt Marion smiled from ear to ear.

"Made by Marion herself," boasted Uncle Virg.

"I could tell," Mama said, "they're beautiful. Let me see yours, Peach!" We put them on and admired each other.

"Thank you, Aunt Marion," I said, hugging my present around my shoulders.

"It's nice on you Carol, really pinks up your cheeks," she beamed.

Next Mama opened a tube of her signature lipstick, and a hankie scalloped in green with yellow daisies embroidered on the corners. The last thing to open was the smallest box of all. It was smaller than a bar of soap, and fairly flat. She lifted the lid, and there were the tickets to the *Funny Face* play for tomorrow night. She studied the tickets, then looked up in amazement.

"I can't believe it!" Mama flung her head back and covered her face. She peeked out at me, then she covered her eyes with her brand new hanky and lay back on the sofa again.

"Are we all going?" She was laughing and crying at the same time.

"Yep, even me!" I jumped up on her lap and put both my hands on her cheeks. "I love your fu--nny face. Your su--nny, fu--nny face!" I sang.

She got up, still holding me, and gave Aunt Marion and Uncle Virgil kisses and hugs, offering thanks and tears at such an outpouring of generosity.

They were just as pleased to be the givers as she was the gracious recipient.

Mama took a deep breath to settle herself, then said, "I'm not the only one celebrating a birthday." She found a small parcel in the bottom of her purse and brought it to Uncle Virg. It looked like a roll of candy, with the wrapping twisted at each end and tied with twine. She handed it to him. Her smile was telling.

"What have we here?" said Uncle Virg as he unwrapped it. "Well, I'll be darned. Grandpa's toothpick holder. I haven't seen this since... I don't think I've seen this since Grandpa died. I used to love this little thing… the way the top slides over the tube, this is some master craftsmanship!"

Mama said, "I'm sure you haven't seen it. I took it off the windowsill the day of his funeral. I knew you wanted it, but I guess I wanted it worse, so I snatched it."

"You thieving rascal!" he said. "I've often wondered where it went."

"Yep, and I forgot to feel bad about it until I found it when I was packing to move. Then I couldn't stop feeling guilty again, so here you go." Mama said. "Finally in the hands of its rightful owner."

Uncle Virg twisted off the top of the toothpick holder. He turned it over and two hand-carved toothpicks fell into his hand, along with a tightly rolled scroll of paper. He slipped off the piece of string that kept it rolled, and carefully peeled the old yellow paper open and read:

"I will be your slave for life if you do not tell Dad. V.S. Hussey."

Uncle Virg burst into laughter and re- rolled the little piece of paper. "I'm keeping this as proof and someday I *will* cash in on this promise."

"What does it mean, Mama?" I said.

"Uncle Virg bribed me about something, I don't even remember what—do you Virgil?"

"No, all I remember is you didn't want Dad to find out bad enough to agree to being my slave for life, and I have twenty years of favors to collect. This could come in handy. Best birthday present ever!" Uncle Virg scrunched his face into a deviant smile.

"Isn't there a statute of limitations?" Mama argued.

"Nope." Uncle Virg kissed Mama on the cheek, then his voice changed to heartfelt sincerity, "thanks Virginia, what a treasure."

Aunt Marion interrupted the sentimental moment, "We have thirty minutes to be dressed and down to the boat for boarding. I can't wait to see you in your dress, Virginia."

We split up to our designated rooms. Mama donned her dress, and I covered up my brown church dress with my new shawl and pulled my bangs back with the ribbon from my present. We all met in the sitting room in plenty of time to praise each other for our stunning attire and set off for an evening on the silver seas.

14

This was more than just a boat. There were two levels, each surrounded by a white-painted wooden-spindle railing. Smokestacks sent steam billowing into the air and flags flipped and floated into the blue sky. When we arrived, the railings were already lined with hatted women and suited men awaiting departure. Some held tight to curious children yearning to climb the railings for a better view.

Once on board, we took a promenade around the upper level. A crew member was giving tours of the Pilot house and I took a turn at the steering wheel. From there I could see the Athenaeum and marveled at my good fortune.

The signal bell rang to announce dinner seating and we all filed into the dining room. A string quartet played from somewhere I couldn't see, and a waiter approached our table.

"Welcome to the Buffalo Steam Boat," he said. He wore black trousers and a black vest over his stiff-collared shirt. He had what looked like a white table cloth wrapped around his waist, with a bar towel tucked in at the hip. We were all very thankful when he read the menu aloud, and explained each dish, as we followed along,

Terrine de Foie Gras Truffle
"A pate' of fattened goose liver and wild mushrooms."
Clear Turtle Soup with Sherry
"Flesh of the snapping turtle in a sherry and herb broth, or we offer a simple onion consommé."

Supreme of Halibut with Lobster Sauce or Rack of Lamb

"The halibut is a light white fish, topped with a cheesy cream sauce, and the lamb, we oven roast and serve in sections of three chops, with mint jelly"

Fresh Buttered Green peas
"Just as it sounds."

Chateau Potatoes
"Crispy baked potato slices," he put a hand up to the side of his mouth and confided, "glorified French fries, they're delicious."

Salade Roquefort
"A small iceberg wedge laced with dill vinaigrette and sprinkled with Roquefort cheese crumbles."

Chocolate Petits Fours
He looked at me. "These I will leave as a surprise of their own."

Fresh Peaches Cardinal
"A half poached peach, chilled and served with raspberry syrup."

Coffee, Tea, or Cocoa

He then leaned down to me and whispered, "And if you wish, we also have macaroni noodles in creamed cheese, topped with meatballs. This is preceded with sliced apples and grapes, and followed by your choice of dessert."

I smiled and blew a sigh of relief. I wasn't able to concentrate much after he said, "turtle flesh", and was sure I didn't want Roquefort cheese smelling up any part of my dinner. "Mac n' cheese aims to please," I said to myself just like the radio commercial.

"Does anyone have a question?" he asked.

I was hoping no one was going to stall because I was starting to get a watery mouth. And after feeding the masses with the miracle of the celery and peanut butter, I'd forgotten to eat much lunch myself. I was famished.

Aunt Marion raised her perfectly manicured index finger in front of her face and asked her stock restaurant question. "Does your chef use bouillon cubes in any of his sauces? I get a terrible headache if I eat anything cooked with bouillon."

"I don't know, but I will find out. Would anyone like more tea or lemonade?" he asked.

We all said yes and he excused himself. I looked down at the array of eating utensils set before me and started taking inventory. To my left were three forks, plus one above the plate. On my right were three knives, plus one on the small plate. Out past the knives was a huge spoon, and above the plate was another smaller spoon. I started stacking the forks to see if they would fit together, but Mama's hand laid gently on mine so I stopped. Uncle Virg lay his menu aside and proceeded to give report about a twelve-foot Calla Lilly that bloomed in the New York Botanical Garden. Mama was staring at the silverware. She hadn't been listening and he knew it.

"What's the problem Sis?" he said.

"I don't know where to begin," she said under her breath, "I'm accustomed to one fork, one knife, and one spoon. I'm going to need a map to get me from salad to dessert, and I'm afraid I didn't bring my Emily Post," Mama said.

Uncle Virg just laughed, but Aunt Marion came directly to the rescue. "Well, let me see if *I* can remember. My mother always said that if you can't remember what it's for, start from the outside and work your way in. The courses should use up all the silver, but let's see...soup, salad, fish, meat. I think that's how it goes. The soup spoon gets used for the soup, go figure, "she smiled," and then the forks and knives should match up, one set for the salad, one for the fish, and one for the meat or main entree. The set at the top of the plate is for dessert and this extra plate and knife are for the bread. If all else fails, do what I do, and we'll all make the same mistakes." She shrugged, unfolded her napkin and laid it in her lap. We did the same, even Uncle Virg.

When the waiter returned he was followed by a man with a tall, white pleated hat. He wore a white tunic and a red scarf around his neck. Before he approached our table he untied his smudgy, soiled apron and passed it off to the waiter. His face was red and his eyes were dark brown.

"Who haz zee inquire of zee cube?" He was not from New York.

"Why that was me, you see, I have a terrible headache allergy to bouillon cubes," Aunt Marion said waving her hand and acting like she was being visited by a celebrity, "And with the various sauces in your recipes, I just wanted to know what was safe for..."

"I am here in zees galley from before you are wake up," he started calmly, "and I sleep only to dream of zee parfait sauce for zee day next." His face turned a shade redder than it already was and his voice rose with each word as he continued.

He crossed his arms over his chest. Aunt Marion puckered her lips and checked the napkin in her lap.

"My pot for stock is nebar empty or bastardized with zee poison of zee lazy kitchen staff of her majesty, zee Queen!" His face was turning purple now and his fingernails were pulling our tablecloth, and everything on it, dangerously close to an avalanche.

I noticed a lady at the next table looking at us over the napkin that covered her mouth. Her shoulders bobbed with silent laughter. Mama and Aunt Marion looked from the chef in his rage, to the woman, then at each other. Their heads moved at the same time, in the same direction. Aunt Marion had her hands in the prayer position with her first fingers touching her bottom lip. She looked back to the chef with furrowed uncertainty. He leaned in.

"NO! I DO NOT USING BOUILLON FOR MY SAUCE!" he said and walked away, flapping the louvered doors to the galley in his wake.

The laughing lady next to us was wiping her eyes. We looked at Aunt Marion. In fact most of the people in the dining room were looking at Aunt Marion.

She addressed the three of us loudly enough for the other diners to hear, "Chef Du Bour has misplaced his wooden spoon and I think if he looks hard enough he will find it stuck up his..."

Mama interrupted, "ass-uming there is no bullion in the sauce, Marion, will you have the soup, or the consommé?"

Aunt Marion and Mama started to snicker, and then outright belly laughs erupted. Uncle Virg looked back and forth at both women. It seemed like he didn't know what to do. I was mortified. I was sure we'd have to leave and I was already blaming Aunt Marion for my upset stomach. The lady at the next table was making small clapping motions as she approached our table and leaned in to speak to Aunt Marion.

"This is my third dinner on board this vessel and each time Chef Du Bour has found some reason to put the fear of the "god of cuisine" into his diners," she said. "I complained of my steak being too rare the first time I was here and was told to 'sit on it'. Believe me, if he weren't such an artist in the kitchen, he would probably be out begging on the streets of France. They keep him for his gift, not his genteel personality." Before we could respond, she squeezed Aunt Marion's hand. "It's worth it. Enjoy your dinner. The Rack of Lamb is to die for." She winked at Aunt Marion and went back to her table laughing with her friends.

"There is a crazy man on board, and he's cooking our food!" Uncle Virg said into his napkin.

Aunt Marion was feeling the walls of the cabin closing in on her, so she and Uncle Virg excused themselves for some fresh air on deck.

"Remind me to never get so good at something that I can't take criticism or question," she said sarcastically as she left the table.

"I was just about sure he was going to pull the whole table cloth to the floor," Mama confided in me after they'd left, "along with all five hundred pieces of silverware!"

"Forty," I said.

"Forty?"

"Yeah, forty pieces of silverware."

"Smarty pants," said Mama.

The minute Uncle Virg and Aunt Marion sat down again, the waiter was there with our soup. He served Aunt Marion, then Mama, then me, then Uncle Virg. This was the pattern every time he brought something new. The soup was not the thin broth that I had expected. It was a small bowl of hearty brown broth with caramelized onions swimming around. A small round piece of toast floated in the middle of the bowl, with a tiny fried egg sitting right on top.

As the waiter gingerly placed each bowl on top of the plate in front of us he narrated, "Caramelized sweet onion soup. The onions are imported from Walla Walla, Washington. Resting on the crouton is a poached quail egg."

I looked down at the unborn quail.

Mama saved me. "Try one taste, Peach. If you don't like it, say no thank you and be done."

I took the teeniest bit, and choked it down, trying not to taste it. I was just getting ready to push the bowl away when the most satisfying flavor reached my taste buds. It was the best thing I think I've ever tasted, and didn't even remotely taste like onions, more like sugar and bread. I ate the whole thing, egg and all.

The next plate to arrive looked like modeling clay. The waiter saw my dilemma. "Would you like your salad now miss?"

"May I have... just pears?" I asked.

"By all means," he said and made a gesture to his helper.

Within a minute, my pears appeared in a pretty white china bowl. I saved the paper doily underneath and put it in

Mama's purse. When the adults got their lamb, I got my macaroni and cheese.

"Macaroni a la crème fromage, avec boulettes de viande," he said when he delivered my plate. The delightful smell was introduction enough.

"Thank you," I said, hoping I still had room after that delicious soup and the sweet pears.

Uncle Virg removed the leather cover from his Kodak Bantam. "I have never considered food to be an artistic medium," he said, "but I am going to take a photograph of this plate." He stood right up and focused in on the delicacy before him.

I was considering my last meatball when the waiter came by and saved me from slipping into a macaroni induced coma. He offered coffee, tea or cocoa, but I had to decline. My belly was challenging the buttons on my dress and I needed a bathroom so I excused myself. Mama, Aunt Marion and Uncle Virg had coffee while I walked all the way around both decks. I had stopped to see the view from the top deck when Mama came to find me. We stood for a while and watched as the lights of the surrounding houses and hotel lit up the window squares. Each window had a story to tell and we wondered about the lady, alone on the balcony of a simple cottage. Mama made up a story about her waiting for her sailor to return from a voyage. I suggested her sailor might be Chef Du Bour. Mama said that accounted for the sad look on her face, as well as her round belly, so we waved goodnight to Chef Du Bour's girlfriend and made our way back for dessert. I managed to enjoy the Petits Fours, which were actually tiny chocolate cakes, and a scoop of ice cream. Oh lands. Being spoiled was painful.

When we arrived back at port, the hotel was lit it up like a fairy castle. The night air felt cool and smelled like honeysuckle. As we walked back up the brick pathway, I could hear people on the porch laughing and talking, and band music coming from inside. In the lobby, we were greeted by Mr. Danielson. He invited Mama to come back and listen to the band with him, as he would be relieved of his duties in just a few minutes. She looked at Uncle Virg, seeking his opinion.

"Sure, Virginia, have a spin on the dance floor," encouraged Uncle Virg.

"I wish I could offer a nightcap," said Mr. Danielson, "but if you haven't noticed, the Athenaeum is dry. Not a drop of liquor to be found anywhere on the grounds. The prohibition of liquor has never been lifted."

"Just my style, Mr. Danielson. I'll be down in half an hour," Mama said.

As I got ready for bed Mama asked me, "Do you mind if I go out for just a little while, Peach? Aunt Marion will be right in the next room if you need anything."

"When are you coming back?"

"I won't be long." She was putting on lipstick in the mirror above one of the sinks.

"Can I stay awake and wait for you?"

"Sure, did you bring a book?" She fluffed her hair.

"Yes. You look pretty."

"I just love my new dress." She spun around and landed on my bed.

"Tell me a story about when you were a little girl."

"All right." She lay down next to me. "Scooch over." She got comfortable and thought for a while. "When my daddy, your Grandpa Hussey, needed supplies for the farm in Ellington, he had to go to Jamestown with a horse-drawn wagon. You know how it takes us about half an hour to drive to Ellington to visit Aunt Honey?"

I nodded, and yawned.

"Well, depending on the condition of the road, it might take us close to two hours to get there with the horses and wagon. You think Ellington is small now, you should have seen it then. It had a small store for flour, rice and soap and things like that, but if we needed seed or tools or medicine, we would need to go to Jamestown. I always wanted to go with Grandpa, but he would only take two of us at a time. And with seven of us kids, there was a pecking order. Aunt Honey was the only one younger than Virg and me. Robert, my oldest brother, was fifteen years-old when we were born, so Virg, Honey and I were way down on the list of helpful town-goers. Usually, father chose Robert or Clifford to go.

"One day when my mother was feeling poorly, she suggested that Honey and I go to town with Daddy. It was a nice warm day, probably August or September. I remember that because we bought apples on the way home and that's when the best apples are ready. Anyway, Honey and I were very excited to go. I was about eight years old, because Honey was four. She always sat in the middle so she wouldn't fall off, and had her own set of reigns to help drive the wagon. She didn't know that they were only attached to the front of the wagon, not the horses, so she paid attention to what was going on most of the time. Daddy would pretend we were going to crash if she started getting far-tracked, then she would pay attention again and not get bored.

"I did my best at playing twenty-questions with her, 'cuz that's what Uncle Virg and I usually did on the way to Jamestown, but she didn't really understand the game. Every time it was her turn, she would choose the exact same thing that I just got done having her and Daddy guess. And if I told her she couldn't use my word, she always chose Abraham Lincoln. She didn't even know who he was, so she didn't know how to answer the questions, but she heard Robert use Abraham Lincoln before, so she thought that would be a good one I guess.

"Anyway, we had three places to go that day and Daddy said that when we were all done shopping, we would get an ice cream cone at the pharmacy. Honey could think of nothing else once Daddy mentioned ice cream. She made up a song: "Ice cream at the pharmacy, ice cream at the pharmacy, ice cream — ice cream — ice cream at the pharmacy," and didn't stop singing it until we stopped in front of the blacksmith.

"Daddy had to pick up a horse bit that he had had repaired. We stayed there a while, keeping plenty far from the fire. Daddy had some conversation with a few men while we sat on the bench out front and ate the licorice whips that the blacksmith had given us. The blacksmiths' son was there helping his dad and I thought he was cute. He must have been a little older than me, at least he was taller, and he wore an apron that made him look like a real blacksmith. I was pretty taken with him, and since his dad was busy talking to my dad, he could take a break and come and show off for us with his peashooter for a while. He put a watermelon rind up on the railing of the porch and started in shooting peas at the rind. He'd put a dried pea in a hollowed-out stick and blow, and the pea would come flying out and imbed into the watermelon rind. He could blow those peas into the rind with perfect aim. He made a cross in one rind, an arrow on another, and then he asked me what I wanted him to make. I said a heart and he made the heart right over the arrow, like cupid, so I was absolutely sure that meant he was in love with me. I asked if I could have a try with the peashooter and he gave it right over with a fistful of peas. He asked me my name, then told me to try to make a "V" for Virginia. I shot my first pea and it must have hit Honey in the head 'cuz she started crying, rubbing the side of her head and ran in to Daddy. That was the end of my pea-shooting career and the last time I saw that particular love of my life, 'cuz Daddy came storming out, with Honey still holding the side of her head, inquiring about what had happened. I admitted to hitting her with a pea, so he checked her face and head and told her she'd live. He hoisted her up on the seat of the wagon, then helped me up and we were off. I felt bad about hitting her with a pea, but really, how bad can a pea hurt?

"Then we went to the Mercantile with the list that Mother had written and I checked off each item as Daddy put it in our basket. We finished our list and I called for Honey, whom I expected was over gleaning grapes, but she didn't answer. I went to the produce wall and she wasn't there. I went to the candy bins and she wasn't there either. Daddy walked one way around the store and I walked the other, still no Honey. I called her name and Daddy whistled his signature whistle that never failed to round up one of us kids if we could hear it. So it was decided that she wasn't in the store, so we put our shopping in the wagon and took off looking for Honey.

"Daddy told me to go up the street as far as the park, and he went the opposite way. The first shop next to the mercantile was the barber shop. No Honey. The pharmacy was next door. I entered and asked the man if a little blonde girl in a blue dress had come in here. He pointed over at the ice cream counter and there she was. Her back was to me and she was tip toed up on a chair, leaning over the ice cream case with her bottom swinging from side to side as she sang, 'Ice cream at the pharmacy, ice cream at the pharmacy.' I walked over, grabbed her by the hand, and told her to jump off the chair. She did, but as soon as we left the store she screamed, 'I WANT ICE CREAM AT THE PHARMACY!' I pretty much had to drag her up the street, and she didn't stop crying and carrying on until I delivered her to Daddy. He had heard the ruckus from half way down the street and was running toward us. As soon as he was sure she was all right and heard my story of finding her, he sat down on the bench in front of the blacksmith's. He laid her over his knees, and spanked her butt one time, hard. Honey was so startled that she stopped breathing for a few seconds, and when she caught her breath she let out a howl so loud the barber and his patron peeked out the door, and the dog lying in front of the bakery started howling. Before she was even done crying, Daddy plopped her up on the seat of the wagon and told me to get up there too and not to let her down or out of my sight. He walked into the pharmacy to get what Mother needed, and was back in no time at all.

"We started home and I asked Daddy about getting ice cream. He said 'little girls who run off don't get ice cream.' I said '*I* didn't run off.' He said 'Yes, but you didn't keep an eye on your little sister, and neither did I, so none of us gets ice cream today!' I couldn't argue with that. We drove home in silence while Honey cried herself to sleep with her head on my lap.

"All this leads to the best part of the story. It's one of the craziest things I've ever seen. About a week after our trip to Jamestown, Honey woke up in the morning with an earache and said she couldn't hear out of her right ear. Mother looked in there and sure enough, a little yellow sprout was growing right out of Honey's ear. The pea from my pea shooter had gone into Honey's ear canal. From the moisture of swimming in the creek, and the warmth of her body, Honey had sprouted the pea."

"Really?"

"I'm one hundred percent telling the truth." She made an X across her chest.

"How did she get it out?"

"Well, Mother tried a turkey baster but it didn't have enough suction, so she sucked it out with her own mouth. She was afraid to stick anything in there, so she put her mouth right over Honey's ear to create a suction and it slipped out. We saved the pea on the windowsill."

"That's icky. I wish *we* had a horse and buggy," I said.

"Horse and buggies are fun for about an hour, then I think you'd change your tune. Takes forever to get anywhere." She got up and fluffed the back of her hair, then kissed me softly on the lips so she didn't leave too much color behind. She stopped at the door on her way out, "give me lovings," she recited.

I blew her a kiss. She caught it and put it in her pocket, then blew one back to me. I caught it and hid my fist under the blanket. Love.

15

When I woke up in the morning I didn't know where I was. My disorientation only lasted two seconds, but so many thoughts went through my head that it felt like longer, and when the feeling was over, I wanted it back. I stretched, scratched my left calf with the toenails of my right foot, lifted my arms way above my head and felt the headboard. Remembering where I was, and knowing I had an entire day and another night here, brought contentment. I didn't have to go anywhere or do any chores. I was a leaf in the wind. The day lay ahead of me with lots of things I could do, but nothing I had to. Swimming might very well be the most taxing activity put before me all day. When I opened my eyes the shadow of maple leaves danced on the wall. They flickered and floated like a penny arcade movie machine. I could hear Mama breathing in the bed next to mine. She sounded peaceful. The quicker I turned over and really woke up, the quicker the day would start, but then it would be over, so I waited and listened to her breaths for a while. I heard Aunt Marion and Uncle Virg out in the sitting room, so I ventured out. They were having coffee and reading the newspaper, side by side on the sofa.

"Good morning, Peach," said Uncle Virg. "You look like a baby bird that has just hatched from its egg."

My hair was sweaty and stuck to my head. I had my blanket wrapped around my shoulders and my long skinny legs hung out beneath my baby-doll pajamas. "Mama's still sleeping," I said and snuggled up to the other side of Uncle Virg.

"I don't expect she'll be up and around for a while," said Aunt Marion, "I think it was a late night for her. How did you sleep, Carol?"

"I can't remember; I was sleeping." I said, yawning.

They smiled at each other.

"Would you be after having a glass of apple juice?" asked Uncle Virg.

"How did you know what I was thinking?" I grunted with my still-sleepy voice, and leaned over onto the arm of the sofa.

"I know you, Peach," he said.

He got up from the couch and went over to a tray with a pitcher of juice and several glasses. He filled two and brought me one, then with the other, slipped into the room where Mama slept. He left it on the bedside table, then returned to his newspaper.

"Yesterday was my best day ever so far," I said dreamily.

"In your whole life?" asked Aunt Marion.

"In my whole life," I answered. There were better times in my life, but never a better day that I could remember. I looked forward to swimming some more today, seeing the friends I had met, and making sure Cornelius had more than peanut butter for lunch.

"What are we gonna have for lunch?" I asked.

"You skipped breakfast Carol. Why are you thinking about lunch already?" said Aunt Marion.

"I was thinking about Cornelius," I said.

"Who in the world is Cornelius?" asked Aunt Marion.

"The one who didn't like celery," I said, "at the swimming area. He looked like all he had to eat the whole day yesterday was the peanut butter we gave him."

"Hmm," said Aunt Marion. "Well, get yourself dressed then, looks like we need to make a trip to the market. Virgil, would you mind driving us to the Red and White?"

"Not at all, soon as I read the funny pages and finish my coffee," he said without looking up.

I kissed him on the cheek and went to get dressed. I succeeded in washing and dressing without waking Mama, and left a note on the bedside table:

Mama, Went to the market.
Be back soon.
Lovings, C.C.

"What shall we have for the picnic? We should make a list so we don't impulse buy," Aunt Marion said from the front seat, ready for dictation.

"Lena got a new kind of ham that's really yummy. It's called Spam. Lena entered a contest to name the meat. We got to taste it and she had the idea to name it *Mighty Meat,* but she didn't win. They chose Spam instead and the guy who named it won one hundred dollars!" I said.

"I've tasted a sample at the market, it wasn't bad, and it will travel well. All right, Spam sandwiches," she said as she wrote the makings on our list.

"And pickles, and cookies, and carrots," I added.

As Usual, Aunt Marion waited for Uncle Virg to open her car door, so I waited too this time. We each took one of his arms and squished ourselves into the market three abreast.

Uncle Virg put himself in charge of choosing the cookies. He decided on oatmeal-raisin and Scottish shortbread. Aunt Marion got a jug of grape juice among other things, and we left with everything we needed for a perfect picnic.

When we got home Mama was sitting in a chair by the window, reading the paper.

"Hey Peach, good job leaving a note. How'd you do at the market?"

"Fine, we're gonna make Spam sandwiches for lunch and share with the knitting lady's kids at the lake." I climbed up on her lap, and wrapped my arm around her neck so I could rub the hangy-down part of her ear between my fingers.

"That sounds like a perfect idea," she said still scanning the news.

"That's what I thought, wanna help?" I said as I slid down off her lap.

"Sure," Mama said, and got up to look in the grocery bags, "looks like Uncle Virg was in charge of the dessert."

When we got done packing our picnic we went down to breakfast, as we had only had juice and coffee so far. We were seated at a table on the porch. After we ordered Aunt Marion got right to it.

"You must have had more than a little in common with Mr. Danielson."

"Why do you say that?" asked Mama.

"Let's just say the evening was not a short one. Did you dance?" Marion said.

"Yes, just for two songs. Then we went down to the boathouse and found three men playing bluesy-swing with old tattered guitars and a guy on harmonica. Mr. Danielson— his first name is Michael—said this was more his style, so we stayed there till the music stopped. I think we got back around midnight," Mama said.

"Well?" encouraged Aunt Marion.

"Well what," said Mama.

Uncle Virg looked at his wife, "Marion, stop interrogating Carol."

"It's Okay Virgil," said Mama, "It's in a woman's nature to want to know the details," said Mama. She winked at me and went on. "So we got back to the hotel and necked on the sofa in the lobby until we got kicked out of the place by the manager, and Mr. Danielson got fired for seducing another helpless woman passing through Lake Chautauqua. I hear he has quite the reputation." Mama took a long drag from her cigarette and blew the smoke in the air with her head tilted up. Then she brought her coffee cup to her lips and took a big gulp. She knew better than to look at her brother.

Mama had kicked me under the table, which is code for, "I'm lying but don't let on," so I was privy, though still embarrassed by even the *idea* of Mama kissing Mr. Danielson. Aunt Marion's expressions ran the gamut from surprised to interested, to embarrassed, and finally shocked. She looked at Uncle Virg to see his response and he was smiling ear-to-ear, shaking his head. Aunt Marion's love of gossip and tendency for gullibility had gotten the better of her again. Realizing this, she had to make up her mind to be either mad or graciously bamboozled. Praise God from whom all blessings flow, she chose bamboozled and erupted with a laughter that was definitely not under the heading of acceptable restaurant behavior. Aunt Marion had a way of carrying her mad around that could have put a damper on the whole day, but as it turned out she only punched Mama in the arm.

Breakfast finished and picnic packed, Mama and I went down to the shore to swim and laze the day away. Aunt Marion went to the Women's' Book Club meeting, and Uncle Virg headed off to the Amphitheater for a lecture from some important French Rotarian. They were back in time for lunch. The knitting lady and her kids were there and didn't skip a beat when offered the extra Spam sandwiches we happened to have leftover. Cornelius ate through the middle of his sandwich like a snowplow, and gave the crust to his mother who held the leftovers like a fancy tea cake. Uncle Virg played football with the boys, Aunt Marion and Mama spent a long time standing in the water and talking, and we the rest of the kids played every version of Marco Polo we could think of. We met some boys with a boat and everyone got a ride around the perimeter of the swimming area. They even let me row. Eleanor, her dad and her sister in the wheel chair, had already left that morning and we exchanged addresses and promised to be pen pals as soon as we both could write a letter by ourselves.

Around three o'clock in the afternoon, Aunt Marion suggested we head up to our rooms for a rest and evening preparations. I didn't complain or challenge the plans that day; I was going to an off-Broadway musical.

***

We had dinner in the hotel restaurant. I had chicken, Mama had steak, Uncle Virg had Lamb and Aunt Marion ordered a salad and nibbled off of our plates, prophesying that there would be too much food and nowhere to store the leftovers. The butterflies in my stomach left little room for food. I was so excited for the play that, I'm sorry to say, dinner was almost a bother.

The theatre was just a short walk from the hotel. Aunt Marion and Uncle Virg were strolling along through the Plaza like we had nowhere to go. Mama, on the other hand, was pulling me along like we were on our way to a fire! I had to skip to keep up with her. When we found Norton Hall, the doors weren't even open yet, so Aunt Marion and Uncle Virg stood in line while Mama and I took a walk. We could not stand still to save our souls.

The houses in the area were stately and perfectly groomed. Mama and I each picked out a lake house to buy when our "ship came in". Mine was a white cottage with green and white striped awnings over every window and a big front yard. Hers was a brown craftsman with more windows than siding, and white wicker furniture tucked into a fern-filled porch.

Even though I was excited beyond belief about going to the show, I can't remember a time when I felt more at peace. Just walking around in this place gave me hope that there was more than just Jamestown. There were longer, more graceful walks than the walk from Tower Street to WCA Hospital. There were new things to learn, way past the doors of Willard Scool. There were bigger swimming holes that the Chadakion River and Conewango Creek. And there were different people, different voices in different languages, different colors, different shoes and hats and a dozen ways to wear them. This place, these people, and even the food sparked a yearning in me to see and do, to explore and take chances.

We walked a long time without talking, and when we came back around to the Theatre, the line was gone so we walked right in and gave the man our tickets. He ushered us way down to the fourth row where Aunt Marion was craning her neck looking for us. We took our seats and Mama nearly squeezed my hand off when the curtain rose. At intermission Mama kept rubbing her cheeks, they were sore from smiling so much. My whole body was tired from making myself stay in my seat. I could not keep my legs still for wanting to dance.

By the time the last song was sung and Frankie and Jimmy had taken their final bow, I was stunned. My head was swimming with music, dancing, laughter, beauty, movement, fast-talking, and knee-slapping. I didn't know how to respond, so I cried. We were walking up the inclined aisle of the beautiful theater and I couldn't see for the tears. Thank goodness for my new shawl to wipe my drippy nose.

Mama asked why I was crying and all I could say was, "I'm too filled up."

Mama had a much more reasonable response. She went on and on about the silliness of the thieves, and how cute Frankie was. I swore to myself that I would never write a diary that I wouldn't want anyone else to read, like Frankie did. Although, I wouldn't mind getting my hands on hers and finding out what all the fuss was. And the music, oh, the music! We sang the songs all the way back to our room. Then and there, I made up my mind to be a dancer. It didn't look that hard.

***

All good things come to an end. Waking up in the morning was the beginning of the end of this magical weekend. I lay in the comfy bed, memorizing the pattern in the ceiling tiles. I counted the curtain rings, noticed the angle of the crown molding and circled my fingers around the banister of the bed to record how big it was. I decided that I would pattern my bedroom after this one when I could decorate a room of my own. I tried to be extra quiet so no one would wake up before I had a chance to soak it all in one last time. I didn't want to leave.

I was looking straight at Mama when her eyes peeked open and the first thing she saw was me. She closed them again and smiled, snuggling the soft cotton sheet up around her face.

"Good morning, Funny Face," she mumbled in her deep morning voice. "Don't tell me it's already Sunday."

"If I tell you it's Saturday can we stay another day?"

"If you told me it was Saturday, we could relive yesterday and I would be the happiest woman on the planet. No wait, I am the happiest woman on the planet already."

Three knocks announced Aunt Marion from the bathroom door. She didn't wait for an answer, just came in and sat at the foot of Mama's bed. "You two ready to head home?" she said.

"No," Mama said, "I think I'll hire some thieves, steal the family jewels, and sell them. Then from the money I make I'll rent a room here at the Athenaeum and Carol and I will spend the rest of our days swimming in the lake and drinking sweet tea on the veranda."

"Perfect, I'll be your thief if you'll let me stay too," Aunt Marion said without skipping a beat.

"Deal," said Mama.

"Mama?" I said from my bed.

"Well?"

"Can we come back here some time?"

"I hope so, Peach."

"Mama?" I crawled in bed next to her.

"What?"

"Can I come and live with you?"

"Not yet, honey," she said apologetically.

"Can I live with Aunt Marion and Uncle Virg?"

"No, it's too far from Jamestown. Plus, they both work all through the school year," she said.

Aunt Marion cocked her head. "But I don't work all summer. Maybe Carol would like to come and spend the rest of the summer at our house, if it's okay with Virgil that is. But I don't think there'll be any problem getting him to agree. In fact, this isn't the first we've thought about it."

I sprung up from the bed, fully awake now. "Really?" The idea started a vibration in my body that sent me running around the room and landing in the arms of Aunt Marion.

She didn't know what to do with me once she realized my presence, so she fluffed my bangs and pinched my cheeks. "A little farm life will put some pink in these cheeks." She patted me on the bottom, "and maybe we can fatten you up a little."

"Oh, Mama, can I?"

"Well, let's hear what Uncle Virg has to say, then we'll see," Mama said.

"Stay here, let me talk to Virgil and let him know what we're planning. It's not likely he'll have any reservations, but he hasn't had his coffee yet either. Let's get some coffee in him before he makes any decisions," Aunt Marion said. She was turning gears in her head as she left.

"Will you miss me too much if I go?" I said, getting my suitcase out with a brand new perspective on leaving.

"No, because I'd have to come see you every weekend," Mama said. "Six weeks without you would be like six weeks without water. I simply couldn't do it."

"Really, Oh Mama this is perfect. If Uncle Virg says no, I don't know what I'll do. I'll just cry my brains out."

"Well, don't go countin' chickens." Her smile showed her confidence in her brother.

Three more knocks came, this time from the door to the sitting room. "Can I come in?" Uncle Virg said.

"Bet yer life!" I said.

He peeked his head in the doorway and looked around, "I'm lookin' for a girl by the name of Carol, 'bout this high, brown hair, loves to pull weeds and make her bed. I hear she's looking for lodgings out Greenwood way."

"That's me!" I climbed up on the bed and jumped several times before I leaped right off into Uncle Virg's outstretched arms. "Thank you, thank you, I knew you'd say yes!"

"Last word's up to your mother. What d'ya say sis?"

"Can I come and visit?" Mama said.

"If you pull your weight around the house, same as Carol," he said, winking at me.

"Guess it's a go then." She came and put her arms around both of us and whispered, "You're my two favorite people in the whole world."

"Me too," I said.

"Me three, but I've got one more. Marion!" he called, "Come in here. We're picking favorites and I pick you!"

Aunt Marion came in and found us all woven together like a twisted rope. She cuddled in next to Uncle Virg, and gave a short squeeze of approval, then re-addressed the business of the morning. "Alright then, if it's settled that Carol's coming with us, let's get a move on."

***

We took the long way home, looping up around the lake and coming down the other side. It took longer than we had imagined since the Sunday motorists were making the same scenic loop.

"So, Virginia," said Aunt Marion, from the front seat. "What about Mr. Danielson? He wasn't there when we left."

"I'm not sure. He knows where I work. He can call if he wants to. I'm not going to hold my breath though." Mama said, as she looked out the window. "Oh, and just for the record, we did not kiss, or even hold hands. He was a perfect gentleman, and I am a *perfect* lady."

16

I spent the rest of the summer with Aunt Marion and Uncle Virg. In the mornings, I'd get out of bed with my blanket in tow, move to the parlor and lay on the window seat, listening to the sounds coming from the kitchen. Sometimes Uncle Virg would be in there having breakfast with Aunt Marion, but usually I didn't wake up until he was long gone.

Uncle Virg was the Superintendent of the Steuben County School district. He also taught math. Aunt Marion was an English Literature professor at the college for teachers. She had the whole summer off, but Uncle Virg had meetings and interviews that kept him busy most of the summer. I went everywhere with Aunt Marion, except to her outings with the P.E.O. I never did find out what Aunt Marion really did with the P.E.O. ladies, besides wear hats and gloves and eat lunch. She wouldn't tell me what the initials stood for so I called it *Pigs Eat Out,* because they were always going out to lunch, taking someone lunch, or planning a luncheon. Even when she wasn't out with "the pigs", Aunt Marion was always busy. She canned anything that would grow, so we picked and canned about twice a week. By the end of the summer it looked like a regular store in the basement.

July was the month of the zucchini. We ate it steamed, sautéed, baked, grilled, breaded, and fried. We made Zucchini bread, ate as much as we could, and froze the rest. We canned any that was leftover, layered with tomatoes. It looked like Christmas in a jar. Cucumbers came on all at once. We ate them peeled and raw, sugar and vinegared, and pickled. I snapped more green beans than I care to conjure up a number for. Blueberries were my favorite picking. We only had a few bushes, but we usually made it over to the farm just out of town and picked all day on a Saturday. My teeth were blue for weeks. At the end of the tomato harvest, usually late August or early September, we stewed, roasted, peeled, chopped and packed into jars, every nationality of tomato known to man.

Aunt Marion taught me that food does not come from the grocery store, it comes from the earth, and every step of the process is important. Dirt under my fingernails meant a job well done, and a little dirt never hurt anyone. As we pulled weeds and drowned tomato bugs and slugs in mugs of beer, we talked about things we might not have otherwise.

Aunt Marion woke me up early on potato-digging day. She liked to can the small new potatoes and leave the others to grow until the first frost. It was light outside, but the sun hadn't reached over the trees to shine on the potato patch yet, so we got busy doing the dirty work before our sweat turned the dust on our faces into mud.

"Is this one big enough?" I asked as I dug.

"Why isn't that cute, that's what the farmers call a fingerling. My daddy always called the tiny ones the babies," she said. "Why don't you put a few of those babies in the colander and we'll have them for dinner tonight."

I got to thinking about babies.

"Aunt Marion?"

"Yes, Carol."

"Why don't you and Uncle Virg have any babies?"

She thought for a minute before she answered. "Well, God hasn't given us any yet."

I thought for a minute before I asked, "Do you have eggs?"

"Not in the house, we'll go check the chicken coup when we're done here. You getting hungry?"

She didn't understand. "Not eating eggs, baby eggs, in your ovaries."

"I hope so, I mean yes, I assume so," she said, a little flustered.

"If the sperm can't meet up with the eggs, they won't grow."

"Did your Mother tell you this?"

"Yeah. She drew a picture. She was telling me how she and Uncle Virg had to share the nest in their mother 'cuz they were twins, and how it took two eggs and two sperm to make them 'cuz they don't look alike, ya know, they aren't the same size."

"What did your mother say about my eggs?"

"Nothin'."

"Then why do you ask?"

"I just wondered. Most people have babies, can't be that hard."

"It's a miracle is what it is," Aunt Marion said.

"Yeah, that's what Mama said. Sure are a lot of miracles walking around though, seems like God could give you one."

"God can do anything He wants to, Peach," Aunt Marion wiped her face and a muddy smudge stayed on her cheek. "He just doesn't always do what we want when we want it. I know this for sure..." she sat back on her feet, "when God doesn't answer my prayers, when and how I want them answered, I know He has something better in mind. Something better than I could ever conceive."

"Okay." I laid three more babies in the colander. "Well, I'm ready to be a cousin. Your baby will be my cousin."

"That's right. But until then, I'll just practice on you," she said.

That didn't sit well with me. I sprung up from my knees and slapped the dirt off my hands, "I don't want to be practiced on! I'm not a baby, and I'm not yours."

Aunt Marion stood up. "Of course you're not a baby. You're almost a young lady. I didn't mean it like that. I'm sorry. I can't wait to have my own baby. I know you're not mine." Tears spilled onto her dusty face and made trails down her cheeks. She walked over to me and took me in her arms and hugged me tighter than I knew she could. "I'm not sure if I'll ever have a baby of my own. But it's sure fun to have you here. And I hope that if I ever do have a child, that she is as sweet as you."

"Sorry, I didn't mean to make you sad."

"It's okay, Carol. You don't make me sad." She let go of me and headed for the house. "I need some tea. Keep digging, I'll bring you some."

When she came back, she was her old self again. I don't know what I would have done if she was still sad. She sat my mug of tea down in the dirt beside me to cool.

"Carol, there's a big slug on the marigold by the tomatoes. Go get the salt shaker," Aunt Marion ordered. I liked the bossy Aunt Marion better than the sad one.

Aunt Marion always planted marigolds along the perimeter of her tomatoes, and it looked so pretty with the orange and golden blossoms protecting the red and yellow fruit. Little did I know, until I helped to plant the marigolds and she narrated while we planted, that they really did protect the tomatoes from certain pests. Slugs and snails love marigolds more than the vegetables. So, on our slug and snail hunt that's where we'd look.

***

The rest of the summer flew by. Aunt Marion said I was welcome to come back next summer, as I was such a helpful and unobtrusive house guest. I guess that was a compliment. So I did. I spent every summer there for the next six years. It became my home away from home, which wasn't really my home at all.

17

After being gone to Aunt Marion and Uncle Virg's for the second summer, I started feeling different about the back and forthness of my life. I'd been changing my mind, or rather, my mind had been changing. When I was six I had just enough sense to be sad about losing my father, homesick about being apart from my mother, and found great comfort in rubbing the silky part of my blanket just under my nose. At nine I was mad about missing my father, heartsick to be without my mother, and the binding of my blanket was mostly worn off.

The mood at Lena and Leonard's had changed also. Lena spent an awful lot of time on the telephone. Some afternoons I'd come home and she'd be sitting on the kitchen stool, full ashtray smoldering next to her, with the phone glued to her ear, listening, but not contributing to any conversation at all, just eavesdropping on the party line. When she was on a legitimate call, I'd eavesdrop on *her*. There was much to be learned from that corner of the kitchen. My ears instinctively perked up when I heard a gasp or an "Oh!" Lena wouldn't tell *me* how she was feeling, but she'd tell the person on the other end of the phone just about anything.

One chilly afternoon in spring, I came in through the front door after school, unwrapped myself and threw my coat on the hook. The wood stove lured me to the kitchen and there was Lena, staring out the window, phone in hand, "Mm-hm...Mm-hm...Mm-hm. I know but...I know, but it's the only offer he's gotten. It's a start and the one good thing about it is we'd have a place to stay until..." I stood a moment, warming my backside, waiting for acknowledgment. She turned around to set her coffee cup on the counter and looked at me in surprise, then shot a glance at the kitchen clock and stood up.

"Hold on a minute," she said, then covered the receiver. "I'll be off in a minute, Carol. Do you have homework?" She didn't wait for an answer. "Good heavens, it's 3:30, I'm gonna have to go," she said to the person on the other end as she opened the back door, stepped outside and shut the door as best she could over the curly wire. She turned her back to the door and spoke in hushed tones. I got the hint and went to my room.

A few minutes later I heard her hang up the phone and come in to my room. "How come you didn't go see your mother?"

"She had a meeting, remember?" I said. I put my book down.

"Oh, yeah...I forgot."

"Did Leonard get a new job?"

"Why do you ask?"

"I heard you say he got an offer," I said.

"Carol, you shouldn't listen to other people's phone conversations and how do you know I was talking about Leonard? I could have been talking about anyone for that matter. Don't worry about Leonard and his job. He has a fine job, and I'll keep you informed if there is anything you need to know."

"Well then, who were you talking about?" I asked, a bit sheepishly.

"It's none of your affair. I'm going to start dinner. Please go get the clothes off the line before it gets dark," she said, "and stop rolling your eyes, you're nine, not nineteen."

It *was* my affair. Where was I supposed to go if Lena and Leonard took off to who knows where? I'd heard her talking about a new place, and doesn't that mean that the new job would be too far from here to drive every day, and wouldn't that mean I'd be farther from my mother? Or did that mean that I'd have to live somewhere else?

18

I saw my father three times in the three years that I lived with Lena and Leonard. All were completely unexpected. The first time, Lena and I were on our way uptown to buy glue. That's another story, but as we walked down Water street, we passed Jerry's barbershop window and there sat Father. Jerry, the barber, was fastening a brown cape around his neck. Father's hair was so long, Jerry had to pull it out from under the collar of the cape, and it curled around his ears, making him look like a little boy. He didn't see me. When Lena realized I was lollygagging in front of the barbershop, she came back to get me. She took one look in the window, and pulled me down the sidewalk faster than quick.

The second time I saw him, I was waiting for the city bus. I'd just turned nine. Mama said when I turned nine I could take the bus by myself to Aunt Marion and Uncle Virg's in Greenwood for a weekend. It was a three hour trip each way and I had to change buses in Amity. I had seventeen minutes to meet my next bus, and already had my ticket, so I found the place where the bus would pull up and sat down on the bench to eat a chocolate chip cookie and read my book. A man came and stood right in front of me. At first I couldn't see his face, as mine was down and he was so close, but I saw his hand. It was extended toward me, and the baby finger was being offered in the manner of a pinky swear. I knew, without looking up, that it was my father. I curled my finger around his before I even saw his face.

He sat down next to me, short hair this time. "How are you?"

"Fine," I said. "I'm going to Aunt Marion and Uncle Virg's. I can travel alone now that I'm nine." My heart was pounding into my ribs.

"Nine." He nodded and looked at the pavement. His voice quivered when he spoke again. "How's your mom?" He covered his mouth and looked at me.

"Good. She's a nurse."

He kept nodding.

"Where are you going?" I asked.

"Gotta go see a man about a job."

"Hmm," I said. I'd heard my mother quote him with this exact phrase. His beard was scruffy and he wasn't even wearing a tie.

The bus for Greenwood pulled up and made it hard to hear or breathe.

"That's mine," I said.

"Yes, well, better be on your way. My bus should be here any minute. Have a good trip then. "He reached in his pocket and handed me something. I put my hand out and he pressed a quarter into my palm, then curled my fingers up around it. "For incidentals," he smiled.

"Thanks." I picked up my satchel and handed him the bag of cookies. "Mama made them."

He started nodding again, bit his lip, and waved as I walked away.

The third time I saw him was during the last week of third grade. It was sunny outside and I was tired of school, so were Paul, Lydia and Beanie. We'd met on the sidewalk in front of my house to walk to school together, as usual. Paul carried a fishing pole propped up on his shoulder, Huck Fin style. Beanie was crying because her shoes were too tight.

"Take 'em off then, cry baby!" said Lydia, who was now fourteen.

"I can't go to school without shoes and these are my only ones," she whimpered. "Feels like my toes are gonna squish right out the front."

"Here, take mine," said Lydia, and threw her brown oxfords at her sister.

Beanie put them on. Her feet swam around with each step she took.

"What are *you* gonna wear?" I asked Lydia.

"Nothin'," she said.

"You can't go to school barefoot—they'll make you wear donation shoes," I reminded her. It was a disgrace to have to wear donation shoes. Only the poorest of the poor wore them. You had to give them back at the end of the school day and walk home barefoot.

"I'm not going to school; I haven't gone for three days," she said with a brag to her voice. "Eighth grade is stupid. I can't bear another minute of it."

"Yer gonna get in trouble. Yer gonna get expelled!" Beanie warned.

"I already expelled myself," she hollered over her shoulder as she and Paul, the middle brother, took off running.

Beanie couldn't run, just kept scuffing along in the too big shoes. I wasn't anxious to get there in the first place, so we walked along taking our time. At the corner we stopped and waited for a big gravel truck and trailer to pass. The truck rumbled the ground, its gears high-pitched and grinding. We didn't hear Lydia and Paul before they abducted us and pulled us through a hedge and into the Anderson's yard.

Lydia had Beanie pinned down on the ground under a straddle. With one hand she was mashing Beanie's face around, trying to cover her mouth while she struggled. With the other she attempted to hold Beanie's flailing arms away from her own face. "Promise you won't tell mom we're ditching," Lydia snarled.

Beanie mumbled something through her nose. Paul had me by the neck in the crook of his elbow. I wasn't trying to speak or escape. I was more surprised than scared.

"Promise and I'll let you go!" Lydia grunted, trying not to yell too loud.

"She can't promise, dip-snot, you're covering her mouth!" said Paul.

"Okay, blink once if you promise not to tell, and two if you want me to throw you in the creek." Lydia laughed at her own wittiness.

Beanie blinked once I guess, because she was released and so was I. It took a few seconds for us to realize our freedom. Beanie sat up and sort of sobbed while she rubbed her sore mouth and I craned my neck to make sure it still turned.

"Where are you going?" I said.

"Fishing," said Paul.

"Take us with you," I said.

"No way!"

"Then I'm tellin' your mother. I didn't promise, only Beanie did."

"You wouldn't," he said in disbelief.

I cocked my head and looked him straight in the eyes. I didn't know where this bravery came from, but I knew Lydia and Paul well enough to know that they didn't go around torturing people, as a rule. Besides, I genuinely wanted to go fishing with them.

"You'll slow us down and get us caught," Lydia protested.

"Have it your way." I turned back toward home. "Go ahead to school, Beanie. I have to make a visit to your mother."

Lydia and Paul looked at each other, trying to decide if I'd tell or not, but not wanting to take the chance.

"All right! Geeze, but we're not waiting for you. You have to keep up!" Paul conceded.

We hid our book bags in the hedge and did our best to sneak around the school and not be seen passing by. Beanie made much better time once she ditched her sister's shoes in an old oak tree along the way. We followed close behind the big kids and entered into a part of the woods where I had never been. The way was thick with trees, stickery brambles, and bushes. We wove along a partially blazed deer path, under branches and around piles of poop. A branch snapped back after Paul pushed it away to get through, and hit me in the forehead. I cried out and he turned around. "Shhh," he scolded with his finger over his lips. I lagged behind a little, worrying my wound. When I caught up, we had arrived at a clearing that opened up to a sandy beach alongside the creek. I found a sunny spot and sat down on a rock to catch my breath. Lydia was holding onto a tree trunk with one hand and pulling splinters out of her foot with the other.

"Give me my shoes back, Beanie," Lydia ordered.

"I don't have 'em," Beanie mumbled.

"What do you mean you don't have 'em?" Lydia stood up and looked around like they might have run there by themselves.

"I stuck them in the tree with the hole in the side, they were falling off," said Beanie.

"They don't fit me either, but I can't go home without 'em, Mom'll pitch a fit! Which tree with the hole in the side, there's hundreds!"

"Quit breathin' down my neck, I'll get 'em on the way home," Beanie whined.

"Maybe I just won't go home." Lydia pulled her dress off over her head and revealed her cut off blue jeans and t-shirt. "Maybe I'll just find a cave to live in and eat berries and fish and become a river rat and never do homework or chores again." She threw her dress on the rocky sand and headed to the water.

Paul was already there, fiddling with the hook of his fishing pole and eating an apple from his lunch. I climbed up onto a giant rock and settled into a crevice that was perfectly formed for my torso and equipped with a rise like a pillow for my head. Lydia and Beanie were at the water's edge skipping stones and blaming their poor results on the shape of the stones rather than the skill of their throw. Each time Beanie picked up a stone she inspected it and then either hurled it out over the water, or threw it over her shoulder into the brush. She wasn't getting any better with practice.

"Aaach! Bloody Hell!" erupted a voice from the brush. All eyes darted in the direction of the outburst. Out of the bushes tumbled a teetering man, hair tousled, his face creased with unfinished sleep. He struggled to see through the daylight. "What the devil are you doing, you nasty little punk, tossing rocks all about at the crack of dawn. There's people sleeping here!"

His voice was familiar, but he didn't look like anyone I knew. He stumbled toward Lydia and Beanie, trying to shade his eyes from the low morning sun, while at the same time, finding the wound on his head and wiping the blood away.

Beanie tried to scream but only managed a weak, breathy, nightmare scream. She ran to her big brother's side, wrapping her body around him like a snake on a stick.

"Come back here you little devil, look what you did to my face. It's bleedin' like water from a spigot. Come here you mischievous imp!" The man shuffled past without seeing me so I left my rock. I didn't think I could single handedly save my friends, so in an attempted to save myself, I climbed onto a low branch of a nearby tree. Hidden in the dense leaves, I watched and listened.

Beanie, Paul, and Lydia were cloistered together on a big flat flagstone jetting out over the river. All eyes were plastered on the madman approaching them with a great determination for justice. Paul dropped his fishing pole and stepped in front of Beanie. Lydia huddled up behind Beanie acting like she was protecting Beanie, but hiding behind her just the same. There was nowhere to go but into the water.

They were trapped. The man worked his way toward them with an unsteady gait and a sour face.

"STOP!" hollered Lydia. "She didn't mean to hurt you! We were just skipping stones. No reason to be bullying a little girl!"

The man slowed down, but continued to walk toward them. He ran one hand through his hair and scratched his head. Lichen and leaves fell from the unkempt mass. The back seam of his overcoat was torn and the cuffs of his pants were crusty from mud. He wore one boot and one dress shoe, but you'd hardly know it because the dried sludge that covered them made them a matched pair. When he reached the place where the flagstone met the shore, he stopped, rubbed his face, then covered one eye and considered his prey.

"You can't skip stones on dry land you worthless vermin!" he yelled. His speech was sticky with the dry tongue of the morning after a bout with the bottle. He stooped to pick up a stone and straightened, grounded his feet, and straightened some more. Then he bobbed at the knees a few times, and hurled the stone out over the surface of the water, skipping it six times. He picked up another. "Stones only skip on the water," he lectured as he expertly slung the stone and skipped this one five times. "And if you had a brain in your head you would know that and not be out here throwing stones on innocent citizens trying to sleep off the night b'fore."

He bent down and scooped some water into his mouth, swished it around, then spit it out. The olders were still holding on to the younger as he stumbled up close to them.

"Look!" he bent his bloody forehead toward them, pointing to the wound and the blood dripping down the bridge of his nose, causing them to recoil in unison.

"She didn't know you were there. She's sorry!" Paul said in a defiant tone.

"Of course you didn't know I was there! No one knows I'm there, that's the beauty of it! You should be sorrier that

you have seen me at all, than sorry that you have impal
me!" He was loud now, a lecturer. "I am invisible to most ar
you are only able to see me because of your evil hearts ar
destructive ways!" Then he leaned in close to Beanie, "A Davi
you are not. Never try to slay a giant like me!" he said
pounding his chest once with his fist. Beanie shivered and hid
her face behind her brother.

The man was anything but a giant. He was barely five
foot six, had no apparent weapon, and proved himself more
and more a fool for harassing a little girl with a stone.

"I am going to let you off this time, under one
condition," he went on. "Tomorrow... at this time, you bring
me breakfast, served on linen with fine silver. Bring bread,
cheese, eggs, fruit and anything else you can get yer hands on.
Oh, and for certain, a bottle of whiskey. Bring me a good
bottle of Irish whiskey. Otherwise I will seek you out and
invade your dreams. You will never sleep soundly again." He
pointed his finger first at Paul. "You will never be free from
the fear that I will show up when you least expect it." Then the
finger moved to Beanie, "do you understand," then to Lydia,
"my request?"

"Yessir!" said the siblings. Paul, covered his nose from
the foul smell of rotting teeth and gut. The man backed away
and left the three clung together like magnets, vibrating in
fear.

"Don't be late!" he yelled, then fished into his pocket.
The children stepped back, not knowing what he might
produce. He laughed at their helplessness, pulled out a flat
bottle, and sucked the last drops of whiskey from it. Then he
sliced the bottle over the creek. It skipped once, floated for a
few seconds, and then sank.

As he turned to go, I got my first full glimpse of his
face. I slung my hand up to cover my mouth, fearful I might
scream or vomit. I lay still and quiet on the branch, dizzy from
my discovery. As he retreated back into the woods, I could

ssing to himself about nothing I could understand, snickering and growling.

soon as my father was out of sight, the three siblings running as fast as they could. They were heading to the tree where I was hiding, so I started my retreat ground. I looked back, hearing another set of running and saw my father, rambling after them at no great l. He was yelling, "give me yer money! Give me yer h, you spoiled brat!" Scared and shaking, I didn't know at to do, but I knew I needed to stop him and save my ends. So, at the moment he was passing under my tree, I vung down, still holding onto a branch, and kicked him flat n the chest. He fell on his back—his head the last thing to hit, making a hollow thud on the muddy ground. I hung there, astonished at my bravery, yet ashamed of my task. My father brought his hands to his head and moaned. He opened his eyes, blinked a few suspicious blinks, and let out another string of swearing I won't repeat. I released myself to the ground, and made a beeline for the forest path. Beanie, Paul and Lydia were waiting for me. We ran pell-mell without regard for deer droppings, thorns or thistles. I followed, not knowing if we were going the right way, fearful that my father might catch up with us again. We didn't speak at all until we dove back through the hedge and landed on the grass behind it, panting, coughing and shaking with adrenaline. I was mortified. They had no idea the forest bum was my father, but I was mortified. I curled up in a ball, and sobbed. I could not comprehend the tragic reality. That man looked and acted nothing like my father, but it was him, of that I was sure.

When she had caught her breath, Lydia said, "Nice move Carol, you knocked the wind so far out of that guy, he'll be lucky if he ever breathes again."

"Oh he'll breathe again alright, right down our necks unless we get busy and do what we're told!" said Paul. "That man's pure evil, I'm not puttin' nothin' past him."

"Think there's any truth to what he said?" said Lydia.

"I'm not gonna spend any time considerin'," said Paul. "We just gotta do what he said and be done. And you two stop yer sobbin'." He pointed to Beanie and me.

"I'm too scared to go back," said Beanie.

"I can't go back," I said.

"You belly-achin' babies better shut up!" he said. "You helped get us into this an' yer gonna help get us out."

"Well, we can't risk running into that crazy maniac again, so I say we take the stuff, but do it before the sun rises, just drop it off and get out of there," Lydia said. She ripped a piece of notebook paper from her sister's binder and tore it in half.

"Good idea," said Paul. "We'll give him the ol' hole-and-corner. Go in under the shroud of darkness."

"Pl-ease," said Lydia. "This isn't a Dick Tracy comic strip. This is real life, be serious!"

He looked his sister in the eyes. "I've never been more serious in my life."

"Alright then, stop using spy language so we can understand you," Lydia searched Beanies school bag and found a pencil. "We need to make a list."

Lydia drew a line down the middle of the page. "Carol, you think you can kype some silverware from Lena's? It has to look fancy and we don't have a full set that matches, plus it's all grey steal, nothin' shiny."

"Yeah. I think so, but he doesn't really need fancy. I don't think he's used to fancy...living out there in the wilderness and all."

Beanie spoke up once she could speak without sobbing. "He said fine silver."

"No, he said fine linen," said Paul.

"No, he said fine silver," I agreed with Beanie.

"Would you all just stop yer' bickerin'. Carol, bring silverware, whatever you can get. A fork, a knife and a spoon," said Lydia. "We'll bring the tablecloth, the cheese and bread. Carol you bring some eggs, hardboiled, and a couple a' apples. Okay?"

Paul snatched the paper out of Lydia's hands and reviewed both lists, "What about the liquor?"

"Dang!" huffed Lydia, "Where are we gonna get Whiskey? We're gonna have to steal it."

"No!" whined Beanie. "People who steal go to jail or hell!"

"I'll be in charge of the liquor," said Paul. "Just don't ask where I got it and you won't get the blame and go to jail *or* hell. Besides, only people who get caught go to jail, and I don't plan on getting caught. If I go to hell for stealing liquor, I guess I was on my way already," he snickered.

"I forgot your shoes," Beanie confessed to Lydia.

"Well we're not going back now, so you better be able to find the tree in the dark, 'cuz if you don't find em in the morning, we're both up a creek," said Lydia, this being the least of her worries right now.

Beanie started crying again.

"What's wrong now!" said Lydia, losing patience.

"It's all my fault. I threw the stone and I lost the shoes and now I am the reason for Paul going to jail, and I didn't even do anything bad on purpose!" Tears, snot, and sweat saturated her dusty cheeks. She picked up the front of her blouse and wiped her face with it. The blouse, now soiled and wet, gave her another thing to cry about.

Paul put his arm around his little sister. "Knock it off. I'm not going to jail, I'm just going to take a little of Mom's whiskey that she keeps for nights when she can't sleep. She gave me a swig of it when I broke my finger, so I know where she keeps it. No one's going to jail or hell. It's not all your fault, either. We're in this together, and after tomorrow, we never have to talk or think of it again. Okay?"

"Okay," said Beanie, feeling slightly comforted.

We couldn't go home yet, because it was only mid-morning and school got out at noon that day, so we lay on the grass, perfecting our plan, and playing "I'm thinking of," until we saw the first kid walk past. Then we headed home.

I don't know what it was like for Beanie, Paul and Lydia, but that was one of the longest afternoons of my life. Keeping secrets was still not a strong point for me. Lena and I made potato salad for dinner. I slipped three extra eggs in to boil so I'd have extra for my secret task. My mind was preoccupied with so many balls to juggle that I couldn't come up with an answer when Lena asked me how my day was. I just froze and looked at her, waiting for her to fill in the silence with her own answer. She asked me if something was the matter and I said no, that I hadn't slept well the night before, and maybe I'd need a little whiskey to help me sleep tonight. She just laughed and asked how I ever came up with the things I did.

I left to visit Mama at three o'clock. The whole way there I argued with myself about what to do with my secret. If I told Mama about ditching school, I would be punished, but I didn't know how badly. I was afraid she might say I couldn't go to Aunt Marion and Uncle Virg's house for the summer, and I was so ready for a change of scenery that I could not bear to hold up for even another week at Lena and Leonard's. I could tell her that I saw him after school, telling only half a lie, but didn't know if I even wanted to bring him up. She got short-tempered and irritable whenever we talked about Father. She seemed much happier not knowing anything about him at all. He didn't come to visit me, like he had promised. He never sent any money, like he had promised. Mama said I was better off without him for the time being, that maybe someday he would "kick in and face his responsibilities," but she didn't recommend holding my breath waiting for it. I didn't want to stir up grief, so I decided to keep the secret, finish the plan, and never lie again. I had lost my father because of lies, so I told myself I wasn't going to lie... unless she asked.

Mama had just woken up and was still lying in her bed when I knocked. I knew, because the door was locked.

"You're early," she said as she opened the door and put out her cheek for me to kiss.

Her hair was mushed down on both sides, and stood up on the top so it resembled a rooster's comb.

"School got out early today," I said. That wasn't a lie.

"Are you hungry?" she asked as she put her little tea kettle on the hot plate.

"No, just thirsty."

She got a Bubble-Up out of the tiny refrigerator under her desk and handed me the bottle and a bottle opener. I sat down on one of two chairs in the studio apartment, put the bottle between my legs and popped the top off. She held her hands out and I tossed the bottle opener to her across the small room.

"Let's take a walk down by the river and have a swim, wanna?" Mama said. She caught the bottle opener and put it back in the basket on the shelf.

"No!" I panicked, my heart beating in my ears. I shivered a little.

She turned around and looked at me with curious eyes, but didn't say anything.

"I already went down to the river today and it's too cold. The water is like ice." I wasn't lying.

"Oh. Who'd you go swimming with?" she asked.

"Um, we didn't actually swim, just splashed around a little. Beanie, Paul and Lydia," I said.

"Okay, well, that was my idea for the day, what do *you* want to do?" She was stirring sugar into her tea.

"We could go grocery shopping," I said. I had never said this before and it felt weird.

"Grocery shopping," Mama said, blowing the steam off her tea.

"Lena needs apples," I lied.

"All right then. To market to market to buy a fat pig..." She went into the bathroom, shut the door and came out a few minutes later, hair coiffed, lipstick on, and wearing a light blue blouse and a dark blue skirt. She walked across the room to her closet, reached into the inside pocket of her plaid blazer and pulled out a roll of bills. Mad money, she called it. She peeled off a five dollar bill, replaced the rest, and off we went.

We held hands as we walked. Mama asked me about my day and I said "boring." I asked her about her night and she said "Busy. Two injuries, one laboring mom and six cases of kids with whooping cough."

"Any head injuries?" I asked, immediately sorry that I had.

"Matter of fact yes," she said, looking down at me, "Why do you ask?"

"Umm, I know a guy who got hit in the head with a rock early this morning, on our way to school."

"My, my. No this young man stood up too fast and too tall under the tractor scoop and split his head wide open. Nineteen stitches. Head wounds sure do bleed though; usually bleeds worse than it really is. This guy was drenched all down his back — looked like mud splatters from not having fenders on a bike."

"Owee," I said, secretly relieved.

"He'll be all right," she said. Mama wasn't fazed by injuries.

As we turned on Water Street, we nearly crashed into Lydia and Paul who were coming from the opposite direction.

"Whoa!" said Mama. We stood face to face with my accomplices.

"Oh, sorry, Mrs. Carlson. Hi Carol." Lydia's voice was nervous and stiff.

"Hi guys, you're in a hurry. Where are you off to at such a pace?" Mama said just to be polite and make conversation.

"Oh, it's our umm, Aunt Mimi's birthday and we got her a table cloth at the resale store." Lydia fake-smiled and opened the bag for me to look in. "It's a little stained, but I thought that if the glasses and sil-ver, "(she reminded me of my responsibility like she was talking to a hard-of-hearing old person)"are set just so, no one will ever see them."

"How sweet and thrifty of you," Mama admired.

"Yep, that's what Lydia and Paul are," I added, "thrifty and sweet."

"So...see ya in the morning, Carol, bright and early!" Paul said as they attempted to slip around us.

But Mama kept the conversation going "Carol said the river was freezing cold today, too bad, but that was nice of you to take her down there with you."

They froze, went sheet-white, and both looked at me, questions in their eyes.

I said, "Maybe we can try again tomorrow after school. We have early release again, right?"

"Uh, sure. Tomorrow. See ya." Lydia grabbed Paul by the hand and they sailed around us like a kite and its tail.

"Lydia seems nervous," Mama noticed.

"She's not a good swimmer," I lied again.

"Oh." Mama frowned.

We walked down the baking aisle of the grocery store to the produce section. I grabbed a paper bag and put three red apples into it.

"What is Lena making with the apples?" Mama asked.

"Pie," I lied. It was the first thing I could think of.

"Well, she'll need more than three apples, and will probably want green ones." Mama took the bag.

I knew that Father didn't like green apples. I also didn't want to have to carry too many apples back to Lena and Leonard's house.

"Sweet apple and berry pie," I said. I couldn't believe I'd just said that. I was becoming an expert liar and felt myself digging a ditch deeper than I might be able to crawl out of, but I went on, "she has the berries, just needs three red apples."

"That sounds good, I'll have to get the recipe from her," Mama seemed amused.

"I'll get it for you." I was going to need a crane or a miracle to see me out of this.

"All right then, what else do we need?" Mama said, looking at the lettuce assortment.

"Can we get some peanuts?" I asked. Father loved salted peanuts in the shell.

"You must need some salt in your diet." Peanuts made Mama think of Father, I'm sure.

I did my best to control the conversation on the way home. I was feeling guilty, but also the littlest bit clever about pulling it off.

"I'm ready for summer," I said.

"Only one more day of school," Mama said.

"Yeah! I can't wait to go to Uncle Virg and Aunt Marion's. I think Lena is getting tired of me," I said.

"Oh? Why's that?" Mama looked surprised.

"Oh, I don't know. Maybe it's me getting tired of her." That was the honest truth.

"Well, I know Aunt Marion and Uncle Virg love having you. Hang on, summer's a coming," she smiled and squeezed my hand.

***

I made it back from visiting with Mama by five-thirty, as expected. On the way, I didn't step on any sidewalk cracks and counted twenty-seven cars. I told Lena that the apples were for my three favorite teachers and asked her if I could have the extra hard-boiled eggs in my lunch tomorrow. She believed and accommodated me. After dinner I took my plate to the sink and shoved my silverware in the waistband of my skirt. Leonard challenged me to a game of Mille Bornes and I felt the stabs of deception every time I moved, until I had the genius to excuse myself to my bedroom for a moment. I deposited the utensils in the top drawer of my desk, where my personal and private things were kept, right next to my hairbrush.

That night I set my alarm clock for five A.M. I put it under my blankets with me to muffle the sound, so it wouldn't wake Lena too early and cause suspicion. The moon shone in through my bedroom window and brought just enough light for me to read the clock. I had a hard time falling asleep. My heart was burbling in my chest every so often and woke me with a bad case of the death pains. I saw twelve o'clock, one o'clock and two o'clock come and go. Somewhere after two I drifted off for a while and woke to the alarm with a start. There could be trouble ahead if everything didn't go just as planned, and I couldn't be sure of success anyway with so many people needing to cooperate, and so many ways the plan could fail.

I had slept in my clothes to make my exit swifter. I brushed my hair, didn't bother brushing my teeth, grabbed the silverware, then went to the kitchen to get my lunch and the apples. My lunch sack was sitting on the counter. On it, Leonard had sketched a cartoon of a girl walking to school, books in hand, and little music notes floating up from her puckered mouth like she was whistling. A big, happy, sunshine face smiled down from the sky. This little girl wasn't me. She didn't have a care in the world. I could only slightly remember how that felt. I grabbed the sack, stuck everything in a large flannel shopping bag, and quietly slipped out the kitchen door. Beanie, Paul, and Lydia were nowhere in sight. We hadn't really talked about where to meet. If it was a normal school day I'd wait on the sidewalk like any normal person would do. But today I couldn't even stand on the side walk in front of my own house for fear of being seen where and when I shouldn't. I walked up the street toward their house, better to look like I knew what I was doing than stand around like a vagrant. I stopped at the corner, and saw them coming, single file, in silence. No one spoke until we were two blocks away.

Lydia came up alongside of me, "did you bring all your stuff?"

"Uh-huh. Silverware, three apples, two hard-boiled eggs and some peanuts. I said quietly.

"Peanuts?" she furrowed her brow, "for who?"

"For him."

"The bum? Look, we're not on a goodwill mission to the guy who threatened to ruin our lives, we're just trying to give him what we need to, to get him off our backs," she scolded.

"I know. I just thought he might like some peanuts," I said.

She let out a big sigh, "I'm hungry, give me some."

I handed over the paper sack of peanuts and she took a handful and passed the bag to Paul. When he and Lydia had taken their share, the bag was half gone. I ate a few and tossed the leftovers back into my flannel bag. He wouldn't miss what he wasn't expecting.

The trail was a little more familiar to us this time, but the going was made more difficult by the dark and the shroud of uncertainty that enveloped us.

"I sure don't want to have another run in with that maniac," Paul thought out loud while he dodged branches and searched for the deer trail.

"When we get there, just drop the stuff on the rock, and I'll set it up while you guys go upriver and wait," Lydia said.

"This guy's a freak," complained Paul, "silverware and linen for a guy who sleeps in the forest, for cryin' out loud. I'm getting madder and madder at myself for even doin' what he asked."

"I want to help set it up," I said.

"What for, you want to get your neck broke?" said Paul. "I'm sure as hell not volunteering." He was even starting to talk like a criminal.

"I just want to," I said. I didn't even know why. Maybe I actually wanted to see that things were done right. Maybe I wanted to make my dad feel taken care of. I felt sorry for him. I'd heard Mama say it a million times, "two wrongs don't make a right."

We arrived just as the birds were starting to wake up. They were so noisy; I worried that they might wake my father. We worked quickly and quietly, then stood back and checked our work. The white tablecloth was laid out on the rock where they had been standing the day before. I placed the silverware all in the right locations, fork on the left, knife and spoon on the right. I lined up the three apples between the utensils and poured the remaining peanuts alongside them. Lydia had brought her supplies in a shoe box. She looked at my apple and peanut arrangement and rolled her eyes. She scooped up the peanuts and slowly sifted them into the shoebox, covered it again and rolled the apples up in a corner of the tablecloth.

"Squirrels," she whispered.

Lydia turned to go and motioned for me to follow her. I nodded, but before I left I slipped my baby ring off of my pinky finger and laid it where the apples had been. My very last lie would be about where it went.

***

Lydia and Paul decided to go back to school that day because it was field day and all we had to do was play Red-Rover and Whip-Lash, and turn in our books. Some of the mothers would bring cookies and lemonade and then we'd get out early so the eighth graders could practice for graduation. Beanie and I gladly followed their lead. I was comforted, knowing I was where I should be. We got there before the bell, but I went into the classroom anyway and found Miss Thurber, cleaning out her desk.

"Good morning, Carol, how are you feeling this morning?" she said, looking up from her task only momentarily.

"Good," I said as I bounced into the room, the heaviness already lifting from my corrupt past.

"Did you bring a note from your mother or Lena?" she asked, still sifting through a drawer full of confiscated nick-knacks, bent paper clips and eraser dust.

"No, I forgot." My stomach got tight.

"That's all right, just go to the office and they can call Lena and make you a re-entry slip," she said, as if it was the simplest request in the world.

I left the room without a word, walked down the hall, past the office and out the door to the playground. I was tired from the restless night before and now I was feeling the kind of exhaustion that comes from keeping invisible ducks in a row. I lay down under the canopy of a big tree, behind the wooden backstop, and looked up at the clouds moving slowly in and out of my line of vision.

The school bell brought me back from a daydream and a hundred kids, ages six through thirteen, were running toward me. I melted into the bustle of activity and never did get a chance to present Miss Thurber with even a bogus note. School got out that noon and I went home thinking I had gotten away with it. Exhausted, I climbed the steps to the front porch and met Leonard standing behind the screen door. He opened the door and stepped aside. The look on his face was stern. As I passed he said matter-of-factly and with very little emotion, "you weren't at school yesterday, and left early this morning. What's the deal?"

My heart sank for the twentieth time that day. I was done for. I dropped my heavy book bag like it contained my burden of dishonesty. Then I pulled out one of the ladder-back dining room chairs, sat down, and buried my face in my folded arms. I couldn't face Leonard. I didn't want to lie to him, but I couldn't tell him the truth either—or could I? If I could tell anyone the truth, it was Leonard. He sat down in a chair across from me and waited silently. When I finally lifted my head he was cleaning the jam out from under his fingernails with his pocket knife. His feet were propped up on another chair. He spoke without looking at me.

"You've been telling some stories lately, as kids your age will do. Lena and I have been patient and discerning as to what to do about it, but Carol, you gave us a real scare this morning when you weren't in bed when I came to wake you up." His voice was controlled, but melancholy, revealing his disappointment. "I went down to Lydia's house to see if you had gone over there, and they were gone too. I have to say that fact was of some comfort to me, as it looked like mischief among comrades rather than tragedy. So as not to scare your mother to an early grave, I have not called her yet. I made sure you were at school this morning before I took any drastic measures. And good thing you were, because they were waiting for you. How did the teachers like their apples?" he paused.

My tired mind roamed around looking for a way out, but it couldn't find one. "The apples weren't for my teachers," I confessed.

"Mmm hmm," He stopped cleaning his nails and looked at me. "Are you all right?"

"Yes."

"Then, let's have it." He took his pipe out of his pocket, packed it with tobacco, walked into the kitchen for a match and scraped it on his knife. He slowly passed the flame over his pipe, threw the match at the wood stove, then sat down to listen.

I told him the entire story from the front. He listened quietly, puffing on his pipe, mostly looking at the floor, or his boots, but occasionally looking at me with understanding eyes. I didn't spare any detail. I even told him about leaving my ring. His head continued to nod long after my story was told, as I anxiously awaited his verdict.

"It's not easy sneaking around with a bushel of lies on your back, is it?" he said.

"No sir," I said

"You feel better now?"

"Yes, I think so." I was wondering how I would feel once I was presented with my punishment.

"You need to get Lena's silverware back." He got up and laid his pipe in the ceramic bowl on the table, tapping the embers out. "Let's go."

I led the way. The fear and anticipation of seeing my father added weight to my steps. I had clearly wanted him to know I had been there, but I didn't want to face him. We found the river, and approached the very spot where we had laid the breakfast. The shoe box with all the food and little Mason jar of whiskey were gone. The tablecloth lay on the rock, folded in a triangle like an American flag, with the silverware tucked into the final fold. Leonard bent down and picked it up and started back toward the shore. A shiny spot on the rock caught my eye; my father's wedding ring. I didn't think Leonard had seen it, so I bent down, picked it up, and slipped it on to my thumb where it was still too big.

"Fair trade," Leonard said, over his shoulder. We walked home single file, Leonard leading, through the woods, and then hand-in-hand once we reached the sidewalk.

19

Leonard told Mama as much as was needed to explain the letters from school and the scratch on my forehead. He told Lena everything and Lena, poor thing, had a tender heart that fretted over the folly of others. It seems my folly put her over the edge and she went straight to bed for a week. She was sick in the morning, sick when she smelled meat cooking, sick if she ate and sick if she didn't eat. Only thing that kept her alive was seltzer water and sucking on popped corn, one piece at a time. She said that for all of this to happen on her watch was proof, in her eyes, that she would never be a fit mother and that's why the Lord had kept her childless. I knew this was hogwash.

Leonard did indeed get a job offer from General Mills in Minneapolis, Minnesota. They would be leaving July 3rd, and told Mama I was welcome to stay until then. We already had it planned that I would again, stay with Aunt Marion and Uncle Virg for the summer, so Lena and Leonard were off the hook. It was hard to leave them. I'd never lived away from them. They were there when Mama and Uncle Virg brought me home from the hospital. I was off to Greenwood for the summer, just like any other summer, except this time I wasn't coming back.

What with the business of my father at the river, and the sadness I felt for making Lena so sick, I couldn't help feeling that I helped them to make the decision to leave Tower Street. As was our habit on Saturday nights, Leonard came in to read to me from the Saturday Evening Post.

Before he began reading he said, "Carol, I took that job a month ago. We just wanted to make sure it went through before we told you and your mother. You didn't do anything to help, or not help us make our decision."

"Well, I'm sorry about making Lena sick and upset."

"Lena's not upset about you. In fact, Lena's not upset at all, her system is," he said. Then he opened up to an article: "Signs and symptoms of pregnancy," he read.

It included, but was not limited to tiredness, an aversion to certain foods, nausea, vomiting, irritability, and short-temperateness. Then he looked at me.

"What do you think, Carol?" he said.

I sat up wide eyed and hopeful, "I think Lena's gonna have a baby!" I said.

Lena peeked her head around the corner of the door. "Me too," she said, grinning from ear to ear. She came over and sat on the end of my bed.

I got out from my covers and leaned over to give her a hug. "Now you won't miss me so much," I said.

"Oh, but I will," she said. "I'm going to miss you a lot, Carol."

"I'll miss you too."

"We'll write letters to keep in touch. No more skipping school, Okay?"

"Okay," I said, smiling just a little.

She got up to leave, took the Saturday Evening Post from Leonard, and handed him a book to read instead.

"*The Birds' Christmas Carol.* Should I read this?" he said.

"Yes," I said.

I blamed all of my tears on the book, not my circumstances. I didn't want to find another place to live. If I couldn't be with my mother full-time, I guess I'd just as well stay with Lena and Leonard, but this was not to be. I would miss Lena, my surrogate mother, my tutor, and my cooking teacher. I would miss her familiar ways. But I was heartsick about losing my personal chauffeur, my fix-it man, my employer, my confidant, and my friend. I'd miss Leonard the most.

Part Two

September, 1941

1

As the country was crawling up out of the valley of the Great Depression, an unstoppable boulder was rolling down. In the early stages, World War Two inspired patriotic songs and high spirits. Big brothers and dads went off to war with hope and gallantry, but war reels and newspapers, acting as our eyes and ears, reported pain and devastation that letters from soldiers would purposely never convey. I wasn't sure if my father was off fighting in the war, as I hadn't heard from or of him since the events down by the river. I assumed he was still down there, skipping stones and strangling the last drop from a whiskey bottle.

After Lena and Leonard deemed it necessary for me to move on, Grandpa Hussey begged Mama to let me live with them. Grandpa and Grandma Hussey had enough room, enough money and enough patience to raise one more girl. Those were his words. Mama said no, on account of him living twelve miles away. She wanted me close so we could see each other most days. So he suggested that Mama inquire with a woman who was an acquaintance of theirs through the garden club. She took in boarders and lived less than a mile from the hospital. The schools would be the same, and I could continue to see my mother after school every day as had been our routine. Before I had a say about a single thing, it was decided that when I returned from my stay with Aunt Marion and Uncle Virg that summer, I would move in with the Lindermans. My quiet minimalist life with Lena and Leonard Harrison was over, and I entered into my own impending war — life with Ruth Linderman.

Mrs. Linderman's father had been a successful trade lawyer and the Mayor of Jamestown in the late twenties. He'd taken all of his money out of the stock market exactly one year, to the day, before Black Tuesday and spent much of his fortune building the house. I learned all of this as Grandpa gossiped openly about the Lindermans during the drive over to their home. He credited Ruth Linderman with the brightest tulips, the tidiest hedgerows, the most stoic iris, and practically perfect pansies. He said she had inherited her father's love of prudent excess, comparative perfection, and prideful discipline; all this to say, I guessed they were rich and snobby.

The Linderman home was a large, brick, six bedroom Georgian Colonial. It had two stories, plus an attic, and a cellar. When Grandpa pulled up in front of the house, I thought he must be kidding. I had passed this house hundreds of times on our way to church or on my bike, if I took the downhill route to the hospital. I'd felt a certain respect for its pillared grandness and multi-paned windows. In my most far fetched fantasy, I never expected to live in a mansion like this. Not now, when some of the boys at school were wearing second generation hand-me-down shoes, re-soled with old cut-up felt hats or Hoover leather (which was nothing more than cardboard used to line a shoe with the sole worn through). Not now, when I had purposely ignored the embarrassed smile of Mrs. Nigren, shivering in the freezing wind outside the grange hall. She and many others waited in line for a brick of cheese, a pound of rice, and a slab of lard. I was a lucky girl. Life in a mansion was very appealing to me. Considering my good fortune, I made an internal vow to aim all of my efforts at being as gracious to the poor as Jane Austen's Emma Woodhouse, and as helpful to the lame as Eleanor Roosevelt.

Grandpa parked on the street. I didn't usually wait to have the car door opened for me, but hesitated this morning, considering my new position at the mansion. Would the neighbor, who was looking out the window, think me less of a lady if I came spilling out of the car without the help of my driver? I sat as Grandpa scooted his ample body out from behind the wheel. When he spied me, still sitting with my hands folded, he hollered, "scooch over to the other side, Peach. There's a puddle in the road here!"

I lifted my legs up and around Jessie's baby buggy, opened my own door, and humbly climbed down off my high horse. We walked up the brick pathway past the perfectly squared hedgerows and masses of yellow marigolds. At the Tower Street house, the brick path was laid in dirt. Mossy, green fuzz grew in between and onto the bricks. Here the bricks were set in grout and not a speck of dirt, or even a leaf, littered the way. There were no steps to the porch, just a gentle incline that rose slowly to the front of the house, perfect for a head start on roller skates. The tall, white front door had a row of seven little windows climbing up each side. As soon as we reached the front porch, I was pretty sure this was the right place for me. If the well-appointed garden was any reflection of the indoors, life here was going to be a routine of orderliness in large areas of uncluttered space. I would surely have a beautiful room, maybe even a handmaiden, a brush and mirror set waiting on the vanity, and my own pair of monogrammed towels hanging on the golden towel bar. I had seen a few movies featuring houses like this, and the little girls that grew up in them were usually spoiled and bratty. I made a pact with myself right then and there to never be a brat, but to hold on to the memory of the hard times of my humble childhood and be a gracious and grateful resident. Grandpa Hussey rang the doorbell, which only made two chimes. As I waited for the butler to answer the door, I smoothed my bangs and looked up at Mama with an approving smile. To my surprise, a woman greeted us.

"Hello George, this must be Carol." She bent down a bit and took my hand in both of hers. She felt cold and bony, a bit fragile, so I didn't squeeze her hand very hard. "I'm so pleased to meet you, do come in."

We walked in and stepped onto a wide expanse of black and white floor tiles, arranged like a huge checker board. The tiles were laid in such a way that they looked like diamonds, rather than squares, as you entered. This was a relief for me, as it made it easier for me to avoid stepping on any cracks.

"Ruth, you know my daughter Virginia," said Grandpa, putting his hand on Mama's back.

"Virginia," Mrs. Linderman held out her hand and they shook, "so nice to see you again. I'm sure that we will get to know each other much better. My hope is that you will always feel as welcome in our home as your daughter does."

"Thank you, Mrs. Linderman," said Mama.

"Please, call me Ruth," she said as she directed us into the parlor off to the right, "and Carol, you may call me Aunt Ruth." Her voice was nasally and slow. When she said my name it stretched out for both syllables and hung on the 'l'. Mama would say her speech was syrupy.

Mama and Grandpa walked across the entryway paying no attention to how many cracks they stepped on. Aunt Ruth avoided every crack between the tiles without even looking.

She invited us to sit down, and we did; Mama and I on a firm, brown, camel-back settee and Grandpa in a floral overstuffed chair. As we waited for Aunt Ruth to sit down, I observed her. She was very tall, nearly as tall as Grandpa, and thin. She was older than Mama, but younger than Grandpa, I think. She wore a ruffled-collar blouse that clung tight to her neck. Her dark brown hair was braided in two braids that each wrapped up over her head and over to the other side, then tucked under each other. It resembled a plaited crown. I wondered if she could yodel, it just looked like a yodeling hairdo. She wore no lipstick on her tiny puckered lips and her face was mostly beige. Pinned to the front of her blouse, just at the base of her neck, was a pretty, light brown and white, oval brooch with a carving of a lady that looked a lot like her. As she sat, she smoothed her black skirt along her hips, and settled, just barely, on the edge of a wooden ladder-back chair with a cane seat. It appeared she didn't want to wrinkle her carefully ironed pleats. I assumed these were her Sunday clothes, as they were so neat and tidy and churchy. If she had been wearing white gloves, they would not have looked out of place.

The grownups talked in polite murmurs as I surveyed my surroundings. I took particular notice of the things artfully arranged on the coffee table in front of me. There was a china tea cup and saucer, set in a special glass coaster that held the plate straight up so you could see the hand-painted roses. I reached out to pick up a small frame that held a coin set in black velvet, but Mrs. Linderman stopped my hand with one finger and asked, "So Carol, what do you like to do outside of school? Are you musical?"

"I like to play piano," I said, as I glanced at the baby grand I had noticed in the adjoining room.

"Oh lovely, so do I," she said as she brought her delicate hands up to prayer position.

"Except I only play by ear and it sometimes takes me a little while to figure out a song, but I really want to learn some of the songs from Funny Face. I love all those songs. Mama and I sing them all the time and we know all the words—but how fun it would be to sing them with the piano," I rambled.

"Funny Face," she repeated.

"It's a play we saw at Chautauqua." Mama saved me with her reference to the Institute.

"How nice for you," she said, the words sliding down her nose. "I should like to help you learn to read music, if it interests you."

"Bet yer life!" I said, smiling up at Mama. I immediately covered my mouth to stop any other unplanned outburst.

"Yes, well." Aunt Ruth smoothed her already perfect skirt.

After that short exchange, it felt as if I were an outsider to the rest of the conversation.

"I hear this house was your father's," Mama said.

"Yes, dear man, may he rest in eternal peace." She laid her palm on her chest and looked up to the ceiling. "He loved his God, his family, and his country, in that order, and without question," she said. She pulled a white folded handkerchief out of her cuff and wrapped it around her finger, brought it to the corner of her eye, refolded it, and sniffed.

"I am sorry for your loss," Mama said, "how long has he been gone?"

"Two years. I am only now able to say his name, or the title of Mayor for that matter, without seeking the respite of a reclining position and a sip of medicinal brandy." She sat back in her chair and looked out the window.

Grandpa skillfully interjected, "Your father, Robert Cooper, was one of the most upstanding men I have ever met: a leader and a gentleman. It's a tribute to him, Ruth, that you keep this house in such impeccable order and offer it up as a refuge for others in need."

This steered Mrs. Linderman back on track, "Thank you, George. He is truly missed in this home and in the community at large, if I may be so bold as to speak for the community at large. Would you like to see the rest of the house and grounds?" she offered, rising from her perch and shifting gears.

I opened my mouth and took a deep breath, then stopped myself from another "Bet yer life!" outburst.

"Of course," said Mama. She took my hand and squeezed it, knowingly.

Aunt Ruth led the way with her long pointy nose. Grandpa followed her directly while Mama and I followed, hand-in-hand, not far behind. We first entered the room with the piano. Aunt Ruth stopped, once we had all entered. A shiny brass tuba rested on a wooden stand in the corner. A display of nine fifes rose up the wall between two doors, and four chairs were grouped in the middle of the room, each equipped with a music stand in front of it.

"This is the music room of course. On Tuesday and Thursday mornings, you will hear the civic string quartet practicing here. I give piano lessons to only three students, and they are all on Thursday afternoon. As a young man, my father belonged to the fife and drum corps. The fifes were his," she explained as she circled around the room pointing out objects of interest.

I reached up to feel the glossy-black surface of the piano. The top was down and the keys were covered. Mrs. Linderman directed us out the door to the next room. As I looked back to see which way we should go, I saw Aunt Ruth polishing the piano where my fingers had touched. She joined us back in the large entryway and slipped her multi-purposed handkerchief back up her cuff. Then she led us across the entryway to the other side of the house, and pointed out a set of double doors on the way.

"These are our private sleeping quarters." She paused, but didn't open the doors. "Mr. Linderman is an invalid and unable to climb the stairs." She used the word "invalid" with little emotion, as if she were telling us that he was a banker, or had brown eyes.

Next we entered a very large dining room with a massive table and ten chairs tucked up around it. A cabinet with lots of drawers and cupboards was built right into the wall. Through the beveled and leaded glass doors I counted twelve big plates, twelve little plates, twelve bowls, twelve water goblets, twelve saucers, and eleven tea cups. I counted again, eleven tea cups. I hoped it was being used and hadn't been broken.

As I stood counting and trying to come up with a reasonable scenario for the missing cup, I was startled back in line with the tour.

"Carol. Carol, this way, dear." Mrs. Linderman was holding the kitchen door open with her fragile frame. Mama and Grandpa were in the kitchen beyond. "Come along dear, don't dilly-dally." Her smile was forced.

We took a turn around the newly refurbished kitchen. Mrs. Linderman introduced the stove and other new kitchen furnishings as if they were friends at a luncheon, gently caressing their cold surfaces with her brittle fingers. I liked the kitchen the best so far. Even though it was equipped with the most modern conveniences, it was more like a real house than the rest of the rooms. It felt warm and inviting. The wood table that filled the center of the room was stained, rutted and worn. A few of the cabinet doors had wear marks around the knobs. The floor was soft pine and made a comforting echo from Grandpa's heavy-soled shoes, like at the hardware store. At the back of the kitchen, an open larder revealed rows and rows of colorful jars. I recognized peaches, corn, green beans, and a dark red preserve of some kind. A pickle barrel sat on the floor in the corner. There was plenty of everything. We circled around the back of the kitchen and I craned my neck to see out to the screened porch. Aunt Ruth gave my shoulder a gentle, guiding pressure, encouraging me to move along.

"I won't bore you with the more utilitarian rooms of the house," she said, "shall we go upstairs?"

We followed her back out to the giant checkerboard and ascended to the second floor.

The stairway was curved and ornate with a stately banister and shiny, dark mahogany steps. Each step had two white, spiral spindles holding up a wide handrail. It made me think of the big wooden slide in the school yard. I wondered how wax paper would work on that railing.

Aunt Ruth talked over her shoulder as we climbed the stairs; "All the other bedrooms are on the second floor. Miss

Platts rents the East room. She teaches at Jamestown High School, and Mr. Danielson lives at the other end of the hall. He is starting as a resident at the hospital this week."

"Mr. Danielson?" asked Mama.

"Yes, Michael Danielson, do you know him?" said Aunt Ruth.

"I know a Michael Danielson, but I'm not sure it's the same person. I wasn't aware he was in medical school," said Mama.

"He's a lovely man. If he's in I'll introduce you," said Aunt Ruth.

I counted sixteen stairs to the top. We turned left at the landing and walked along a series of fringed, oriental rugs until we reached a door at the end of the hallway. Aunt Ruth reached in her pocket and pulled out a red ribbon tied to two identical skeleton keys. She unlocked the door without opening it and stepped back.

"Would you like to show your mother and your grandfather your new room?" she said as she gracefully retreated to the back of the line.

I turned the white marble doorknob and slowly opened the door to my lodgings. A flush of goose bumps rose up my back as I took in the first impression of the room. It smelled strongly of fresh mint. The first thing that caught my eye was the bed. It had an eighteen inch organza ruffle draping down from the canopy frame above. The mattress itself was covered in a white comforter so filled with down that the throw pillows looked like little pink pebbles sunk halfway in snow. A white eyelet bed skirt dressed the bottom half of the bed all the way to the dark mahogany wood floor. I entered the room and slowly approached the bed. The top of the mattress was right at my hips.

"This may be necessary," Aunt Ruth brought over a two- tiered stool and set it next to the bed, motioning for me to use it."

I tiptoed up to the second step, trying very hard to move as daintily as this room deserved. Then I turned around and lifted my bottom up to the fluffiness of the duvet, and sunk all the way to my waist in the loft.

"Carol, I'm not sure about this," Mama said lifting herself up onto the bed beside me, "I think this was supposed to be my room. How about we trade and you live at the hospital?"

She smiled and put her arm around me, and when our eyes met, they agreed that I was certainly the most fortunate girl on the planet.

"This will be your desk, and your bureau. This half of the closet is all yours, the other half I use to store out of season clothing for Mr. Linderman and myself," Aunt Ruth explained as she walked around the room, "The bathroom is shared between the upstairs bedrooms, so we will get a morning routine figured out as soon as everyone is sure of their schedules. I suggest evening bathing for you, Carol, as I know that Miss Platts is a morning bather. There is a more rustic toilet out in back of the barn, if you have urgent need and the lavatory is occupied."

I could not imagine myself having any urgent need while being a resident of this lavish estate.

After the tour of my room, Grandpa went out to the car to retrieve my suitcase and my few other belongings. When he returned, laden with all my worldly possessions, a familiar face followed him into the room carrying Jesse in her buggy.

"Mr. Danielson, so good of you to help Carol with her things," said Mrs. Linderman.

Mama and I stared at him in realization that this *was* the same Mr. Danielson that had worked at the Athenaeum. He carefully set the baby buggy down in the corner of the room, and then looked up, not expecting to see anyone he knew, and immediately locked eyes with Mama.

"Virginia?" he said, "land sakes alive in Mississippi on a Monday! What are you doing here?"

"Why, Mr. Danielson," Mama blushed.

She held out her hand to shake his. He took her hand in both of his and continued to look into her eyes.

"Are you going to be living here?" he asked.

"No, no, no, Carol, my daughter is going to be staying here. I still live at the nurse's residence." Mama released her hand from his firm grip and guided me in front of her, between the two of them.

"Yes, I remember," he stammered a bit, "I didn't remember, I mean I remembered, but I forgot which hospital it was and well, it's been awhile. Wow, it's good to see you"

"I had no idea you were in training to be a doctor," Mama said.

"No? Well I am, I only worked at the hotel during the summers while I was at the University," he said.

"Oh," said Mama. She looked around the room and realized we were all watching and listening to their conversation. "I'm sorry, Father, this is Michael Danielson. Michael, my father George Hussey." They shook hands and smiled, "and you remember my daughter, Carol."

"Of course, nice to see you again, Carol. Guess we'll be house mates." He smiled at me. His light blue eyes smiled too.

Aunt Ruth interrupted, "The world gets increasingly smaller every day!" She had been standing, watching the exchange with her arms folded and her lips scrunched to the side, biting the inside of her bottom lip. Our happy reunion had taken some of the wind out of her sails of introduction.

"Delightfully small," said Mr. Danielson, "I look forward to seeing you later—probably sooner than later, actually. Are you working tonight Virginia?"

"No, not until Monday night. I usually have weekends off to be with Carol," she explained.

"Good then, see you Monday. I'm on 2-West for my first month." He backed out of the room, spun around with a flair, and headed down the hall to his room.

His absence left a quiet lull. I walked over to examine Jessie, lifted her out of her buggy and brought her back to the bed, resting her against a pillow like she was a display at a toy store. Mama went over to have a look out the window.

Aunt Ruth broke the silence. "I'll leave you to help Carol get settled and when you're ready, come to the parlor and we will see to the final arrangements and signatures."

When she was gone Mama closed the door, leaned her back against it, and released a big sigh. Grandpa sat down on the sun-soaked window seat. He rested both elbows on his knees, and winked at me with a nod of fruition.

"I think I'm going to like it here," I said as I unlatched my suitcase.

"I'm glad," Grandpa said, "Mrs. Linderman is a very nice woman. I still say you could come and live with us, but your mother likes the idea of having you closer."

"Carol will do famously here, Dad, and we'll come to your house for visits on weekends," Mama assured him.

"Make sure you help Mrs. Linderman around the house," Grandpa instructed. "She expects you to pull your weight."

"I will, Grandpa." I smiled, knowing he was just kidding.

I had no idea.

2

After Mama and Grandpa left, Aunt Ruth and I had tea from a real tea cart in the china tea cups from the dining room. We ate brown bread with butter and little raisin cakes. I offered to help clean up but she said no, that I could go get used to my lodgings and explore out in the garden, but to be down to dinner at precisely six o'clock. As I stood up to go, she stopped me in her fragile grasp, and looked me in the eyes.

"Stay on the property, and don't go past the hedge. Do not go into the mint field or anywhere near the house in the middle of it. Never, ever. Mind what I say, and don't ask questions. This is for your own protection!" she said, squeezing my shoulders for emphasis.

She might as well have challenged me to a game of truth or dare.

I went outside to look around. The arborvitae hedge separated us from the mint field and the "house of the knowledge of good and evil". A brown cow stared at me from a stick-made, fenced-in area. I squelched my desire to investigate the forbidden house for the time being, and went straight up to my room and set my alarm for five-fifty-five, so I would be sure to be on time. I read for a while, re-organized my dresser drawers, alphabetized my books on the shelf above the desk, and then sat on the window seat with Jesse. I opened the double hung window to the minty breeze and sensed the dawn of new adventure. I was excited, but I felt lonely. I wondered what Lena and Leonard were doing. I thought about my mother, alone in her room. Out the window, I watched the little white house. It was about a quarter mile away and all that separated us was the mint field and the hedge. A cloud of dust followed a tractor that was turning the rows that had recently been harvested. The smell was delightful and refreshing. I wasn't really hungry for dinner, having had two raisin cakes with my tea. I reminded myself to be more reserved at tea time in the future. I was thinking about chocolate mint ice cream when my alarm went off and nearly catapulted me out the window. Along with my alarm came three brisk knocks on my door.

"Dinner in five minutes," Aunt Ruth reminded in a high, hilly, sing-song voice.

I sprung up to turn off my alarm, then stopped in the bathroom to wash up before going downstairs. I was still wearing my blue cotton play dress, and thought it looked fine in spite of the faded line that revealed the fact that the hem was taken out to make the dress grow with me. Seems I was getting taller, but not fatter. The dress was still above my knees, but the only place it was truly tattered was at the sleeve where it was coming apart a little at the seam. I didn't think it mattered so I descended the stairs, checking the slipperiness of the handrail on the way down. Pretty slippery.

Miss Platts, the other boarder, was there, but Mr. Danielson was not. I was sorry he was absent, as I had gained a considerable amount of confidence thinking there would be someone present that I knew, even remotely. I paused at the archway to the dining room. Mr. Linderman was seated at the head of the table.

"Enter child," he commanded and motioned from the far side of the room. "No need to be timid, you will sit here to my left."

Miss Platts stood up and gestured to the seat to her right. I found it strange that Mr. Linderman didn't stand up, until I saw the wheels on his chair and remembered he was "an invalid". He held one arm out to the side and made a circular motion toward me.

"Take a spin 'round, let's have a look at you!" he said in a British accent.

I felt like a dog in the circus. I turned around, worried that the torn seam would show. Then I slid silently into my seat.

"Ruth! Bring double portions for this one," he hollered in the direction of the closed kitchen door, "she looks as if a slight breeze might blow her out the window!" He chuckled at his joke.

I thought how true he was, remembering how close I had come to being blown out the window from the buzz of the alarm clock.

Aunt Ruth entered through the swinging door carrying a bowl in two pot holders. She was followed by a small, brown, young woman. Her hair was twisted into a very long braid down her back. She set a steamy bowl of rice on the table.

"Basi, bring the meatloaf, then you may go and I'll see you tomorrow," Aunt Ruth said.

Basi disappeared through the doorway, gracefully reappearing on the third swing of the door, with a plate of sliced meatloaf and onions. She offered the plate to Mr. Linderman. He took a big helping with plenty of onions. Then she walked around the back of Mr. Linderman and offered the plate to Aunt Ruth.

"Thank you Basi, we can manage from here," Aunt Ruth took the plate from her.

"Tank you," Basi said, smiling.

"Thank you, see you tomorrow," Aunt Ruth said again, emphasizing the "th" sound in thank.

"Tank you," repeated Basi as she backed away from the table with tiny steps and glided out through the kitchen door again saying "Tank you," and nodding her head.

I wasn't sure if she knew I was there. She never even looked at me. She never looked any of us in the eyes.

Aunt Ruth handed the plate of meatloaf to Miss Platts. Miss Platts took a small piece, no onions, and lay the plate down next to me. I copied her exact serving of meat, then rice, and vegetables. I was happy not to have been pressured with trying an onion, even a "no thank you" bite.

"Who's that girl?" I asked referring to the person called Basi.

"That's Basi," said Aunt Ruth, "she is the daughter of Liang who owns the Chinese restaurant in town. He came to America to work on the railroad and has made quite a name for himself with his skillful cooking. He and his wife have three children and Basi is their oldest. I think she's nineteen."

"Does she live here?" I asked.

"Oh heavens no, she lives with her parents. They keep to their own kind," said Aunt Ruth.

"What kind is she?" I asked.

"Why, Chinese. I already told you. They are very private people. They still practice many of the primitive ways of their ancestors," she said, not revealing any of those primitive ways, but appearing to be very knowledgeable. "How was your afternoon, Friend?" said Aunt Ruth as she buttered her rice.

"Fine," Mr. Linderman and I said in unison.

All three adults looked at me. Mr. Linderman's left eyebrow came to an elevated peak. He snickered as he studied me over the rim of his spectacles.

Aunt Ruth put her fork down and produced a pitying smile, "Mr. Linderman's first name is Friend, Carol."

"Oh, I'm sorry." I slumped back in my chair.

"No need to be sorry," he said to me, "and to answer your question, Ruth, my afternoon was splendid." He tucked his cloth napkin into his stiff, rounded collar. "The roses needed a good pruning and spraying—looks like we'll have one more round of blooms coming before the frost. And the agapanthus is stealing the show out front. If there ever was a proud bloom, it's the agapanthus." He spoke with an authoritative bellow.

Aunt Ruth put her napkin in her lap, folded her hands over it, bowed her head and, and waited in silence.

Mr. Linderman heaped a pile of rice onto his plate. "The petunias are looking a bit sheepish, time to—" He stopped abruptly when he noticed that Aunt Ruth was frozen in prayer position. He cleared his throat. "Bless us oh Lord and these, thy gifts, which we are about to receive, from thy bounty, through Christ our Lord. Amen."

We all said, "Amen" and the polite clicking and tapping of sterling silver on China plates filled in for the conversation.

Mr. Linderman picked up his fork from the left and knife from the right and cut his meatloaf into bite-sized squares. He never switched his fork to the right hand like I was taught. He held his fork in his left hand, upside down, and speared a square of meatloaf. On top of that he piled rice, two carrot medallions, and several peas. Lastly he dipped the whole concoction into a generous pool of gravy, and lifted the loaded fork to his mouth with deliberate precision. So slowly did he move his fork that I was worried he'd lose the entire creation on the way to his mouth. I held my breath and leaned forward in my chair silently willing the peas not to jump off onto the starched white linen napkin. His jaw hung open and patiently waited for the food, which was flawlessly delivered without drip or drizzle. I should have had more confidence in Friend; He had obviously done this before. He continued through the remainder of the meal using the same methodical pattern of loading and launching, never losing a single pea.

"How do you find your lodgings, Carol?" he asked me between launches.

"My room is lovely," I answered, noting how perfectly the word "lovely" rolled off my tongue and how perfectly English it sounded, so I used it again, "the whole house is lovely, Friend."

Mrs. Linderman stopped her fork in mid-air, "You may call him Mr. Linderman," she corrected.

Mr. Linderman cleared his throat. "Lovely, so it is, glad you like it. Tell us about yourself then," he said in a fast, curt, formal manner.

I spoke slowly at first, concentrating on the words I needed to avoid like "Friend" and "bet yer life." I told them what I felt would be beneficial. I sang the praises of Leonard and Lena and said how much I'd miss them, but followed that up immediately with the presumption that I'd like it here just as well. I told them all about Aunt Marion and Uncle Virg and how I always spent summers with them. I mentioned my excellent grades, my tidy housekeeping, and my tendency for early bedtime hours and provided ample evidence for the strong possibility of my being allergic to okra. I didn't mention my father.

Miss Platts asked me about my favorite subjects and when I mentioned my love for reading, we dominated the rest of the mealtime talk with discussion of our favorite books. We had some in common, like *The Peterkin Papers*. We both agreed that the "Lady from Philadelphia" single-handedly kept the Peterkin family out of dire straits more times than we could count, and laughed about the time Mrs. Peterkin put salt in her coffee instead of sugar. Mr. and Mrs. Linderman were not familiar with *The Peterkin Papers*. Mr. Linderman suggested *Moby Dick* as the greatest adventure story of all time. I didn't admit that I had tried to read it but had to put it away as I started having dreams about drowning. Mrs. Linderman boasted *Wuthering Heights* as her favorite, which I had not attempted, and which Miss Platts described as "way over her head" in high school, but liked it much more when she had tried it again in college. She suggested I try it when I get in high school, because I seemed like an advanced reader. Miss Platts spoke to me like I was in high school already. I liked her.

I rose from the table when Aunt Ruth did and started clearing the table, as Mama had suggested. This time Aunt Ruth didn't discourage my efforts, but watched closely as I piled plate upon plate with a stray fork or knife stuck in between causing a couple of the plates to sit crooked.

"Carol, please set the plates down," she said.

I did. I was expecting a servant to come rushing through the door and whisk the dishes away without comment or commotion.

"Remove the silver, re-stack the plates, and take them to the kitchen please," she said.

She did not smile, assist me, or try to ease the humiliation I felt from my mistake. Miss Platts followed me with the silverware and the leftover meatloaf. Aunt Ruth held the kitchen door open for us and her gaze followed as I put the plates on the right side of the sink, next to the drainer.

"The plates go to the left of the sink, Carol," she said, "we keep the dirties on the left, and only the clean on the right of the sink." I understood completely, it is exactly how we did it in Lena's kitchen, but still, I felt stupid for not assuming it beforehand. Surely she thought me careless, incompetent, and flighty.

She excused me from any more kitchen duties that night and gave me the choice of listening to the radio for an hour, or retiring to my room with a book. I chose the radio. Little Orphan Annie was wrapping up the case of the missing cowboy hat, and I knew that Harold was hiding something. Turns out there was no mystery about the hat at all. The hat had been misplaced in the cellar of Mrs. Andrew Thurston, but so had the money from the recent bank robbery in Copper City. Thousands of dollars were buried beneath the fashionable hats and coats of Mrs. Andrew Thurston and she didn't even know about it. The new mystery was upon us in the form of finding out why she didn't know, and who possibly could. Harold was still the prime suspect. Annie's life was *so* much more exciting than my own.

3

I slept like chocolate melted onto a hot sidewalk, seeping into every crevice of mattress and soaking up every billowy inch of coverlet. From nine o'clock at night to seven o'clock in the morning my dreams were my only occupation. When I woke I was rested, but reluctant to get out of bed. Then I remembered that this was my last day of summer vacation. Tomorrow was the first day of school and as much as I looked forward to the new year, I also knew I would miss the lazy mornings of summer and the warm sun of the season of leisure. I added a pillow under my head and opened *Anne of Green Gables*, the book that Aunt Marion had started reading to me that summer. I read several chapters and only left my comfortable nest when I heard voices from downstairs. It was a bright sunny morning, so I put on my yellow dress.

As I entered the dining room, Mr. Linderman was sitting alone at the dining room table just like I had left him the night before. He was drinking coffee and reading the paper. I slipped into my chair, thinking I had been unnoticed, but he lowered his paper and considered me silently.

"Good morning, Mr. Linderman." I said

"I guess you could say so, living the life o' Riley like we are here in the heart of God's country. You might not say that if you lived with my sister in London. Bombs was what greeted them for their good morning. Bombs and destruction." He lifted his paper again and continued to talk." You'd think a man could learn from the mistakes of others, from the history books and their fathers and grandfathers. I don't know if she's dead or alive, her with the beautiful little Tessa and naughty

Simon just learning his numbers." He folded up the newspaper and laid it by his plate, then picked up an opened letter. "Give me a go at that murderous monster, I don't need a bloody army behind me, I could filet him with a butter knife if I had half a chance." He threw the paper on the floor next to him. "Bloody Hitler!"

I did not know what to say, so I nodded.

"Won't be long now. Your own father will likely be off to Germany, or beyond," he said.

"No, I don't think so," I pouted. My stomach turned.

"Hmmm," he stirred sugar into his coffee.

"Mama says he couldn't pass the physical. She told Uncle Virg that his eyes had gone yellow and his pee ran red." I couldn't believe I said that. My stomach got tight like I needed the bathroom. I started to excuse myself…

"The jaundice," he said nodding his head. "A weak liver coupled with a weak will. My sister's father-in-law died with the yellow eyes. Shame. I like a nip of the whiskey myself, now and again, but never saw the need for a draw in the daylight."

"Will your sister be all right?" I asked. The pain in my belly subsided a little.

"If that isn't the million-dollar question. They made it through the worst bombing of Buckingham Palace, which is ever so close to where my sister used to live. She and her two children hid out in the train station for over a month until they got an invitation to stay with an aunt in the country. They've recently gone back to London, but today another bombing has the city in chaos, and I have no news. I've invited her to come here, but sometimes people have a hard time leaving what's familiar. She gets the sea sickness so bad, I'm not sure she could make the trip with two little ones to look after." He looked out the window in a day-dreamy stare.

I sat still, not knowing what to say, and was exceedingly grateful when Miss Platts came in and sat down next to me. She poured herself a cup of coffee from a pretty silver pot, added several spoons full of sugar and took a tiny sip.

"Mmmm. The coffee here is worth the entire cost of room and board." She held the dainty cup under her nose and inhaled. "Thin the soup, leave out the meat, skip the sauces and stretch the casserole, but don't water down my coffee."

She reminded me of Br'er Rabbit trying to get thrown into the briar patch, except she really meant what she said. I poured myself a cup, as my stomach was growling and I didn't mind a cup of coffee if I added a lot of milk and sugar. I had just swallowed my first sip of perfectly-cooled, sweet, creamy coffee, when Aunt Ruth appeared at the kitchen door and propped it open with a wooden wedge at the bottom. She went back to the kitchen and reappeared with a bowl of steamy scrambled eggs. Basi followed with a large bowl of oatmeal. It made me think of the choking incident in the Nigren's kitchen. That thought, along with the smell of the oats, the upsetting story of the sister and her children, and the strong coffee on my empty stomach, started my insides churning.

Basi poured tiny glasses of orange juice and placed one in front of each of us. I took a sip, hoping to settle my stomach, but the juice acted more like ipecac syrup. I covered my mouth, hoping to stop anything from coming up, and crossed my legs, attempting to barricade anything from going out. I swallowed, burped, felt the acid of the juice sting my throat, and abruptly excused myself to the bathroom. The rumbling in my bowels needed immediate relief. I ran to the upstairs bathroom. The door was closed and I could hear the sound of the shower running and an off-key rendition of "*You Must Have Been a Beautiful Baby*," being sung by Mr. Danielson.

I remembered Aunt Ruth saying something about a bathroom out in back of the barn, so I ran down the stairs, past the dining room and kitchen and out the mud room door before anyone could ask me where I was going. I clutched my stomach, reciting over and over again to myself, "Just in back of the barn, just in back of the barn." I got to the back of the barn and saw a small lean-to that I figured must be the toilet. I kicked open the door and surprised a neighborhood of sitting hens. They clucked and flapped their disapproval and sent a great tornado of downy feathers and chaffed hay through the air. The morning beams of light through the slats in the wood gave a cartoon quality to the flurry. A car-sick feeling came over me, so I quickly closed the door and searched for anything remotely resembling a toilet. Fifty feet from the hen's maternity ward was a short, longish building with a moon on the front. Hallelujah! I never was so happy to see an outhouse in my life.

Once inside I was faced with a bench equipped with two circular cutouts as places to sit. I chose the one closest to the door and tried my hardest not to put my full weight on the dirty board. My efforts were in vain and I relaxed onto the wooden seat as my stay was not a short one. I decided, as I sat there, that a hole in the forest would have been a better choice. I didn't have to visit the outhouse very often after that. Praise God from whom all blessings flow!

I ate a small breakfast in the kitchen that morning, cold eggs and dry toast, as I had missed the group breakfast in the dining room. No questions were asked. I think Aunt Ruth and Basi understood my dilemma. This started an unsettled period in the case of my stomach. I never knew when I'd need a toilet and when I did, it came with little notice. It was as if my fear of the unexpected or any bit of anxiety announced itself through my bowels. It changed the way I ate, the distances I traveled, and the choice of my desk at school. I ate only small servings of the blandest foods I could choose, and still my bowels betrayed me.

Aunt Ruth asked me to clear the dishes after breakfast, which I was more than happy to do. I was thankful for the second chance so I could show her that I knew the right way now and would never again even *think* of putting the dirties on the right side.

"I need you to go to the post office for me this morning Carol, then you may go visit your mother if you like," Aunt Ruth said as we moved around the kitchen. She handed me a damp rag, and a dry towel. "This one is for wiping and this one is for drying. Go wipe down the table, but don't let any moisture sit for long. The finish is very fragile. This table was shipped here from England by Mr. Linderman's father as our wedding present. It is one of my most prized possessions."

"Can I go to the post office later this afternoon?" I called from the dining room to the kitchen beyond the swinging door.

Aunt Ruth pushed the door open enough to squeeze her head through "Please, don't holler through the house, if you need to speak to me, come and speak to me face to face."

"Sorry," I said.

"Do you have plans for this morning?" she asked.

"No." I was doing a really good job on the table.

"Then you may go to the post office," she said. She was forgetting something.

"I'd be glad to go to the Post Office this morning, but I can't go to see my mother until this afternoon. She sleeps until 3:15 on weekdays. I usually go wake her up after school, remember?" I said, passing her in the doorway.

"Oh. Yes. Well, I suppose this afternoon will be fine. That will leave time for you to get started on a project I have for you," she said as she followed me through the kitchen. She picked up the rags that I had put on the dirty side, carried them out to the mud room and deposited them in a wicker laundry basket. I made a mental note of it.

"Can I play piano?" I asked. I wasn't sure about a project.

"I don't know, can you? Did you mean 'may I'?" I was under the impression that you didn't read music. If you have a piece you'd like to try, I suppose it would be all right for you to practice for a while. Perhaps we can have a proper lesson after we've done something productive. Yes, go along; tinker around for a bit, I'll find the beginning piano books later."

I went to the piano. Something inside me told me to play a hymn. I wanted to practice a new song I had heard on the radio, but an intuition would only allow me to play *The Old Rugged Cross*. I hadn't played it for a while, so I started out slowly, making sure the tune was right, just barely touching the keys to keep quiet. With a little practice behind me, I played with more confidence, adding more chords, more melody, more feeling. I was lost in the song, picturing a group of black-clad mourners standing around an open grave, a scene I recalled from a movie. The song was sad, but hopeful. I didn't hear Aunt Ruth come up and stand behind me, don't know how long she had been there, but she repeated the last line of the chorus, a cappella, after I had stopped playing.

"And exchaaaange it someday for a crowwwwwn," her shaky voice belted out.

I turned around as she was drying the corner of her eye. "Carol, that was truly a tribute of praise. God has blessed you with a gift that needs to be shared. I am going to arrange for you to meet the music director at church and see about sharing your gift with the congregation."

"Oh no, Aunt Ruth, I don't want to play at church. I can't play in front of people," I protested.

"When God gives you a gift, you should use it for the edification of the body. Don't hide your light under a bushel, Carol. Don't bury your talent so it cannot gain interest. You are a gifted little girl!" she said very fast.

"I just like to play for myself. It makes my heart happy," I said.

"Well, you could make a lot more people happy if you'd get over your stage fright," she ridiculed, "we'll see."

I sat with my hands on the keys, too nervous to continue.

"Follow me," she said. "It's time you start your chores."

I rose from the piano bench and followed her to the mud room where she handed me a few rags and a tin of Murphy's oil soap. She led me to the stairs and showed me the exact method to use on the different areas of the wood. The white spindles needed to be cleaned with a damp cloth. The bare wood was washed with a light coating of the oil soap, then rinsed, then thoroughly buffed to remove all the dust, dirt, and stickiness. She showed me her technique; small circular motions that made the wood shine. It smelled good. The banister was the best part. It felt like the banister at the Athenaeum Hotel, well cared for and slippery as black ice.

It took me three hours to finish the stairs. I was bored to death the whole time and could only think of Grandpa's last words to me before he left, "She expects you to pull your weight." Well, I had pulled more than ten times my weight by the time I finished those stairs, and left a goodly amount of skin from my fingertips behind in the process. At the top of the stairway I paused. Mr. Danielson was either sleeping or at the hospital, of that I was fairly sure. Miss Platts was surely at school, preparing for the students' impending arrival the next day. Mr. Linderman was trimming the hydrangeas; I'd seen him from my bedroom window rolling around his wheel chair as if it caused him no inconvenience whatsoever. Aunt Ruth was apparently planning an outing. Her gloves and hat were sitting on the round table in the middle of the wide entry hall.

I watched from the top of the stairs until Aunt Ruth swept into the entryway with Basi close on her heels. "Basi, make sure to prick the zucchini bread before you take it out. I shouldn't be but an hour or so." She smoothed her skirt and donned her hat and gloves, the addition of which made her look more prudish than pretty.

"Yes, okay." Basi handed her a basket and shut the door after her.

With Basi safely back in the kitchen, I went to my bedroom to find my corduroy overalls. They were almost too small, but if I fastened them on the last button they would work perfectly for my plan. I slipped a pair of cotton socks on my feet and grabbed my mittens. Making sure the coast was clear, I swung my left leg up over the perfectly oiled and buffed banister railing, and hung on to one of the spindles to stall my descent. I looked down behind me, took a deep breath and let go. Immediately, I knew I was going too fast. I tried to grasp the railing tighter, but my mittens were performing their task perfectly. I reached for the spindles under the railing, but they only slapped my mittened fingertips as they flew by. I was thinking my best escape would be to just fall off onto the steps, but never had the time to follow through with that plan. My tail bone hit the balustrade and I was brought to an abrupt stop with an explosive grunt. As soon as I could take a breath, I let out a blood curdling scream that brought Basi flying through the kitchen door to my aid. I hurt too bad to crawl down, so I hung there crying.

"Oh, no-no-no, okay, okay?" Basi found me and stood dumbfounded with a kitchen cleaver in one hand and a chicken leg in the other. Realizing her dilemma she laid them on the bottom step and attempted to help me down.

Mr. Danielson descended the stairs two-by-two and hollered, "Don't move her Basi!" He gently slipped his hands under my arm pits and slowly moved me up the banister a bit. I was sobbing, spilling tears and drool all over my excellent polishing job.

"I'm going to take your sock off Carol, hang in there for a minute." He spoke calmly and close to my ear. I literally was "hanging in there" and was going nowhere fast unless someone moved me. "Can you feel this?" He ran his finger along the bottom of my foot and knew the answer before I had a chance to say anything. My toes curled in from the tickle and I pulled my leg away.

"I'm going to lift you up, just hold on around my neck," he said as he slowly lifted me up to his chest. "Wrap your legs around my waist if you can, then I won't have to put any pressure on your tail bone." I tried but it hurt to move my legs much. I hung on to his neck and he carried me up the stairs.

"Basi, go find Mrs. Linderman," he ordered.

"No!" I hollered "don't tell Mrs. Linderman!" My cries turned back into sobs.

"Okay, hush. Be still, no harm done, except to yourself," he smiled.

He laid me on my bed and examined the wounded area.

"Were you sliding down the banister?"

I nodded, yes.

"I think it's just a bruise. You might be walking a little slow for a while, but it doesn't appear to be broken," he said and dried my tears with his hanky.

"Think you'll try that again soon?"

I shook my head, no.

"I'll see what I can find for the pain, be right back."

My bottom end was throbbing. I wasn't sure I could walk to Mama's. Even breathing hurt. I prayed that Mrs. Linderman wouldn't find out. Then I prayed that Mr. Danielson and my mom would fall madly in love and marry each other.

Mr. Danielson came back with an aspirin and a glass of water like he said he would. "Is it better than it was a few minutes ago?"

I nodded.

"Good. I'll go have a chat with Basi. Maybe we can keep this between the three of us."

I smiled in appreciation, despite the pain.

He had me get up and walk around to check my injury and said I would live a long and prosperous life, as long as I gave up banister-sliding.

"I'll be at the hospital all afternoon if you need me," he assured me as he left my room.

I hobbled around my room a few times, changed my clothes and went downstairs. I didn't want to supply Aunt

Ruth with any reason to question me. I needed to see my mother.

As I descended the stairs, I noticed that Aunt Ruth's gloves weren't on the round table by the front door. "Thank you," I silently prayed. In the kitchen I found Basi layering apple wedges into a pie shell.

"Okay in bum?" she asked with a knowing smile.

"I think so, but it really hurts," I said.

She held her finger up. "Wait," she said.

Basi shuffled across the kitchen to the ice box. She chiseled off a chunk of ice and wrapped it in a napkin. "Here. Cold good."

"No thanks Basi, I need to get..."

"Take away pain, cold good!" she insisted, starting to lift the skirt of my dress.

I took the ice pack and shoved it down the back of my panties. She cocked her head around and smiled. "Good. No see."

"Okay," I said. "I'm going to see my mother."

"Okay," she bowed.

"Okay," I curtsied.

She smiled at my attempt at such formalities and went back to her apple layering.

As soon as I got out the door I ditched the ice pack in the bushes. I was limping slightly as I headed for the Post office. Aunt Ruth appeared as I rounded the corner.

"Did you finish the stairway Carol?" was her only greeting.

"Yes, Aunt Ruth," I replied, concentrating on not limping or scrunching my face from the throbbing in my bottom.

"Good. Have a nice visit with your mother. Don't dilly-dally to the post office. Dinner is at six, be home by five-thirty to set the table." And she walked on.

When I reached the door of my mother's room I found it ajar. I could hear voices and laughing and assumed it was the radio. As I entered I was pleasantly surprised by what I found. Mr. Danielson and Mama were sitting at the little table drinking coffee. Mama was stubbing out her cigarette and blowing smoke up in the air while she giggled. Her cheeks were blushed and her eyes were sparkly. Mr. Danielson was straddling his chair, resting his arms and chin on the curve of the back. He too was laughing. Mama saw me out of the corner of her eye and immediately got up and came to me.

"Hi, Peach," she surrounded me with her arms, and her smell, and her voice. "I hear you had an incident," she squatted down and looked in my face, "how's your coccyx?" Mama always called a spade a spade.

"It hurts," I said, and buried my face in her neck.

"Not the best last day of summer vacation, huh?" she consoled.

"Hm-mm," I said unable to open my mouth. Tears came. I sniffed.

Mr. Danielson rose from his chair, spun it around on one leg and slid it up to the table. "I'll be on my way," he said without expecting a response. "Glad you're up and doing." He winked at me and spoke to Mama, "see you tonight!"

I felt her hand lift from my back and knew she was waving.

We spent most of the afternoon playing our own made-up version of "Criss-cross words," which was an early version of the game, Scrabble. In our version, any word was allowed as long as you could site the definition and use it in a sentence. Even made up words were allowed, as long as they made sense in the sentence. My high score of the day came from a word my mother used often, but wasn't in the dictionary, J-O-M-M-E-L. Defined: To mix something up. Sentence: I like to jommel up my crackers in my soft-boiled eggs. Mama acted like she didn't even want to play after that because she didn't think she could top my word. As it turned out, I won by four points and Mama gave me a kiss and four pennies for how smart I was.

By the time I headed back to Aunt Ruth's, my injury was done throbbing, and it only hurt if I pushed on it or sat down hard. I still had to walk slowly, but got home in plenty of time for table-setting, dinner-eating, and dishwashing. I was looking forward to going back to school.

4

I loved fall and the seasonal pull to the preparations of a new school year, a fresh start. I was ready for fifth grade before it was ready for me. I missed the physical act of practicing penmanship, missed the callous on my middle finger from holding my pencil. I loved school. I loved schedules, lines, taking turns, set lunch times, and the sound of the bell, just as the big hand bounced straight up to the twelve, every time.

The first day of school was on a Tuesday. By Friday I was used to the routine. I made fast friends with a pretty, tall, blonde girl named Pauline. We both walked the same route, though I wasn't sure where she lived because she kept walking after I stopped at the Lindermans'. She had a brother named Neil who was younger than us and had one eye that didn't look at you when he looked at you. He didn't talk much, and when he did it was mostly in quiet mumbles, into his sister's ear. She always picked him up from his second grade class after school, so I usually waited for her and we'd walk together. Every day, as soon as we started walking, Neil would grab hold of the hem of Pauline's dress. Then, little by little, he gathered the fabric of the skirt into his fist, until he had made his way half way up the skirt and her thigh was showing. She'd just push his hand down and keep walking, but he would start again and do the same thing over and over again. She didn't seem to mind and acted like it was perfectly regular that her brother should do this. Her dresses were always wrinkled on the right side, which was his side.

The following Monday, Neil stayed home sick from school. In his absence I ventured to ask, "Pauline, what's wrong with your brother?"

"He's sick at home today, bad night," she answered.

"No, I mean, what's *wrong* with him, you know, in general?"

"Nothin's wrong." She seemed irritated.

"Well, something's different," I insisted.

She was silent for a full minute. "He's got the gift," she said, not looking at me.

"What gift?" I asked.

"Have you noticed his eye?" she said.

"Yeah, it's googly," I said. "Ya ever heard the song? Barney Google, with the goo-goo-googly eye."

"No."

"I always pictured Barney Google's eyes to look something like Neil's," I tried to explain.

"You may think they're googly, but that ain't right. Ya see, he talks to angels and always has one eye on heaven. He has a special connection with God," she said, whispering the last part.

"Is that right?" I said, looking at her for a sign of sarcasm. "Is he an angel?"

"No, acourse he ain't no angel. You can see him can't cha? And plus, he ain't got no wings," she said with such conviction that I knew she was dead serious. "Outa all us kids, he's the only one who gots the gift. He don't need to try in school 'cuz he'll never use his learnin'. He'll prob'ly only live to be twelve and then poof! Straight up to glory, sittin' at the feet of Jesus while the rest of us kids are left strugglin' with our multiplication tables and pickin' mint 'till our hands are green as a Martian! Mint green ain't so pretty as people say. Fact is, it's more the color a bile."

"Shut *UP*!"I stopped and slapped her on her arm with the back of my hand. "That's not nice; you don't know he's going to die when he's twelve."

"Yes, I *DO*." She slapped me back on my arm with the word *DO*.

"How?" I said, stopped now, facing her.

"My mother, she had a brother just like Neil. Same heavenly eye, same name, same fits, same dreams, same look. The faraway look of him with the gift. She should know. She spotted it in him when he was two years old and we've all knowed it ever since. It's his destiny," she said, and continued walking.

"But what if he *doesn't* die when he's twelve, what if he...what do you mean fits?" I said.

"He has fits. His whole body gets stiff as a board, and both eyes roll around in his head like marbles. Mother puts the wooden spoon in his mouth so he don't bite his tongue off. He usually stops in a matter of a short while, and then sleeps for a good long time, and can't go to school the next day 'cuz he's worn out like a wrung rag."

"Is that what happened last night?" I asked.

"Yep."

"Is he Okay?"

"Yep."

We walked the rest of the way in silence until we reached Aunt Ruth's house.

"You want to come in?" I offered.

"Nope."

"How come?" I asked, sure that I had offended her by calling her brother googly-eyed.

"Old lady Linderman has made it crystal clear to my mother that we ain't welcome on her porch, or anywhere near her pew at church. She is sure the devil's what kicks around in my brother from the inside, and's skeert to death to be near him or any of us, for that matter. Moldy mint share croppers, is what she called us. Moldy-mint share-croppers." She leaned into me and slowly articulated each of the descriptives. Then she stepped back from me and looked at the big brick house, "Why do you live here anyhow?"

"My mother is a nurse. She works nights at the W.C.A. Hospital. I see her every day, usually, but she doesn't want to leave me by myself all night long so I stay here. When I'm thirteen we're getting an apartment together 'cuz I'll be old enough to stay by myself," I explained.

"Where's yer dad?"

"I'm not sure. Getting ready to go to war to fight the Nazis, probably, everyone else is," I lied.

I added up all I had learned about my new friend and changed the subject, "Do you live in the white house in the mint field?" I said.

"Yep, all eight of us," she bragged.

I was remembering Mrs. Linderman's orders not to go near the white house.

"Did your mother tell Mrs. Linderman about the gift?" I said, surprised at my own understanding.

"People like Ruth Linderman don't deserve to know about the gift, wouldn't believe it if we told her," she answered.

"She's not that bad, really. I mean, I think she means well," I offered.

"That old piss-ant is selfish and greedy. She don't mean well for anyone but her own slimy self. I'd get outa there as soon as I could if I're you. You'd be better off at a work farm than with that witch. I gotta go, see ya around." She walked away, and this time I watched her go, down the street, across the mint field and through the unpainted wooden door of the small white house.

***

That afternoon I walked to the hospital to see my mother. During my short familiar journey, the Barney Google song would not leave my head. I tried singing the Star Spangled Banner to get my mind going on another song, but even the Star Spangled Banner ended up in the tune of Barney Google with the goo-goo-googly eyes.

Mama and I were playing a championship game of Criss-Cross, as both of us had won one game the day before.

"Mama?"

"Well?"

"What does it mean when a person has googly eyes that roll around like marbles in the sockets... and their body goes stiff... and you have to put a wooden spoon in their mouth? Then they fall asleep for a long time, and wake up feeling like a squeezed out rag?"

"That could be a number of things." Mama re-arranged her tiles and laid down the word *comfy*. "To feel cozy and comfortable. That's three, four, plus three doubled is ten plus four is fourteen and "Y" with a double letter is.... Twenty-two." She wrote her score under her name.

"Well, what if a person has a gift? Say they're special, and act unusual because they have a direct line to God, kinda like John the Baptist," I explained in a perfectly logical manner.

Mama pushed her letters aside. "Well, I don't know. Who do you know that has googly eyes and a direct line to God?"

"Neil."

"A friend of yours?"

"The neighbor boy that lives in the mint field, in the little white house. Did you know that eight people live in that house, Mama? It's barely bigger than Aunt Ruth's chicken house."

"The house that you can see out your bedroom window?" she asked.

"Yep, the forbidden house," I said wiggling my fingers up near my face, using a spooky voice.

"The what house? You're going to have to start from the start," she said.

I told Mama the whole story about Aunt Ruth saying I shouldn't go over to the white house in the mint field. Then I told her about how I made friends with Pauline, and how she told me all about her brother with "the gift".

"Then Pauline told me that Mrs. Linderman thinks there is a demon in him. She thinks that's why he acts like he does, and flails all around and needs a wooden spoon in his mouth to stop him from biting his tongue off, or worse, someone else." I made up the part about someone else.

"Goodness gracious," Mama said. She lit a cigarette and walked over to open the window. "Sounds like he might have seizures of some kind. He certainly is not demon-possessed. There is medicine to treat this. They probably don't take him to the doctor because they can't afford it." She seemed concerned.

"Can you give him some medicine?"

"No, I'm not a doctor, but I'll talk to his mother and see if Dr. Danielson would be willing to see him," she offered.

"That would be lovely," I said, having delivered my first good deed as lodger at the Linderman estate.

Mama looked at me over her glasses, smiling. "Lovely?"

"Yes," I said, "perfectly lovely."

5

On a Saturday morning, about a month after I had moved in with the Lindermans, a knock on my door woke me from a dream about teaching Aunt Marion's dog, Butch, to read. Mrs. Linderman poked her head in and instructed me to have some oatmeal off the stove, and wait for her in the kitchen for some housekeeping. I wasn't sure what this meant but it sounded like chores to me. I got up, dressed in shorts and an old blouse, went to the kitchen, but skipped the oatmeal. Instead I grabbed a bunch of grapes and ate them while I waited at the kitchen table, which was more of a work table than a dining table. It was made from one huge slab of wood, about three inches thick. One end had just the slightest indentation, as if a large cat had been sleeping there for a hundred years. Five unmatched chairs bellied up to the table. All were well-worn on the seats and the rungs, a noticeable contrast to the formal dining room where all the chairs matched and were perfectly polished.

The kitchen was as clean as a whistle, but worn in, almost homey. An earthenware bowl full of beets with their greens spilling over the side, sat in the middle of the table. On the floor along the wall was a row of pumpkins, looking like they were standing in line for their turn. The whole house smelled of baked pumpkin. There were pots hanging from iron hooks on a stone wall, and different sized ladles hanging from the stove's hood. The floor was wood, the rugs were braided, and the curtains were made of embroidered dishcloths. An ice box still stood in the far corner, even though an electric refrigerator buzzed nearby. Four large glass canisters with wooden tops took up a good amount of one counter, each storing something white or beige and powdery. I tried to guess: flour, sugar, cornmeal, rice? No probably not rice, but maybe tapioca, hopefully tapioca, but probably oatmeal.

The sun had shifted its window-sized beam and crept slowly across my back. The warm rays, and the smell of pumpkin cooking made my still-sleepy head feel heavy so I laid it down on my crisscrossed forearms and closed my eyes until the the slam of the screen door startled me to attention . In walked Basi with a load of cucumbers hammocked in her apron. She balanced a basket of cherry tomatoes on her head, one arm up to steady it as she turned to shut the door with a push of her foot. She didn't see me until she started across the kitchen to set the vegetables on the table. I stood, thinking there was probably something I should do to assist her in shedding her bounty.

"Do you need help?" I asked.

"Tank you," she said, and she squatted down to the floor on one knee and motioned for me to take the basket from her head.

She bowed twice in thanks. Then she carefully and methodically unloaded the cucumbers from her apron onto the table, then went back outside to give herself a good dusting off. She clapped her hands, shook her apron, and promptly returned. She washed her hands with a big square of beige soap that sat beside the sink, air dried her hands with a graceful wavy dance, and retrieved a big brown bowl from on top of the refrigerator. She brought it over to the table and took the towel off the domed top, revealing a swollen dome of light brown dough. Basi gave it a pat-pat, then inserted two fingers into the dough before she coaxed it out of the bowl and into the indented, cat-sleeping-place, at the end of the table. She cut it in two, laid half of it aside, and started kneading the other half. Only then did she look at me and smile.

"Can I help?" I pointed to the other half.

As she handed me the dough, Aunt Ruth entered through the swinging door leading from the dining room.

"Good morning Basi," said Aunt Ruth.

"Goot moling, yes," said Basi. She bowed two more times "tank you." When she stood up her head bobbed a little from all that bowing.

"Looks like our little vegetable garden is producing more than we bargained for," said Aunt Ruth. She took a quick inventory, smelling tomatoes, thumping pumpkins, and popping two cherry tomatoes into her mouth. "Mmmm, warm and sweet." She walked over to the oven, grabbed the fork from the counter and peeked in at the four halves of pumpkin. She poked one, announced it needed ten more minutes and shut the door.

Aunt Ruth looked around, assessing the kitchen. Then her eyes fell on me. "All right... Let's see... Carol," she said. She sat gingerly on the most anterior edge of the captain's chair at the head of the table. She then lifted a pair of spectacles from a chain around her neck, positioned them at the tip of her nose, and addressed me over the top of them. "Carol, please have a seat, Basi can knead the dough. We need to talk about your role here." She waited for me to sit down, then referred to a sheet of paper in front of her. "I believe your first month here has been a success. I find you very amiable and capable, in keeping with the general good nature of our home." Her hands were in front of her on the table, fingers folded into each other. "As you know, your mother has entrusted your care and well-being to me. She is paying me something to keep you, but is not able to pay my full rate. I have agreed to provide your food and lodgings and supervise your daily routine and until now, you have done very little in the way of chores. This has been a trial time. From now on you will be responsible for regular household chores and local errands when I need help." She removed her spectacles, folded them, and lay them to dangle on her chest. Then she looked at me. "I expect you to behave with obedience and respect. I will not tolerate tardiness or mouthiness. I will do my best to fulfill the desires of your mother and provide a safe and healthy place for you to grow and learn. Do you understand and do you have any questions?"

"Am I in trouble?" I asked. I was trying to figure out if someone had divulged my sliding-down-the-banister ordeal.

"No. In fact, you are being rewarded for your good behavior. The trial time is over and I have decided you may stay. Do you have any questions?" she said.

"I get *more* chores for good behavior?"

"It's like becoming more a part of our family." She cleared her throat. "You get more responsibility. I can't expect you to understand, The Harrison's seemed to have spoiled you over there," she said. "I don't have time or patience for a spoiled little girl, and I will see to it that you don't turn into one. It's the least I can do for your mother, as she hasn't the time to bring you up by hand. Do you have any other questions?"

I felt like I was getting a lecture about my bad behavior that hadn't even happened yet. My tongue stuck to the dry roof of my mouth, and the back of my hands felt tingly so I stuck them between my knees. "No," I tried to say, but no words came out, so I shook my head and my bangs fell in my face. That's the closest I could get to hiding.

"Good then. From now on, after school, I will expect you to check in with me, do your homework, and do the assigned errand or chore for that day," she continued, "On most days you will be able to finish your chores in under an hour. We will eat dinner at six o'clock every evening and I would like you here to set the table by five-thirty. Your mother says you will continue to spend most weekends with her, but just in case you are here on a Sunday, we attend the eight o'clock service and our Sunday meal is at two o'clock."

I stopped listening as soon as I heard the words "chore for that day." "What about visiting my mother after school?" I asked.

"You may visit your mother on weekends and holidays. During the week your responsibilities are here." Her mouth puckered and her eyes shifted from me to Basi.

I pressed my thumbnail into the fleshy part of my other hand until it made a series of red indented arches. "But my mother expects me at the hospital at three fifteen every day," I said, trying desperately to choke down the sobs that bubbled up in my throat, and control the anger rising in my chest.

"Your mother will just have to agree to this new arrangement, or we will have to make other plans for you. These are uncertain times. Oh, and we will be moving you up to the attic room. Mr. Linderman's sister will soon be arriving on passage from England and we will need your room for her. Her two children will sleep upstairs in the attic with you. I've ordered three cots that should be delivered next week. You will enjoy the companionship." She smiled a closed-lipped grin, got up, and went back to the stove to check on the pumpkins. "Perfect. Basi, take these pumpkins out of the oven and set them on the shelf in the mud room to cool. I'll be back in two hours. Mr. Linderman is in the garden. Carol, are you going to your mother's?"

"Yes." I sure as Pete wasn't staying around there.

"Basi will show you how to hang the laundry, then you may go. We'll see you on Sunday then. I've sent your mother a letter concerning the things we've discussed this morning," she said.

Mrs. Linderman left through the same door she had come in and stopped the swinging of the door after only one pass.

I sat in the silence. Neither Basi nor I spoke as she lowered the first lump of dough into the bread pan. I couldn't get up. I could only stare at the sun ray on the table and try to swallow the rising tightness in my throat. This was not my real life.

Basi was starting on the second loaf. I rose and sidled up to Basi. She moved away, clapping floury dust from her hands and took my place in the chair. I kneaded, then pushed, and punched the dough, crying and dripping tears onto the lightly-floured surface. The dough became Ruth Linderman's face. I inserted my fingers into the squishy mound, poking out Aunt Ruth's eyes. Pauline was right; this old piss-ant was gonna take me and my mother for anything she could get. I was no longer her lodger, but her hired help, just like Basi. I lifted the bread dough up over my head and smashed it onto the floor as hard as I could. It landed with a satisfying thud. Basi put her arms out and I melted onto her little frame. She hummed and rocked me in her sway, trying to accommodate my long, bony body on her hard, unfeminine chest.

"Okay...Nooo...Shhhh...is okay now." She wiped my face with her apron, whispering, "is okay...is okay now."

When I stopped crying Basi released my hot, soggy face from her front and motioned for me to sit. She cleaned up the dough, then tended to the pumpkins and came back from the last trip to the mud room with a bowl full of steaming hot pumpkin. She set it on the counter and pulled down a tin canister from the cupboard. After she had smothered the pumpkin with brown sugar, she found a can of fresh milk. With a little ladle, she scooped off the separated cream and generously covered the sugary pumpkin with it, then sprinkled a little more brown sugar over the top.

"Mmmm...okay now...goooot, is goot," she said.

She set the bowl down in front of me and sat down across the table. It smelled heavenly. I looked up to find her round, brown eyes watching me with excited anticipation.

"Eat," she said, nodding her head. She leaned over the table and loaded the spoon with sweet, creamy pumpkin.

My stomach wasn't feeling particularly hungry or healthy right then, but I felt I might break her heart if I rejected her sure cure, so I succumbed. Had I not intercepted the spoon from her, I am sure she would have fed me without question, but I took it from her fingers that were no bigger than my own, and blew on it for only a moment before devouring the entire bite. If anything can take your mind off despair and destitution, this was it. Pure goodness! I rolled my eyes around with abandon to show my delight. I licked the dripping cream from my lips and loaded my spoon for another bite. She was satisfied.

"Okay, goot," she said "is goot for you?"

I nodded slowly.

She smiled and bowed, then went outside to wring and hang the laundry. I finished my pumpkin, licked the bowl and set it in the sink, then headed out the back door to find Basi so I could thank her. She was still hanging clothes. There was one basket of laundry near her feet, and another at the foot of the steps. I hoisted it up onto my hip, like I had seen Lena and Mama do, and joined Basi at the clothesline. The laundry smelled fresh and sweet. The wind sent a sheet billowing into my face and I thought of summer afternoons helping Mama hang the socks and Father's handkerchiefs. Basi worked quickly and skillfully. Each clothespin held the terminal end of one piece and the beginning of another. I observed that before attaching any piece of wet laundry, she first gave it a shake that made a loud snapping noise and sometimes made a rainbow in the misty sunshine. I picked up a piece of laundry from my basket and shook it. No rainbow. The clothes line was a manageable height for me, as Basi was probably only two inches taller than me, so I started my own row on the next clothes line.

"Thank you Basi," I said as I clipped my first clothespin over the corner of a dish towel.

"Yes, tank you. You yike punkin, is goot?" she said as she worked.

"Very good," I said, peeking around a towel.

"Velly goot," She said, and smiled and nodded her head. "Okay, you?"

"Yes, I'm Okay." I lied.

***

From that day on, my days were much different. Mama promised that as soon as I was thirteen I could move in with her, but for now I would need to do my best to help Aunt Ruth and try to be the best girl I could be. What she didn't understand was that Aunt Ruth was turning me into the worst girl I could be. I lived for my weekends with Mama. The times we spent with Grandpa and Grandma, or Uncle Virg and Aunt Marion were like holidays that I wished would never end. Saturdays went too fast, and Sundays, though they should have been a day of loving God and eating pot roast, only represented the last day before going back to the wrath of Ruth Linderman. I tried not to speak to Mrs. Linderman unless I had to, and couldn't bear to call her Aunt Ruth anymore. If I had to address her at all I called her Mrs. Linderman. She was not my aunt. When she spoke to me it was always with instruction or reprimand. She used a cold voice and a false smile. Mr. Linderman was nice to me and seemed to understand how I felt, though he never said so. Miss Platts and Mr. Danielson were extra nice to me after that, like buffers in the space around the meanness. Miss Platts often said she was too full for her piece of pie after dinner and would give it to me, as mine was usually about the size a mouse could pick up and eat. When Mr. Danielson was home, he and I played cards after dinner, or he helped me with my homework if Miss Platts wasn't available. I felt like a prisoner doing time in a jail. I started to count the days until my thirteenth birthday, but stopped, knowing that the number would be far too high for me to bear. I figured if I could make it to the next day I could probably make it to the next day after that, so that's what I did, counted to one every day.

6

The impending arrival of Mr. Linderman's sister and her children brought a burst of activity to the house. All of my belongings were moved upstairs to the attic, and my old room was made ready for Mrs. Joy Taylor.

They arrived on a Tuesday. I ran home from school, not even thinking of waiting for Pauline and Neil, and burst through the kitchen door. I found Basi cutting carrots.

"Are the refugees here?" I inquired, using the title Mrs. Linderman had given them.

"Shhh. Sleep," she warned.

I left the kitchen and was headed upstairs when Mrs. Linderman's voice slapped me in the ear.

"Carol!" she half whispered, half yelled. "Come back here!"

At the bottom of the stairs she took my hand and led me into the sitting room. I hadn't been in that room since my arrival day. Mrs. Linderman closed the pocket doors that led to the entryway. Then she sat closer to me than she ever had before and it felt as if we were going to have a real conversation. Her face had a serious worry to it.

"They're here — the refugees," she started.

I nodded.

"I had no idea." She pulled the hanky out from her sleeve and made ready for the tears that were welling up in her eyes. These were not the well thought out tears of a person trying to make a point or emit some sort of reaction from another. These were genuine, heartfelt tears. She had to soak these tears up with the full body of the hanky; a fingertip covered in a corner of the cloth would not do. "The newspapers didn't let on how bad it was. The newsreels didn't show...I don't know how these people lived through the devastation, and I've only heard a very small part of the story. They've had bombs dropping on their neighborhood for months. The little girl, Tessa, walked off that train with one shoe on, Carol, one shoe. The other one's lost in London."

"Were *they* fighting in the war?" I didn't understand.

"Well...no. But they might as well have been. From what I can tell, this is not a battle between soldiers. The Germans are bombing anyone they can reach and having no preference for rank, age or gender. They're just bombing London, indiscriminately. I don't understand it myself, so I don't expect you to," she was finding her normal voice, "but I wanted to let you know how fragile and tired they are before you met them."

"Are they hurt?"

"They don't appear injured. The hurt might be more inside than out."

"Why would they try to kill kids?" I asked.

"I don't know, Carol."

"Who started the war, anyhow?" I was baffled.

"The selfish and greedy," she said.

For a split second I felt like I wanted to give Mrs. Linderman a hug. She seemed so vulnerable and unlike the hard-shelled task master I'd come to resent. Then I remembered Pauline using those same words to describe Mrs. Linderman. Selfish and greedy.

"Hmmm," I said. Saying "hmmm" helped me to not open my mouth and say something I might regret.

"So Carol, try to be as charitable and helpful as you can be. We've moved your things up to the attic," she said. She shoved her vulnerability back up her sleeve with her handkerchief and stood to signal that our conversation was over.

***

The salvation of the refugees, which in theory was sacrificial and humanitarian, turned out in reality to be a great source of frustration for Mrs. Linderman. It also lit a simmering flame of conflict between Mr. and Mrs. Linderman. The most obvious benefactor, other than the refugees themselves, was the garden. Mr. Linderman found solace out of doors. If a stray leaf could be snatched with his reaching contraption, or a hedge could be rounder or squarer, he found reason to excuse himself from the ruckus of the children, and the forced formalities between his sister and his wife.

Aunt Ruth started a habit of murmuring. She complained to no one in particular, and I'm sure I wasn't meant to hear her murmurings at all, but she kept quite a constant conversation going with herself under her breath. In response to Mrs. Taylor's frequent dislike of the weather, she said, "What on earth! If it's not too hot it's too cool, or too humid or too dry..." I didn't hear the rest because she stopped at the top of the stairs and fixed the fringe on the rug and grunted the rest of her lamentations to her chest and the floor. Another time she came storming through the kitchen door, mimicking a whiny British accent, "I don't *care* for creamed soups," and then as she poured the contents of a mug into the scrap bucket, "I'll cream her soup." I actually had to turn and hide my face at this one so she wouldn't see my smile. Aunt Ruth's feathers were being severely ruffled. More than once I observed her counting backwards from ten and taking a deep breath when she reached one. When she wasn't murmuring her complaints, they just seemed to seep out of the wrinkles in her forehead. I would have loved to give her a taste of her own medicine and suggest a Bible verse to help her curb her rebellious spirit.

I didn't mind the attic after all. It was at the top of a steep, narrow staircase and was, by design, not easily accessible to adults. It became a refuge from the rest of the house. Even though it was colder and darker than the main part of the house, it had a sunnier disposition. My roommates were younger than me. Simon was four. He had gingery red hair with lots of cowlicks that made it stick up in every odd way. He didn't speak at all. He would laugh if he was tickled or scream if he was mad, but he didn't use words. Tessa was seven. She had hair the same color as Simon and wore it in a braid down her back. She never stopped talking and teased Simon incessantly. Mama and I named them "The Ginger Snaps" because of the color of their hair.

I slept on a cot next to Tessa. Simon's was in an alcove near the window. When I asked Tessa about their home in England she started to hum, then sniffle. Then she bit her lip until it bled, so I didn't ask again. I never found out exactly what happened, but I can't conceive of what would cause a woman like their mother to stare out the window for hours on end, or make a four year old stop speaking altogether. Their reality was surely worse than the most tragic event I could imagine. I thought of other memories we could share about our early childhoods. We learned each other's finger plays and clapping songs, and I sang all the nursery rhymes I knew to Simon. I taught Tessa, *A sailor went to sea, sea, sea...* and she taught me one about *walking 'round a garden like a teddy bear.* For the first few weeks after their arrival, their mother was very sad and pale. She spent most of her time in a chair by the window, reading Aunt Ruth's collection of book club novels, dozing between chapters. She wasn't the least bit helpful with the wash or cooking, or any real companionship to Ruth Linderman. Her kindest offering to me was a weak smile of thanks when I made it my responsibility to occupy the children as they caroused around the house or got on her last nerve. I was happy to corral them most of the time, as it kept them out of Aunt Ruth's way and she didn't bother me about as many chores if I was entertaining The Ginger Snaps.

7

About three weeks after their arrival, Mrs. Joy Taylor came out of her funk. She got up and got dressed and announced that it was Thursday. After that, Tessa, Simon, and their mother spent every Thursday after school at the war relief volunteer hall. They rolled bandages, sewed on buttons, or packaged supplies for soldiers. I didn't get to go; I did laundry on Thursdays.

One afternoon when we had finished hanging the laundry, Basi took both baskets and set them by the back door. Then she took me by the hand. "Come," she said.

We walked around to the side of the house and across the mowed lawn. A tall arborvitae hedge divided the yard from the mint field beyond. Basi stopped at a hollowed-out place in the hedge and pulled me through. I stopped and pulled back on Basi's hand, knowing this was the way to the white house, and that it was forbidden ground.

"Come, try swing," she said as she tugged on my arm.

"No Basi, I'm not supposed to go near the white house. Mrs. Linderman said never to go over there."

"Is okay. No kids. Swing is good," she said, and pulled me along.

The field smelled all the more minty as we tramped on the stems of harvested plants and headed to the huge oak tree in the distance. Once there, Basi held the wooden seat and I hoisted myself up onto it. It was suspended by smooth thick rope which was looped into the wood through two holes, drilled at each end. My feet hung about two inches from the dirt, where a trough had been created from thousands of feet starting and stopping. Basi ran around in back of me and took hold of the ropes. She pulled me back, then ran forward under the swing and didn't let go until she had pushed me as high as her slight stature could manage.

"Weeeeeee!" she yelled and ran around in back of me again.

She pushed and I flew back and forth through the air. The sky came closer with every swing. Basi came around and sat on the ground in front of me as I pumped the swing by myself. She smiled as she watched me and sang a song in Chinese. I swung my feet back and forth to the beat, which slowed me down a little, but I couldn't help it; the tune was contagious. When I jumped off, she clapped for my daredevil feat.

"Your turn," I said.

She lifted herself up onto the swing and I ran around and gave her the biggest under-doggie I could. She screamed and giggled and actually looked a little scared for a moment, but she was laughing the whole time. I ran around to watch her and she kicked her feet up and her little slippers flew over my head and landed way beyond me with a puff of dust. She slid off the swing and went to retrieve her shoes, so I went back for one more turn. As Basi turned back from getting her shoes, she froze. She was staring past me as if she'd seen a ghost. I looked over my shoulder and saw Pauline and Neil walking toward us. I waved my arms and hollered for them to come and swing with us, but was interrupted by Basi pressing into me like a linebacker and pushing me off the swing and beyond.

"Go—go home, we go home!" Basi took off running, quick and quiet as a deer, bare footed, across the dusty field. I followed, looking back once when we reached the hedge and saw Pauline, standing on the seat of the swing with her feet spread out and her arms stretched high on the ropes. She looked like an X. Neil was squatting down on the ground writing something in the dirt. They watched us retreat and made no effort to call us back. Basi ran into the house. I followed, confused. Basi slammed the kitchen door behind me. Mrs. Linderman was at the kitchen table peeling cucumbers.

"Where *have* you two been? And Basi! Why, your toe is bleeding!" Mrs. Linderman dipped a corner of her kitchen towel in a bowl of water, flung it over her shoulder, and walked toward Basi to assess the damaged toe.

"Bad kids!" bellowed Basi.

"Are they home already?" Mrs. Linderman asked. She was referring to the" ginger snaps."

Basi pointed toward the way we had come.

"The white house kids?" Mrs. Linderman covered her heart with both hands and gasped, then her face turned pale and her forehead furrowed.

"Yes," said Basi between panting breaths.

"They know better than to set foot on this property, where are they?" she grabbed a long cast iron hook that hung over the stove and started for the door.

"No!" I hollered. "We were swinging." I grabbed the hook, trying to slow her down. "They were in the mint field! They just wanted to play!"

Aunt Ruth stopped, jerked the heavy hook from my grip, and studied me with a perplexed look. Then she backed up searching for a chair to sit in. She wiped her forehead with the damp end of the towel, (never mind Basi's bloody toe) and stared at me as a sentencing judge might look at a convicted murderer.

She sat for a moment, wiped her own chronically drippy nose with a freshly ironed hanky from her sleeve, then sat straight up on the edge of her chair. Her hands were shaking and her eyes showed white all the way around the iris.

"NEVER say NO to me!" she yelled, still maintaining the perpetual pucker in her lips. She took a few deep breaths, then squeezed the rest of her words out through rigid vocal folds. "I told you never to go anywhere near that white house, and I meant it." Her hands were fisted around the kettle hook and she tapped it on the ground with each syllable. "Carol, you have no idea what kind of savages they are over there," her voice was low and controlled now, like she didn't want anyone to hear her. Her face was getting redder and redder and sweat beads appeared on her forehead. Basi took a cookie sheet from the pantry and fanned Aunt Ruth with it. "Basi and I have seen the evil spirits that live in that youngest brother. They fly around in him and shake him up. I've seen it more than once!" Her voice choked and she teared up.

I looked at Basi. She nodded her head in agreement. "Evil."

I backed away from Aunt Ruth, "He is not an evil boy. He's a sick boy! He's special! He doesn't have an evil spirit, he has an angel. You're the one with the evil spirit!" I stood still then, in utter amazement of my true, but reckless comment.

Aunt Ruth leaned over as if I had punched her in the stomach and let the cast iron hook fall to the floor with a heavy thump. When she regained her breath she rose from her chair and stepped toward me with her index finger aimed at my chest.

"Go to your room and don't come down until I call for...no better yet..." She grabbed the muscle between my neck and my shoulder and corralled me over to the kitchen sink, then clenched the hair at the base of my neck with one hand, and a bar of lie soap with the other, and shoved it into my mouth. I tried to turn my head, but she twisted her finger in my hair. I could hear some of it ripping out behind my ear. She ground the bitter bar into my teeth and when she was satisfied with the amount of soap deposited and the extent of my broken will, she led me into the mud room and undid a rusty latch on a short door that led to the cellar. She leaned into the darkness and pulled a chain. The bare light bulb did not respond, but the light from the kitchen revealed a steep wooden stairway. With her fingers still securely tangled in my hair, she led me to the doorway. "I told you on your first day here not to go near that white house. Now you may go down into the cellar and think about whether or not you will take me at my word in the future." She pushed me through the door of the cellar and I felt for the railing. There wasn't one. I stepped down one step then turned around. Her silhouette stood in the small doorway.

"Aunt Ruth, I'm sorry. I didn't mean to disobey you. Basi just wanted to show me the swing, we were having fun." I drooled and spit chunks of soap as I spoke.

"Don't grovel! And let the bad taste in your mouth remind you to refrain from EVER saying NO to me again," she said. "I believe there is a candle at the bottom of the stairs." Then she slammed the door.

I heard her slide the latch and walk away. The combination of soap and saliva churned in my throat and my whole body seized as I gagged and spit over the edge of the steps. I had no water to rinse my mouth out so I began digging the impacted soap out of my teeth with my finger nail. I gagged and vomited over the side of the stairs splashing the soapy remains of my lunch all over the concrete floor. It didn't smell good, but the force of the evacuation actually helped to clean out my mouth, so the bulk of the soap was gone. I sat on the steps and continued to spit with any saliva I could make. I don't remember ever being so angry. I stared at the door, thinking she would open it at any minute. She didn't. I hated Mrs. Linderman. If there was a way out of this cellar, I had to find it and get away from her. I was scared to stand up on the stairs and go any deeper into the darkness, so I scooted on my bottom, down to the fourth step. I had to wrap my arms around my knees to keep my legs from shaking, not from cold, but from fury. My limited knowledge of cellars was that they were cold and damp, but this place was hot and dry and stunk of moldy potatoes and furniture oil. I felt nautious. I didn't need a toilet, but I feared that I would. Just the thought of it started a cramp in my middle. I wiped my face on my shirt and tried to stop crying.

From the far wall a window let a scant amount of light into the cellar. It was covered with ivy on the outside and scummy dirt on the inside, so I couldn't tell how big it was for sure, but it looked like my only way out. I scooted down the stairs, one step at a time, making sure I stayed close to the wall so I wouldn't fall off. Just as Mrs. Linderman had said, a box of matches and a candle were sitting on the windowsill. I pinched out a wooden match and scraped it along the rough side of the box. Nothing. I tried again, still nothing. My hands were shaking so bad that I was afraid of dropping the whole box. I walked back up to the door and called again for help. There was only silence, so I sat down on the step and tried the matches again. Fire. Finally! The candle was still at the bottom of the steps so I tucked the box of matches under my arm and slowly carried the lit match to it. The flame reached my fingers before I reached the candle, and the pain released my fingers from the matchstick. It landed on the concrete floor into what looked like a puddle of water, but most certainly was not. It was probably the source of the oily smell and it immediately ignited into a pool of blue flame. I jumped back and stood in shock for a moment, then ran up the stairs, retreating from the growing blaze and toxic black smoke. The dark cloud chased me up the stairs, launching me into a coughing fit. The oily fire trailed to a stack of old newspapers and ignited them with little effort. Instantly the air at the top of the stairs was too thick for breathing and I was feeling faint. I retreated to the foot of the steps and took a deep breath of not-so-smoky air, then again, struggled up to the door.

"Aunt Ruth, I'm sorry! I'm so sorry. Aunt Ruth. Basi!" Mucous and tears ran into my mouth and my fists throbbed with each attack at the door. "Help! Fire! Help me!" I pounded and slapped my palms against the door. My hands, lungs and eyes stung. I couldn't yell or scream anymore because every time I took a breath I just started coughing. I threw up again, this time on the stairs, and slipped on the slimy film. I was going to die. I thought of never seeing my mother again and my fear turned to rage. As a last effort, I threw my whole self into the splintery door. It didn't budge. I tried again, this time with *less* force, but I flew through it with no resistance at all and came crashing to an abrupt stop into the iron feet of the washing machine. Volcanic clouds of smoke billowed from the cellar door.

"Fire! Ruth, ring up the fire department, the cellar is on fire!" called a voice hovering over me. My eyes were blurred from the smoke and tears, so I couldn't see, but someone picked me up and laid me on my back. It felt like I was being strolled in a baby buggy through the kitchen and adjoining rooms. With a bump, we rolled over the threshold and out to daylight and air that could be breathed.

"I've got you, Carol," assured my rescuer. It was Mr. Linderman.

I couldn't speak, couldn't see, and could hardly breathe. Above the repetitive wrenching of my coughs, I could hear Aunt Ruth screaming unanswerable questions and yelling useless orders to no one.

"Stay here," He laid me on the front lawn, away from the house and disappeared through the front door. Within seconds he reappeared with a huge black cat in his lap. He wheeled over near me and the cat jumped down, disappearing through the hedge. I had lived here for three months and didn't even know they had a cat.

Within minutes, three men appeared from out of nowhere, hauling buckets of water. Not long after that, a siren announced the arrival of the fire truck. They ran past me and into the house carrying bags of sand and buckets of water, back and forth and back again, tracking soot and mud all over Mrs. Linderman's fancy tiled entryway. Two firemen drug a huge flat hose up the brick path. A few moments later the hose was round with water. I felt a surge of hope thinking the fire could be stopped, then I felt an equally strong hope that the whole house would burn to the ground and Mrs. Linderman with it. Through the hedge I saw Neil's face watching the commotion. All of a sudden he catapulted through the hedge and was immediately followed by two older boys, a bucket of water in each hand. They barely missed stampeding their little brother and splashed across the lawn. I saw Neil's face, yelling something in anger or maybe terror, but I couldn't make it out for all the other noise around. They barreled into the house without invitation. Neil got up, spun around and dove back through the arborvitae. I watched through the hole in the hedge as he ran, looking back a few times, falling once, and finally disappearing through the door of the white clapboard house.

Behind me I recognized the voice of Miss Platts. I got up and fell into her, wrapping my arms around her little waist.

"There's a fire in the cellar!" she naively informed me. "Did we all get out? Where are the other children? Sir, there are more children in the house, and an invalid! Sir! There are people in there!" Only one stopped to listen to her, it was Neil's brother Will. He ran back into the house. We watched firefighters run back and forth, expecting to see them carrying Tessa or Simon with each exit. Mrs. Linderman escorted Joy Taylor out and across the street to Mr. Doyle's house. She had that glazed look back in her eyes and just stood, staring out the window, wrapped in a blanket.

The upstairs attic window opened and Will's voice bellowed through the smoke, "I'VE GOT THE CHILDREN!" He tossed Simon onto a close branch of a huge tree. The four year old effortlessly slithered down like a lizard. A firefighter attempted to help him but he was down before the man could intercept him, so the rescuer climbed up to help with Tessa who was hysterical. She held onto the casing of the window, resisting all efforts from Will or the fire fighter. When she'd made a big enough fuss I heard Will yell, "DO YOU WANT TO BURN TO DEATH, OR RISK A BROKEN LEG?" She immediately, though reluctantly allowed her body to be passed to the able arms of the fireman. Will jumped to a lower branch and from there directly down to the grass and back into the house.

Mr. Linderman approached Miss Platts and stopped, "I am NOT an invalid!" he said, and rolled away.

She gathered me closer, this time for her own comfort more than mine. I put my head under her thick gray sweater. I was shivering from shock. She walked me away from the line of traffic, and peeked under her sweater to find my face. She saw it and frowned when she saw my bloodshot eyes and sooty face.

"What happened?" she shrieked and bent down to get a better look at me. Over her shoulder I could see Mrs. Linderman, her face in a snit and her fists clenched tight, barreling across the front yard with a purpose only I could fully know. Before she closed the gap, I escaped from under the safety of Miss Platts' sweater and followed Neil's path. I too dove through the hole in the hedge and ran with a force that I didn't know I had. My skinny, bruised legs, powered by pure adrenaline, sprinted the three blocks to the Hospital without any deliberate help from me. I ran the familiar route with blurry eyes and stinging lungs, making it to my mother's door, too weak to knock. I fell in front of the door with my face in the half-inch gap at the bottom and called as loud as I could, "Maaa-maaa!"

Before I finished my next breath, the door opened and my mother picked me up. She carried me to her bed and lay down without letting go. She stayed right next to me and held me, not asking, not scolding, just breathing and saying, "I'm sorry baby, I'm sorry. Dear Jesus, I am so sorry, Oh Carol, my baby."

I sobbed a wet patch onto the pillow. Mama turned me onto my back, gazed into my dirty, sweaty, face, and wept.

"I couldn't get out of the basement." I whined breathlessly. "I never want to go back there."

"You never have to. Can you tell me what happened?" She wiped her nose on her sleeve.

I didn't know where to start. My voice was raspy and weak. "I couldn't get out of the basement, the door was locked and the match fell and I couldn't open the door and no one came, but then Mr. Linderman opened the door... my head hurts."

"It's okay now, it's okay. I'm so sorry, Peach, you smell like fire."

"I couldn't get out." I sobbed and she held me until I could start from the start.

She listened, asking very few questions as I spoke. I tried to think why Mrs. Linderman would get so mad at me. I tried to think why anyone would get so mad about anything.

When Mama spoke she said, "Ignorance. That's why people do things like that." Then she rocked me in her arms and hummed a sleepy tune and let me finish crying.

The knock we were both expecting came next—a quiet underhand tap with one knuckle. We knew who it was and neither of us moved. She held me tighter. The knock came again, this time hard and fast, business-like. Mama went to the door.

"I assume Carol is here," Aunt Ruth started in as soon as Mama started to open the door.

"Yes, she is, and she is very distraught. It's not a good idea for you to be here." Mama held her foot against the door. "I question that you are of sound mind, Mrs. Linderman."

"That's ridiculous. My mind is sound enough to know that Carol has not listened to my instructions and has therefore come face to face with life-threatening danger twice this very day!" She spoke in overly dramatic terms with her palm pressing to her chest, just under her brooch. "Carol was specifically instructed not to go near that god-forsaken white house in the mint field, and she did!" Ruth Linderman tattled.

Mama turned to me, "Carol, did you go over to the neighbor's house after being told not to?"

"No," I said.

"Well," continued Aunt Ruth, "she may not have gone *to* their house, but she went near it and I have forbidden any contact with those unruly and unhealthy children. It is for Carol's own safety and well-being."

"One of the big brother's from the white house saved Tessa and Simon from the fire!" I said. All of my courage to speak as such came only from the fact that I knew my mother was my protector and defender.

Ignoring my outburst, she went on, "Besides this, she blatantly told me 'no' to my face. She is a defiant and unruly child! She started a fire in my basement! She could have burned my house down! It would have been *her* fault if those children had perished!" she clucked, still standing in the hallway.

"Why was my daughter in the basement?" Mama asked, already knowing the answer.

"A child needs discipline for blatant disobedience!" Aunt Ruth pushed the door open and took three steps into the apartment. Her face was getting red again. She stopped short, clearly taken aback by my disheveled appearance. I sat up in the bed and got up on my knees.

"I was not! I was not being disobedient. I was just playing, and Basi ran—and you were mad—you put me in the cellar and it was dark—and I was scared—I couldn't ... I wanted to come and find you Mama. The door was locked, I couldn't get out." I pulled the blanket up over my head and buried my face in my mother's fragrance, pressing my hands over my ears and sobbing into the already soggy pillow.

"Mrs. Linderman, we are not finished discussing this, but you are finished as Carol's guardian. I will send my father for her belongings. That will be all." Mama pushed Mrs. Linderman out the door, then slammed and locked it behind her.

Later, after I had brushed my teeth four times to get all the soap out, and was soaking in a warm bubbly tub, mama sat on the toilet seat and asked me a series of questions to fill in the gaps of the story. She didn't gasp or frown or murmur at my answers, she just tucked them away and added up her conclusion.

"Do *you* think you were disobedient?" she asked.

"No, Mama. I didn't go near the house and that's all she ever said was don't go near the house."

"Good. Do you think you were disrespectful?"

I thought for a few seconds. "Yes," I said.

"Do you think you need to apologize for that?" she said.

I thought for a few seconds more. My Sunday school self said yes. That we should respect our elders and not lash out at people, no matter what they do to us. But my own self, my gut and my heart, said no. "I probably *should,* but I don't want to," I said. "I can't stand the thought of standing in front of her and her being able to look down her nose at me and feel like she did the right thing and I was the bad one."

"All right, I understand. But I'm going to ask you about it again in a month. We'll see how you feel about it then," she said. "I'm not saying she did the right thing. I just want to make sure you do."

8

The question of my future whereabouts hung like a heavy layer of fog over the weekend. We maneuvered through it, ignored it, breathed it in, rolled it around in our minds, but never spoke of it. Monday morning, Mama walked me to school.

"See you around three," Mama said after she bent to kiss me.

"At your apartment?"

"Yeah, I'll leave the door unlocked, I might take a nap. I have to work tonight." She forced a smile. "Have a bully day!"

"Okay." I turned to go, but didn't move. I turned back, "I love you," I said.

"A bushel and a peck!" she said back and walked on.

The day seemed fifty hours long. Everyone wanted to know all about the fire, but I didn't want to let on that I had started it, so I said I didn't know. I avoided Neil and Pauline after school and took off running down Willard Street as soon as the last bell rang. Mama was still asleep when I got to her apartment. I snuck in and sat at the little table where a plate of gingerbread wheels was waiting, and ate three, all in a row. When Mama's alarm went off at 3:10, I shut it off and crawled in with her. Halfway through chapter seven of *Little Women*, I slipped into a cozy slumber and neither of us woke up until we heard a knock on the door.

"Who is it?" Mama hollered at the door.

"Dad." Grandpa walked in.

"Oh, Dad. Hi."

Mama was in a bit of a sleepy fog until she looked at the clock which read 6:30. She sprung out of bed and landed in front of her dresser, pulled out a pair of white stockings, her garter belt, a bra, a slip, and a folded pair of white cotton underpants. "I'm going to be late. Carol why'd you let me sleep so long? Thanks Dad. Did you pick up Carol's things?" she said, not waiting for an answer. She opened her top drawer and carefully removed a flat, starched nurse's cap and a small cardboard box with little drawers on its sides. She handed the whole lot to me. "Peach, be the peachiest and put my hat together for me." She filed through half a dozen white dresses in the closet, chose one and sailed into the bathroom.

I knew how to fold the stiff fabric and secure the button into the three button holes to make the flat, linen square become a tidy white pyramid. I straight-pinned the velvet ribbon onto the flipped up front and voila; a nurse's cap! I had done this many times, but in her hurry, mama was fully dressed in less time than it took me to fold the cap.

"Carol, you go with Grandpa," she said in between puckers in the mirror as she applied her orange lipstick, "he will drive you to school in the morning and you can come back here after school. I've scheduled a visit with a family who is interested in having you stay with them." My heart sank. She turned to me with a tissue between her lips, when she removed it she let it go over a small trash can, but missed. She bent and fake kissed me on the cheek so she wouldn't ruin her perfectly blotted lips. "Okay?"

"I want to live with you," I frowned.

"We'll talk about it tomorrow. I have to go. I love you." She slipped her navy blue wool cape over her shoulders, lit a cigarette, blew Grandpa a kiss, and left.

Just seconds later, she poked her head back in the door. "Thanks, Daddy, lock the door when you leave, would ya?" She blew him another kiss and shut the door again. We both took a deep breath and waited a moment before either of us spoke.

"Sorry about Ruth Linderman," Grandpa said.

"It's not your fault," I mumbled to my dirty fingernails.

"Didn't take you long to peel away the onion skin," he said.

"What?"

"Didn't take you long to find out what Ruth Linderman was really made of, what she was like inside," he explained. "I've known the woman thirty years and never, well, never really knew her I guess."

"She's evil. She's heartless and evil," I said with conviction.

"Yes, I suppose she is."

"I hate her."

"I'm sorry about that, but I don't think she's worth the energy, Carol. Best to let the Judge of the universe see to her."

I went into the bathroom and when I came out he picked me up and hugged me in his gentle arms, then set me down and touched my cheek.

"I'm glad you're all right," he said, and wiped a tear from the corner of his own eye.

I smiled as best I could.

"All right, Peach, what d'ya say we get going? Grandma's got some dinner waiting, and I think she made a pound cake for dessert." He jingled his keys in his pocket.

"Okay," I willingly surrendered. Dinner didn't interest me, but pound cake did.

When we arrived in Levant, Grandma was waiting for us. Dinner, a warm fire, and the familiarity of this safe refuge calmed my sad and tired heart. Everything I owned sat on a small corner of their guest room. Everything smelled of smoke.

"Where's my baby buggy?" I asked.

"Don't know, Carol, she didn't give it to me, just what's here. Maybe it burned."

"It didn't burn! It was in the hallway upstairs. I need it back, Jesse's in there!" I cried.

"I'll go back tomorrow, Carol. I'll phone her tonight and ask her to look for it," Grandpa said.

There was no answer at the Linderman's that night, but Grandpa went over to The Linderman's the next day. He got Jesse back, but they couldn't find her buggy. How on earth a thing as big as a baby buggy can get lost in a house is a mystery to me. Jesse was safer in my arms anyway.

***

I stayed with Grandma and Grandpa in Levant for a whole week. Mama called it my forced vacation. When I returned to Jamestown the following Friday morning, Mama was awake and dressed in her blue, long-sleeved, all-business dress. Her eyes looked tired, and her face wasn't the right color. As soon as I saw her, ready and waiting for me, I felt my heart jumping around in my chest, trying to come up through my throat. She was trying to act casual, normal, like we were going shopping for school shoes, but we weren't. We were going shopping for a new place for me to live.

"Mama, I have two requests," I said.

"Well," she said.

"I want to be out of smelling range of the mint field, and I would like it if there were other kids."

Part Three

November, 1941

1

On the last warm day of autumn, we started our search. Mama gave my hand a squeeze. "This looks like it. Yep, number three-thirty-three." She confidently guided me up the dirt driveway, past a chain link fence that separated us from a barking dog and three kids. They were all younger than me. Their fingers grabbed the crisscross of the fence like prisoners in jail. Six curious eyes followed us as we walked by. From the looks of it, they had taken one full set of clothes and divided it up between the three of them. The youngest, a girl, was wearing shoes, socks, and underpants. The elastic in the waist was nearly worn out and she kept tugging at them to keep them up. Next in line was the tallest, a barefoot boy. He wore only trousers and a half smile. The last, another boy, had on too-big cowboy boots, and a button-down, long-sleeved shirt of faded orange and gray plaid. Mama smiled at them and said hello. They didn't answer. The boy in the cowboy boots sidestepped along the fence as we walked on, following us all the way to the house.

Three-thirty-three Baker Street was a two-story yellow farm house. The front porch was shady and swept clean. There was a rocking chair and a few wooden school chairs lined up under the front window. A very plump lady was busy deadheading the spent flower buds from a hanging fuchsia basket and throwing them over the porch railing. As we neared the front steps, the boy in the boots monkeyed up the front railing of the porch and hopped over, landing with a loud thump on the wood slats, just moments before our arrival.

"COMPANY!" he yelled, still squatting like a frog.

The plump lady turned around and acknowledged us with a wide welcoming smile. She wiped her hands on her apron and approached us quickly.

"Welcome, welcome! Oh my, you snuck up on me." She untied her apron, looped it over her head and tossed it over the back of the rocking chair. Then she planted both of her hands on her billowing waist, took a deep breath, and looked me right in the eyes. "Hello," she said, smiling.

Mama and I both returned the greeting.

"Abe Joe, go get Axel and Ellie," she said, over her shoulder to the boy in the boots.

He sprung up, hopped back over the railing and took off running, yelling for his siblings at the top of his lungs.

"I could have done *that*," she smiled apologetically and opened the front door. "Please come in, come in, did you walk over? Of course you did... it's so close and such a nice day... would you like some tea? I bet you would, if you like tea... Carol, do you like sweet sun tea? I love sweet tea. If there's one thing I love and look forward to on a warm afternoon, it's a tall glass of sweet, cool, tea."

We didn't have a chance to answer because she kept on talking, answering her own questions as if she could read our minds. She led us past a sitting room, through the dining room and into the kitchen. "Have a seat," she said, as she motioned toward the kitchen table.

The front screen door slammed and all three kids tumbled into the kitchen. The little girl had lost her underpants altogether by this time and squatted down to pull up her socks.

"Carol, this is Abe Joe," His mother pointed to the agile boy in the boots. He looked like he was about six, but seemed older. Abe Joe lowered his head and moved his lips to say hi, but I couldn't hear him. She pointed to the taller boy. "This is Axel. Axel, say hello to Carol."

"Hel-lo Car-rrol." His voice was slow and melodic. He covered his bare chest with folded arms and started biting on his knuckle.

The little girl was twisted up in the folds of her mother's huge flowered skirt, so only her eyes and forehead peaked out.

"And this is Ellie, she's almost three. Where's your teeny-pants, Ellie? A lady needs to keep her panties on especially when company's coming." She laughed, unfolded the naked toddler from her skirt and picked her up. The tiny girl landed on her mother's soft, adequate hip, and burrowed her head into her even more adequate bosom. She said nothing and stuck her two middle fingers in her mouth. "Axel, be a dear and go look on the line for a dress and a pair of teeny-pants for Ellie."

Axel took off out the back door and came flying back, only moments later, with a light green pillow case and a pair of underpants.

"Put your arms up, Ellie," she said.

Ellie's mother slipped the pillow case right over her and out popped Ellie's arms and head, through holes cut in the top and sides. She handed the underwear to Ellie, instructing her to give it a try.

Mama and I had hardly uttered a word so far. We just watched as orders were given and followed. Tea spoons were laid, glasses set out, hands washed, and chairs pulled from corners so that everyone had a seat. Ellie climbed into a high chair and laid her hands open on the wooden tray, "Cookie, please." Her mother gave her two, one for each hand, and gently pinched the snot from under Ellie's nose with her bare fingers. Ellie rubbed her arm furiously all over her face, smearing around any remnant. After washing her own hands, (and thank you God for that, or I would not have been eating *any* of those cookies) the woman finally sat down with a sigh, and giggled.

"I haven't even introduced myself!" she said, "I'm Glory McDonald and I know that you are Carol, and you are Virginia, and I have absolutely no manners to speak of, and what little I might have I seem to have thrown overboard with the fuchsias." She giggled again. "Seems I've forgotten the tea. Axel, be a love and bring the tea jug up from the basement, would you? Careful, it's heavy."

"It's a pleasure to meet you, Gloria," said Mama, offering a hand.

"No, just Glory," she corrected. She took hold of Mama's outstretched hand with both of hers and started shaking. "Just call me Glory. That's what my daddy named me, said it was the first thing that came out of his mouth when he saw me all purple and prune-like just after I was born. 'Glory be!' is what he said. Carol, you can call me Glory too. No fancy Mrs. McDonald title, that's my mother-in-law." Only then did she let loose of Mama's hand.

"Well Glory, looks like you have your hands full around here," Mama said, making her first attempt at giving Glory a chance to back out of the deal.

"These three? They're only half of our blessings. The other three are likely lolly-gagging their way home by way of the baseball diamond. They'll be here soon enough. Anyway, wouldn't want to overpower you with all six at once. Isaac and Elizabeth are twins, ten years old, same as you, Carol. Orion's our oldest. He's thirteen, smart as a whip. Can't find Orion? Look in that tree fort out there. He'll be up there reading some book about something or other; airplanes, gangsters, kidneys, you name it. He'd rather read than eat. Only thing he likes better than books is baseball." She opened the cookie jar and offered it to me first, then Mama, then the other kids. She took two for herself before she set it down and continued. "Mr. McDonald and I made a deal with each other that we would take as many children as the Lord saw fit, and the Lord has blessed us above and beyond." She ladled the cool tea into the various, unmatched glasses.

"Mama's gonna grow me a brother," Abe Joe informed us. He had crawled up in back of his mother and was sitting on the window sill with his arms wrapped around Glory's neck.

Glory smiled and brought her hand up to his, "Abe Joe wants a little brother," she explained.

"I need a brother," Abe Joe corrected, then looked at me, "are you gonna be our new sister?"

I looked at my mother. I didn't know what to say, so I said nothing. Abe Joe crawled down over his mother's shoulder and settled into her lap, then turned his attention to me. His voice was slow and meandering. "Elizabeth said she would go off and live in the forest if she didn't get a sister next time around, but I really need a brother. So if you live with us you could be Elizabeth's new sister and the baby could be the brother."

"I'm delighted you have it all figured out Abe Joe, but no one's even sure there will be a 'next time around'." said Glory, kissing the silky yellow curls that rolled down his forehead.

Abe Joe slipped down under the table and crawled out between me and Glory. "Can I have another cookie Mama?"

"Yes, Abe Joe."

He carefully chose the best one, took one bite, slipped the rest into the pocket of his shirt, and headed for the kitchen door.

"Where you going, Abe Joe?" asked Axel.

"I gotta go find my gun."

Axel got up to go with his brother, but stopped before he closed the door. "You wanna see the tree fort?" he asked, looking at me.

Again I looked at Mama. She nodded, so I pushed my chair back, making a grinding noise on the wood floor, and followed the boys out the back door.

"Last one there's a rotten egg!" yelled Axel.

I was the last one, of course, but no mention was made of me being a rotten egg, or even that I was last. They climbed up the ladder, hardly slowing the pace, flipped up the trap door in the floor of the fort, and hoisted themselves up. I took my time climbing the tree-branch ladder. It didn't look trustworthy. It was made of two long, fairly straight branches with shorter branches tied on with twine, and nailed in for steps. I tested each rung as I climbed, and held on tight with my hands just in case.

"Hurry up! We're being followed," Axel said in a loud raspy whisper.

I looked around and saw little Ellie toddling toward us. Lifting myself up onto the floor of the fort was not as easy as they made it look. As soon as I cleared the door, Axel flipped it back over and carefully secured the latch. I looked through the slats and saw Ellie, sidetracked now, following a small yellow kitten. I took a look around the fort. It was tall enough for standing up, probably even for a grown up. The floor was made partly of branches and partly of thin plywood, painted green in some areas. It was not perfectly even, but looked like four kids could probably lay down with their legs stretched out. Good place for a camp-out. Abe Joe lifted himself up and over a big branch inside the fort and crawled on his hands and knees through an opening in the ceiling. When he came back he had a small, L-shaped stick in his hand.

"Found it," he said.

Axel retrieved a spiral notebook from a nail on the wall. "We have a rule book. You gotta follow the rules if you want to be part of the fort club. Do you?"

"Sure..." I said apprehensively. I wasn't sure I really wanted to be part of the club, but I wanted to hear the rules.

"Put yer hand up like this and repeat after me." He raised his palm up in an oath taking position next to his head. I raised my hand. "I Car-rol," he began.

"I Carol," I repeated.

"Do solemnly swear."

I paused, "I *don't* swear."

"Not like cursing-swearing. Promise-swearing." Axel sounded insulted.

"Do solemnly *promise.*"

He let out a big sigh, "to keep all the rules in the book."

I paused again and looked back and forth to each brother.

"Say it, Car-rol," said Axel.

"No. How can I promise something I don't even know what is?" I lowered my hand. "I'm going back in." I scooted toward the exit.

"Okay. You can hear 'em, but you can't tell anyone else the rules, even if you don't join the club." He flipped the tablet open.

"All right, 'cause I'm not joining anything I don't know the rules to."

"Listen carefully," he said. "Abe Joe, put yer gun down during the rule-reading and pay attention." He ceremoniously remained standing, flipped through a few pages of the book, and began to read. "One: Must have access to a secret squadron decoder."

Abe Joe looked at me with a self-satisfied smile and flipped up the collar of his shirt, revealing a silver Captain Midnight decoder badge. "Check!" he said.

Axel seemed irritated that the attention was off of him, and continued. "Two: Must be able to pass special initiation tests. Three: No fighting between fellow members. Four: Must be able to get a little dirty while playing." At this point he looked up and addressed me. "So far, so good? I mean, you got some other type of clothes I hope."

"Yeah, go on," I said.

"Five: Must be able to run fast enough to ditch somebody." He stole a glance at my shoes and continued, "Six: Must start each meeting with calisthenics. Seven: If caught by the enemy, do not reveal any secret information. Eight: There will be a test each week with Secret Squadron-type words. Nine: No swearing. Ten: No being a wise guy."

"No being a wise guy, *seeee*," Abe Joe mimicked in a gangster voice.

"Abe, that *was* being a wise guy," Axel continued. "Eleven: If you don't have a penny for monthly dues, you must do chores assigned by the head guy. Twelve: Nobody act big, nobody act little, everybody act medium."

"Hmm... That's a lot of rules," I said. "I'll have to think about it."

"You could be like Joyce!" said Abe Joe. "She's Captain Midnight's right hand girl!"

"I like rule number twelve," I said.

"That's actually Mom's rule, but it works ever-where," said Axel.

"What about the rule saying "No Girls"?" Abe Joe asked. But Axel didn't have time to answer.

The strong, clear ring of a dinner bell echoed from the direction of the house. Abe Joe immediately prepared to disembark, but Axel paused.

"You guys go ahead, I need to make some revisions to the rules," Axel said.

I followed Abe Joe up the back steps. He walked past the kitchen door to the double-hung window and raised the bottom half. He motioned for me to enter over the low-hung sill while he held the window, so I did. Then he slipped through himself and shut the window behind him.

"Why'd we go that way?"

"I prefer it," he said, and led the way to the kitchen.

Two boys, one big and one medium, (they made me think of rule number twelve) were elbow deep in the cookie jar. When they heard us enter, they turned around.

"Hi, Carol," said one, then the other.

"What do you mean "*hi Carol*?" Introduce yourself!" Glory scolded.

"We already know her, Mom," said the younger brother, who I recognized from school. "She's in Elizabeth's class. She's really good at math and *really* bad at kickball." Both brothers made snorting snickers under their breath.

I immediately melted under a sinking feeling. I hadn't put two and two together and just now realized my dilemma. I prayed the first foxhole prayer of my life. "Please not her, dear God...please, please, please! I will change all my bad thoughts into pure, all my evil deeds into good, all my selfish desires into volunteer hours at the poor house, just don't let it be *that* Elizabeth McDonald!" as if there could be another. I opened my eyes, which I didn't even know I had shut, and there she was looking at me with her head cocked just so and her lips puckered up a little like she was getting ready to announce her opinion, but she just stood there.

"Lizzy, I hear you and Carol are already friends," said Glory, a huge smile on her face.

"Who told you that?" said Elizabeth.

"Isaac said you're in the same class," said Glory. "Carol, do you two know each other?"

"Kind of," I answered.

Glory looked at her daughter, "Well, looks like you might just have all the time in the world to get better acquainted if Carol moves in."

"Moves in?" Elizabeth acted as if this were the first time she had heard of the arrangement. "Hope she likes sleeping in a dormitory full of boys, 'cause there's no room in with us, is there, Ellie?"

Ellie dipped her cookie in her tea and sucked on it.

"Elizabeth! You may go to your room now. If you're going to act hateful, you can sally-forth right upstairs and ..." Glory stopped lecturing because Elizabeth was already stomping her way up the stairs in cadence to her muffled exploits.

"I'm not sharin'... nothin'... not as if we don't have enough mouths..." Elizabeth's voice trailed off behind her.

"That girl has got such a case of the princess syndrome, got it from the McDonald side. Never mind anyway, she'll get over it," Glory said.

Mama was still sitting at the kitchen table. "Mrs. Mc... I'm sorry, Glory, it really appears you have your hands full. I'm not sure you have the space or the time to take on the care of another child. I think this might be too big a burden on your family," Mama attempted one more tactic of escape.

Glory sat down sideways in the chair next to Mama and leaned into her, "I have thought this over long and hard," she said. "I think it will be good for Elizabeth to have another girl her age around, take her off her high horse. Plus Ellie will be sleeping in with me and Sir—Jim—Mr. McDonald that is, I just call him Sir—it's a long story. Anyway, we need the money while Sir is out of work, and I can't offer much in the way of employment outside of this house. We need Carol as much as she needs us."

"Well," Mama said, "I'll have to pray about it."

Mama always used that to close an argument when she thought she was right. How are you supposed to argue with, or try to convince, someone who only wants what the Lord ordains?

"Good idea. I've been praying all along for a girl just like Carol, and here you are!" Glory stood and started clearing the table, "If it's the will of God, He will lay it on your heart, same as He did me." She poured a glass of milk and dug a cookie out of the bottom of the cookie jar. "Axel, take this up to your sister. I think her blood sugar's low."

"It's too full Mama, I'm gonna spill it," Axel said, looking for a way out of his errand.

"Well then, drink a little, but wipe off the milk from your lip. She won't drink it if she knows it's been drunk from," Glory said, and shooed him out. Then she looked at me again, "So, Carol, tell me about yourself."

"Not again," I thought.

2

As soon as we got back down the driveway, Mama started laughing.

"What's so funny?" I asked, surprised.

"That is one wild household." Mama was smiling and frowning all at the same time. "Why'd you tell her you were allergic to okra? You aren't allergic to okra."

"I *hate* okra."

"I know you hate okra, but that's no reason to tell a bald-face lie. Do you think she'd make you eat okra if you told her the truth—you hate okra?"

"I don't know. Might be all they had."

"If all she had to feed you was okra, she'd likely mix it up with a little maple syrup, sugar coat it, and roll it in chocolate shavings. She seems to like you already," Mama said.

"Her daughter doesn't," I said.

"I noticed. Why not?"

"She's stupid," I said.

"Well, that's obviously not true. She's not stupid, what is she?"

I thought about it and kicked a rock into the street, "She's stuck up and mean."

"Mean to you?"

"Was."

"Well then, start from the start," Mama said, like she always did when she wanted the whole story.

So I told her from the start, which was the very first day of this school year. I'd seen Elizabeth at school before, but never paid her much attention. She wasn't the type of girl you could just walk up to and say hi. She wasn't approachable, I don't know how else to say it. She had some friends, but even they seemed careful around her. People laughed at her jokes too much, and surrendered the best things from their lunch if she looked interested. She wasn't particularly pretty or well dressed, just freckled, with long blonde hair that curled up on the end like it had never been cut. She was tall and thin. She had a forehead that crinkled easily and a mouth that smiled sarcastically.

That first day of school, a new girl named Cindy walked up, plopped her lunch on the table, and sat down right next to Elizabeth. That's another thing; even though she had six friends at her table, no one sat right next to her. Elizabeth backed away a little bit and said, "You're going to have to move, Miss Priss, you're crowding me."

The lunch room seemed to get a lot quieter, but maybe it was just my ears plugging up from all the blood rushing to my head. I felt trouble brewing. I wanted to, but knew I couldn't stop it. Elizabeth stood up, grabbed Cindy's lunch bag, and tossed it over to the table where I was sitting. I took off my glasses and slipped them in the pocket of my skirt, then picked up the lunch bag and threw it back. It landed on Elizabeth's milk carton, tipping it over and splashing milk all over her freckled face, yellow hair, and sky-blue blouse. Elizabeth didn't cry out like most girls would have. She froze, and then slowly erupted. Her freckles disappeared as her face turned dark red. The crinkles in her forehead turned to furrows, and her eyes glazed over and threatened to pop right out of their sockets. Her cheeks puffed up and her lips puckered to release a slow, continuous stream of invisible steam. Then she turned to Cindy, the new girl, and looked inside her lunch bag. She pulled out a chicken leg wrapped in wax paper and handed it to her. She spoke into Cindy's ear, slow and low so that I couldn't hear. Cindy's brow furrowed while listening. She shook her head, no, and then her face turned sad as she continued listening to Elizabeth's whispers.

Next thing you know, Cindy walked over to our table and sat down directly across from me. There were tears in her eyes.

"Open your mouth," Cindy said as she removed the chicken leg from the wax paper. The girls at Elizabeth's table were leaning any way they had to, in order to see the goings-on. A few were smiling, one was covering her mouth, and the others were snickering, anticipating what was coming.

"No, I'm not going to open my mouth," I said, loud enough for all the girls to hear.

Cindy looked back at Elizabeth.

"Tell her to sit on her hands and open her mouth!" Elizabeth fumed.

"You heard her," said Cindy. Then she whispered, "Just do it."

"No," I said, and attempted to furrow my brow as deep as Elizabeth's.

Elizabeth flipped both legs over the picnic bench seat and before I knew it, she was standing in back of Cindy. She took hold of Cindy's ear lobes and started pulling. Cindy flinched at first, trying to get away.

"Don't struggle, Miss Priss, 'cause every time she says no, I'm gonna pull harder," Elizabeth said with a most un-genuine smile.

"Please, open your mouth," she pleaded to me, unable to move.

I opened my mouth a little.

"That's not wide enough," Elizabeth said, and gave a noticeable tug to Cindy's ears.

"Wider!" Cindy said, tears streaming down her face.

"Good. Now sit on your hands!" Elizabeth snapped.

I did. Elizabeth leaned over and whispered in Cindy's ear.

"Close your eyes," Cindy said.

"Come on!" I said, and started to get up.

Cindy gasped with pain.

"She said, close your eyes and open your mouth. Big!" Elizabeth scolded.

The room was nearly silent. I sat there, mouth open, sitting on my hands, with my eyes mostly shut. Cindy shoved the chicken leg in my mouth and left it there. I started to pull my hand out from under my butt.

"SIT-ON-YOUR-HANDS!" yelled Elizabeth. "Now, sit there and don't move or I will pull this girls' ears clean off her head and it will be your fault!"

Anger burned in my chest.

"Count to one hundred, then you can take it out," Elizabeth chided.

"I ca' cou'," I mumbled.

"Yes you *can* count, and you'd better get shakin' or you'll be sitting there with that chicken leg and drool dripping all down your ugly brown dress for the rest of the day!"

I started, "Un, du, shee..." When I finally got to ninety, my face was slimy with salty tears and snot, and my chin was covered with slobber and chicken drippings.

Then Elizabeth shouted to her table of followers, "Everybody! Ninety One, Ninety two.... Count, Miss Priss!... Ninety three..." But only Elizabeth was counting for the last few numbers to one hundred.

Elizabeth gave one last tug on Cindy's ears, spun around, and then froze. Her face was six inches from Mrs. Anderson's chest.

"Elizabeth McDonald," Mrs. Anderson said, grabbing *her* by the ear. "Come with me."

***

The next day when we got to class, there was a new seating chart on the wall and names taped to every desk. Elizabeth McDonald's name was in the front row, center aisle. I was to her right and Cindy sat to her left. Benjamin

Rosenberg sat directly in back of her. All of her friends were distributed several rows back, but no friends sat side-by-side.

On the blackboard, in beautiful curling cursive were the words: *Surround yourself with people of integrity.* That morning our assignment was to write what we thought this meant. I was noticing that to my right was Frank Thomas. He definitely didn't fit my definition of integrity. But to his right was Ben Van Hoffer, a very nice boy who didn't talk too much, and lived with his grandma. I could see a pattern and started to appreciate my new seat. At least as I thought Mrs. Anderson saw it.

"Good morning Carol. Good morning Cindy," Elizabeth said as she took her seat without looking at us.

I could hardly believe my ears. Cindy and I leaned around Elizabeth and looked at each other and then at Mrs. Anderson. She nodded and gave a knowing smile.

"Good morning, Elizabeth," we both managed to say.

***

"How come you didn't say anything to me earlier?" Mama said, after several seconds of soaking it all in.

"I was going to, but then she didn't bother me anymore. She even picked me and Cindy to be on her team for kickball. She probably had to, but still, she stopped being so mean, pretty much just left me alone, so I just forgot about it," I explained.

"Well, you certainly don't have to live there. We'll find somewhere else," Mama said.

"I think I might *want* to live there," I said.

"Why?" Mama was surprised.

"I want to see what it's like to live with a big family. Axel and Abe Joe are nice," I said. "Elizabeth is just a bully. I can stick up for myself, I think."

"You're a brave girl," Mama said.

The rest of the way home we played "I'm thinking of," and she couldn't guess what I was thinking of, an alligator. She said crocodile, but not alligator, so I won.

3

Mama said I could try living with the McDonald family for one week, and if I didn't like it we would figure out something else. I liked it just fine. Elizabeth didn't pay much attention to me for a long time. In fact she pretty much ignored me for the first month. She finally broke her silence one Sunday night when we were getting ready for bed. I had been at Mama's since Friday. Maybe Elizabeth had gotten used to me not being there and felt the intrusion all over again. Maybe she missed me. I doubt it.

"Why are you here?" she asked. She was sitting on her bed putting a second pair of socks over the first.

"Why are you putting on two pairs of socks?" I said.

"I'm cold." She rolled her eyes and sighed. "Why are you here?"

"My mom and dad are divorced," I said.

"So what, why don't you go live with one or the other of 'em?"

"Well I can't live with my dad, that's for sure," I said.

"How come?"

"'Cause I'd be living in a ram-shackle down by the river," I said, thinking I'd said too much, but she didn't skip a beat.

"What about yer mom?"

"My mom works nights and lives at the hospital. She's a nurse. She doesn't want to leave me alone all night while she works, and she sleeps most of the day, 'til I get home from school. So... it just doesn't work out right now." I was starting to resent having to explain my situation, when I really didn't understand it fully myself. "I just need a place to stay until I can move in with my mom when I'm thirteen," I explained, trying to ease her anger with the idea that it was only for a few years. "I'll be gone most weekends and holidays. I'll try to stay out of your way."

"Why do you dress like that?" She lay back on her bed with her hands behind her head.

"Like what?" I was hanging my new skirt on a wire hanger with clothes pins.

"All fancy and perfect with your pleated skirts and those stupid brown shoes." She pointed to my skirt with her foot.

I didn't answer. I hung up my skirt, put my shoes in the closet and shut the door. I was getting ready to leave the room to go brush my teeth, when she uttered the last words I'd ever expected to hear.

"You think you're better than me, don't you?" she said.

I turned around slowly, "What?" I said, shaking my head and frowning.

"You think you're better than me. You dress nicer, you get better grades than me, you never get yelled at in school and you walk around here like a princess, helping the poor little children of poverty."

"I do not."

"Do to."

"I DO NOT!" and I stormed downstairs to brush my teeth.

If anyone in this world carried an air of superiority, it was her. She criticized everyone, and made fun of anyone. When I went back upstairs, I was so full of rage at her accusation that I had an entire speech ready, complete with quotes from the Bible, my mother, and our teacher Mrs. Anderson. I took a deep breath before I entered the room and started, "I am sorry if you think..." I stopped. She wasn't on her bed where she was when I'd left her. I pivoted around to scan the small room and found her standing by the closet. She was wearing her bathrobe and quickly tied it up as she turned to leave. I noticed the empty hanger swinging in the closet.

"Where's my skirt?" I said, blocking the way to the door. She tried to push past me, but I stood my ground.

"I'm wearing it. See?!" she said and abruptly untied her tattered robe. She jerked it open, laying her hands on her hips to reveal *my* skirt over her nightgown. She stood there, left hip darting out to one side, daring me to say another word.

I wanted to rip that skirt from her waist, tie it around her neck and strangle her with it, but instead I heard the most unusual words come out of my mouth. To this day I will swear it was Uncle Virg speaking through me. He is the only one in the world who would know to say this.

"Now *that* is fancy! The perfect look for you. I love what you've done with the nightie!" I said, using my best movie star voice.

She huffed, unbuttoned the skirt, stepped out of it, and threw it on my bed. I picked it up and threw it on hers.

"Keep it," I said.

"Shut up. I don't want your hand-me-downs," she spat.

"It's not a hand-me-down if I've never worn it. Keep it, it's too short for me," I argued.

She walked over to her bed and put it up to her again. "Only if you don't want it."

"I want you to have it," I lied. I really liked that skirt; I was planning on wearing it to school the next day. Mama bought it for me as a reward, on account of my good report card.

"Fine," she said, like I was doing her a favor.

"Fine," I said and got into bed.

It wasn't long before Elizabeth's breath was deep and slumbery, but I couldn't fall asleep for a long time. My mind was sailing around somewhere between bitter defeat and humble heroics.

In light of the idea of "being the bigger person," I started to think of Mrs. Linderman. Mama had said she was going to ask me about her in a month, and knowing Mama, she would. I didn't want to be asked. I'd rather bring it up and be done with it, than have to endure another series of questions examining my integrity. I couldn't sleep, so I got up and wrote my note of apology to Ruth Linderman. The final copy was on plain white paper, folded in thirds, and written in my best penmanship. But my first draft looked something like this:

Mrs. Linderman,

~~My mother~~ I wanted to write to you and let you know that I did not mean to speak to you with a disrespectful tone. It just came out that way because I was so mad. I am asking for your forgiveness. ~~I should say I'm sorry, but I'm not, so I'm not going to lie. You didn't give the family in the white house a chance and I can't believe you think Neil is demon possessed.~~ I never meant to make you mad. The fire was an accident. I didn't mean to do it. ~~Though sometimes I feel like I wish you would have been~~ I'm thankful that nobody got hurt in the fire. If you find my buggy please give it to Mr. Danielson. ~~I left it in the hallway by the stairs to the attic and I know it didn't get lost or burned, why are you so mean that you would take my buggy?!!!~~

~~Good riddance~~ Sincerely,
Carol Carlson

I gave the final copy to Mama to read. She said it was perfect because it was honest and not syrupy. She should have seen the first copy; she thinks I'm a lot nicer than I am.

***

Glory and Jim McDonald treated me like all of their other kids. I had chores, but not too many. I had to eat what I put on my plate, but wasn't forced to take anything I didn't want. Glory was a great cook. Some days she cooked all day. If you wanted to find Glory, and she wasn't in the kitchen, she was likely in the garden. Her garden was a sight to behold, especially from the upstairs window. From the ground it was colorful and bountiful, to be sure. But from the upstairs window, it was a work of art. The rows and beds were laid out like a puzzle where the pieces never totally interlocked, but had little pebbled rows between ever changing colors and textures. The green beans grew on poles that made little tee-pees, six feet tall, and all around each tee-pee was a circle of orange marigolds. The tomato plants rested their heavy limbs on cages made from tree branches, strapped together with twine. Four apple trees, each with a different type of apple, sat at four corners in the middle of the yard. In between the trees, rows of impatiens made rolling mounds of pink and green. And in the middle of the square was an old claw foot bath tub that overflowed with water lilies and acted as a breeding ground for tadpoles and mosquitoes. A hammock was draped between two of the apple trees. That hammock is why I know so much about this part of the yard. If the house got too noisy for me, or it seemed like I was keeping someone from acting like they might act if I wasn't there, I'd head for the hammock. I liked the way the sides wrapped around me and rocked me just a little. I felt safe in the McDonald house. I felt like a kid.

From an onlooker's point of view, the McDonald household could give the impression of pure chaos. There were always kids hollering and running here and there, unfinished games of cards on the kitchen table, and never a lack of random orders being spewn about from Glory's loud, but loving voice. But the truth was, it was incredibly organized, mostly in Glory's brain, and there was an inner sense of peace that calmed my predisposition for an anxious chest. Glory had a grocery list, a chore list, and a book called *What to do in your Northeastern garden in the Winter, Spring, Summer and Fall.* She had tea towels for each day of the week, which were always used on the correct days. Chores even had their own particular day. Mondays were washing, Tuesdays were ironing, Wednesdays were baking, Thursdays were mending and sewing, and Fridays were cleaning. Saturdays the beds got changed and everyone got a bath. Sunday, if I was there, we went to church, and had Sunday Chocolate pudding after dinner.

At the McDonalds' I knew what to expect and what was expected of me. I knew that on Mondays I'd fold clothes, and on Wednesdays we'd be kneading bread. I knew that Mr. McDonald had a cup of tea at four-thirty every evening, and bedtime was nine o'clock. I knew which days I had to help with the dinner dishes, and which days I could laze around and enjoy the toil of another's labor. At night, we were tired. In the morning we were roused with anticipation for a new day. Things needed to be done and we were not allowed to lolly-gag around allowing someone else to carry our load. It was fair. I don't know how Glory did it. It seems like it would have been easier to allow us to goof off and stay out of her hair, but she was a ring leader and had our best interest in mind, I'm sure of it. She didn't boss us around, she taught us with kindness and high standards. I wanted to be like her when I grew up.

4

When I moved in with the McDonalds, Abe Joe was seven. In the three years that I lived there, I learned a lot from him. He was the youngest boy in the family, and possibly the wisest person I'd ever met. Abe Joe didn't lie. He didn't even smooth out the truth to make it easier. He was pure and simple, truthful and honest, speaking the truth in love, like Jesus did. Nothing wrong with that, it's just that sometimes he said things you wouldn't expect to hear, especially out of the mouth of a young boy.

One baking day, Abe was in the kitchen with Glory, kneading dough. Elizabeth and I were doing our homework at the kitchen table. I was just about to ask Glory how many 'l's' in the word collateral, when I heard Abe Joe say something way more interesting than my inquiry.

"Mom, my body is telling me something," he said, pushing his hands into the soft dough.

"Oh? What's that Joe?" said Glory, unassumingly.

"My body is telling me that I want to marry a bad girl that loves God," he said, straight-faced and intent on his work.

"Well." Glory paused. "What exactly is a bad girl that loves God?"

"Not sure. But there's none good. No, not one," he said, turning the dough.

Glory stopped her lips with the tip of her tongue and turned her head so he wouldn't see, but he didn't look up, just kept on working.

Elizabeth and I looked at each other, eyes wide and ready to bust a gut laughing. Then we looked at Glory, standing in back of Abe Joe. She saw our red, pre-eruptive faces, smiled at us, and winked. Abe Joe kept on kneading.

Recognizing the truth in the girl he was considering, and the serious demeanor of his revelation, I took a deep breath and asked Glory my question about the 'I's'.

Abe Joe didn't skip a beat. "Look it up in the dictionary."

That gave us license to respond, and whether we were laughing at the bad girl, or at the patent dictionary response, it didn't matter. Abe Joe was a listener and a thinker, and sometimes it was just funny to hear what was going to come out of his mouth next.

"I know exactly what you're talking about Joe," said Elizabeth, still breathless from laughing. "I don't do the things I know I should, but do do the things I shouldn't."

"Apostle Paul," he said.

Elizabeth paused a second, "What?"

"Apostle Paul said that."

"Sure he did." She looked at me like he was crazy. I looked at Abe Joe and smiled.

Jim came through the back door right about then and tossed a headless chicken into the sink.

Glory put a pot of water on to boil and said, "Abe Joe, tell your daddy what your body told you."

Abe Joe told him.

Jim said, "That's what I did," and went back outside.

***

In December, eight baby lambs were delivered in a stinky old farm truck. Abe Joe waited at the bottom of the makeshift ramp while they clumsily made their way into the McDonald barn. As they disembarked he named each one, and the names stuck with them their entire lives; Bumper, Lou, Fred, George, Buck, Lilly, Bee and Goliath. Goliath was the last off the truck and the smallest of the bunch. I mentioned that historically Goliath was a giant of a man. Abe Joe said he was a giant only in stature, but his heart was dumb and small. I couldn't disagree. He loved those lambs. He fed them with bottles and endured their head-butts with good natured reprimand.

In the mornings when we left for school, the little lambs followed Abe Joe all the way down the fence line, and when the fence ended, they crowded into the corner of the chain link, nearly crushing each other. One day Goliath squeezed under the fence and got out. When we were walking up the steps to the school, there was Goliath, trotting right along beside Abe Joe. We had a heyday singing, "Abe Joe had a little lamb, little lamb, little lamb...it followed him to school one day, school one day, school one day..." Abe Joe just smiled, like the song was truly about him, and how nice of us to make up a song for him and Goliath.

It's strange to me how different two people in the same family can be. As kind and gentle-spirited as Abe Joe was, Isaac balanced the weight on the other side. Like his twin sister Elizabeth, Isaac was ornery and selfish. I don't know what happened to those two. Glory must have lived on a diet of vinegar and thistles when she was pregnant with them, they had such sour and splintery dispositions. Isaac was a liar. He lied to get people in trouble, lied to get more pudding, and told grand stories in convoluted detail that always delivered him up smelling like a rose. I understood most people to have a mean streak if they had a mind, like Mama just having an off day or Father when the liquor ran his life. Aunt Marion had her share of snits, though I never do remember Uncle Virg getting mad or being mean toward anyone. I guess everyone had their days, but Isaac, he was a caution.

On Saturday mornings we had extra chores. Saturday mornings were also baseball games in the dirt lot. Isaac liked baseball more than chores, and more times than not, could finagle his way out of them.

"Mommy," Isaac said. Manipulative and syrupy might come close to describing his voice.

"Yes, Love." Glory called everyone she loved, "Love".

"Can I borrow seventeen cents, just until I sell my tomahawk to Steve Rice? He's gonna pay me twenty cents at least for it, if he'll pay a dime," he said.

"What do you need seventeen cents for, Isaac. I need every penny we have around here to keep a bone in the stock pot. What's seventeen cents gonna do for you?" She said, automatically like she always did when someone asked for money.

"Oh never mind, I just was hoping...never mind."

"Hoping what?"

"Well, one of the kids at the ballpark doesn't have any shoes for running the bases, and I, well...us guys thought it might be nice if we brought seventeen cents each, then we could take him to The Salvation Army Surplus and get him some shoes," he lied.

Glory turned around with weak shoulders. "What a sweet boy you are, Isaac. Was this your idea?"

"Kind of, I mean... yes, but all the other fellas were just as willing to ask their parents. This kid, his name is Brad, he's a great hitter, but has sores on his feet from the holes in his shoes, so he can't run so good, and well... his family is so poor that he don't dare ask his dad for new soles, if they can't even afford enough food for the baby." He went on, and on, and on.

She asked some more questions, and he told some more lies, and she believed him. He went on his merry way with seventeen cents jingling in his pocket for the poor.

Glory got a big sore heart for Brad's family and spent a good amount of the rest of the day creating a basket of provisions that were better than what we ended up having for dinner ourselves. That was Glory's way. She had true compassion for those less fortunate than herself, of which there were few, so when she found one she lavished on them.

She lectured us as we parceled-up what should have been our dinner, for the family in need.

"When you give a gift, give something you yourself would like to have. Whether it's a birthday present or a love offering, always give your best, not your leftovers." She stood back and took inventory. The box was billowing with a coffee can full of buttery mashed potatoes, a loaf of corn bread wrapped in newspaper, nine carrots, and six fresh eggs. She checked her secret stash of horehound candy, and put a handful in the middle of a square of wax paper, then twisted both ends so it looked like a giant piece of candy in a fancy wrapper. "There," she said, pleased with the offering.

Then she started a pot of salted water on the stove for our dinner. When it was simmering she added a bunch of chard, a bay leaf, two cut carrots, and a lone potato. "Stone soup," I thought.

When Isaac got home he was in high spirits. He reported all about how the shoes fit perfectly and they even had enough money for some socks. Glory was so pleased, as were the rest of us, and we were all anxious to present Isaac with the dinner we had prepared for Brad's family. He backed into the kitchen corner and stuck his hands in his bulging pockets. He smiled, said how nice it all was, and insisted he take it to them himself, so they wouldn't feel like needy poor people in front of our whole family. He loaded everything into the little wooden wagon with one bad wheel and slat sides, and set out for his second mission of mercy for the day. Abe Joe watched him through the kitchen window, then jumped down off the counter and headed for the kitchen door.

"I'm going with him, Mama!" he announced before she could respond.

She hollered out the window, "Take some apples too, Joe."

Abe lifted the front of his shirt, tossed in half a dozen apples from the bushel basket, and took off running in the direction of his brother. I followed, without him knowing, keeping my distance and hiding behind bushes along the way. He ran half a block before he alerted Isaac with his gallop.

"Go home, ya little tag-along, I don't need yer help!" Isaac said, struggling along with the rickety wagon.

"Mama said to take some apples," Abe Joe said, as he jogged alongside the wagon. "Stop!"

Isaac stopped reluctantly, and waited for Abe Joe to release the apples. "Hurry up! Now go home. I said I didn't need yer help."

Abe Joe crouched down in a squat to catch his breath and stayed there until his brother disappeared around the corner. Breath caught, he sprinted like a gazelle to the end of the block where the sidewalk started and peeked around a fence. Abe Joe followed at a sufficient distance to remain unnoticed. I followed Abe Joe in an equally cautious manner. When Isaac got to the baseball field, he headed directly toward the bench where two boys were tossing a ball back and forth, and a few others were just sitting around talking and kicking dirt. Abe Joe had taken a seat on a low branch of a tree, in perfect view of the ball field. I watched from behind a low wall.

"Din-ner!" Isaac hollered through cupped hands.

The boys on the bench looked curious and the ball-tossing stopped. A tall boy got up and spat a good collection of tobacco juice out the side of his mouth, then sauntered over to Isaac.

"Whacha got?" he called, wiping tarry drool from his chin.

I couldn't hear Isaac's answer, but as he uncovered the feast, the rest of the boys hustled over to the wagon to investigate. Dodging each other's elbows and shoving greedy shoulders, each boy dug in, devouring the mashed potatoes with their fingers, and tearing into the corn bread like dogs. Ten minutes was sufficient time to consume the hours of work and sacrifice that Glory and the rest of us had made for a needy family. My heart ached. Abe Joe didn't move, just sat up on that branch still as a scared squirrel, with his arms wrapped around his legs.

The sated boys slapped praise and thanks on Isaac's guilty back. He smiled, but hid his sorry eyes under his baseball cap. The tobacco-spitter picked up an apple, "First one to catch it at twenty yards gets it!" he announced.

***

For dinner that night we had homemade rye flour rolls, thin soup, and Apple Betty for dessert. Glory silently glowed with the knowledge that she had not only provided for the needs of her own family from such minimal resources, but for those in need. Because she didn't care about being rewarded for her generosity, she never asked how the meal was received. I hoped she would just assume it was greatly appreciated and cherish it in her heart as a gift given in secret. Abe Joe never ratted on Isaac as far as I know, and he got quiet for a few days after that.

Isaac came home that day a victorious liar. He appeared to pull into himself for a time. He didn't look Glory in the eye, though I'm not sure she noticed, having so many sets of eyes looking to her for so many things. If he'd had a tail, it would have been curled up tight between his legs. He mumbled more, laughed less, and stopped playing baseball. It made me mad to see him crumbling under the weight of his own folly. I knew what it felt like to keep a secret sin trapped in a bundle deep in my chest. I also knew that confessing the secret and telling someone eased the burden.

***

As Abe Joe's lambs grew, they got more stubborn and harder to handle. Abe's head hardly rose higher than that of the flock. One morning before school, Abe was out with the sheep trying to herd them into the barn for breakfast and having little success. He came into the house, frustrated and out of breath.

"Dad, can you help me with the kids?" he said.

Jim smiled. "They're sheep not goats Abe. What's the problem? They giving you a hard time?"

"Yeah, they're being rebellious," he said, serious as the parent of a wayward child.

Jim smiled bigger still, trying to hide it behind his coffee mug. "Isaac, go help your brother corral the kids, would you?"

Abe Joe spoke up. "Dad could you come? The sheep don't trust him; they can smell his bad mood."

"You in a bad mood Isaac?" asked Jim.

Isaac shrugged and rose to go with Abe Joe.

"I'm serious Dad. I don't want Isaac around my sheep. He's not genuine," said Abe Joe.

"Abe, are you nine or thirty-five?" said Jim, as he waved Isaac off and followed Abe Joe.

Abe didn't answer, but led the way as his dad followed him out the kitchen door.

"What do you think that meant, not genuine?" I asked Isaac after they'd gone.

"Don't know. Don't care either. Probably 'cuz I don't smell like hay and sheep shit like he does."

But I knew different. I'd noticed Abe Joe being careful around Isaac, even avoiding him. Neither of them knew that I had observed the entire scene at the baseball diamond. Each of us hid our knowledge with a unique perspective. We navigated around the lie like skillful riders leading their horses through an obstacle course.

The next morning, Glory was making pancakes, I was separating the cream off the top of that day's milk, and Elizabeth was writing a last minute book report on a book she'd barely read. As Isaac walked through the kitchen on his way out to feed the chickens, he bumped the kitchen table and caused Elizabeth to put an overly exaggerated tail on a 'g'.

"Isaac! You jerk," she yelled.

"What'd I do?" he frowned, not looking at her.

"You know what you did, you ruined my paper,"

"I didn't do anything," he mumbled and opened the door.

Glory turned around to stop the bickering, but Jim had followed Isaac into the kitchen and beat her to it.

"Isaac. Just say you're sorry, it was an accident," Jim said.

"What'd I do?"

"Isaac, say you're sorry then sit down," Jim said calmly.

"Dad, I gotta feed the chickens."

Jim walked across the worn wood floor, took a firm hold on the top of Isaac's shoulder, and navigated him down into a kitchen chair.

"Geeze, it was an accident," he mumbled, shrugging his father's hand off of him.

Jim patted the pockets of Isaac's coat, and said calmly, "Where'd you get all that?"

Glory, Elizabeth, and I stopped what we were doing and directed our attention to Isaac.

"I got it from the guys at the diamond."

"Empty your pockets."

Isaac paused, then shoved his hand into his coat pocket and pulled out a fistful of penny candy.

"All of it, and anything else you have in your pockets."

Isaac pulled his pockets inside-out over the table. A few more pieces of candy rolled onto the table, along with two pennies, a bottle top, and a half-smoked, hand rolled cigarette.

"Where'd you get all this?" he asked again.

"Dad! I won it at the baseball diamond. We had a contest for the farthest hit and I won most of the rounds," he continued.

"Are you sure you were throwing baseballs and not apples?" Jim asked and folded his arms.

"I didn't throw the apples, Jeff Augustus..." he stopped short. Trapped.

"Passing the buck to Jeffry Augustus, huh? Funny, because he didn't tell the story that way when I saw him at the diamond last night. He couldn't stop raving about your pitching arm, especially your skillful delivery of apples."

"Dad, it wasn't like that," Isaac said, "I just stopped to throw a few balls and..."

"I happen to *know* that you weren't throwing baseballs, and that there were no new shoes for Brad, and that his family never received the dinner your mother so graciously provided." Jim spoke in a low, controlled voice, but his face was turning red. "I also know that you were not raised to be a liar or a thief, so it's time you stop acting like one."

Isaac lowered his head to his hands and let out a windy breath. He sat there half a minute, then finally mumbled, "Sorry, Dad."

"I hope so, Son, but it's your mother deserves the apology."

Isaac meandered into the kitchen. Glory's face was so low I wanted to push it back up with my own two hands. She looked like a rag doll, just propped up against the kitchen sink.

"I'm Sorry, Mom," Isaac said. He sounded sorry for once.

Glory looked deep into his eyes, reached out and touched his cheek, but didn't speak. He tried to hug her to avoid her eyes, but she pushed him back and held him at arm's length, staring at his face like she was trying to figure out who he was. She attempted to speak, but her sobs took over.

Jim spoke. "Now get your sorry self out to feed the chickens and don't make any plans for the next month. You'll be busy learning how to make mashed potatoes and corn bread. You'll be the only dishwasher, the only milker, and the only pig-slopper. That and whatever else needs to be done that might teach a boy to bite a tongue bent to lying, and hold tight to a hand that is tempted to steal. There is fun in sin for a season, Son. But when the season's over, the fall comes fast. Time to start diggin' yourself out of the pit. And don't forget to say sorry to your sister."

5

Jim didn't get much work that winter. He'd leave before the sun came up every morning, but was often back before we even left for school. He spent a lot of time out with the chickens and the sheep. Jim ate pitiful little during a meal. He'd eat one chicken drumstick for dinner, or cut up an apple for the kids and eat the core. He never acted hungry. He always washed his own dish and put all the leftover scrapings in a green glass bowl for the chickens. I wondered if he gleaned from the chicken feed, but that's none of my affair. I suppose a man's got more right to the scraps from his own kitchen than the chickens do. After dinner he'd usually retire to a straight back chair by the fireplace. If there was tobacco, he'd roll a cigarette and smoke half, pinch off the cinder and save the rest for the following day. He'd stow the stinky half-smoked butts in a place where the chink was crumbling out between the bricks of the chimney. After that he'd read to us. Sometimes if we had chapters to read for school, we'd give them to him and he would read in his comforting, smoky voice and we would lay around on a pillow or the belly of a dog and soak it in.

Jim was nice. There was nothing bad to say about him, but I could understand how Glory got frustrated with him. Glory was always working so hard, planning, organizing and making sure everything was running smooth. She had to; she was the mother of six children, plus me. We didn't have everything we wanted, but she made sure we had everything we needed.

***

One afternoon, out of the clear blue nowhere, Glory came storming into the kitchen wearing her church shoes. Jim was sitting at the kitchen table.

"I am leaving, Sir. I won't be gone long, but you may have to rustle up something for these children to eat and I don't have any suggestions." She opened and closed the door of the refrigerator in one smooth movement. "I cannot stand one more minute of whining and bickering. I've spent the better part of my life trying to raise these children up in the way they should go, and they don't seem to be catching on! And you, Sir, are no help with your carrying on about all manner of whatever ails you. They can't stop complaining about how overworked they are around here, while you sit lamenting your loss of work. I'll give you work, there's plenty a' work to be done around here, starting with the leaky roof and following right up with the soggy basement." She was slamming the frying pan into an overcrowded cupboard, talking over the clatter, having no problem being heard. "And when you're not carrying on about the job market, you're blaming someone else for this current state of affairs. Why don't you take this "forced time off" as you call it, and *do* something about it! Start a newspaper, run for office, write an article, volunteer somewhere, but stop your complaining about how bad the economy is and how incompetent the leaders of this country are." Glory's voice was shaky and little beads of sweat glistened under her nose. She slammed the cabinet door, picked up her purse and headed for the kitchen door.

"Wow," Jim said, looking like he'd just learned of his wife going off to join the army.

Glory was halfway out the door when she turned around. "Don't look so surprised. This is just the steam comin' off a kettle that's been simmerin' for a long time. I need time to cool down. Don't wait up." And she was gone.

During the commotion, several of us kids had filtered toward the kitchen from different parts of the house. I snuck an eye around the door jam and saw Jim rubbing his head, seemingly trying to smooth down the folds on his forehead. He sensed our presence.

"I'm not sure what that was all about, but you kids have chores to do, especially you Isaac, so stop yer gawkin' and see to 'em!" These orders were unfamiliar coming from him. "Lizzy, keep an eye on your sister. Orion? Where's Orion? Somebody find Orion and tell him I want to talk to him."

My job should have been the dishes, but Isaac had gotten that job for his punishment, so I quietly dug around in Glory's recipe box for the cold-water buns card. I thought that would make Jim happy. They were his favorite part of any dinner, and who knew what dinner was going to look like with him in charge. I'd never seen him do any kind of cooking past opening a can of sardines. Jim sat on a kitchen chair, elbows on his knees, head down. I did my best to focus on my task and not look back or listen to his mumbles. My hands were shaking so bad that I was afraid to measure the salt for fear of dumping the whole box into the slurry. After a few minutes he got up, but I kept on with the mixing and rolled the dough out to knead. Next thing I knew he picked up the chair he'd been sitting on and carried it out the kitchen door. He went halfway into the back yard and stopped. I expected him to set it down and sit in it like any normal person who needs to get away and think would, but he didn't. He stood steadfast in the middle of the yard and raised that chair above his head a few times, then took it in his right hand and drew it way back like a javelin and flung it with all the force of a volcano, straight up into the air. I had to lean out through the open kitchen window to follow it. Faster than it went up, it came down and landed on top of the tree fort, crashing through the rickety roof and spearing two of its legs through the floor of the fort.

"Ahhhhhhhhgg," came a howling from the fort.

At first I thought it was Jim yelling out of anger, or maybe embarrassment, but then I noticed a third leg—a real leg with trousers on it—hanging through the floor of the tree fort, right there with the chair legs.

Abe Joe ran out of the chicken coop looking this way and that for the source of the crash and hollering. Axel stopped short and turned around, losing most of the water from the bucket he'd filled. Elizabeth ran down the stairs, dropping her basket of dirty laundry in the kitchen, and then flew out the kitchen door without closing it. I couldn't see Isaac, but heard him holler from an upstairs window, "Holy cow! Orion! You in there?" Then I heard another loud thump, and saw that Isaac had jumped out of his bedroom window, and landed square on the back porch. Without skipping a beat, he took off running and got to the tree fort before anyone else really knew what had happened. I stood watching the goings on, paralyzed except to cover my mouth in disbelief with my trembling hands. Jim was right behind Isaac and swiftly climbed up the makeshift ladder to the tree fort.

"Ahhhhhhhhgg! Ahhhhhhhgg! Help! We've been bombed!" Orion hollered.

My fear and curiosity cured me of my paralysis, so I pulled my head back in through the window and followed the rest. I stopped halfway to the scene, climbed up on the top support beam of the picket fence, and held onto a tree branch that rose above. They were bringing Orion down from the fort. He was bellowing out a spooky howl like a wounded hyena. His screams of pain cut through me as deep as that chair smashed through the roof. As Jim carried him to the house I saw Orion's leg dangling off to one side, blood soaking his jeans and agony distorting his face. I felt dizzy and tried to hold tighter to the branch, but as I looked up to steady myself I saw the sky turn white, then blue, then black.

***

Tiny hands warmed each of my cheeks. "Caro." The words echoed in my head. Something tickled my nose so I tried to scratch it but couldn't lift either arm. My left arm hurt so bad I couldn't move it, and something was holding down the other. I opened my eyes and was startled at the blurry image of Ellie's little face, nose-to-nose with mine. Her breath smelled like peanut butter. "Caro," she said again.

Her little legs were straddling me and one of her knees was balancing on my right arm. My left arm was strewn out to the side in an odd angle, and at first I didn't recognize it as my own

"Oh Ellie," I moaned. "Go get your mommy".

"Mommy went bye-bye," she said. She wiped away the tears that had started to roll down my temples into my hair.

And then I remembered. "Where's Daddy?" I asked.

"Orion got hurt," she said, "Daddy took him in the truck."

"Is he OK?"

"He's all bloody."

"Where'd they go? Are they going to the hospital?"

"They went in the truck." She put her tiny hand on my forehead. "Are you sad?"

"Yeah, I'm sad. My arm is broke. Get off me, Ellie, I gotta get up," I grunted, breathlessly.

"Don't go away."

"I'm not, just get up."

She pushed on my chest to lift her tiny self and a stabbing pain ran down my arm.

"OWWW!" I screamed.

She looked at my face with terror and confusion and started to cry.

"I'm sorry, Ellie, come here," I held out my good arm and she slowly stepped into it and let me hug her. "It's Okay El. Let's go find Daddy." My broken arm was killing me. It hurt so much I hardly had the energy to cry, but the tears kept streaming down my face all the way into the house. We made it as far as the braided rug by the stove. That was far enough for me. I sat down on it and cried.

"Whatcha doin' Car-rol?" Axel stood over me, hands in pockets.

"My arm's broke, where is everyone, what happened to Orion?"

"Ummm, they took him to the hospital. His leg's busted and he was screamin' real bad. Elizabeth and Abe Joe went to find Mama," said Axel, in his slow monotone voice.

"I need to go to the hospital too, who's here?"

"Me 'n you." He paused and looked around, "And Ellie. Yer arm looks weird."

"You know the little house by the church, the white one in the mint field?" I said to Axel.

"Yeah, I think so," he said.

"Well, go over there and tell them I need help," I said. "If you hop the fence out back it's a straight shot. Run!'

Axel stood there for a few seconds, "Okay, what should I say?"

"I don't care, tell them whatever will get them over here as fast as possible, tell them I'm dying. Go!"

***

Other people's memories told me what happened after that. But when I woke up, I knew where I was, even before I opened my eyes. I could hear hospital sounds, and I could smell my mother.

"Hi Mama," I said with my eyes still closed.

"Hi Peach." She kissed my cheek. "How you feeling?"

"My arm hurts."

"I'll bet that's an understatement. You really did a job on that arm. What happened?" she said.

"Orion fell," I said.

"I know all about Orion, he's down the hall. What happened to you?"

"I fell off of the fence. I think I fainted," I said. "How'd I get here?"

"Neil and Pauline's big brother Will brought you," she said, looking confused.

Just then Axel peaked around the curtain that was around my bed.

"Axel, did *you* go get Will?" Mama asked.

"Kind of, he was already on his way," he said.

"Why?" Mama asked.

"He said Neil told him there was trouble. He said Neil knew there was something wrong and made him come over with the truck," Axel said. "He let me ride in the back."

Mama and I looked at each other.

"The gift?" I said.

"Must be," she said, smiling and nodding her head.

***

Orion was going to have to stay in the hospital so they could monitor his busted-up leg and make sure he didn't get an infection. This didn't bother him at all, because he got to be king of the hill, eating on a tray in bed and reading any book that passed under his face. I, on the other hand, was bandaged, cast, inoculated, and medicated, then sent home to my mother's apartment with her. My arm was broken in two places but I was perfectly happy to suffer my wounds if it meant spending a few days with my mother. We did all the things we love to do when we are housebound. I painted her toenails, she painted mine. She let me win at Criss-Cross Words, and I legitimately won at Gin Rummy. I wrote a thank you note to Will and Neil, but didn't mention The Gift. I missed two days of school and then had to go back and learn to write with my left hand.

Turns out, Orion had to stay in the hospital for two weeks. His leg was in far worse shape than they thought, so they had to do surgery to patch it up. Mama was his nurse part of the time so she took him Beemans gum and popsicles. We could visit him two at a time in the afternoons after school. Mr. McDonald went to see him every day, sometimes two times, and on Sunday he stayed all day. He worked odd jobs, welding or building stuff for people, but when he wasn't working, he was right by Orion's side. Glory went to the hospital whenever Jim wasn't there.

Glory had come home on the evening of the chair throwing incident, and found Ellie, all alone in the house, asleep under the kitchen table. From that day, until the day they brought Orion home from the hospital two weeks later, I didn't hear her say two civil words to Jim. If he asked her a question she'd answer uh-huh or hu-uh. She was nice to all the kids, but acted like Jim wasn't even there. She didn't call him for dinner, out the back door, like she used to, and talked around him, not to him, even when he was in the room.

"Elizabeth, will you please close the window," Glory said. She was sitting in her chair by the woodstove rolling yarn from a skein that I was holding.

Elizabeth was in the kitchen scrubbing out the spaghetti pot, "Daddy's sittin' right there by the window, my hands are all soapy, can't you ask him?"

"I asked you, Lizzy, if you can't do it, you ask him," she said without looking up.

"I've got it, Elizabeth," Jim droned. He leaned over and closed the window, looked over his reading glasses at his inattentive wife and went back to his book.

"Lizzy, when you're done, will you get the afghan for me? It's still chilly in here," Glory called to her daughter a little later.

Elizabeth rinsed the pot, laid it upside down on a towel, and dried her hands on her apron. She walked over to her father's chair, pulled the afghan off the back of it and laid it on her mother with a huff. Then she put her hands on her hips and stood looking at her mother for a moment. Glory looked up at her and smiled, said thank you, then went back to her yarn rolling. Elizabeth looked at her dad. He shrugged and shook his head. The house was quiet, most of the kids were upstairs doing homework or sleeping already, but I could feel a storm rising and I sensed that someone was about to stand up and rock the boat, if not tip it over all together.

"Mama?" Elizabeth started, timidly.

"Yes Lizzy," said Glory.

"Would you just put me down," Elizabeth did that thing she did with her mouth when she was fed up.

Glory looked up at her daughter, "Put you down?"

Jim put his book down, lit his pipe, crossed his arms and his ankles, and watched.

"You're carrying me around like a fly swatter, using me to slap anything and anyone that seems to be bugging you, particularly Daddy, and I don't like it. It makes me feel guilty for something I didn't do."

Smoke drifted up from Jim's mouth. He looked directly at Glory. Glory rested the ball of yarn in her lap and stared at it. I stopped unrolling my spool and concentrated on breathing. My heart pounded nine times before Glory's shoulders started to bobble up and down. She took a deep breath then started to bobble again, crying a silent cry.

"Girls, go get ready for bed, I'll be in to read to you in a few minutes," Jim said, rising from his chair.

I couldn't get out of there fast enough. I left my spool of yarn on the floor and ran up the stairs, skipping every other one, and slid into the cool comfort of clean, line-dried sheets. Elizabeth crawled in right after me. She wiped her nose on my sheet. I gave her pat-pats on her back.

"Mrs. Anderson said that," she said between sniffles.

"Said what?"

"About the fly swatter," she said. "Ya know, when I was mean to you at school?"

"Yeah." I remembered. "That seems like a long time ago."

"I'm sorry," said Elizabeth.

"Thank you."

That night Jim continued reading to us from the book of Proverbs. We were reading from chapter 21. We'd read verses 1-10 the night before, so tonight we were on 11-20. I do not think he meant to, but Jim gave out a suppressed snicker after reading verse 19. "It is better to dwell in the wilderness, than with a contentious and angry woman." He went on to verse 20, then tucked us in, smiling the whole time.

"Think it might be time for a fishing trip," he said, as he shut off our lamp.

6

When Glory got over her mad, Jim got a job. Or maybe it was the other way around. Either way, they started talking to each other again, and things got back to normal.

When Jim got his first paycheck we had a roast beef on a Wednesday and all the McDonald kids got new shoes, even though it wasn't a new school year. Mama was forever slipping five-dollar bills into Glory's apron pocket to help out where she could. Glory would look straight at me when she found it, and funny, she always found it when I was in the kitchen. "Praise God from whom all blessings flow!" She'd say.

Jim wore bib overalls most days. He had a pair of black man-pants that he wore when he went to church on Sunday, but otherwise he wore a plaid, long-sleeved shirt and overalls every day. If it was cold out he wore a floppy yellow leather hat and a canvas overcoat that smelled like pipe tobacco. The hat was stained from the sweat off his brow so it always looked wet around the rim. Jim's overalls were like a filing cabinet. There was a chain of safety pins; no less than eight in a row of various sizes. The straight pins he'd weave through the shoulder straps. A chain of rubber bands were tucked into one pocket, and string of any length could be found from in his back pocket. Jim was thrifty, but not stingy, wise, but not old. He was handsome, but not flirtatious. He loved his children and instructed them in the simple, yet important things of life. He indulged his daughters, and disciplined his boys. September 4th was just as sacred to him as December 25th. He never had a career, he had a ministry. He said that.

I decided I wanted to marry a man a lot like Jim, so I set out to be a lot like Glory. She taught me how to fold laundry; corners all come together and edges meet. I watched her every move as she orchestrated a meal in her kitchen, taking mental notes for my future. If Abe Joe's arm got tired of grating cheese, she would quickly move him into the silverware sorting job and ask me or Elizabeth to finish the cheese while he set the table. Glory was afraid of grating her knuckles, so she never grated cheese. Just before dinner she would peruse the table and usually holler for one or more missing items, like, "Ellie, grab a serving spoon and Lizzie bring the pepper." Jim loved pepper. He put it on everything, even pancakes. I ate more pancakes at the McDonald house than I could ever count. We had pancakes with Karo syrup for breakfast, pancakes rolled around a wedge of cheese for lunch and pancakes covered with hamburger gravy for dinner. I concluded that eating three meals of pancakes, and being tucked in with a kiss and a good story at this house, was far better than steak and mashed potatoes and a cold shoulder from Mrs. Linderman. I still love pancakes.

***

One morning in May, Jim woke up later than usual. He stumbled down the stairs with his hand shading his eyes and a furrowed brow dominating his forehead.

"Something's wrong with my brother," he said, feeling for the coffee pot with his eyes half closed.

"What's that, Sir?" asked Glory.

"Not sure Glory, just got that feeling in my chest."

"Hmmm," was all Glory said.

I was eating toast with marmalade and finishing math. All the other kids were still waking up or getting ready for school, except Isaac who was out in the barn. My eyes went back and forth, first to Jim, then to Glory.

"All night I dreamt about Louis. He had a bump in his eye."

"What's that mean, a bump in his eye?"

"Not sure but I suppose I'm gonna find that Louis has an actual bump of some sort and I hope he isn't going blind or worse. Suppose I'll find out when I get there."

"Get where?"

"Florida."

"Florida." Glory cocked her head in an Elizabeth-ish, teen-agery sort of way.

"Yep, that's where he lives; Florida," said Jim.

"Florida? Sir, you just got settled in your new job," Glory said.

"Yes ma'am."

"And I have news of my own."

"What's that?" said Jim.

"Well, I didn't want to tell you over a sink full of dishes, while you were heading out the door like a snowbird, but we're expecting."

I kept pretending to do my math.

"Oh. That explains it." Jim smiled big enough to reveal a missing molar.

"Explains what?" said Glory.

Jim paused. "That explains why you are looking so ravishing this morning." He snuggled up to his wife and gave her a kiss. Then he backed away and laid his hands on her belly, which looked no different than usual. "When's number seven coming?"

"June, I think."

"Well, I should be back by then," he chided.

"How on earth are you going to travel to Florida with no automobile or money for train fare?"

"Not sure, but I can't wait to find out." Jim looked up from his coffee to the ceiling, then folded his face into a thoughtful smile.

"We cannot afford another one of your wild goose chases," Glory said as she skimmed grape jelly onto seven pieces of brown bread.

"So we can't."

"That's right."

"That's right," and he picked up a stale crust from the loaf of bread and walked out the door.

"That man," Glory said. She put down her knife and looked straight ahead. "Can two walk together, except they be agreed? You tell me Lord, 'cuz I'm askin'." She spoke to God like He was sitting right on the kitchen stool while she sliced bananas. "You might not tempt me beyond what I can handle, but that man...Lord, help me." She popped the end of the banana into her mouth. "Who wants peanut butter and who wants jelly!?" she hollered.

A few voices hollered back, but she didn't really listen. She already knew. I wanted both and said so.

Before we left for school that day a man drove up to the house in a fancy brown car. He got out and stood around for a while in the drizzly rain, talking and laughing with Jim. Then he left and Jim came in through the front door and went upstairs. When he came down his hair was slicked back with pomade and he was wearing his black church pants. He carried a suitcase and his floppy hat. By this time all of the kids had convened in the kitchen to collect lunches and head off to school.

"Mr. Pearson commissioned me to build him a wall—gave me seventy-five dollars to start, soon as I get back," Jim announced, as he entered the room.

"Back from where?" Glory said, hardly looking up from her wax paper sandwich packages.

"I told you, Florida."

Glory looked up. "Right now?"

"Yep." He put a twenty dollar bill under the salt shaker, kissed Glory on the lips and on the belly, stopped to hug or kiss each of us, and then stopped and faced us all. "Listen to your Mother. Don't be storing up whippings for when I get home because I don't care for giving 'em out. I'll be back in ten days, either way."

He closed the warped kitchen door without a sound, which was almost impossible to do.

Before the movement of the morning re-commenced, Ellie walked up to her mother and kissed her belly.

"Why's everyone kissing your stomach Mom?" said Elizabeth, suspecting the answer before she had an answer.

"Either Abe Joe is getting his brother, or you are getting your sister. We'll know in June," she said, smiling.

Orion was the only one who didn't respond with excited anticipation and a kiss or a pat-pat on Glory's belly. He shook his head and said something about a full quiver and left early for school.

I don't know about anyone else, but I was sort of sad to see Jim go. He had a calming effect on the household. But I was also excited for him. Jim had a sixth sense about stuff and the mystery of the bump on his brother's eye had my mind entertaining all kinds of possibilities.

At dinner that night we all shared our opinions of what might be the problem with Louis' eye. Glory didn't say if she thought her husband was a kook, or a prophet of God.

"Sir just does things different. It's hard to judge a man when he is doing what he thinks is right," she said, "but whatever you do, when the bank comes to give us our forty five days, which I'm expecting any day now, don't let on that Dad is off gallivanting. No man in the house, they'll pack us up and send us to the tenement faster than quick."

Orion changed the subject to baseball after this, and the rest of us finished our noodles and chicken gravy, without chicken, in silence.

***

Jim had been gone three days when Glory received a letter from Aunt Lorraine, Louis' wife. She read it to us after dinner:

> *Dear Jim and Glory,*
> *I write to petition your prayers. I won't bother with niceties or small talk, but get right to the issue of need. Louis has a bump in his right eye that has been getting increasingly larger over the past few months. We went and saw the doctor last month, and he thinks it is a cancerous tumor and must be removed. We have scheduled the surgery for next Wednesday. I will send further word as soon as I know more, but for now we ask that you cover us, especially Louis, with your most fervent prayers. I know Jim will want to come down and show his support, but for now it might be best to save the trip until we know what the outcome is. No fair worrying, just pray. Thank you.*
> *Love,*
> *Lorraine*

This was Wednesday, surgery Wednesday. Louis had a bump, just like Jim had dreamed. Mama was always saying how the Lord works in mysterious ways, but holy cow! As soon as the letter was tucked back into Glory's apron pocket, she took hold of the hand of both children seated beside her. We all followed suit and bowed our heads in unison and started praying as if we were a sanctified order of obedient monks. We prayed out loud and all at the same time, no one stopped to listen to the other, we just prayed to God, who we knew healed in the days of prophets, and since we seemingly had a prophet in the family, we trusted him to hear and answer our prayers. Pastor Sorenson always said that God will heal one way or another. God either heals a man here on earth to continue in the things he is obedient to do, or He gives him a brand new body and takes him home to heaven to start in on whatever it is He has for him to do up there. There was no denying that God was doing something miraculous.

The prayers slowly faded. It was Abe Joe who finished last with: "...Daddy home safe. In Jesus' name, Amen", then we all sat in silence for a few seconds.

"That man!" Glory broke the silence. "I don't know how he got it, but I am convinced he has a direct line to the Almighty himself. I can't explain it."

"The Holy Spirit got into him Mama," said Axel.

"So he did, Axel. Hallelujah!" said Glory.

***

I might have lived my whole life believing *in* God but not really *believing* Him. But this was the day that God showed me His mighty power. It was a great length for Him to go—what with Jim having to travel so far, and Louis having to endure the hardship of a cancerous tumor and, but that was the day for me. I'd like to think that the rest of the McDonald family had a similar awakening that day, but they all just kind of went along without acting any different or needing to. I was the outsider, being the one who was amazed at God doing what God did. I thought maybe I should introduce Neil and Jim to each other.

Just before we left for school the next morning, a man came to the door with a telegram. Glory opened it before she even closed the door.

Surgery went fine stop Jim leaving Friday stop
Thank you for praying stop
Diane stop

My death pains didn't come back for a long time after that. It's as if Jesus himself was holding my heart in His hands. So when people suggest that God isn't real or that prayer doesn't help, I can honestly say I know different now. Not only do I know different, I see different. Bad isn't always bad when God has His hand in it. Joseph getting thrown into the cistern and then being sold, by his brothers, to a band of traveling salesmen was certainly a roundabout way to make him the governor of Egypt. I suspected, at this point, that God might have great plans for me when I grew up.

When Jim got home the pomade had worked its way out of his hair. He looked like his old self again, except the lines around his eyes were deeper, and his face was brown. We were all ready and waiting to hear the details of the surgery, but Glory told us not to ask any questions until after Jim had eaten dinner.

"Jim," I asked, the minute he put his fork down and picked up his tobacco pouch, "what made you know that your dream was true, that your brother really had a cancer bump on his face?"

"Well, it's hard to say, but I get these pains in my chest, like a real anxious feeling, when God is trying to get my attention. Problem is, I am so far-tracked most of the time that I don't usually pay attention," he said. "Seems this time the Lord put it on my heart and knocked me over the head with it in a dream too. It was a good thing I went."

"What do you mean, Daddy?" said Elizabeth.

"Well, I haven't seen my brother for a couple of years, and I missed him, one." He shuffled around in his seat and rolled a cigarette while he kept on talking, "They got the tumor in full they believe. But the truth of the matter is..." Jim got up to look for a match and stayed standing in the kitchen.

We all turned around in our chairs to wait for the truth of the matter. "The surgery left him blind in both eyes, something about the optic nerve."

"Oh my!" said Glory, "Lorraine said it all went fine."

"No one knew until the day I left, his eyes were both wrapped up."

"That's terrible," said Orion.

The rest of us nodded or shook our heads in agreement.

"Guess it was the fault of the surgeon," Jim said, "They found out after that he was drunker than a skunk. Two of the nurses turned him in, now there's a lawsuit. Looks like Louis might be a millionaire."

"That's great!" said Elizabeth.

We all got over our sorrow for Uncle Louis' eyes pretty quick hearing about his chance for becoming a millionaire.

"Well, how many of you would sell your eyes for a million dollars?" Jim said.

No one said they would.

Abe Joe spoke up, "I wouldn't sell my eyes to a doctor for a million dollars, but I'd give 'em to Uncle Louis for free."

"I'm sure you would Abe Joe," said Jim. "Well anyway, I'm glad I went, so's my brother could see my homely face one more time, and I could see the recognition in his eyes." He teared up and went out the back door.

***

Two weeks went by and Jim didn't wash his hair on either Friday, which was his usual hair washing day. It looked like he'd started in with the pomade again, but it was just slick down with its own grease. He went to work sad and came home sad. When he read to us he sounded sad and when he prayed for the dinner he sounded mournful, not thankful. One evening Glory followed him out to the back porch after dinner. Isaac's penance was over by this time, so I was washing dishes by the open window.

"Sir. Why are you still moping around and being so melancholy. You've been off your feed ever since you got back from Florida. There's nothing we can do to bring back Louis' eyesight. The Lord gave it, and the Lord took it away."

"This was not the work of the Lord, Glory. This was the work of a careless drunk," he said. "I know we can't see into the future, but I just don't understand any way this could deliver a happy ending. Louis is an artist, he needs his eyes."

"I know darlin', but you can't punish yourself by letting the joys in life pass you by. You have six reasons for joy right in the house and number seven will be along soon enough. And we have each other," she said. They were silent for a while.

"This is no way to live," he said.

"How's that?" she said.

"Up at five, out by six, home for dinner, then back at it the next mornin'. It's no way to live."

I couldn't see them, but I heard the creak of the porch swing and smelled the smoke from Jim's cigarette.

"You've got a case of the blues, Sir. You're carrying too much burden in your heart. You need a break," she said.

"I need a fishing trip," he said

"What's keeping you? For crying on a hanky, Sir, go fishing!" Glory raised her voice. "If fishing is what's on your mind, do it. Maybe you'll bring us some dinner," she encouraged.

"Only problem is… worms."

"Worms?" Glory sort of laughed.

"Bait and tackle shop's closed down, up at Celoron. Not enough tourism, and you can't get a good worm around here, ground's so muddy this time of year," Jim mumbled, defeated.

"You want worms? Axel and Abe could get you a full bucket o' worms in no time if you'd promise to take them with you. "You should take 'em, Sir, they'd jump at the chance."

"I'll think about it." The squeak of the porch swing stopped. "Gotta build that wall first."

7

Glory was moving especially slow by the end of May. Her already bulging frame took on the look of a too-risen bowl of bread dough. Even her cheeks and feet were puffy. When I asked where the baby would sleep Glory said it would sleep in with her and Jim until it took to kicking, at which time they'd probably make an odd bed in the corner for a while until the child needed corralling. Of course I asked what then and Glory looked at Ellie and asked, "Ellie, how would you like to have a room with the new baby?"

Ellie answered, "Nope. No boys allowed."

Glory pressed down a giggle and replied, "Guess we'll cross that bridge when we get to it."

That night at dinner, Jim asked Glory, "How long do you think before the baby comes?"

"Well, the doctor says any time now, but two weeks from now is the due day."

"I don't mean that," he said, "I mean how long do *you* think until the due day?"

"Twelve days," she answered after a short pause.

"Then I'll be gone for seven days and I'm taking the boys with me, all of 'em," he said

"And where are you traipsing off to with me in such a state and the boys having three days of school left?" said Glory.

"We're going fishing."

"Fishing," she said.

"Yep," said Jim.

Jim finished his dinner in silence while the boys made plans and anticipated adventures that would fill the corners of their memories with reasons to have children of their own someday.

"You boys need to provide the worms for bait," said Jim. "We'll leave at the break of dawn tomorrow morning, so we'll need to make some torches for night-crawler hunting tonight."

You'd have thought that the roll had been called for the Jamestown infantry, the way these boys got to hootin' and hollerin' over digging up worms in the middle of the night. It resembled the scene in *Gone with the Wind* where the young men rallied to the call of the Confederacy. They wolfed down their soup and bread and immediately started collecting the essentials they would need for their excursion.

"Momma!? Orion called over the railing from upstairs, "Have you seen my flint kit?"

"It's in the junk drawer!" She hollered back.

"Momma?" called Isaac from outside the kitchen window.

"What is it Isaac?" she responded, leaning over the kitchen sink.

"Do we have four empty tin cans?"

"Yes, in the basement."

Isaac came barreling in through the kitchen door, left it open, cranked open the heavy basement door, left it open, and galloped down the wooden plank stairs to the basement singing "Oh Suzanna, won't you cry for me..."

"Momma!" called Isaac through the heating vent.

Glory jumped in surprise because the vent from the basement echoed the sound so it seemed that Isaac was right behind her. She bent over the vent and answered, "What!"

"Can we take a few jars of these pickled eggs?"

"Don't bother with the food, I'll pack a chuck wagon box for you boys, just get your grip together!"

Abe Joe walked into the kitchen and sat up on the kitchen stool. He tucked his feet onto the rungs, and rested his elbows on his knees and his chin in his hands. His face was forlorn.

"What's the matter, Joe?" asked Glory.

"I can't go fishing," he mumbled through his pouting lips.

"Why's that?"

"Crossing duty."

"Can't you get someone to cover for you?" offered Glory over her shoulder.

"Nope."

"Why not?"

"Just can't, too short of notice. Mr. Graves said two days notice so he can get a suitable replacement or you don't get to be crossing guard again," he said.

"Well, what if you got your own replacement? I'll do it for you Joe, or Elizabeth or Carol could do it," encouraged Glory.

"You don't know how Mom. And Elizabeth's too bossy; they told her she couldn't do it anymore."

"So, what about Carol?"

Abe Joe looked at me with his nose down and his eyes peeking out from under his curly blonde hair. He didn't say anything, but it was clear he was mentally dressing me in a yellow vest and hat.

"What do you think?" he asked me.

"Sure," I said.

He perked up a little and got up from his perch. "Say this... 'Signs UP!'" He pantomimed holding a crossing-guard stop sign and marched toward me. I mimicked him the best I could.

"Louder," he said.

"SIGNS UP!" I hollered.

"No, not SIGNS UP! Signs UP!" he corrected.

I tried it again, "Signs UP!"

"Get ready to crossss...signs OUT!" he instructed, with the body language of a drill sergeant.

I did my best to imitate his diligence and passed the test.

"You gotta be there by seven-forty tomorrow morning," he said.

"Okay," I said.

"It's not an easy job," he went on.

"I know, Abe Joe. I cross with the guards every day and I see how hard they work and how much concentration it takes," I said, half sarcastically.

"It takes a lot of patience, and you'll be five minutes late for morning rally, and you gotta get a note to be marked not late, and if you don't have gloves they loan you a pair."

"Okay," I agreed.

"Okay," he shrugged. "Guess I'll go fishing." Then he looked at his mother's pregnant figure, "You could probably do it, but that baby would get in the way." He left out the kitchen door and jumped one step at a time, down the porch steps till he got to the bottom, then took off running toward the barn.

Clothing packed, supplies collected, plans made, and shifts covered, the male half of the household retired to an early bedtime so they would be ready for pre-dawn worm hunting and an early departure. Glory, Elizabeth, Ellie and I sat on the front porch, shelling walnuts for the boys to take on their trip. Ellie ate more than shelled.

"I'll be glad to be rid of the lot of them for a few days. It'll give me time to get ready for this baby," she said rubbing the small of her back and smiling. "I feel like I'm ready to tip over from the weight."

"What does it feel like to have a baby?" I asked.

"Oh, it's just glorious. You never know how much love you have to go around until you look in the eyes of the newest one and know you will be able to love him, or her, just as much as the rest. Funny thing, love is. There's always enough to go around."

This was a nice thing to hear and a comfort even, but that's not what I meant. "But how does it feel, like when the baby comes out?" I asked, a little reluctantly.

"Oh, well. Hmm..." Glory looked down at her round belly. "It hurts. At first it feels like a really bad stomach or back ache and then, just as the baby comes out it feels like an Indian burn, but you don't really care that much because the hard and painful work is only for a while. The baby is forever," she smiled.

"What are you gonna name the baby?" asked Elizabeth.

"I was thinking about Zedekiah," she answered.

"Zedekiah?" Elizabeth and I said in unison, looking at each other with furrowed brows.

Glory broke into such a belly laugh that the baby bumped up and down under her billowing blouse. When she was done laughing, she said, "Zedekiah! Get that chicken off yer head and get out of the pig pen!!" It was a line from one of our favorite stories, *Zedekiah's First Haircut*. We all laughed so hard that we woke up Orion, who slept in the alcove above the porch.

"Keep it down! You sound like a bunch of cackling chickens!" he hollered through the open window.

This only made us laugh harder, especially with the reference to the chicken. We finished our nut cracking among muffled snickering and more ridiculous quotes from the book.

"Zedekiah! Take that pot off your head and put the water on to boil!" and, "Zedekiah! Take that diaper off your head and put it back on the baby!" and on and on and on, until we ran out of things that would fit on a person's head to cover a bad haircut.

I didn't think Zedekiah would be a bad name for a baby boy. When he was a man he would have a strong name that wasn't shared by many. But we never got off the subject of things Zedekiah could put on his head long enough for a serious discussion on baby names. So when the baby finally came the name was a complete surprise to us all, even Glory I believe.

8

The boys were long gone before I woke up in the morning, and when I came down the stairs I could hear Glory in the kitchen. Elizabeth and Ellie were still sleeping. Glory was stirring something and whistling "Mama's little baby loves shortnin' bread." I lay down on a sunny patch of the window seat to finish waking up.

"Want some apple juice, Carol?" offered Glory.

I nodded so she could see me, but wasn't ready to talk yet. She poured it and sat it on the counter. I watched as a squirrel played soccer with a walnut on the grass outside and then secured it in his mouth for easier transport—such a big mouth on such a little creature. This made me think of Elizabeth and the chicken leg, and I started getting mad at her before she'd even woken up. I got my apple juice off the counter and brought it back to the window seat. When Elizabeth came into the kitchen a few minutes later, I had compiled a mental list of the many wrongs inflicted on me by Elizabeth McDonald: cheating off of my homework, the skirt incident, the chicken leg, always having to be first, get the best, and always having the last word, to name just a few. By the time I finished my apple juice, my chest was simmering with anger and resentment. To top it off, she was wearing my bathrobe

"Take my robe off. You're dragging it all over the floor like a dust mop," I blurted out.

She looked my way and rolled her eyes. "So what? It'll wash."

"Lizzy, if Carol doesn't want you to wear her robe you need to go put it back," said Glory.

Glory looked at me out of the corner of her eye like she was measuring the chip on my shoulder.

Elizabeth let the robe fall onto the floor and kicked it my way. "There, you stupid, selfish orphan!"

Such welling up of anger, I had never felt before. It started in my fists and spread like wildfire up my arms, over my shoulders, and into my forehead. My fury erupted into an explosion of uncontrollable physical tirade, leaving all rational thinking back on the window seat. Without a second thought, I flew across the room in search of revenge. I ripped the thin cotton sleeve from her nighty, pulled clumps of hair from her head, scratched her face, and left a track of three stripes, raw and bloody, down her cheek. The whole time I cried and yelled, "I'm not an orphan! I have a mom! I have a dad! I'm not an orphan!" Elizabeth was caught completely off guard. So much so that she could not fight back, only cower from my repeated lashings-out. Glory got between us and took hold of my wrists. "Stop it!" she hollered into my face. When I realized that she was protecting her child from me, I melted onto the floor in shame. Salty tears streamed down my face into my running nose. I curled up like a ball on the hard wood and waited for retaliation. I expected a kick or the switch of a stick, or at least a verbal reprimand that would bring me back to my senses and out of this terrible cave of despair. But when I looked up I saw two faces staring down at me that might as well have seen a ghost. I was a stranger to them. I was a stranger to myself.

"Go wash your face, Carol" said Glory, tears welling up in her eyes.

I got up and ran to the bathroom and locked the door. I looked in the mirror and didn't like who I saw. I filled the bathtub, got in and closed my eyes, hoping soap and water could wash away the mean. When I opened my eyes I saw my skinny legs floating in ribbons of pink and red. Alarmed, I checked myself for wounds and found the source of blood between my legs. No! No! No! I wasn't ready for this. Not today. Not me. I was a girl, not a woman. I liked being a girl. I attempted to make a deal with God. If He would delay this curse, I would never be mean to Elizabeth again, and I would forgive and forget all the bad things stacked up in my brain against her. I got out of the tainted water. God didn't take my deal.

Mortified, I snuck up the stairs to my bedroom and did my best to remedy my problem. I stuck an unmatched sock in my underwear, got dressed, and curled up on my bed, facing the wall. Glory came in. She sat on the bed and rubbed my back.

"You're right, Carol, you're not an orphan," she said like a real mother would say to her own daughter. "Would you like to go see your mother?"

I nodded my head.

"Pack a bag and stay a few days. You and Elizabeth need some cooling off time, but when you get back, we need to talk this thing through. Sisters don't behave this way, blood or not," she said.

I started to cry, "How did you know?"

"Know what?"

"About the blood."

"What blood," then she got it, "oh... no I didn't know. I meant blood as in family. You are part of our family, Carol, weather you were born from my body or not. You'll always be a part of our family and we love you. Families have fights and say things they don't mean and do things they didn't plan on doing. You need some space to find some forgiveness for Elizabeth. She needs the same. Take your time getting your grip together. I'll walk you over to your mothers when you're ready."

"Okay," I whispered through a deep sigh.

"I'll bring up what you need for the other. Do you know what all this means? The bleeding?" she gently inquired.

"Yeah," I said with finality. Glory shut the door without another word. When I went back into the bathroom later there was a plain paper sack on the floor by the toilet. I was embarrassed even by these discreet tactics. Inside I found an elastic loop, about the size of a belt. It had two metal safety pins dangling from it. There were also three, thick, 3x8 inch pillows with ends that made them look like a hammock. I did my best at figuring out the mechanics and hid the paper sack in my school bag.

The damage I had done took seconds to commit. The scars on Elizabeth's face would take several weeks and a good amount of vitamin E oil to heal. But the most tragic causality was in me. I was afraid of my own anger. I punished myself. I didn't trust myself. I questioned if I should ever have children.

***

Those three days with Mama were exactly what I needed. My mood was better, I laughed more, cried less and felt like a few pounds of lead had been removed from inside my chest. I stopped feeling like everyone was out to get me for no good reason, and I loved the peace and quiet of Mama's apartment. She had to work the first night and sleep part of the next day, but other than that, we spent every waking moment together. We talked about serious matters for about an hour that first day; mood swings, Kotex, pimples, showers, extra hair, and swimming. She gave me a blue box of hammocks, a tube of light-pink lipstick, and a salt lick the size of my fist, to rub under my arms. She told me I was no more a woman now, than I was a week ago, and to go ahead and keep acting like a girl all I wanted 'cuz that's what I was. My body was just practicing making a nest for a baby to grow in when the time came that I decided I wanted to have one. Then she reviewed how the whole conception process works, which I assured her I never planned on doing anyway, and drew some pictures of fallopian tubes and gave me some sticky stars to put on my calendar every twenty-eight days. Then she assured me I wasn't alone and to try and enjoy myself in spite of the inconvenience. After the menstruation lecture she asked me if I had any questions. I said no as fast as I could without even thinking about it, because I was tired of talking about it, thinking about it, and dealing with it. I couldn't imagine this was going to go on for the best part of my life.

For the rest of the weekend we just acted silly and did things we loved doing, but didn't usually do. We had root beer floats for dinner and went to the theater and saw *Frankenstein Meets the Wolf Man*, which to this day is the scariest movie ever made, no doubt. We woke up without an alarm clock, my mother's most cherished luxury, and ate when we were hungry. I got a good taste of what it was going to be like to live with her when I turned thirteen. I couldn't wait.

When it was time for me to go back to the McDonalds', Mama walked with me and we sang "Faro-la Faro-Li" from the Frankenstein movie. I held my book bag and Mama carried my suitcase. We held hands and swung them to the cadence of the song as we marched along. We stopped at the grocery store on the way. Mama said we'd be there around dinner and should take an offering in case she was invited to stay.

In 1943 you couldn't just walk into a market and buy a chicken because you had the money and the desire. You needed a red stamp. A red stamp bought meat, oil, or cheese. When you used up the red stamps, that's all the chicken, oil, or cheese you got for that month. This was so everyone in the nation got some chicken, and the soldiers fighting the war got some too. Meat was not the only commodity that was hard to come by, sugar was even more scarce. Mama gave most of her food coupons to the hospital, because they fed her most of the time. And she gave my coupon book to Glory, because she fed me most of the time. But at the end of the month, if Mama had any of her own coupons left, she'd use them all up and give most of the food to the McDonalds. She kept enough sugar to have a teaspoon in her tea once in a while, and she kept a can of condensed milk in the fridge for the same reason.

Mama had enough red coupons left to buy a chicken. We also bought a bag of rice and two boxes of corn flakes, which to the McDonald kids was better than ten chickens, as long as there was sugar or Karo syrup to put on it. At the checkout counter, Mama said I could pick out a treat for the kids. I put a roll of Necco wafers on the counter.

"Get one for each of the kids, and you too," she said.

I lined up seven rolls and smiled from ear to ear knowing what a treat it would be for each of the McDonald kids to have their own roll of Neccos, and that no one would have to do extra chores for the chocolate ones. I promised myself I would eat them one at a time as they presented themselves from the roll, and not to go digging for the pink ones, which were my favorite. The other challenge was to suck on a wafer until it melted in my mouth, no chewing. This didn't happen very often.

"I'm sorry Ma'am, only one per family," said the man checking our items. "We only get one box a week, gotta make them last." I felt greedy for a minute, then I felt jipped.

I felt nervous going back into the McDonald house. I knew that Glory had a graceful and forgiving heart, but I wasn't sure about Elizabeth, and what's worse, I wasn't sure about me. No one was in the kitchen when we entered through the unlocked back door, so we headed upstairs to put my things away. On my bed, propped up on my pillow was an envelope with my name written on the front. It was Elizabeth's handwriting. Mama saw it but acted uninterested and excused herself to go to the bathroom. I opened it.

Dear Carol,

I'm sorry for calling you names and making you mad. You are not selfish, or an orphan so that makes me a liar, which I don't want to be so please forgive me. My face is okay and I can grow more hair, but I will never have another friend like you so

please be my sister-friend and I will stop being mean to you. I
washed your bathrobe.   *Elizabeth*

I showed the letter to Mama. "It's going to be all right," she said.

We went outside and found Glory, Ellie and Elizabeth picking the first few strawberries of the season. They were not surprised to see me and acted like nothing ever happened. I bent down next to Elizabeth and started searching for ripe berries.

"Sorry for going off like that," I said. I avoided looking at her face.

"Guess we're even," Elizabeth said.

"Thanks for the note," I said.

"Sure," she said. And that was it. She turned and smiled at me like we were true friends. It felt like she was glad to have seen the worst of me, like I was more human and approachable now that I had proven my imperfect character.

"You girls make up over there?" Glory put a basket of berries in a wooden wagon, then came over to us. She had a bit to say about growing up and self-control and acting like ladies, which I liked a lot better than acting like grown women. Ladies seemed like an in-between place to be for now. She talked about the beauty of forgiveness and the richness of grace. She explained how un-forgiveness is heavier for the one carrying it than for the one on which it is imposed. I'd never thought about it that way but I understood it just as she said it, and felt the weight of guilt and anger release through a deep breath. I smiled with a heart of humble remorse and looked up at Glory.

"I'm really sorry," I said.

"I'm glad," she said quietly. Then louder she said, "I'm ready for a rest and a cup of tea."

We loaded our berries into the wagon. Mama pulled and Ellie found a place to sit, next to our harvest.

Mama was indeed invited for dinner. Glory fried the chicken, Mama made biscuits, and Elizabeth, Ellie and I washed and trimmed the strawberries. After we ate, Mama and Glory promised us a game of gin rummy as soon as Elizabeth and I got the dishes done, which we did in record time and headed out to the porch. Glory sat down last. The relief showed in her face. Mama got a stool to prop up Glory's feet. Her ankles were the same size as her calves.

As Glory was bending forward to lay down a run of diamonds, she gasped. She looked down at her middle and moaned a moan that sounded like the "Mmmm Hmmm" that Uncle Virg makes when he has just taken a bite of Aunt Marion's chocolate cake. Glory took a deep breath, laid all of her cards down, not just the ones that counted, and closed her eyes.

"That one felt genuine," she said, and relaxed her shoulders down from up around her ears. She sat back and smiled, "Maybe I'll have this baby today."

"Oh! Don't do that, Daddy's not here!" Elizabeth said.

"Well never mind, I can't help it," and she got up.

"Where you going, Glory?" asked Mama.

"For a walk. If these are real pains, they'll get more real. If they're not, they'll stop," she said.

We all took off after her, partly for support and partly out of curiosity. Glory didn't stop until we reached the sidewalk at the corner. She stood, looking back at Ellie who was trying to catch a moth among an outcropping of bright green ladies mantle.

"Well?" Mama said.

"Nothing yet, guess I'll head back," she said, seeming a little disappointed.

Mama suggested we all take a walk down to the hospital while Glory still could. "Walking's good for your progress, and Dr. Snow could have a look."

"A mother knows better than any old doctor! I'm not going to the hospital," she said. Then she lowered her voice and said, "Ellie was the only one so far born at the hospital. They filled me so full of the sleeping gas I don't remember much about the birth or the look about Ellie when she was born. I'm having a baby, not some kind of surgery. I'll call the midwife and have her come when it's time."

"Oh Glory, don't be so old fashioned. The hospital has all the modern equipment and anything you might need in case of an emergency; of *course* you'll go the hospital. I have seen some difficult situations that could have ended in disaster!" said Mama.

"I'm more inclined to think that the disaster was induced by the hospital and them trying to tell a woman how to have a baby. Women have been having babies without doctors for longer than we know. I'll be having this baby in my own bed with the help of Mrs. Dickson," she insisted.

"Very well," Mama said. Her feelings and her professional opinion were obviously bruised. "I'm sorry to interfere, you've had more personal experience with childbirth than I have, being that you're on your seventh, but I have observed many crucial moments when a child was saved by a skillful surgeon."

"Thank you for your concern Virginia, but I assure you, I am perfectly able," said Glory.

The two women were quiet for the rest of the walk, but Elizabeth and I made up for it with our continued offerings of possible baby names. I liked Esther or Elijah. Elizabeth protested, saying Esther was for old ladies and Elijah would probably be called Eli for short which was too much like Ellie. She liked Sylvia or Leonard, which she wanted to shorten into Sylvie and Lenny. But by the time we made it back to the house nothing was settled. Glory said she knew the name of the child and would reveal it at the proper time. At this Ellie spoke up, "Baby Zedekiah!" Glory looked surprised and the rest of us broke out laughing.

The sun was low in the sky. Mama didn't have to work that night so she offered to stay and wait to see if "Baby Zed", which we called the child until its birth, would in fact show his or her face.

"Yes, Virginia. I'm stubborn, but not stupid. I'd be ever grateful if you could stay and see us through the night," she smiled, then took hold of the kitchen chair and squatted down slowly. "Mmmmm Hmmmm," she said again, followed by little whistles that made me want to help her breathe. "Elizabeth, go on over to the Silverstein's house and see if you can use their phone to call the midwife." She got out a piece of paper and wrote down a number she knew by heart. "Call Mrs. Dickson and tell her I'm having pains about ten minutes apart and we'll call again when they're closer to five," Glory groaned as she lifted herself up from a squat, "This is the day that the Lord has made for this child."

9

When Elizabeth got back from the Silverstein's house she made her report.

"Mrs. Dickson's at another birth, so I left a message with her daughter," she said.

Glory came in from the sitting room and lowered herself onto a kitchen chair. She had a quietness about her. Her smile was thin and knowing.

"So, Virginia, ever delivered a baby by yourself?" Glory said.

"Bet yer life!" Mama said.

"How many?" asked Glory.

"Lots. Fifty, maybe more."

Glory got up again and waddled into the hallway. Mama started sorting through the pots and pans, found the one Glory used for spaghetti noodles, filled it with water and put it on to boil. She asked me if I knew where she could find a new shoe string and a pair of scissors. I went to my room and fished around the top drawer of my dresser until I found the extra pair of laces that came with my P.E. shoes. I took them to Mama and she put one right in the water.

"What's that for, Mama?" I asked.

"To tie off the umbilical cord, where's the scissors?" she said.

I brought her my school scissors and she lowered them into the hot water also. "To cut the cord," she said.

Glory paced around the main rooms of the house in a continuous circle from the kitchen, to the hallway, to the sitting room, to the dining room. She stopped every once in a while and held onto something, breathed deeper, moaned a little, then kept on walking.

Mama took me and Elizabeth aside and made a list. She gave it to me and sent both of us off to the hospital with Glory's two wheeled shopping cart.

"Don't dilly-dally. Talk to Reynolds and tell her we're doing this at home and to keep an ear out for a call from us if we need assistance. Make sure she gives you everything on the list," she instructed.

We ran as fast as we could, the empty cart bumping along behind me. Mama had gone over and used the neighbor's phone to let them know we were coming, so when we arrived the gathering of supplies was well underway. They filled the cart and rushed us back out in no time at all. When we got back from our errand it was ten o'clock at night and all the lights were on in the house. The stove in the kitchen was fired way up and made the house feel warm and close. As soon as I bumped the cart across the threshold, Mama unpacked it, all the while talking to herself. She took the bundle of sheets and put them straight in the oven, then closed the damper on the stove to slow the coals. She laid all the other supplies on the table in the order in which they would be used. I knew this because she laid each thing and then re-arranged others and all the time kept a running inventory in her mind saying "and then this and then we'll need that and then this, this and that."

There was a brown bottle, a white bottle, a package of 4x4 gauze squares and a big set of tongs that didn't look like something I'd want to see getting anywhere near a baby.

A timer went off and she turned the fire down under the spaghetti pot and told me not to open that kettle no matter what, unless I was asked to. Then she went in to check on Glory. I followed and we found her squatting down with her elbows leaning on the hassock in the sitting room.

"She's praying," I whispered.

"Good," said Mama, "that's actually the most beneficial way to birth a baby. The Indians did it that way."

"Praying?"

"No, squatting," Mama said.

"How do you know all this?" I asked.

"Every mother has a birth story. That's what women talk about at a birth. I've probably helped deliver three-hundred babies, and each one is unique, but certain things hold true for most deliveries, squatting's one."

When Glory's breathing changed, she rose very slowly and looked our way with the same smile she'd been wearing for the past hour. Her voice was breathy.

"Let's start timing them," she said, with calm authority.

Mama checked the underside of her wrist. "It's 10:16. Let me know when the next one starts. Carol, get a piece of paper and write down 10:16."

I stood up and pondered where the closest pen and paper might be.

"In my desk," said Glory.

I got a pretty piece of stationary and a pen and headed the paper: "Glory's baby pains", then wrote 10:16, along the left hand side. I sat at the dining room table, pen ready, feeling good about having such an important job.

"Where's Ellie and Elizabeth?" asked Glory.

"I sent them upstairs. Elizabeth's going to read Ellie a story and see if she can get her to fall asleep for a while. I promised to wake her up when it gets closer," said Mama, winding her watch.

But it didn't get closer. I waited in perfect secretarial position, legs crossed, pen and paper at hand, but minutes, then half an hour, then an hour passed and no more pains came. Glory dozed in the chair. Midnight came and went. Mama made some black cohosh tea which I tasted and didn't care for one bit. It was supposed encourage contractions, and maybe it would if a person could get it down their gullet, but it tasted like dirt!

Glory managed to get the whole cup down like a jigger of medicine. Mama made her a second cup and suggested we all get some rest until Zedekiah was ready to join us. I left my pen and paper and went upstairs. Mama made an odd bed on the couch and Glory went into her room, which luckily was on the main floor so she didn't have to haul that stubborn baby up all those stairs. I was kind of nervous which made it hard to sleep, so I went back downstairs and shared Mama's narrow bed. I knew when she fell asleep by the way her breath was noisier and faster on the way out that on the way in.

***

I woke to the whistle of the tea kettle. It was still dark outside. A spoon clinked on the sides of a tea cup interrupting my attempt at dozing off again. I couldn't see her in the kitchen, but I could follow Mama's every step by the way the floorboards creaked as she shuffled around from sink to table, back to the sink again, then silence, after the careful scuff of a kitchen chair. I heard the strike of a match followed by Mama's slow, smoky exhale.

"Mama?"

"Well..." she answered.

I didn't have a question, just wanted to make sure she was there. I peeled myself off the couch, and wrapped the blanket around my shoulders like a cape. I found Mama in the kitchen reading *Recipes for Today*. She balanced her cigarette on the edge of the table and held her arms out for me to come and sit on her lap. I didn't fit like I used to. I curled my legs up and hugged my arms around myself to make myself smaller, but that just made my bony hips gouge into her thighs and she grunted.

"Glory's still sleeping," she whispered.

"No baby yet?" I asked.

"Nope."

"Maybe he's waiting for Jim and the boys to come back," I said.

"Maybe."

"Can babies hear us from inside a mom's tummy?"

"Yes, they can," Mama answered unwaveringly.

"Yeah, he's just waiting for his dad."

"Probably," she assured me. "Hungry?"

"No," I said.

"Think I'll make this bean and bacon soup. It can cook all day and will be good protein for Glory after the baby comes," Mama said and slid me off her lap onto the next chair. She got up and went to the stove, took the lid off the big spaghetti pot and fished the contents out with a pair of long kitchen tongs. She laid the sterile shoelace, scissors and washcloth on a cookie sheet, stoked the fire, and poured the beans right into the same water. I guess there was nothing wrong with that, but it didn't seem quite right to me. Shoelace soup.

***

Not many memories are as vivid in my mind as the one I have from that day. The soup pot was simmering and the kitchen windows were steamy, painting a blurry orange glow on the horizon. My eyes felt itchy and tired, but my body was buzzing and unable to rest. Mama was cutting an onion and I was watching the fat on the bacon turn golden brown when there came a howling from Glory's bedroom. The sound literally launched me into my mother.

"Sounds like Zedekiah's ready to meet us." She gently moved me aside and went to check on Glory, I waited.

Glory gave out some humming noises, then hoo- hoo-hoo, like an owl, then more humming.

"Carol," Mama called to me, "make a new pot of water and put it on to boil, put the scissors and the shoe lace in the new pot and bring me the towels from the stove." She wasn't hollering, but her voice was authoritative. "No, bring me the towels first."

When I got there with the towels, she was putting her stethoscope to her ears with one hand and rubbing Glory's back with the other. Glory was on her hands and knees swaying back and forth to her humming.

"Glory, turn over so I can listen to the baby's heart," Mama said.

"Wait till he's born!" she growled.

"That's the point Glory," Mama smiled, "I want to hear while the baby is still in there," she said, coaxing Glory to her side.

Glory rolled down onto her left side but kept her knee up. Mama checked her watch as she listened to Glory's belly. A grunty howl from Glory brought forth a flood of blackish-green fluid from between her legs. Some of it squirted onto my jammies. Mama was quick with the towels. I stood paralyzed.

"Glory? You got any urge to push?" Mama asked.

"Not really, maybe."

"Well, let's take a walk, or would you rather squat?" said Mama.

"No," said Glory.

"Why don't you try and squat."

"I can't," said Glory.

"You need to; this baby wants to come out. There's meconium in the water, it's not good for the baby, we need gravity to help," Mama encouraged while she shifted Glory's huge body against its will.

Glory rolled up to a sitting position and breathed through another contraction.

Mama gave me a shove to get my attention, "Carol, go get the things I laid out on the table and check if the water's boiling. I need the thing that looks like a short turkey baster. It's a rubber bulb with a metal tip."

I reluctantly left my post and went to the kitchen. There I found Ellie sitting on the kitchen table with a butcher knife and a whole loaf of brown bread. She'd successfully cut off a big chunk and was buttering it with the giant knife.

"Here Ellie, let me help you," I attempted to get the knife out of her hand and she started to bellow.

"No! I do it!"

"You're using the wrong knife." I pried her fingers off of the handle while she flailed and hollered. She kicked my arm with her foot and I dropped the knife. It fell, point into the floor, landing only a quarter of an inch from my bare foot. "Here try this," I said as I handed her a butter knife and pushed the butter closer.

Glory continued making owl sounds in the next room and I was far too invested to miss the event, so I hoisted Ellie and her breakfast up onto my hip and was just about to head across the hallway when I heard noise behind me. Before I could maneuver myself and Ellie around to see what it was, a gust of wind delivered the smell of earth, fish, and boys. The heavy sound of tired boots trudged through the porch and erupted into the kitchen.

I hurried toward them with my index finger over my mouth, "Shhhh!"

"Don't Shhhh me missy. All I want is a hot cup of cocoa and my bed. Where's my mom?" Isaac said as he dropped his tackle box on the floor with a clank and hoisted a bucket of smelly fish into the sink. "How's about trout for breakfast!"

"Shhhh," I said again, this time with a frown and a more threatening shake of my finger. "Zedekiah's coming!" I whispered loudly.

"Who's Zedekiah?" asked Abe Joe, chucking his wet socks into the general area of the laundry basket.

"The baby!" I said in an exaggerated whisper.

Jim dodged the boy barricade and made a beeline to the bedroom. His four sons stood in the kitchen, looking puzzled.

"Your mom is having the baby," I said knowingly, and retreated back to the bedroom.

Orion was the first to peek his head in the doorway. Under him three more sets of eyes peaked around in order of height.

Glory looked at the boys and managed a smile. Jim lifted her hand and kissed it. She sniffed, then scrunched her nose up and coughed and sent him away to bathe.

I could see Mama's brain sorting things out through her eyes. "Glory, scoot down here to the bottom of the bed. Ellie, if you're gonna sit up on the bed you've gotta stay on Daddy's side, Mama needs room. Abe Joe, go wake Elizabeth. Orion, check the fire under the pot, see that it doesn't boil over. Axel, put a log in the woodstove, and Glory, honey, see if you can push."

Mama looked at me and smiled as I laid out the things from the table onto the side of the bed.

"Think I'll push now," Glory panted with the next wave.

"Good idea, Glory, gentle though. Give a slow, gentle, steady push."

Silence loomed while Glory's face turned purple as a plum. Her eyes bugged out and her toes curled up. Then all of a sudden she let it all out through her puckered lips and made a whistle that sounded like a steam boat, stopped it for a second, then continued on as if the baby might come out through her mouth.

Mama threw the soaked towels aside and added others under Glory to make a nice fresh landing pad for the baby. When Glory had finished the next prune-faced push, Mama smiled and motioned for me to join her at the foot of the bed.

"Glory, won't be long now, you're doing great" Mama pushed Glory's feet up closer to her bottom. "Keep breathing glory, you are the baby's oxygen supply; nice, deep, slow breaths."

Glory followed Mama's directions and slowed her breaths until the next contraction. I had been looking mostly at Glory's face up till this time and partly at her belly, wondering how a person was gonna come out of that giant belly through a little hole between her legs. Nothing could stretch that much. I didn't feel quite right staring, but Mama insisted I come and have a look and when I did I couldn't believe my eyes. What looked like a wrinkly ball was pressing out from inside of Glory. Mama squirted some olive oil on her fingers and rubbed around the skin by the baby's head.

"The baby's crowning. Good work, Glory."

Glory couldn't talk 'cuz her face was all red and serious again. She gave a grunt and then gasped for air and the baby disappeared. I looked at Mama, worried something was wrong with the baby going back where it came from.

"Excellent, Glory, he's almost here, a couple more pushes," Mama encouraged.

"Is he OK?" Glory asked.

"Top of his head looks good!" Mama winked at me.

The bigger boys had gone to take a bath, probably unsteady about seeing their mama in such a state. Elizabeth had come down, wrapped in her quilt, and took her place next to Ellie on Jim's side of the bed. She ran her fingers through her mom's hair and hummed a quiet tune. Abe Joe and Axel sat against the wall in the hallway, each eating a giant pickle.

"Here he comes, Glory, keep it up, just breathe. Breathe again. Now when you feel the next pain, bear down nice and steady."

Glory didn't open her eyes this time. She was inside herself. There was a furrow on her brow and she hardly made any noise. When Glory's legs started to shake I held on to one and Elizabeth took hold of the other. Jim, smelling much better now, stepped over the boys in the doorway and arrived with the timing of a dancer. He knelt down by Glory and whispered in her ear. She lost her grimace and replaced it with a smile. I watched in nervous anticipation for the baby's head to appear again. The wrinkly head looked like the cow brain that Mr. Longstreet kept in a jar in the seventh grade science room. I couldn't watch after that because I was so scared that the tiny boy would have no skin at all and would come out looking like a skeleton with a brain. I was glad I had Glory's leg to hold onto or I may have fainted dead away from the thoughts rolling around in my head.

"Look Carol, here he comes," Mama said.

I pretended to look, but just scanned the area and went back to my leg holding. I watched Glory's face as she did the hardest job a woman has to do. She made a long, guttural grunt. Mama leaned in, ushered the tiny baby into the world and cried with delight, "Good job, Glory. Hello sweet child."

I refocused my attention just as the baby's feet were slipping from their journey and saw the slimy pink flesh make its last descent from Glory. Hallelujah, the baby had skin—I was so relieved. I knew about the cord that connected a baby to the mother for food while it was growing, but I wasn't expecting it to still be attached to Glory after the birth. Mama put the baby up on Glory's chest and rubbed the baby's back with more vigor than I thought she should. The baby coughed a little, then let out a tiny squeaky cry. Mama seemed satisfied and stopped her rubbing. Glory tucked the baby's head up under her chin and the tiny hand took a firm grip on Glory's finger. Glory and Jim were all smiles and contentment as they stared into the face of their new child. Glory whispered praises to Jesus, while Jim wiped the tear that escaped down his cheek

After a few minutes Mama tied off two places on the umbilical cord and got the scissors ready to cut in between. I gasped.

"Isn't that gonna hurt?" I asked.

"No, not one bit" Mama said, as she cut through the rubbery strands.

"This makes number three, Dear," Jim announced.

"Three?" Glory said.

"Well, I never heard of a girl named Zedekiah, but this is definitely our third daughter," Jim smiled and kissed his wife on the temple.

Glory took a closer look at Zedekiah and started in to giggle, "Well look at you little girl, fooling us all this time! I'm naming you Sassy!"

Jim raised his eyebrows and tilted his head.

"You're just gonna have to trust me on this one, Sir," Glory said as she helped little Sassy cuddle in and start suckling.

10

In the first year after Sassy was born, I learned several things about living in the same house as a baby. First, the baby is in charge of what time we eat dinner. Things might be rolling right along; potatoes in the oven, chicken frying, water on the boil for the corn, when a tiny cry from the warm corner by the woodstove brings the entire production to a screeching halt. Potatoes crack, the chicken grows a skin of congealed grease, and the corn never makes it to the boiling pot. So I realized that either I had to learn to cook, or be satisfied with raw corn and overcooked potatoes. Many a night, Glory orchestrated the finishing touches of our dinner from her nursing chair, often passing little Sassy off to one of us for the burping. I'd rather cook than burp the baby for some reason. I don't know why, just like cooking I guess.

Second thing I noticed was that boys act different around babies. Isaac's voice rose up like a soprano when he spoke to his baby sister. He washed his hands without being asked and caught himself from using crass slang or bitter words around her. He smiled. He whispered when she slept and tip-toed when he walked past her cradle. Little Sassy took him outside of himself and introduced him to a nurturing heart, eager to escape its hard shell. The other three boys were just as sweet with her; only the contrast wasn't as severe.

My third observation was that the old baby is no longer the baby. Ellie went from being all cuteness and ease, to resembling a mule getting a tooth pulled. She seemed to need something nearly every time Glory sat down to nurse the baby. She used old charcoal to color all over the wall in the hallway and she stopped taking naps altogether. For several days in a row, all she would eat was soft-boiled eggs, mixed with butter and saltine crackers, made *only* by Glory. She had lost her position as the littlest princess and was not a gracious loser. In fact, she seemed to be stepping into a position that was frighteningly like her older sister when I first met her, except it was all the more disconcerting given the fact that she was only four years old. Ellie started having extraordinary temper tantrums. Glory tried being patient and attentive during Ellie's fits of rage, then she tried ignoring her altogether. She tried singing "*Home home on the range,*" to mask the irritating whining and make the rest of us laugh, but this made Ellie even madder and she'd wail with new found fervor. If Glory let Ellie hold the baby, in hopes she would bond with her, Ellie would pinch Sassy and make her cry, then lie about pinching her.

I watched month after month as Ellie's whole demeanor changed. After a while she even looked different. She refused to let Glory, or any of the rest of us, comb her hair so it knotted up underneath and looked a lot like a lion's mane from the back.

Glory was tired. That baby needed a lot of attention, even more than Ellie. Sassy started walking before she was one, and after that she was like a tornado, destroying any sense of order that entered her path. When the chore board hadn't been changed for three weeks, I got a sure sense that things were really falling apart. Elizabeth erased her name from the board altogether, and Glory didn't even notice. I'd been gathering eggs and cleaning chicken beds all that time and was very thankful that this extension didn't happen on a week that I was assigned to dish drying. I'd take dish *washing* for three weeks—just something about the drying that bored me to death. Orion had been assigned to weed patrol and had simply stopped doing it. Said he'd pulled all the weeds in the yard twice already and if they came back he'd torch 'em. He had better things to do. So, what with the slack delegations and the lack of supervision on the part of Jim and Glory, many things were left undone and the house took on an air of dishevelment. The only exception to this was the front porch. That was Ellie's job. Despite her rantings and general change of character, she didn't miss a day of sweeping the front porch and checking it off her list. Jim had taken an old house broom and sawed off the handle to make a miniature broom, just right for Ellie. She used that broom with purpose and fervor, intent on a job well done. It became, after a few weeks of sweeping, her territory. On occasion, when she wanted to have a tantrum, but knew everyone was too busy or preoccupied to care, she'd grab her little broom and go at the porch two or three times in a day, sweeping up spent fuchsia petals and knocking down the spider webs that reappeared daily.

Despite the general lack of organization, Thursday's were still pancake day. Ellie had recently lost her high chair to Sassy and now ate her meals on the kitchen stool, pushed up to the table. One Thursday morning, when she wasn't quite awake, she inserted her two middle fingers upside-down into her mouth and was staring into her pancakes. Her other hand was twisting up in one of the rats nests at the nape of her neck. The pancake had started out hot and the butter had melted over the edge. Every once in a while she'd stick her fingers in the butter then re-insert them into her mouth. Axel, now nine years old and growing like a weed, asked if he could have her pancake if she wasn't going to eat it. She looked at him but didn't answer, so he helped himself. He speared it with his fork, plopped it down on his plate and started smothering it in Caro syrup and raspberry jam, both. The wailing that followed surpassed anything I'd ever heard from a human being of any age. Ellie started in to hollering and hyperventilating worse than I'd ever seen her do. She seemed sad more than mad. All of a sudden she took a deep breath and plugged her mouth with her fingers again. Then she closed her eyes and stopped breathing. No one seemed to know what to do when her face turned red, then reached a shade toward purple. Eventually she tipped right off her chair and onto the floor.

"Holy Nellie!" said Abe Joe, "Ellie Sue done hit rock bottom!"

"So she has," said Jim as he rushed around the table to find Ellie laying on the floor looking bluer by the second.

He shook her and called her name, but she didn't move, so he swept her up and carried her to the kitchen sink, turned on the cold water and stuck her face right under the faucet. She shrieked, and came to with so much snorting, and sniffing, and carrying on—you'd have thought she was a monkey in a poacher's trap. But she was breathing and Jim was holding her tight while she convulsed. "I'm all wet! I'm all wet!" she cried with so much drama and indignation you'd just like to slap her. And that's what Jim did. He slapped her right on her bare leg, leaving a bright pink picture of his fingers. She quit her fit and melted onto Jim in sobs and tears. I'd never seen Glory or Jim lay a hand on any of their children in anger or fear. We were all as surprised as Ellie, I'm sure. Glory stood up, as if to take Ellie from Jim's arms, but Ellie clung tight to him like a koala bear. He took her out onto the porch and passed Orion on the way. Orion didn't say anything, just looked at the two of them as if this were an everyday occurrence, which unfortunately, wasn't far from the truth.

When Ellie calmed down, she and Jim came back in and went upstairs. Ten minutes later they were back in the kitchen. Ellie was dressed in her yellow pillowcase dress with a pair of blue jeans underneath. Nothing had been done with her hair because she just wouldn't sit still long enough for a comb to run half way through. Plus, it was so matted underneath that I doubt you could have anyway.

"We're going on a date, Ellie and I. We'll be back for dinner," Jim said, and they left out the kitchen door.

***

That day after school, I went to see my mother and told her all about Ellie and her pancake temper tantrum and thanked her over and over again for not having another baby after me. What if I was the big sister, having to give up my place in the big bed and sleep with another sibling or in an odd bed in the corner? I'd feel slighted too. I liked having my mother all to myself and, even though Glory swears there's always enough love to go around, I would argue that there aren't always enough arms, beds or cookies.

Mama listened attentively while I did my best to deliver a true and un-exaggerated account of Ellie's antics. She stopped her knitting three different times and looked up at me to say "really?" and I would say "really!" and go on.

"Well then, what do you think you and I can do to help?" Mama slipped a black loop onto her knitting needle to mark the place to start pearling.

"I don't know, Mama. It's like she's going crazy. It's the oddest thing." I got my protractor out to do my math homework.

"That child has lost her perch," she said, "she's bored."

"You mean spoiled," I said

"No, I really think she was used to chorin' around with Glory, helping with this or that, and now she doesn't know her place. She's full of energy and bored to death. That's a bad combination. She needs a purpose. She has too much time on her hands."

I got back to the McDonald house just as Jim and Ellie were walking up the gravel driveway. They heard my footsteps in back of them so they stopped and waited for me to catch up.

"Evenin', Carol," said Jim.

"Evenin', Jim. Hi, Ellie." I was trying not to stare at Ellie. Her head was shaved, clean as a bowling ball.

"Have a good day?" asked Jim.

"Yeah."

"How's your mother?"

"Fine, and yours?" I said without thinking. I couldn't stop wondering about Ellie's bald head.

Jim just laughed and said, "Dead. How do you like Ellie's new hair cut?

"It's all gone. But you have a nice-shaped head Ellie." It was the only nice thing I could think to say. It was just plain painful looking at it, all scabby and red.

"I had bugs," she said, "we went to the barber shop."

"Bugs," I repeated.

"Yep, bugs," she said.

"They all gone now?"

"Are they all gone now?" she asked her dad.

"Hope so," Jim said. "Mama's not gonna be happy though. We're gonna have to shave everyone, or put kerosene in their hair to kill the bugs."

"Me too?" I asked.

"Mmm Hmm."

Elizabeth was the next one to see Ellie. She pulled her chin back into her neck and gasped. "What the..."

"Easy, Elizabeth," said Jim, and gave her a hug. "You're next."

"What are you talking about?"

"Head lice. Everyone either needs a shave or a treatment, and Ellie chose the shave, on account of the tangles," he explained. "Everyone out of the house!" yelled Jim to all inside. "No one's allowed back in until they've had a shave or a douse with the kerosene and a thorough combing out."

It took no time at all to get rid of the lice on the boys; Jim just shaved their heads clean and applied olive oil to the newly shorn skin. Glory, Elizabeth, and I, on the other hand wanted to keep our hair, so we spent the rest of the day dousing with kerosene and picking nits out of each other's hair. Mine wasn't too bad, but Elizabeth was pretty infested, which only made my nit-picking harder. She hollered at me every time I pulled too hard, to the point that Glory told her if she made one more peep, she'd give the job to Orion. After that she held her tongue. Glory didn't seem to have one single bug. She said God knew exactly how much she could handle and a head louse was not one of them. She treated herself with kerosene all the same, and Elizabeth combed her hair with a fine-tooth comb. Sassy's baby fine hair didn't attract any lice, but Glory found that the nit comb worked famously on her cradle cap. Afterward we washed our hair with Drene shampoo and rinsed it out with vinegar. Once the boys were bald, they went about stripping the beds and started in on laundering the overwhelming piles of bedding that needed de-lousing.

When Jim was done with the hair cutting, he went to work in the barn. When he came in for dinner that night he was carrying a huge piece of plywood, scored with a wood burner into 48 squares. Down the left hand side he had burned each of our names into the wood, even Sassy. Across the top were the days of the week. Each square had a nail pounded into the top at the center He set it on the window seat and took his place at the table. Many inquired as to what the board was for, but Jim kept quiet until we were all seated and prayers for the food and praise for the eradication of the head lice had been lifted.

"This is the new chore board," Jim announced before he took his first bite of sweet potatoes. Then he pointed to a box of wooden discs. Each disc was about three inches wide and had a hole drilled through the edge. They looked like they could be painted and used for Christmas decorations. He picked one up and hooked it onto one of the little nails in the boxes. "This counts for one chore. Mom and I will decide on what chores get written on each disc and you will be responsible for the ones that hang in the boxes by your name." He gave a little push to the disc. It swung back and forth on its nail. He smiled, noticeably taken with his project. "If you're wondering why the new system, it's because there are now officially too many of you for us to keep track of, and you've got to start doing the track-keeping. Your mother and I will delegate the chores for the week, and you can check the board daily for your responsibilities. If there is any fussin' about fairness or hardness of chores, you get more, not less work to do. If one has five chores and one has only two, it's because your behavior reflects that you have too much time on your hands and your chore load will increase. We will start the week out with everyone having two chores per day and as the week goes by, if you display extra time to say...have a temper tantrum, then you will receive an extra chore." Everyone looked at Ellie. She was smiling. "So, what do you think?" asked Jim.

"I think it's a lovely idea!" said Glory, "thank you, Sir!"

"I think it's stupid," said Orion.

"That's the kind of attitude that earns extra chores. Take heed. We start using it tomorrow and I will monitor it myself," said Jim.

"I want lots of circles!" said Ellie. "I want the dishes with the bubbles, and the porch sweeping, and the baking, and going to the market with Mama and..." she went on and on about the things she wanted on her list all the while rubbing her naked scabby head.

"Sounds hard," said Axel.

"That's 'cuz yer lazy," said Abe Joe. He left the table and hooked a few blank discs on the nails in a zigzag pattern, "sounds good to me."

"That's 'cuz you're little and have easy chores," said Orion, "sounds like a communist plot to me."

"Will the chores rotate from person to person?" asked Elizabeth.

"Mostly, as age and ability allow," said Jim, "Carol?" he nodded his head toward me.

"I can do anything for a year," I said, and speared a carrot coin.

The chore board suited most, but thrilled Ellie. After the system was put into place, she stopped being such a terror. She took on the role of making sure everyone was up to date on their chores. Orion didn't like this at all, so when she got on him about his responsibilities he'd say, "Yes, Grandma," and do what he wanted anyway. This frustrated Ellie to no end. One time she went after Orion with her short porch broom, acting more like an old grandma than ever. It was one of the funniest sights I can recollect at the McDonald house. He just stood there laughing his head off while Ellie wailed on him with her broom.

As it turns out, Mama was right about Ellie being bored. And the itching from the head lice, I believe, was literally driving her crazy. That, along with her limited access to Glory's attentions, was turning her into a whirling dervish with no purpose or direction, and her personality could not bear it. She liked a list, a hand to hold, and a pat on the back for a job well done. She always had the most discs on the board and thrived from it. Consequently, the McDonald household reclaimed its organized chaos and sense of well-being. Amazing what a good de-lousing and a chore board can do.

11

The gift of routine and the necessities of daily life filled my days so thoroughly that I had little time to pine for my mother and our impending reunion. During the summer of my twelfth year, I stayed with Aunt Marion and Uncle Virg, as usual. Summers in Greenwood were usually very predictable. Aunt Marion rotated the crops in the raised beds — whoopee! — ensuring that the soil wouldn't be overstressed and risk producing smaller than expected Romas, or late Early Girls. There was never any discussion about *if* we'd go to church on Sunday; we always did. I didn't have any standing chores, just helped out when I was asked. Summers in Greenwood were usually a welcome break from my otherwise busy, noisy life at the McDonald's. Therefore, finding Aunt Marion feeling poorly, and myself installed as nursemaid and head cook during the summer between seventh and eighth grade, put a crook in my tail. Aunt Marion took ill shortly after I arrived and didn't get off the couch until I left ten weeks later. She was tired all the time and could hardly stay awake for a game of gin rummy or Criss-Cross. During my first week there, she ate only chicken broth, dry toast points, and hard candy. *I* did the ironing, *I* did the dishes, and *I* had to take care of that spoiled brat of a dog that needed her eggs scrambled and her meat cut. I hate to sound ungrateful, but I had an agenda for this particular summer and was given little time to pursue it. On the other hand, the fact that Aunt Marion wasn't watching my every move may have been a blessing in disguise. There was a boy named Mark that I had met at Uncle Virg's church during Easter vacation. He was going into ninth grade and wanted to be accepted into the private high school, but had to take an entrance exam and score high enough to show himself a worthy applicant. Uncle Virg tutored him every Saturday morning from eight to ten o'clock and these sessions were to continue throughout the summer. The first Saturday morning I made sure I was dressed and ready for the day by seven so I could offer tea or cocoa to the tutor and his student. They both accepted my offer, so I made a second entrance to deliver the drinks. I nonchalantly informed Uncle Virg that I needed to go to the pharmacy to pick up a digestive for Aunt Marion, but would wait until after they were done so Uncle Virg could be available for Aunt Marion. I didn't mention that I knew the pharmacy was on Mark's way home...and that I planned on leaving precisely when he did...and we might even strike up a conversation and walk the whole way together...and, I just happened to have money for Cokes.

My plan was executed without a catch. I wore my polka dot skirt and my bangs stayed down. He wasn't a fast walker, so I didn't trip in my church shoes. He didn't have money for a Coke and wouldn't let me buy him one, but said he'd have a sip of mine from a separate straw. I saved the straw. Phase one of my plan ended in victory. He said he would see me next week and would bring money for Cokes, if I thought I could get away again. I smiled until my cheeks hurt and spent the rest of the week waiting for next Saturday.

As much as I prayed for a miraculous healing, Aunt Marion did not get any better. The next week she moved on to eating boiled macaroni and an occasional slice of peach. She was continually sucking on ice. I'd heard about people being this sick, but had never been around it. Why hadn't someone told me about this before? Should I even be in the same room as her? What if I caught what she had and never made it to my thirteenth birthday? What if I took sick this very week and missed my first date with Mark? My first date ever! I called Mama on the phone and voiced my concern. She just laughed.

"Mama, this is not funny! Aunt Marion is wasting away to nothing and Uncle Virg isn't doing anything about it. He just does pat-pats on her hand and winks at her like she's an old dog who needs to be put down. I think she might be dying and I'm worried about it being contagious! What if..."

"Peach!" Mama interrupted my lamenting, "What she has is *not* contagious. Aunt Marion is pregnant," Mama said, still giggling.

"Oh." I paused for a moment, separating in my mind, an infectious disease from pregnancy. "Does *she* know it?" I asked.

"Of course she knows it. She told me she thought she was, but this confirms it."

"Well why didn't she tell me?" I whined.

"It's a sensitive subject for her. Aunt Marion has had three miscarriages, and she probably doesn't trust this one to go full term. But it looks like her secret is out. It's a good thing you're there, Peach. Help her all you can, she wants a baby in the worst way," she said with a smile in her voice. "I'll be over for dinner on Sunday; I'll talk to her again."

"She could have told me," I said, "I was just about ready to suggest to Uncle Virg that he take her to the hospital. If this is what being pregnant is like, you can count me out!" I assured her.

"Well, good then." Mama said this when she partly agreed and partly disagreed with something someone said, but it wasn't worth fighting over.

"So what should I do about Aunt Marion?" I asked.

"There's nothing to be *done* about Aunt Marion. Aunt Marion will be better in eight weeks, mark my words. Just make sure she drinks enough and has a good supply of Melba toast and soda crackers. Try to get her to eat some almonds or cashews, she needs some protein—and some fruit once in a while too," she said.

"All right, Mama. See you Sunday."

"I'll meet you at church. Love you."

"Love you too. Miss you. Bye," I hated goodbyes, even phone ones.

"Bye- bye."

So the dreaded disease was a baby. After I hung up the phone I stared out the window and kept my hand on the receiver for a few minutes, digesting this new information. Now that I knew the truth I could relax, knowing that if I didn't run to Aunt Marion's bedside every time she rang her bell she at least wasn't going to die. She might throw up, but heck--she could keep a pot by her bed for that. There was a chance I might be able to get away once in a while after all. Not only did I have Mark to persue, I also had piano lessons and a sewing class. I had made a personal promise to myself to actually learn to read music and use a sewing machine this summer. A girl needs goals. Mama said that. I could endure the smell of chicken broth and could even take on the task of being the cook for Uncle Virg and myself, but I didn't want to miss my summer classes.

That night in bed I was thinking about having a little baby cousin and how fun it would be next summer when the baby was born and that maybe I should make a baby quilt in my sewing class. Then I started to giggle. I was laying there all alone giggling uncontrollably. I was thinking about how babies were made and how funny it was that I thought Aunt Marion's sickness was going to rub off on me, and how I'd never have to worry about being sick and pregnant because I would never do *that*. Then I had to start singing '*When the roll is called up yonder*' in my head because I started thinking about all the people that had children that I knew and how absurd it was that they had all done *that*. I thought of Mr. and Mrs. Fitzgerald, him being over six feet tall and so big and fat, and her being shorter than me. Poor lady. I couldn't imagine Aunt Marion and Uncle Virg doing *that*, much less Jim and Glory. When I start to think about things that I know aren't mine to think about, I just sing a song in my head, preferably a hymn, and it's like washing my mind and starting fresh. Mrs. White taught us to do that in third grade Sunday school class and it became one of my most practiced disciplines. I can't begin to imagine where I came up with some of the things that popped into my head, but it was good to know I could chase them out.

12

Harsh weather came on early that year. Some weekends I didn't even go see Mama because of the wind, rain and ice. Jim seldom had work, and some days we stayed home from school simply because we couldn't get through the snow drifts. Mama and I went to Aunt Marion and Uncle Virg's house for Thanksgiving. Aunt Marion was finally looking pregnant and was much more mobile and happier than when I stayed with them in the summer. We had a fun weekend. Mr. Danielson went with us, and their pastor and his family also came. Going between Aunt Marion and Uncle Virg's house and then back to the McDonald house was like night and day. Uncle Virg wore shiny shoes, ironed pants and a hat whenever he went out. Jim wore tattered overalls, dirty boots and usually couldn't find a hat fit to wear in public. Glory was all love and hugs, no matter who you were; Aunt Marion was cold, until she knew you. Glory praised me and my accomplishments; Aunt Marion found fault. Uncle Virg was jolly; Jim was melancholy, but I loved them all. The Hussey house was too warm; the McDonald house was too cold. There was never enough gravy at the McDonalds; there were always leftovers at Uncle Virg's. Dog; no dog. Table cloth; no table cloth. Quiet; noisy. But each had a richness that I loved. I guess it's more the people than the house.

This would be my last winter with the McDonald's. December 16th I'd turn thirteen and finally move in with my mother. I wanted to do something special for the McDonalds. I'd made a plan and shared it with Mama on the drive back to Jamestown after Thanksgiving weekend.

My hope was to have a dinner party like the one that Carol Bird had in my favorite book, "The Bird's Christmas Carol". I presented my idea to Mama from the back seat of Uncle Virg's car, with hopeful enthusiasm.

"Mama?" I said.

"Well," she said.

"I've been thinking."

"Uh oh," Uncle Virg chimed in.

"What's that Peach?" Mama said.

"Ya know the part when Carol Bird throws a party for the Ruggles' in the rear?" I said.

"Yes," she said. She knew exactly what I was talking about.

"I want to have a Christmas party like that for the McDonald kids," I said. "I've read the book so many times that I can pretty much make the menu from memory, if you'll help, and I know just what present to get each one. I even have it mapped out in my head where each kid will sit."

"You've been thinking about this for some time then, huh?" she said.

"Well, just since last night when I read the book for the hundredth time," I said.

"What kind of gifts are you thinking about?" she said.

"I know I don't have enough money, but if I did I'd want to buy each one a new coat and maybe a book. I was thinking that if people didn't buy me presents for my birthday or Christmas, but gave me the money they would spend instead, I could use it to buy the McDonald kids their presents."

"Well, I've never heard of a more Christmassy idea. We could have the party on your birthday," she said.

"Yeah, a double birthday party for me and Jesus." I was surprised at how effortlessly she agreed to my plan. "We could have the party in the church hall at the big table, and the kids could ride in the horse-drawn sleigh if there's snow."

"Well then, let's do it. I'll buy the food if you can raise the money for the gifts," said Mama.

Uncle Virg chimed in from the driver's seat, "I was only going to give you a pair of cotton socks this year, what with the baby coming and all, hope thirty-five cents will be enough from me." I knew he was kidding, but never expected his generous offering of twenty-five dollars, which he entrusted to Mama for safe keeping.

For the rest of the ride home we made lists of coat sizes, book ideas, menus and games. I got a little overwhelmed at the grandness of the task and all that had to be done in less than a month. The buying, the cooking, the secret keeping, not to mention the continued commitment to my own selfless and generous attitude, of which I seemed perfectly able right now, but what if I saw something I really wanted for Christmas, or my birthday, and couldn't ask for it, or even dream about it. This would take a strong will and humanitarian heart, not to mention the mental energy it was going to take to keep all the secrets.

For the next month, my mind was consumed with thoughts of the Christmas party. My afternoons with Mama were spent shopping for the coats, deciding on the perfect book for each child, and deciding between hard or soft sauce for the desserts. In the end Mama said we could have both. With every spare moment I worked on Sassy's gift; a hand-knit ear warmer. Mama said if you buy everything it doesn't show so much love.

One morning while we were getting ready for school, Elizabeth looked in the bathroom mirror and frowned, "I look terrible in brown!" Then she pulled her sweater off over her head. "I'd rather freeze to death than be seen in that old brown sweater one more time. When I'm married I'm only wearing pink. I'm not going to even consider marrying a man unless he can buy me a new pink wardrobe, shoes and all! "She stormed out of the bathroom to find her only piece of pink clothing; a blouse that was so worn in the elbows that she ended up putting the brown sweater over it after all. I could hardly contain myself that day, for though the coat I had chosen for Elizabeth was navy blue, it had pink satin lining that would show if she didn't button the top all the way. I couldn't have been more pleased with myself, and it showed.

"What are you smiling about?" Elizabeth shouted after me as we walked down the stairs.

I didn't answer her. When we got to the kitchen she stuck her tongue out at me, but it didn't make me mad at all.

"You look so pretty in pink," I said.

She said, "I know," and pulled her collar up closer to her face.

Abe Joe already had the warmest coat of any of the other kids because it was patched and reinforced in so many places that the fabric was almost triple thick. He wore that coat from dawn until he went to bed, so it never got into the wash pile that whole fall and winter until he traded it for the junior bomber jacket that Mama and I picked out for him. We found a sailor style P-coat for Axel that fit his shy but sure personality just perfectly. Both Orion and Isaac would get fleece-lined denim jackets and a jar of lanolin for waterproofing so they could ride their bikes to school in the rain, and not end up with a soaked back. But my favorite coat of all, the one I would have chosen for myself if I had gotten a new coat that year, was the one we got for Ellie. It was red wool, buttoned up the front with silver heart-shaped buttons, and had Scotty dogs embroidered all along the bottom. The collar was made of rabbit fur and it came with a matching hand muff, lined with rabbit fur. I knew it was going to make her want to suck her fingers and rub that fur under her nose 'cuz it almost made me want to, and I had long gotten over my thumb-sucking tendency.

13

In the McDonalds' mail came an invitation. It was addressed to all the McDonald children by name. Glory propped the letter up on the salt and pepper shakers in the middle of the table to act as the center piece. We were made to wait until after dinner to open it, and as there was no return address on the envelope its origin was the constant topic of conversation during our hurried meal. I concentrated on chewing and kept my knowing eyes directed at my plate. When Glory and all of the children were done eating and our plates had been taken to the kitchen, Jim took seconds — which was highly uncharacteristic for him to the point that I felt he was doing it on purpose, just to watch us squirm. A communal sigh of disappointment erupted from around the table as we were convinced that our patience had officially run out and we couldn't bear to watch Jim eat one more single solitary pea without ripping into the mystery letter. I had taken great pains to make the invitation as formal and bona fide as possible. I used a folded sheet of Mama's linen stationery and drew a pencil sketch of a Christmas tree on the front. Aunt Marion let me use her Royal typewriter to type the text inside, and in the end I only had one mistake, which I found too late and figured it was such a small mistake that it didn't really matter; they'd surely never notice. Glory asked Jim if he cared if we went ahead and opened it before he was done eating. He said it was none of his affair, being it wasn't addressed to him, and suggested I be allowed to open it since I wasn't invited either. I assured him my feelings weren't tried in the least and handed the envelope to Orion. I thought he had the most expressive reading timbre and would deliver my invitation with the most finesse. He licked off the butter knife, then dried it off under the armpit of his shirt, slid it under the flap, and made a perfect slit in the top of the envelope. He read:

```
        You are cordially invited to a
      Christmas & Birthday dinner party.
    Please join me for a night of remembering
      Our Savior's Birth and my birthday.
        Dinner will be at Four o'clock in
          the parish hall of Grace Chapel
                to be followed by
          Christmas songs and games
              December 16th, 1944
                No gifs please.

          This is my way of giving back
          to you, for sharing your home
             and your lives with me
             these past four years.

                Respectfully,
            Carol Suzanne Carlson
```

"You spelled gifts wrong," said Orion.

"Yahoo!" hollered Abe Joe, "I love me a party!"

"And I don't want you to bring anything, only yourselves." I said, ignoring Orion's critique.

"What a grand idea. Can I do anything to help?" offered Glory.

"Nope." I said, afraid to say anything more for fear that I'd blurt out the surprises we had planned.

So the day was set aside for my dinner party, and just in time too because the following day there came another invitation from the Saint Vincent de Paul requesting the McDonald family to serve soup at the poor farm on December 16th. Glory loved nothing better than volunteering at the poor farm. She found great satisfaction in showing her children how fortunate they were to have a roof over their heads and more than thin soup in their bowl. She openly debated the importance of serving others as opposed to being served, and had the children nearly convinced of their folly in wanting to accept the invitation from me, when Isaac reminded her that it wasn't honest to go back on your word and that they had already promised me of their intentions for my party. Wasn't there another day they could feed the poor so they could have a turn to be fed also? Everyone agreed that it would be insensitive to disappoint me. Glory crossed her arms over her chest and considered her pleading children. She had no intention of letting her children miss out on this special event, but gave out a sigh of resignation and pretended to be cajoled into a moment of weakness. It was agreed that she would arrange for them to volunteer at the St. Vincent de Paul the following week. Even Orion and Isaac were eager to help with the less fortunate, knowing how close they had come to almost missing the only event ever announced to them by formal invitation.

Sassy was invited to the party, but Glory decided she should stay home so no one would have to have the responsibility of watching after her. She said a two-year-old was the fastest way to turn a dinner party into a three-ring circus. I had mixed feelings but figured Glory knew best.

***

I had to purposefully disengage my thoughts from the Christmas party so I could pass my examinations, ensuring that I would be able to move in with Mama during Christmas break. I doubt that Mama would have truly kept me from moving in with her if I flunked my exams, but I didn't want to test her. I do know that it made her very happy when I made good marks and I was trying my hardest to start my new life with Mama under the very best circumstances. After proving how much I knew about the reconstruction after the Civil War, in an essay of no less than three hundred words, all I had to do was finish memorizing my lines for the Christmas program and I would be free from any obligations except the placement of name cards, wrapping of gifts, and deciding which games to play at the party. I had two days to give all my attentions to the preparations, gather my few belongings around the McDonald home, and make ready for my long-awaited move.

When the party day arrived, I walked over to Mama's apartment in the Nurses' housing.

"You gonna miss your apartment Mama?" I said.

"Not in the least," she said, "and you are going to love our new digs! The kitchen isn't in the living room, and you can close the bathroom door without turning sideways. It's a regular Taj Mahal compared to this."

"Where's all your stuff?" I said.

"Grandpa came for the last few boxes this afternoon. There weren't many to begin with. Other than this suitcase, I'm moved out."

We finished making the name cards when we arrived at Grace Chapel and then started cooking. We dressed the duck and put it in the roaster. I peeled enough potatoes to feed the Army and Mama made three pumpkin pies; two for the party and one for Jim and Glory. There were jars of green beans donated from Aunt Marion's pantry and a jar of pickled beets from the market. I cut the potatoes and dropped them in the boiling water. Mama put the bread dough up to rise. Then we sat down and had a cup of tea to reward ourselves for being so industrious.

An hour before the festivities were to begin, we changed into our party clothes. Mama kept our agreement not to buy me any Christmas presents, but she said I needed to have a dress for the party, so we had gone to Bigelow's' and picked out a practical, but lovely dress for my special day. It was blue, with a white collar and cuffs, and would most definitely double as my first-day-of-high-school dress.

Mama let me wear her real pearls and I applied a light smearing of her orange lipstick. I begged her to have a new dress herself, but she said no, not this year. She wore her gray pleated skirt and a red sweater with her holly scarf tied in a square knot around her neck. She added red lipstick and emerald green earrings. The result was very Christmassy; she was beautiful.

We were ready for the six McDonalds when they arrived in the red wooden sleigh. The weather had cooperated and there was just enough snow to ensure a smooth ride. Mr. Danielson drove the team and when they arrived Mama and I were waiting on the front porch. Piles of blankets had been layered on each row of three kids deep, so we went down to help dig them out of their warm, wintery coach.

The McDonald's attended church at Grace Chapel every week, so when they arrived they weren't shy about coming in and making themselves at home in the fellowship hall, which was really no more than that—a hall, but it sure looked pretty with candles and all the fancy glasses filled with pink punch, and the shiny silverware lined up like toy soldiers. Each McDonald found his or her name on a card and eagerly took their seat. Smacking lips proved they had saved big appetites for this feast. Elizabeth was put at one end and I to her right. I put Ellie on my right between me and Mama so we could help her cut her dinner. The boys all sat on the other side of the table looking ravenous as Mama and I presented each dish to each one individually, encouraging them to take as much as they wanted, and reminding them that there was plenty for seconds or thirds, and to make sure they tried everything, keeping in mind the pumpkin pie and puddings.

When the last dish was offered and refused, we retreated to the Christmas tree in the sanctuary. They hadn't seen it yet, and the surprise on the faces of all the children was my greatest reward. Abe Joe dove directly under the tree and surfaced with the biggest box, which, being the biggest was for Orion.

"I was thinking the youngest should go first," I said, "and since Sassy isn't here, that would be Ellie."

Abe Joe went scavenging again and brought Ellie a medium-sized box. She ripped the paper off, then paused and looked up at her siblings.

"Open it!" said several voices.

She looked at me and I nodded with an encouraging smile. Slowly opening the lid, she peeked in, so nobody else could see. When Axel could stand it no longer, he flipped the lid over, which made Ellie furious and she started to cry. Mama got up and led Axel to the piano bench where they sat until it was his turn. Ellie, satisfied with the removal of her brother, opened her eyes and saw what everyone else was already staring at; the red coat with the rabbit-fur collar. I helped her pick it out of the box and she fell into me, rubbing her tear-stained face in the fur. She immediately stuck her fingers in her mouth, just like I thought she would. She removed her fingers from her mouth long enough to get her arm through the sleeve, then tiptoed over to Elizabeth and plopped down on her lap. Axel wanted to pet that collar in the worst way, but Mama kept him corralled as to not upset Ellie again.

Next, I handed Abe his box and he ripped into it like a dog digging an escape route; paper and cardboard flying hither and to. Each took their turn with the undivided attention of the rest. When it came to Elizabeth's turn, she removed the tape from the paper with the care of a surgeon and folded the wrapping like fine linen. Every McDonald child wore their coats for the remainder of the evening, through the games and the dessert. A more satisfied group of siblings I had never encountered. Each one thanked me and Mama at least twice, and compliments were liberally exchanged between themselves. When the games were over and no one could eat another bite, I handed out the wrapped books, instructing them to open them at home with Jim, Glory and Sassy. I gave Elizabeth the little-kid's gifts, knowing they shouldn't be trusted with such a difficult challenge of honor. I know because I would have peeked if it was me.

Isaac was first in line to head out the door, but he stopped short, causing a pile-up of McDonalds. He turned out of line and walked back to Mama. "Mind if I pray?" he said.

"Why no Isaac, I'd love for you to pray," Mama said.

He cleared his throat and bowed his head. "Dear Jesus, we don't deserve the goodness of Carol, or Mrs. Carlson, or of you. We are sure thankful that you continue to call out to us—in the way of giving us blessing, even when we don't especially deserve it, or if what we really should be getting is a whooping or a lecture. God, thanks for being patient. Thank you for the Christ child who grew up and became like us for a while, but didn't ever sin. Thanks for blessing some so they can bless others. Amen."

"Amen!" was the resounding response.

Each sibling gave us one more hug, even Elizabeth, and then reluctantly piled in the sleigh for the chilly ride home.

In Carol Bird's book, this was where she died. All the children went home and she went to bed happy. As she lay remembering the grand day, and listening to the choir from a nearby church, "the wee birdie flew away to its home nest."

I was ready to fly. I was thirteen.

Everyone was gone and it was just Me washing and Mama drying. When the dishes were just about done, Mama lit a cigarette and hoisted herself up to sit on the counter. She rested her head back against the cabinet and blew the smoke up toward the light and watched it swirl around.

"What's that?" she said.

She laid her cigarette down on the edge of the counter and jumped down. I picked up the cigarette, doused it with water and threw it in the trash can. She poked her face through the slightly open door of the nursery and then looked over her shoulder, smiling.

"What?" I said, wringing out the dish rag.

"Come here." She was smiling and frowning, but I could tell she was pleased.

I dried off my hands on the way. She stepped away from the door, allowing me to see in. I looked back at her, puzzled, but I too was smiling. "No way! Not in a million years did I think I'd ever see my old buggy again."

"Wow." Mama walked back to find her cigarette and lit another.

"How do you suppose this got here?"

"I don't know, but it was sure nice of Him," she said. "What a perfect birthday present."

"I'm amazed," I said, and walked over to examine the buggy

"Good. Never cease being amazed." She picked up a plate and continued drying.

The handle felt smaller and smoother than I remembered. The paint was chipping off the wicker and the lining was torn inside; but I was almost positive it was my buggy, Jessie's buggy. Just to make sure I looked underneath and saw where I had written "Thou shall not steal", still legible in purple crayon.

"Look, Mama."

She came back to the nursery. I pointed out my six-year-old inscription.

"That's yours all right," she said.

"Can I take it home?" I asked.

"I think that would be all right. You have somewhere to keep it now," She said.

"Will the church think I stole it?"

"I'll tell Pastor *** the story, or maybe you should. They'll understand. I think you need your old buggy."

"Jesse is going to be so happy."

Mama smiled. "All right then, let's get this place closed up."

We had planned on taking the leftovers from our feast to Neil and Pauline's family in the white house, and the buggy made the perfect vehicle for transport. We loaded it up and made our way over the icy sidewalks. Mama and I had to carry the buggy as we got closer to the white house because it wouldn't maneuver over the un-shoveled snow. The white house family wasn't expecting us, so when Neil's mother opened the door and saw us she was startled and inquired what could the matter be. We assured her we had come with no needs or implication, just wanted to bless them with a good dinner, complete with an entire pumpkin pie that we never even cut.

Neil and Pauline's mother insisted we stay for tea and led us to a cozy, though wooden, seat by the fire.

"Virginia, I have thought a million times of how to thank you for the medication your doctor friend provided for my Neil. He hasn't had one seizure since he's been taking it," said Neil's mother.

"To know he is better is all the thanks I want," Mama said.

"The medicine comes every month. A courier brings it but he won't let me pay him. He'll take a cookie or a biscuit, but he won't let me pay him a dime. I am so filled with gratitude that I don't know what to do with it. Just makes me want to pass it on, you know, just smile at everyone I see," she said.

"What a perfectly lovely thing to be filled with, and how nice that it's spilling over," Mama said. She was wearing one of her knowing smiles. I knew not to ask.

When we were ready to go, Neil's older brother Will pulled the truck around to take us home. Mama protested that it wasn't that far, but he'd already put the baby buggy in the bed of the pickup and was waiting for us when we had finished our good-byes.

"Where'd you find that buggy?" Will asked as he drove with one hand and wiped the fog from the windshield with the other.

I felt nervous, like he knew we'd taken it from the church without asking. "In the church nursery," I said. "It was mine when I was little. Last time I saw it was at the Linderman's before the fire, then there it was tonight in the Grace Chapel nursery. I know it's mine from the writing on the bottom."

"That's how I reco'nized it too," said Will, "It was the last thing I threw out the window the day of the fire, figured it belonged to the scared little girl. The fire never got that far gone, but just in case."

"Well I don't know how it ended up at the church nursery, but I'm glad it did. My father gave it to me for Christmas seven years ago," I said.

"Come full circle, huh?" he said.

I just smiled, realizing how much God loves me.

***

Will hauled my baby buggy up the stairs to the new apartment and I wheeled it over the bumps of the threshold. That was my first view of my new home. It was across the street from the hospital, on the second floor. There were two bedrooms and a bathroom in between, like at the Athenaeum Hotel. From the living room window you could see the windows of the North wing nurses' station, where Mama worked.

All of our things were already in the apartment. Uncle Virg and Grandpa had moved it all and set it up for our homecoming. My room was mostly spring green and white. The window looked out the same way as the living room, to the hospital. My room. My own room, for the very first time.

My clothes were in my closet. My brush was on my vanity. My towel was on my hook. My mom was in the next room.

I went in to see her room and she was already in bed with the comforter hugged way up around her neck.

"I'm gonna have a little lay-down," she said. "I have to work tonight."

"Okay, Mama. I love you." I kissed her cheek and turned off the bedside lamp. "I love my room," I said.

"Oh good. It looks like you, doesn't it?"

"Yes, it's grown up," I said. "Night, Mama."

"Night, Peach. Wake me up in an hour."

"Love you," I said, and closed the door gently.

***

I had waited for this moment for seven years and now I had not the slightest idea what to do with myself. Here I was, right where I had longed to be since I was six, but I felt no different, really, than when I had lived with Lena and Leonard, or with the McDonalds. (I didn't like to think of how I felt at the Linderman's house, so I didn't.) I still felt slightly anxious in my chest. I still wished I could be sitting on my dad's lap. I wondered what tomorrow would bring and how it was going to be, living with Mama. I still wanted the door locked and the window cracked open a little. I was thankful when I opened it and it smelled like snow and not mint.

I put Jesse in her buggy and set the correct time on my clock. Above my bed was the same picture that had been above my bed in the basement on Tower Street. It was a painting of a boy and a girl, walking over a rickety bridge during a storm. The kids were holding each other, fearful of the storm. But hovering over them, where they couldn't see, was a guardian angel. Everything in my room was new, except this picture. It looked exactly the same as when I was little. Thank you, Mama.

316

Mama worked the 11:00-7:00 shift at the hospital, so I woke her up at ten o'clock with a cup of hot tea. I sat on her bed and put the buttons in her hat while she got ready. She was rummaging around in her jewelry box for a velvet ribbon to put on her hat, and pulled out a ring.

"This was the ring I got when I graduated from nurses training; see if it fits you, my knuckles have gotten too big," she said.

I slipped it on. It fit perfectly.

"You may have that. It looks nice on you. Happy birthday."

"Thanks, Mama," I said as I studied the inscriptions. "1925, gosh that was a long time ago."

"You're not kidding. I'm glad it's today and not 1925. I wish I didn't have to work tonight. You gonna be all right all alone here on your first night?"

"Yep. I'm ready. Is Nancy home next door?" I asked.

"Yes, you need anything just ring her doorbell and she or her poodle will save the day. You'll be fine Peach. Remember our signal?"

"Yes."

"All right then, I'm off to my job. Kiss." She bent out, not down, to kiss me and left just a smudge of orange on my lips. "Listen for the train."

"Okay, Mama. See you in the morning."

I shut the door after her, then opened it and watched as she turned the corner. After locking the door I immediately felt the death pains weigh down my mood. I was old enough now; that's what Mama said. Why did I feel six again? Why did I fret over the strength of the lock, the sound in the hall, the bark of a dog—surely warning me of an intruder? My mind knew I was safe, but my heart was beating out of control, sending me into a panic that I knew all too well. Glory came to mind. When she was in a tight spot she almost always had a scripture come tumbling out of nowhere to address the given situation. I missed Glory. Her voice whispered in my ear. "Be anxious for nothing." Easier said than done I thought, but her voice went on, "tell God what you're thinking."

I tried to find words. My thoughts drifted around, and when they caught up with me again, I shivered.

"God, I'm scared of being alone."

I expected immediate relief but none came. Then Mama's voice reminded me, as it had a thousand times before. "Say thank you."

"Thank you?" I said out loud. I wasn't thinking about what I was thankful for, I was thinking of what I needed, what I was lacking. "All right, thank you. Thank you for this new apartment...thank you for my mama and for me being thirteen and for this day finally arriving." I felt sort of foolish talking out loud to God, still standing there by the door, afraid to move. "Thank you for how hard this is so I don't try to do it on my own. Thank you for hearing me and not..."

The distant train whistle interrupted my prayer and reminded me of my responsibility—my signal to be ready. When I peeled my hand off of the doorknob I had a new sense of peace and confidence. I felt less alone. The lights of the hospital were the only thing piercing the black night as I approached the picture window. The whistle of the 11:05 came and went as I stared through the darkness. Her white figure appeared. Mama waved through the second floor window. I waved back, then quickly went to the light switch on the wall and switched it off and on three times. I waited and watched as the light from the hospital window went off and on three times. We were safe.